G.I. JOE

A REAL AMERICAN HERO

VOLUME 10

G.I. JOE: A REAL AMERICAN HERO, VOLUME 10

Writer: Larry Hama

Artist: S L Gallant

Inkers: Marc Deering (Ch. 1),
Juan Castro (Ch. 2), and Brian Shearer (Ch. 3-5)

Colorist: J. Brown

Letterers: Neil Uyetake and Shawn Lee

Series Editor: Carlos Guzman

Cover Artist: S L Gallant

Cover Colorist: J. Brown

Collection Editors: Justin Eisinger & Alonzo Simon

Collection Designer: Claudia Chong

Special thanks to Hasbro's Mike Ballog, Ed Lane, Joe Furfaro, Heather Hopkins, and Michael Kelly for their invaluable assistance.

ISBN: 978-1-63140-154-1

17 16 15 14   1 2 3 4

Ted Adams, CEO & Publisher
Greg Goldstein, President & COO
Robbie Robbins, EVP/Sr. Graphic Artist
Chris Ryall, Chief Creative Officer/Editor-in-Chief
Matthew Ruzicka, CPA, Chief Financial Officer
Alan Payne, VP of Sales
Dirk Wood, VP of Marketing
Lorelei Bunjes, VP of Digital Services
Jeff Webber, VP of Digital Publishing & Business Development

www.IDWPUBLISHING.com
IDW founded by Ted Adams, Alex Garner, Kris Oprisko, and Robbie Robbins

Facebook: facebook.com/idwpublishing
Twitter: @idwpublishing
YouTube: youtube.com/idwpublishing
Instagram: instagram.com/idwpublishing
deviantART: idwpublishing.deviantart.com
Pinterest: pinterest.com/idwpublishing/idw-staff-faves

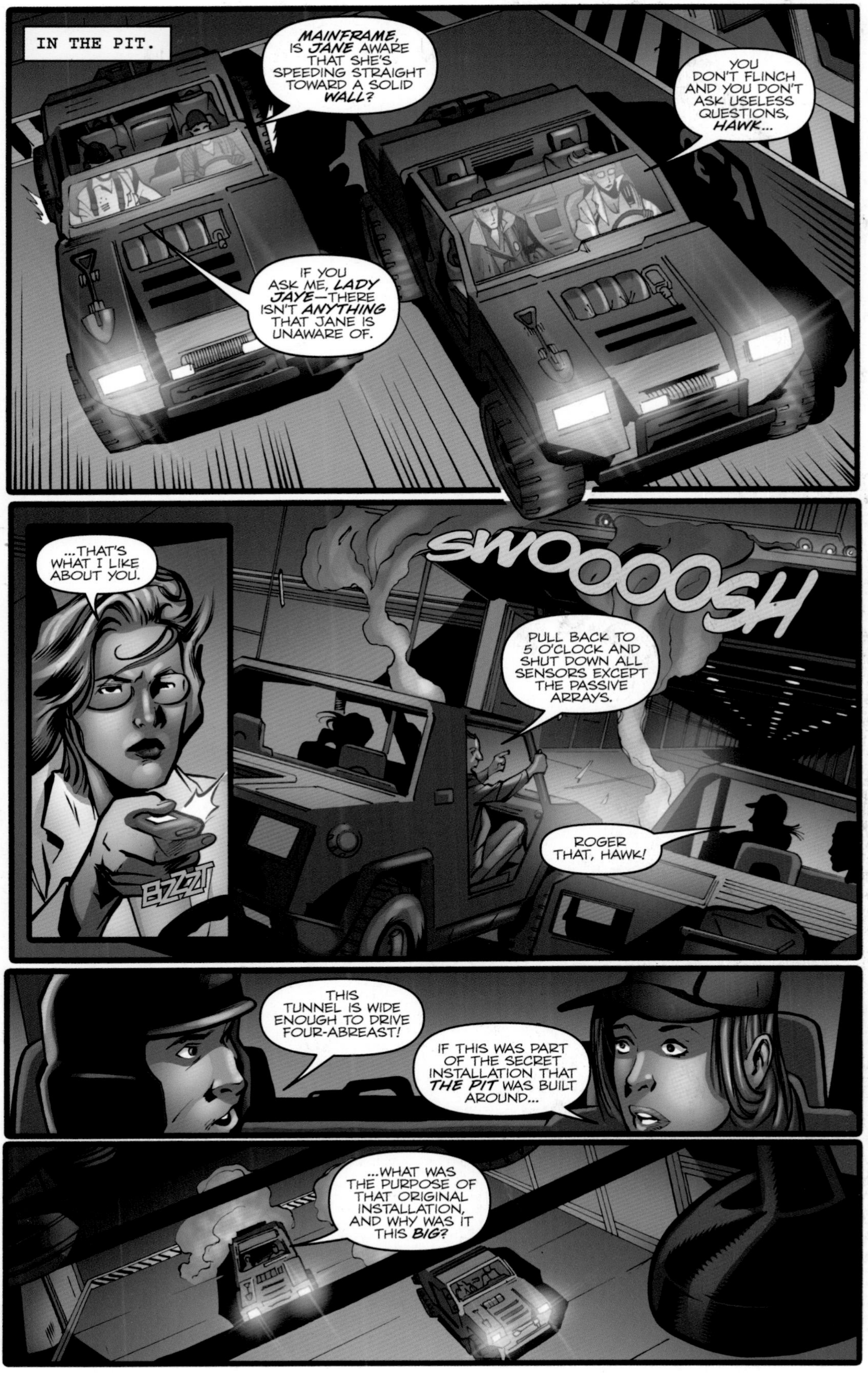
IN THE PIT.
MAINFRAME, IS JANE AWARE THAT SHE'S SPEEDING STRAIGHT TOWARD A SOLID WALL?
YOU DON'T FLINCH AND YOU DON'T ASK USELESS QUESTIONS, HAWK...
IF YOU ASK ME, LADY JAYE—THERE ISN'T ANYTHING THAT JANE IS UNAWARE OF.
...THAT'S WHAT I LIKE ABOUT YOU.
SWOOOOOSH
PULL BACK TO 5 O'CLOCK AND SHUT DOWN ALL SENSORS EXCEPT THE PASSIVE ARRAYS.
ROGER THAT, HAWK!
BZZZT
THIS TUNNEL IS WIDE ENOUGH TO DRIVE FOUR-ABREAST!
IF THIS WAS PART OF THE SECRET INSTALLATION THAT THE PIT WAS BUILT AROUND...
...WHAT WAS THE PURPOSE OF THAT ORIGINAL INSTALLATION, AND WHY WAS IT THIS BIG?

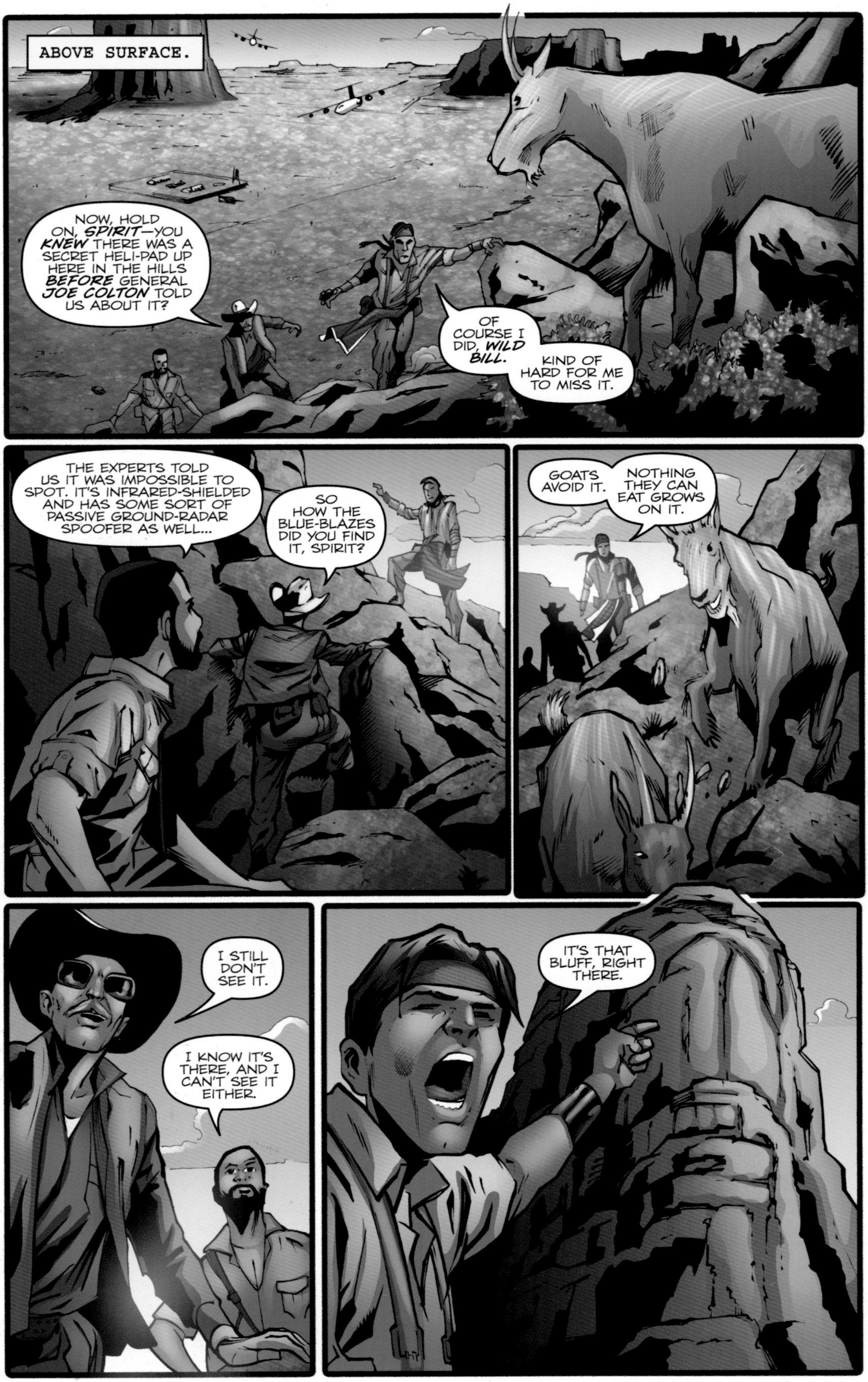
ABOVE SURFACE.
NOW, HOLD ON, SPIRIT—YOU KNEW THERE WAS A SECRET HELI-PAD UP HERE IN THE HILLS BEFORE GENERAL JOE COLTON TOLD US ABOUT IT?
OF COURSE I DID, WILD BILL.
KIND OF HARD FOR ME TO MISS IT.
THE EXPERTS TOLD US IT WAS IMPOSSIBLE TO SPOT. IT'S INFRARED-SHIELDED AND HAS SOME SORT OF PASSIVE GROUND-RADAR SPOOFER AS WELL...
SO HOW THE BLUE-BLAZES DID YOU FIND IT, SPIRIT?
GOATS AVOID IT.
NOTHING THEY CAN EAT GROWS ON IT.
I STILL DON'T SEE IT.
I KNOW IT'S THERE, AND I CAN'T SEE IT EITHER.
IT'S THAT BLUFF, RIGHT THERE.

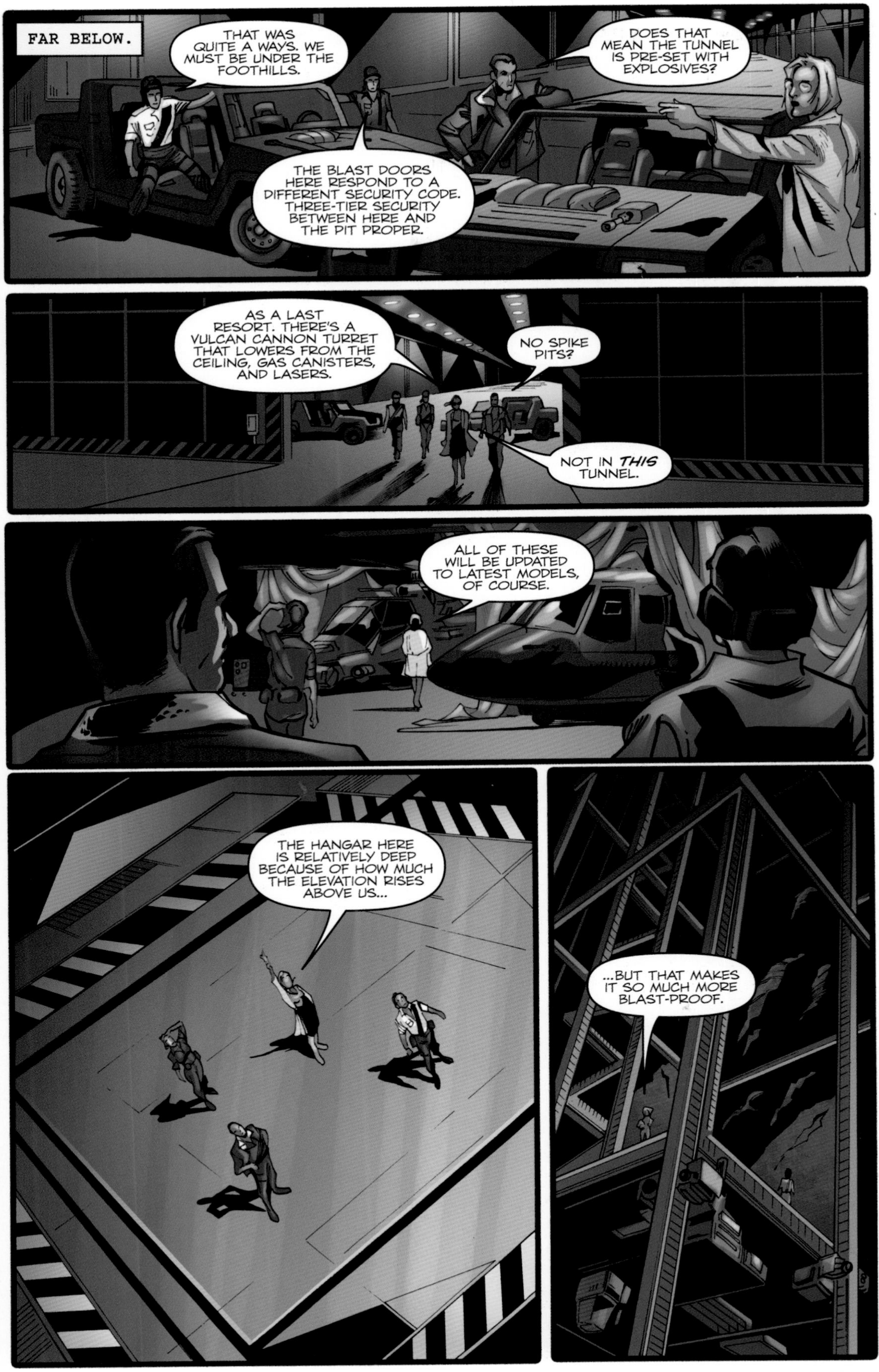
FAR BELOW.
THAT WAS QUITE A WAYS. WE MUST BE UNDER THE FOOTHILLS.
DOES THAT MEAN THE TUNNEL IS PRE-SET WITH EXPLOSIVES?
THE BLAST DOORS HERE RESPOND TO A DIFFERENT SECURITY CODE. THREE-TIER SECURITY BETWEEN HERE AND THE PIT PROPER.
AS A LAST RESORT. THERE'S A VULCAN CANNON TURRET THAT LOWERS FROM THE CEILING, GAS CANISTERS, AND LASERS.
NO SPIKE PITS?
NOT IN *THIS* TUNNEL.
ALL OF THESE WILL BE UPDATED TO LATEST MODELS, OF COURSE.
THE HANGAR HERE IS RELATIVELY DEEP BECAUSE OF HOW MUCH THE ELEVATION RISES ABOVE US...
...BUT THAT MAKES IT SO MUCH MORE BLAST-PROOF.

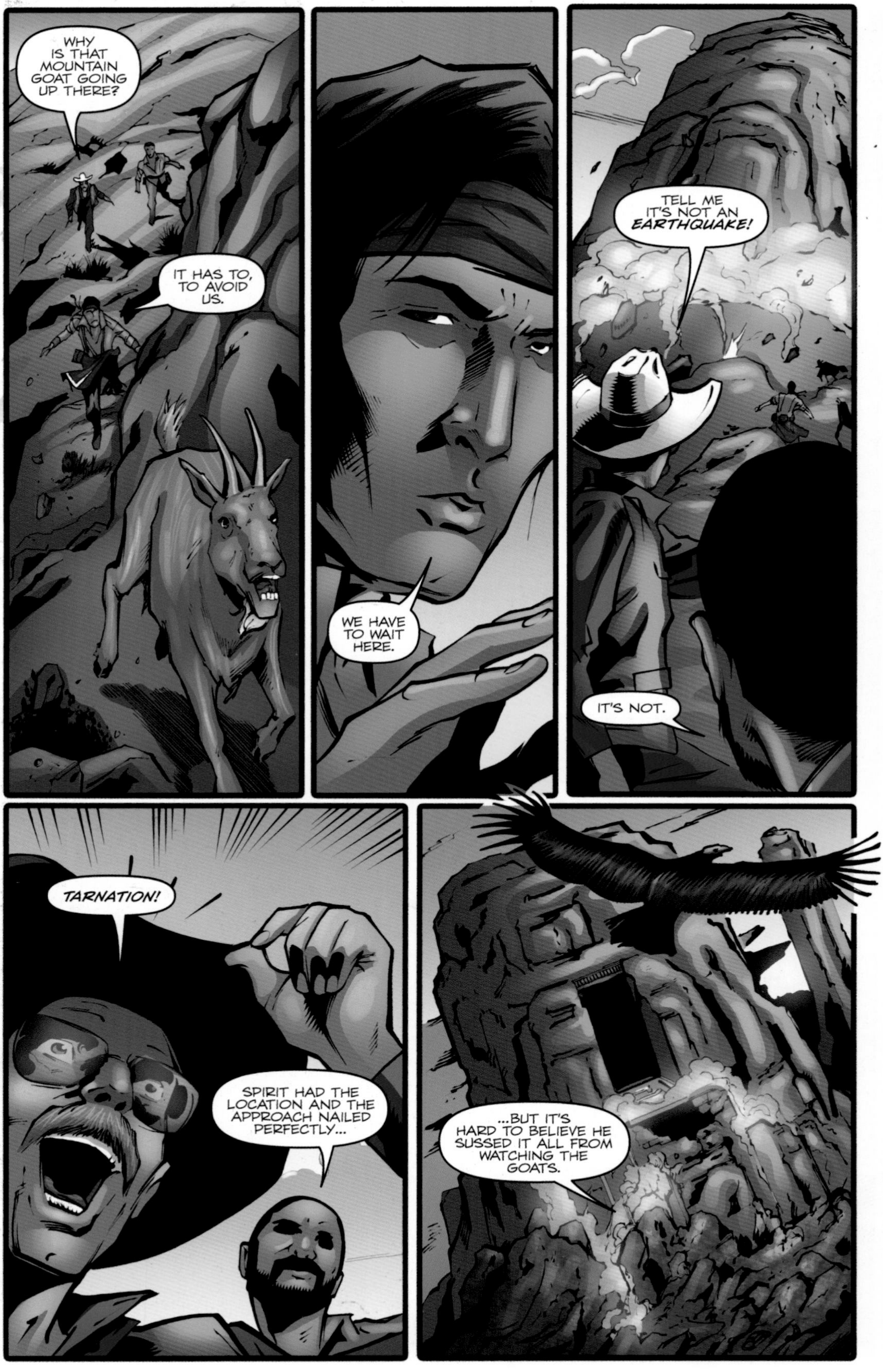
WHY IS THAT MOUNTAIN GOAT GOING UP THERE?
IT HAS TO, TO AVOID US.
WE HAVE TO WAIT HERE.
TELL ME IT'S NOT AN EARTHQUAKE!
IT'S NOT.
TARNATION!
SPIRIT HAD THE LOCATION AND THE APPROACH NAILED PERFECTLY...
...BUT IT'S HARD TO BELIEVE HE SUSSED IT ALL FROM WATCHING THE GOATS.

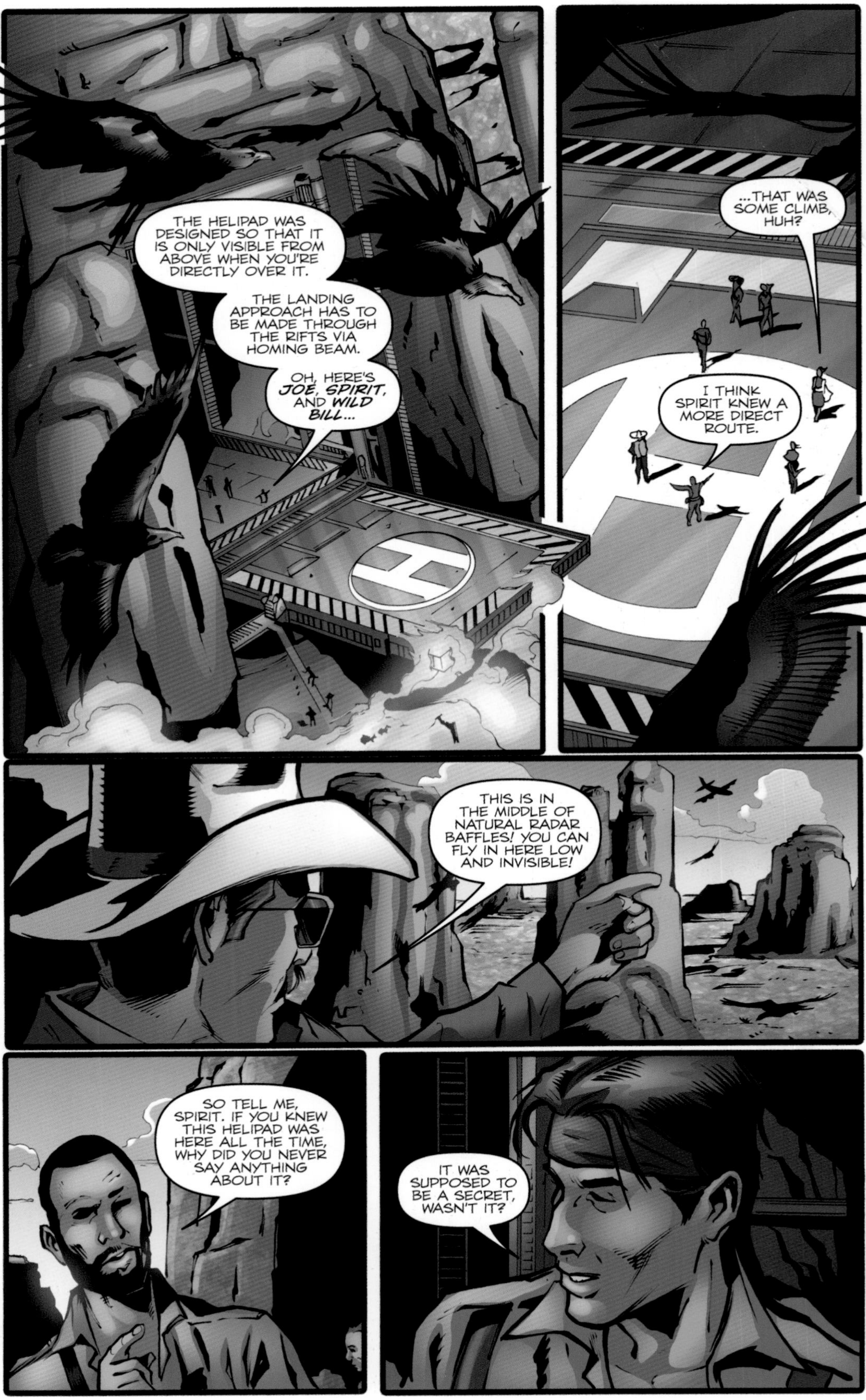
THE HELIPAD WAS DESIGNED SO THAT IT IS ONLY VISIBLE FROM ABOVE WHEN YOU'RE DIRECTLY OVER IT.
THE LANDING APPROACH HAS TO BE MADE THROUGH THE RIFTS VIA HOMING BEAM.
OH, HERE'S JOE, SPIRIT, AND WILD BILL...
...THAT WAS SOME CLIMB, HUH?
I THINK SPIRIT KNEW A MORE DIRECT ROUTE.
THIS IS IN THE MIDDLE OF NATURAL RADAR BAFFLES! YOU CAN FLY IN HERE LOW AND INVISIBLE!
SO TELL ME, SPIRIT. IF YOU KNEW THIS HELIPAD WAS HERE ALL THE TIME, WHY DID YOU NEVER SAY ANYTHING ABOUT IT?
IT WAS SUPPOSED TO BE A SECRET, WASN'T IT?

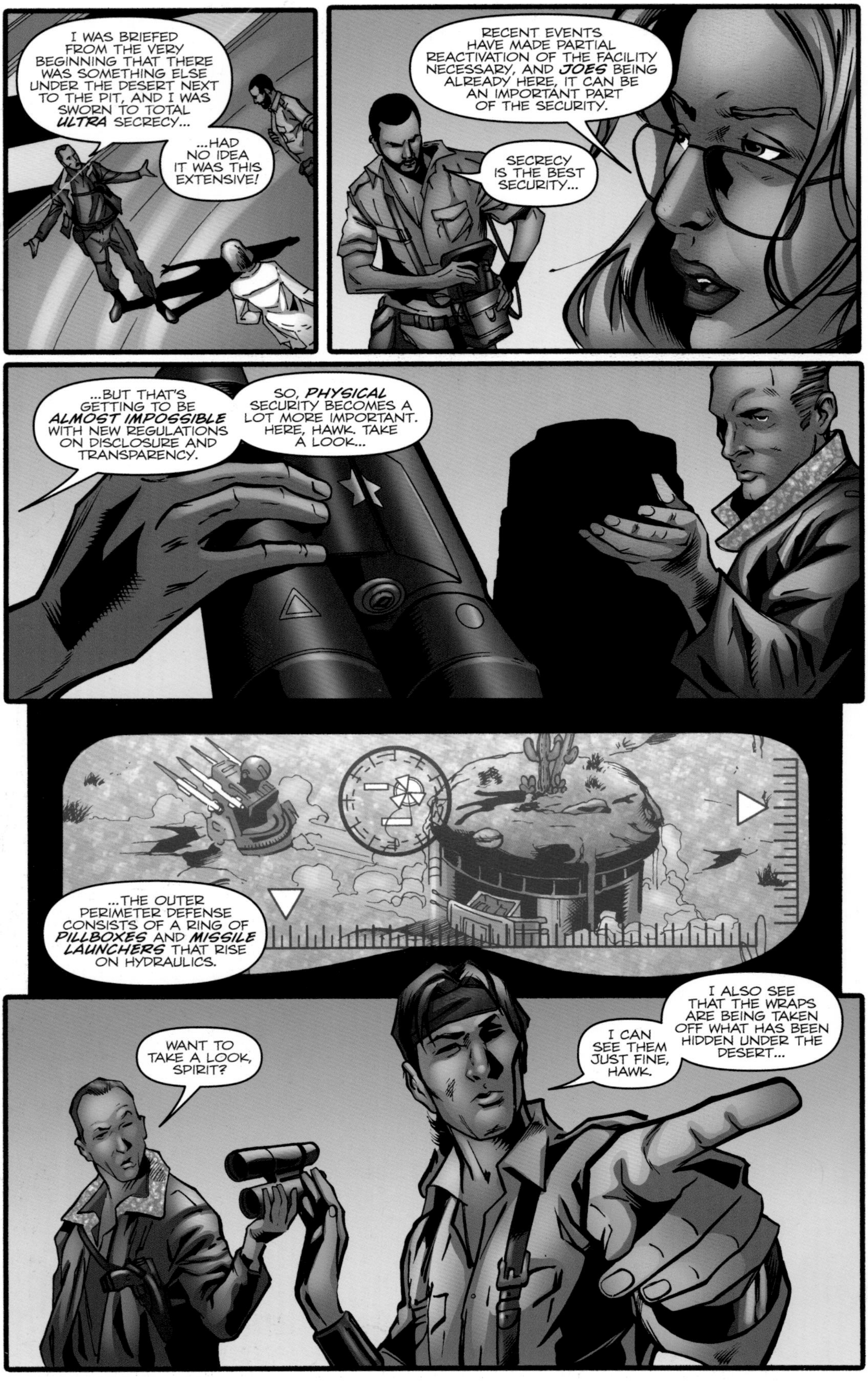
I WAS BRIEFED FROM THE VERY BEGINNING THAT THERE WAS SOMETHING ELSE UNDER THE DESERT NEXT TO THE PIT, AND I WAS SWORN TO TOTAL ULTRA SECRECY...
...HAD NO IDEA IT WAS THIS EXTENSIVE!
RECENT EVENTS HAVE MADE PARTIAL REACTIVATION OF THE FACILITY NECESSARY, AND JOES BEING ALREADY HERE, IT CAN BE AN IMPORTANT PART OF THE SECURITY.
SECRECY IS THE BEST SECURITY...
...BUT THAT'S GETTING TO BE ALMOST IMPOSSIBLE WITH NEW REGULATIONS ON DISCLOSURE AND TRANSPARENCY.
SO, PHYSICAL SECURITY BECOMES A LOT MORE IMPORTANT. HERE, HAWK. TAKE A LOOK...
...THE OUTER PERIMETER DEFENSE CONSISTS OF A RING OF PILLBOXES AND MISSILE LAUNCHERS THAT RISE ON HYDRAULICS.
WANT TO TAKE A LOOK, SPIRIT?
I CAN SEE THEM JUST FINE, HAWK.
I ALSO SEE THAT THE WRAPS ARE BEING TAKEN OFF WHAT HAS BEEN HIDDEN UNDER THE DESERT...

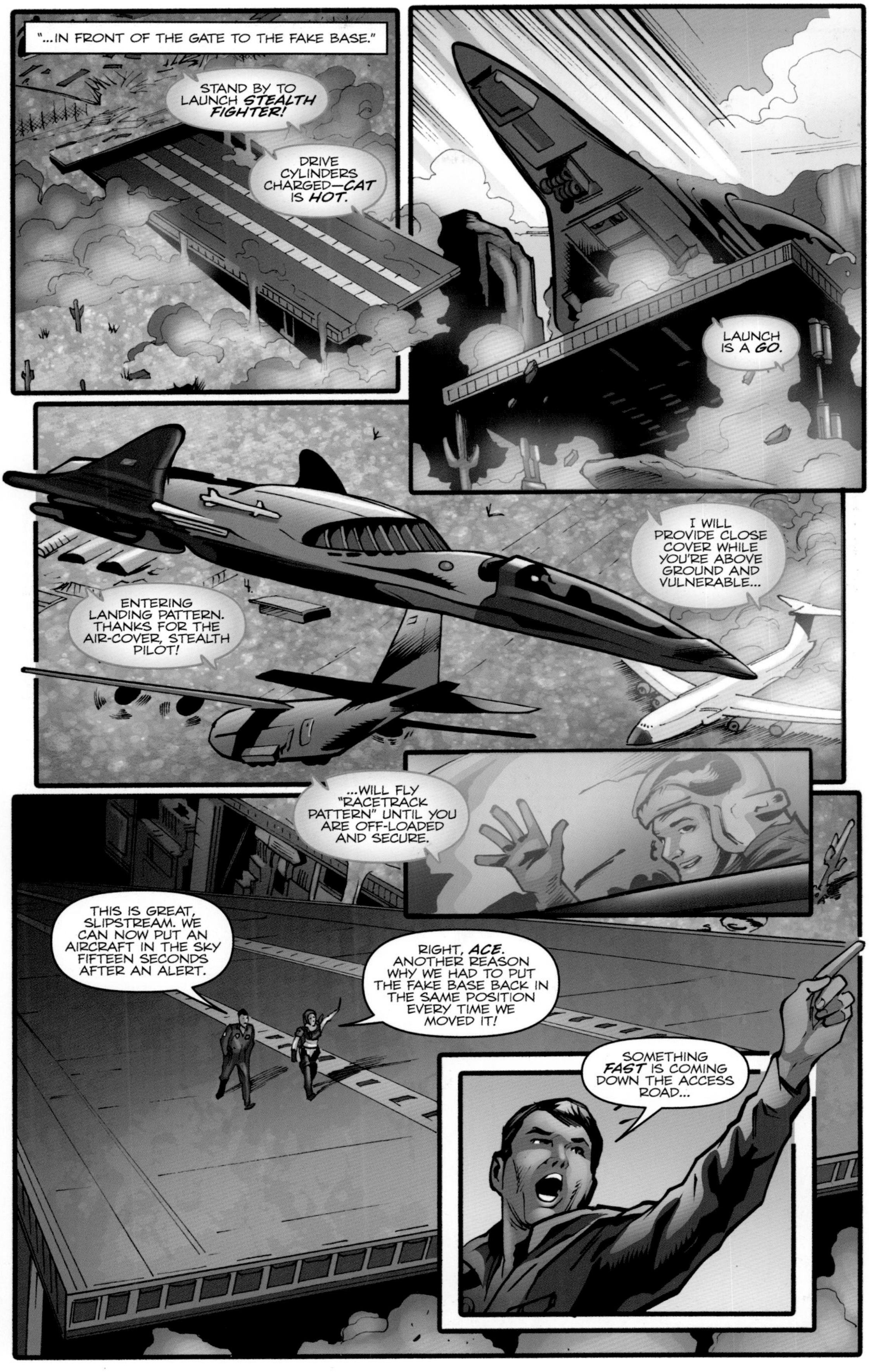
"...IN FRONT OF THE GATE TO THE FAKE BASE."
STAND BY TO LAUNCH STEALTH FIGHTER!
DRIVE CYLINDERS CHARGED—CAT IS HOT.
LAUNCH IS A GO.
I WILL PROVIDE CLOSE COVER WHILE YOU'RE ABOVE GROUND AND VULNERABLE...
ENTERING LANDING PATTERN. THANKS FOR THE AIR-COVER, STEALTH PILOT!
...WILL FLY "RACETRACK PATTERN" UNTIL YOU ARE OFF-LOADED AND SECURE.
THIS IS GREAT, SLIPSTREAM. WE CAN NOW PUT AN AIRCRAFT IN THE SKY FIFTEEN SECONDS AFTER AN ALERT.
RIGHT, ACE. ANOTHER REASON WHY WE HAD TO PUT THE FAKE BASE BACK IN THE SAME POSITION EVERY TIME WE MOVED IT!
SOMETHING FAST IS COMING DOWN THE ACCESS ROAD...

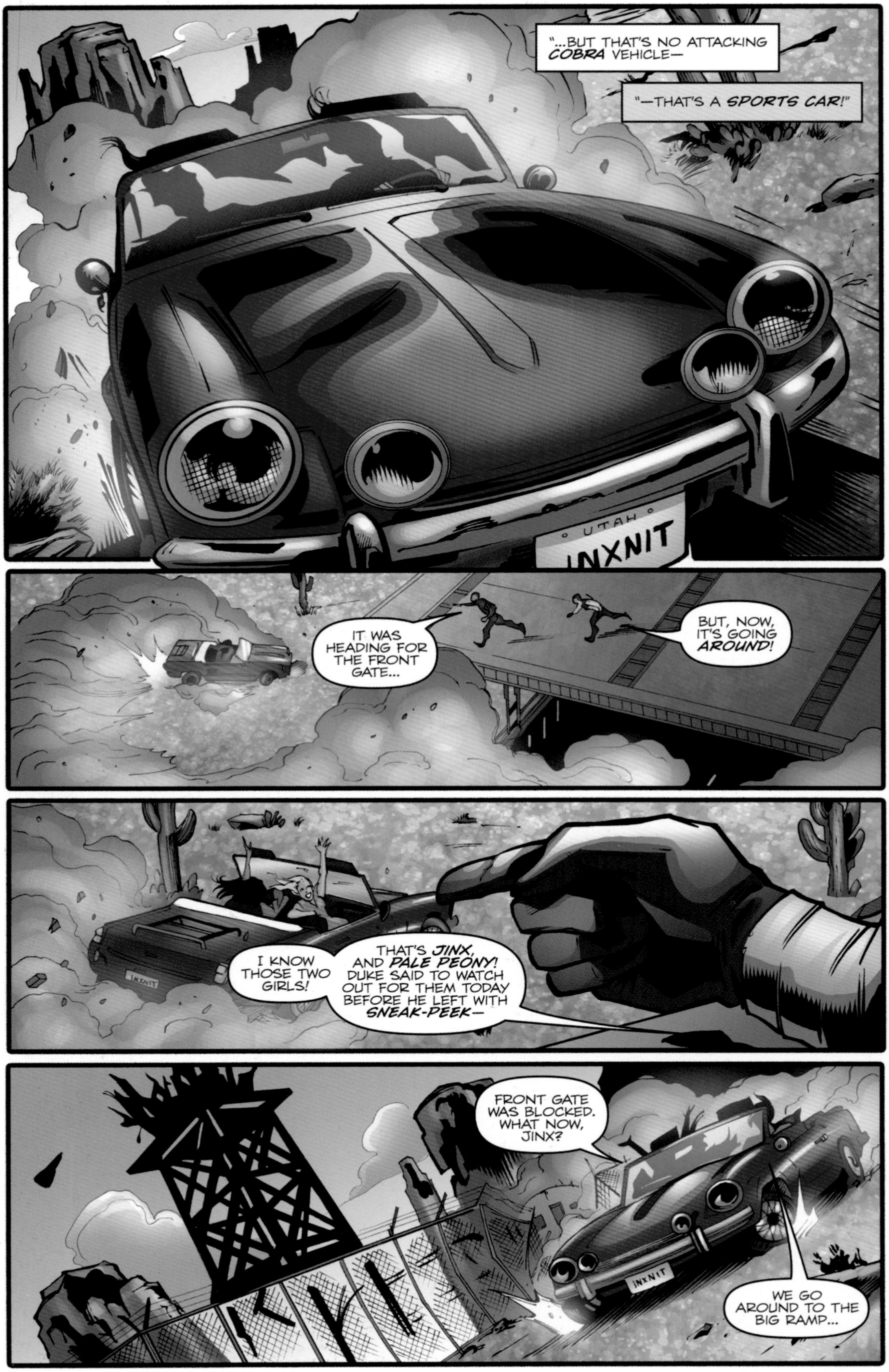
"...BUT THAT'S NO ATTACKING COBRA VEHICLE—
"—THAT'S A SPORTS CAR!"
UTAH
JNXNIT
IT WAS HEADING FOR THE FRONT GATE...
BUT, NOW, IT'S GOING AROUND!
I KNOW THOSE TWO GIRLS!
THAT'S JINX, AND PALE PEONY! DUKE SAID TO WATCH OUT FOR THEM TODAY BEFORE HE LEFT WITH SNEAK-PEEK—
FRONT GATE WAS BLOCKED. WHAT NOW, JINX?
WE GO AROUND TO THE BIG RAMP...

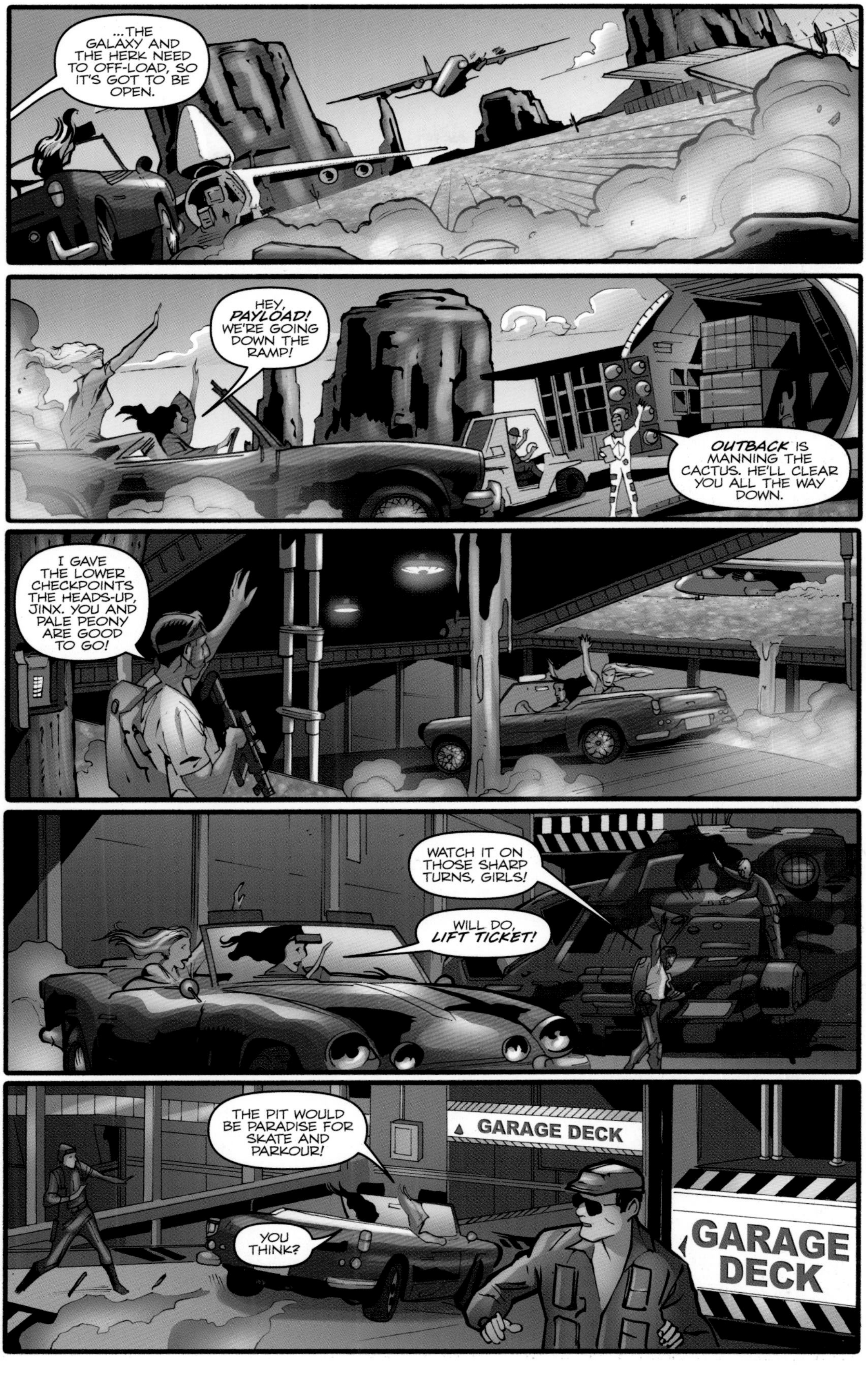
...THE GALAXY AND THE HERK NEED TO OFF-LOAD, SO IT'S GOT TO BE OPEN.
HEY, PAYLOAD! WE'RE GOING DOWN THE RAMP!
OUTBACK IS MANNING THE CACTUS. HE'LL CLEAR YOU ALL THE WAY DOWN.
I GAVE THE LOWER CHECKPOINTS THE HEADS-UP, JINX. YOU AND PALE PEONY ARE GOOD TO GO!
WATCH IT ON THOSE SHARP TURNS, GIRLS!
WILL DO, LIFT TICKET!
THE PIT WOULD BE PARADISE FOR SKATE AND PARKOUR!
GARAGE DECK
YOU THINK?
GARAGE DECK

SAY HEY TO *DUSTY* AND FROSTBITE, *PEONY!*

HEY, GUYS!

WHOA!

WATCH IT ON THE NEXT LEVEL! LOTS O' CONSTRUCTION AND REMODELING GOING ON DOWN THERE!

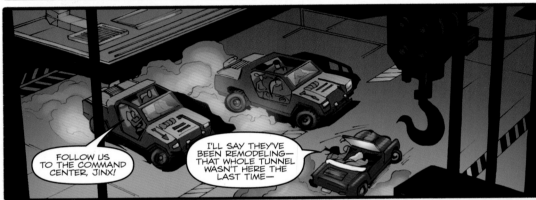

FOLLOW US TO THE COMMAND CENTER, JINX!

I'LL SAY THEY'VE BEEN REMODELING— THAT WHOLE TUNNEL WASN'T HERE THE LAST TIME—

MAINFRAME, WE NEED TO SET UP TO DEBRIEF THE GIRLS ON THEIR *OLLIESTAN* MISSION.

I'VE ALREADY GOT THE FILES COLLATED.

AND SINCE OUR COMMAND CENTER HAS BEEN TOTALLY UPGRADED...

...WE MIGHT AS WELL BREAK IT IN.

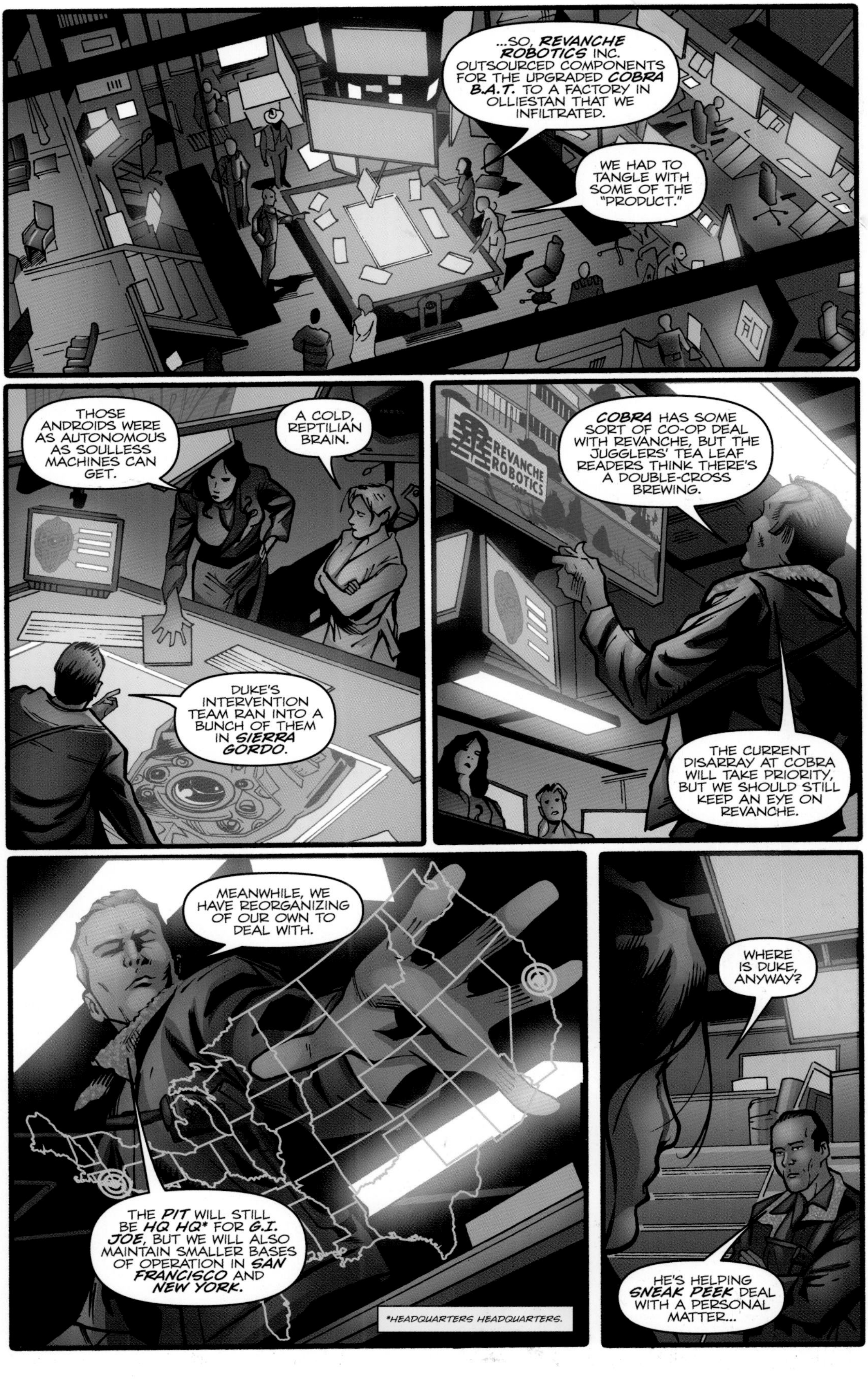

...SO, REVANCHE ROBOTICS INC. OUTSOURCED COMPONENTS FOR THE UPGRADED COBRA B.A.T. TO A FACTORY IN OLLIESTAN THAT WE INFILTRATED.
WE HAD TO TANGLE WITH SOME OF THE "PRODUCT."
THOSE ANDROIDS WERE AS AUTONOMOUS AS SOULLESS MACHINES CAN GET.
A COLD, REPTILIAN BRAIN.
DUKE'S INTERVENTION TEAM RAN INTO A BUNCH OF THEM IN SIERRA GORDO.
REVANCHE ROBOTICS CORP
COBRA HAS SOME SORT OF CO-OP DEAL WITH REVANCHE, BUT THE JUGGLERS' TEA LEAF READERS THINK THERE'S A DOUBLE-CROSS BREWING.
THE CURRENT DISARRAY AT COBRA WILL TAKE PRIORITY, BUT WE SHOULD STILL KEEP AN EYE ON REVANCHE.
MEANWHILE, WE HAVE REORGANIZING OF OUR OWN TO DEAL WITH.
THE PIT WILL STILL BE HQ HQ* FOR G.I. JOE, BUT WE WILL ALSO MAINTAIN SMALLER BASES OF OPERATION IN SAN FRANCISCO AND NEW YORK.
*HEADQUARTERS HEADQUARTERS.
WHERE IS DUKE, ANYWAY?
HE'S HELPING SNEAK PEEK DEAL WITH A PERSONAL MATTER...

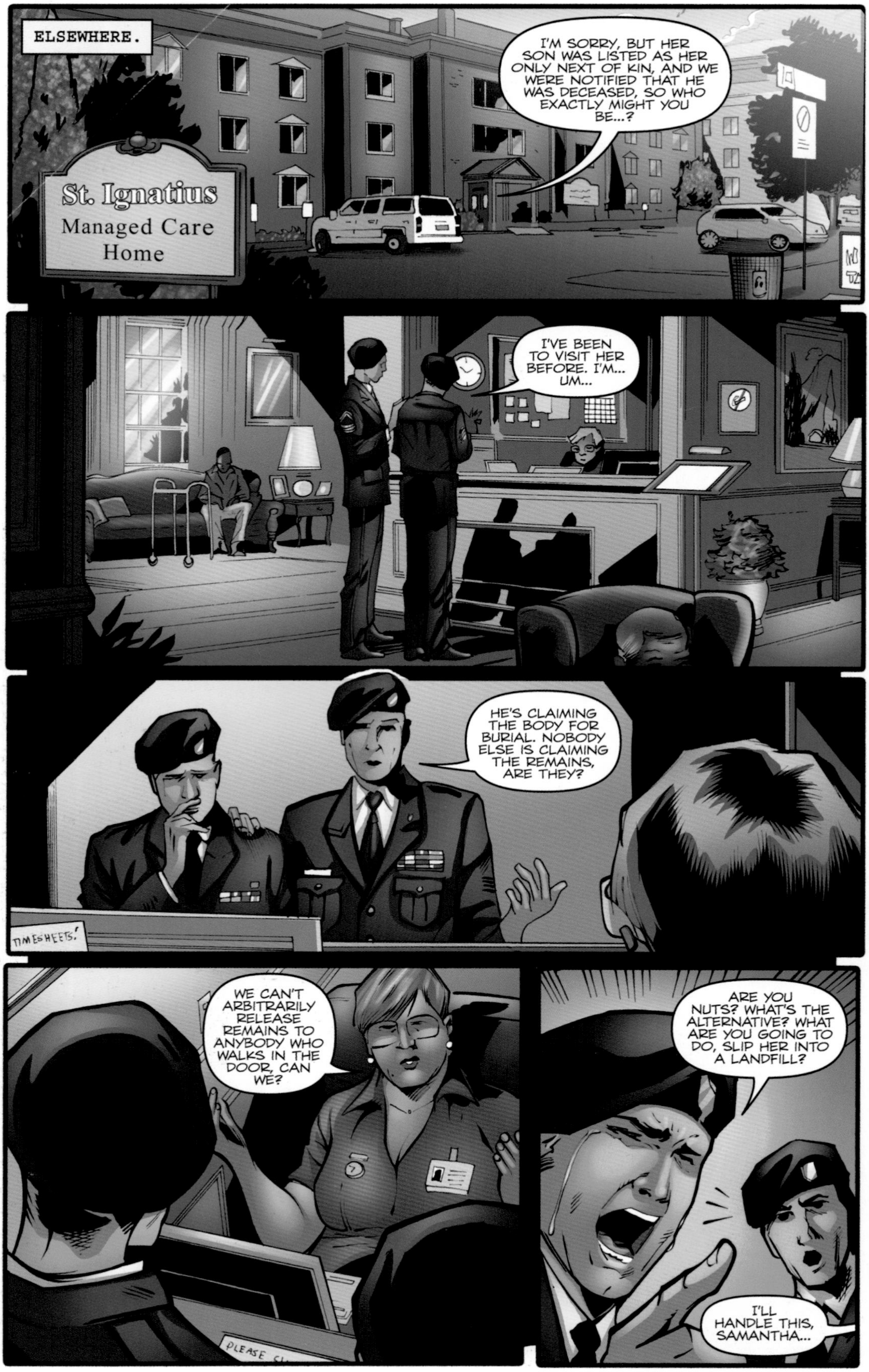
ELSEWHERE.
St. Ignatius Managed Care Home
I'M SORRY, BUT HER SON WAS LISTED AS HER ONLY NEXT OF KIN, AND WE WERE NOTIFIED THAT HE WAS DECEASED, SO WHO EXACTLY MIGHT YOU BE...?
I'VE BEEN TO VISIT HER BEFORE. I'M... UM...
HE'S CLAIMING THE BODY FOR BURIAL. NOBODY ELSE IS CLAIMING THE REMAINS, ARE THEY?
TIMESHEETS!
WE CAN'T ARBITRARILY RELEASE REMAINS TO ANYBODY WHO WALKS IN THE DOOR, CAN WE?
ARE YOU NUTS? WHAT'S THE ALTERNATIVE? WHAT ARE YOU GOING TO DO, SLIP HER INTO A LANDFILL?
I'LL HANDLE THIS, SAMANTHA...

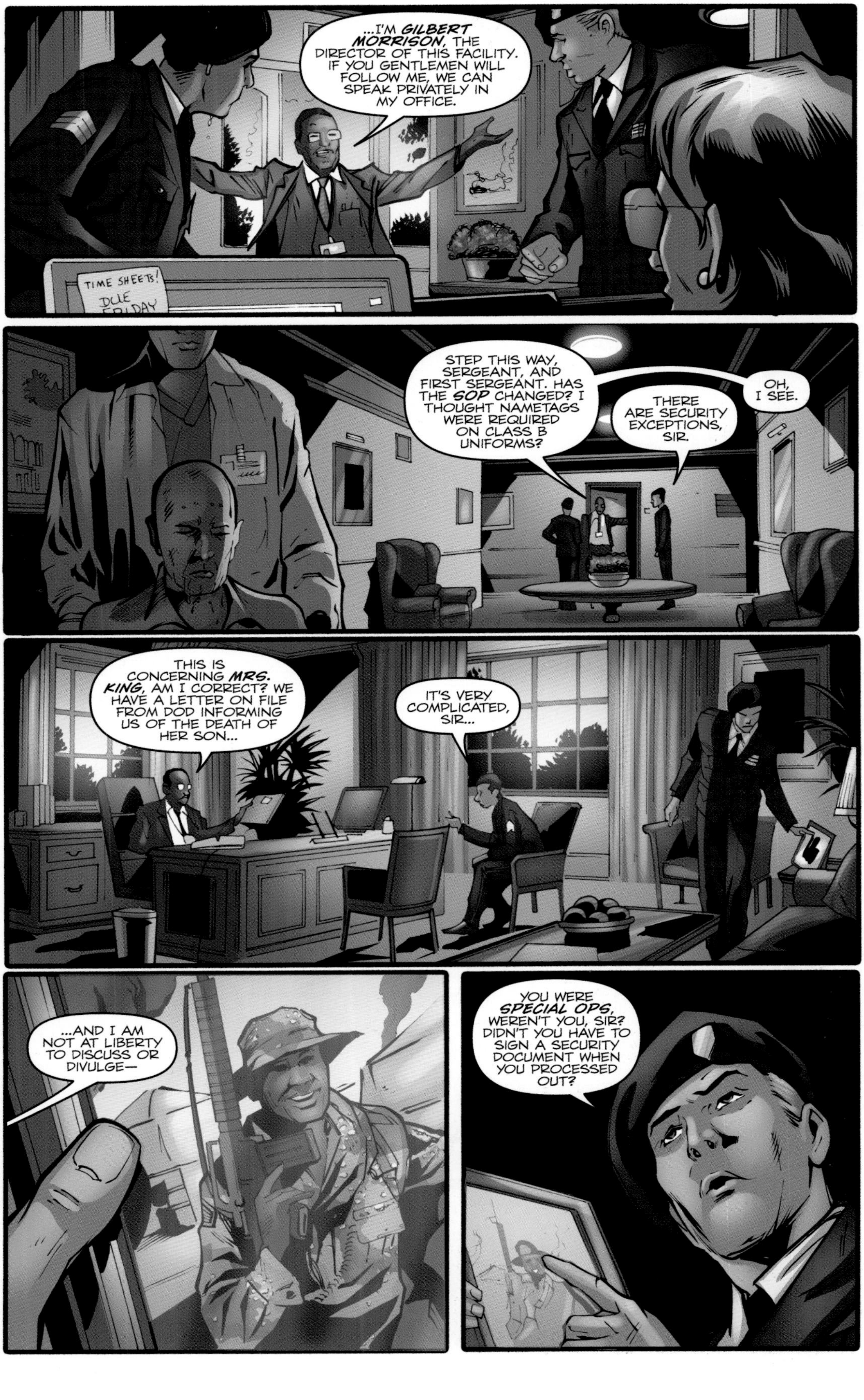
...I'M GILBERT MORRISON, THE DIRECTOR OF THIS FACILITY. IF YOU GENTLEMEN WILL FOLLOW ME, WE CAN SPEAK PRIVATELY IN MY OFFICE.
TIME SHEETS! DUE FRIDAY
STEP THIS WAY, SERGEANT, AND FIRST SERGEANT. HAS THE SOP CHANGED? I THOUGHT NAMETAGS WERE REQUIRED ON CLASS B UNIFORMS?
THERE ARE SECURITY EXCEPTIONS, SIR.
OH, I SEE.
THIS IS CONCERNING MRS. KING, AM I CORRECT? WE HAVE A LETTER ON FILE FROM DOD INFORMING US OF THE DEATH OF HER SON...
IT'S VERY COMPLICATED, SIR...
...AND I AM NOT AT LIBERTY TO DISCUSS OR DIVULGE—
YOU WERE SPECIAL OPS, WEREN'T YOU, SIR? DIDN'T YOU HAVE TO SIGN A SECURITY DOCUMENT WHEN YOU PROCESSED OUT?

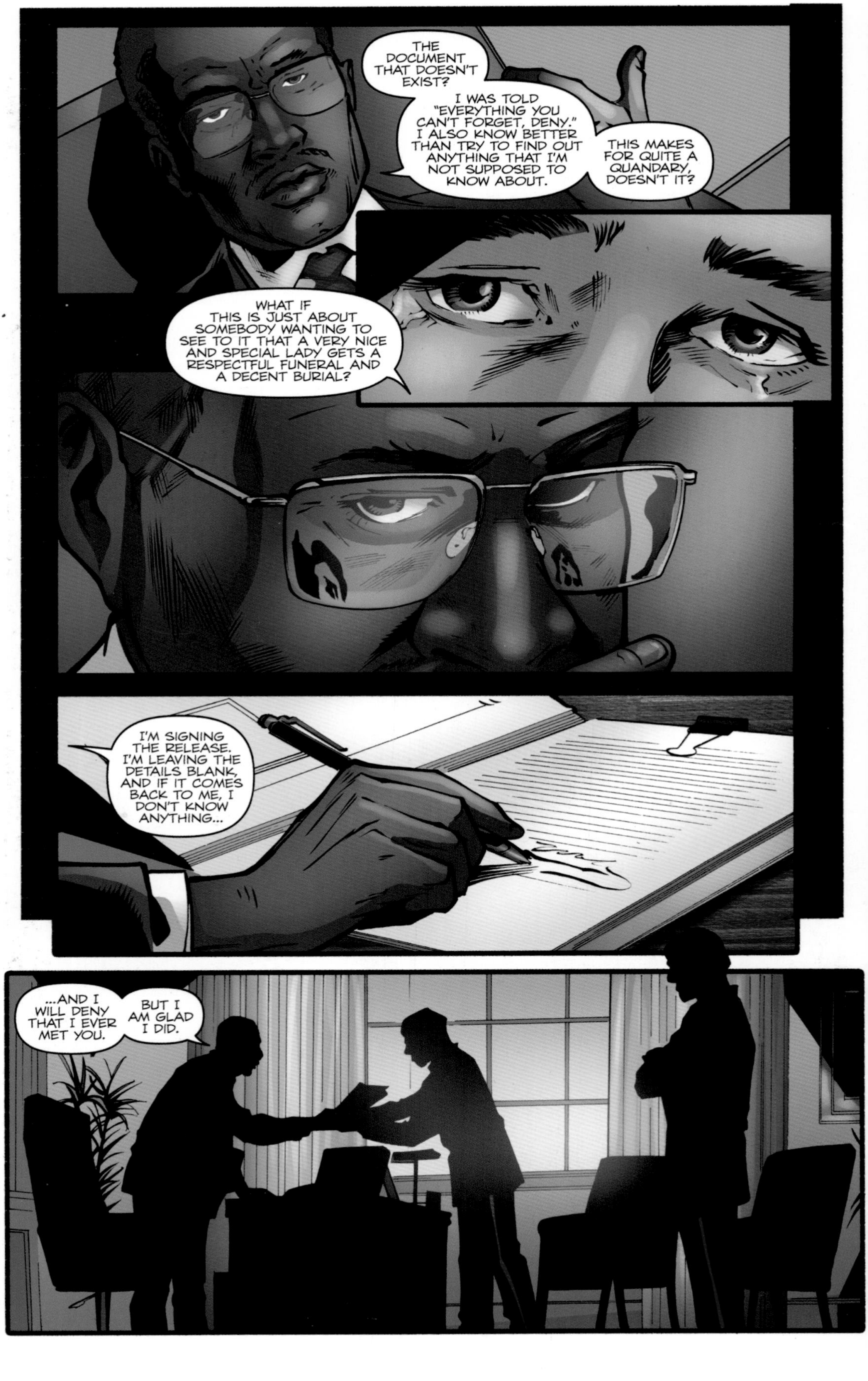
THE DOCUMENT THAT DOESN'T EXIST?
I WAS TOLD "EVERYTHING YOU CAN'T FORGET, DENY." I ALSO KNOW BETTER THAN TRY TO FIND OUT ANYTHING THAT I'M NOT SUPPOSED TO KNOW ABOUT.
THIS MAKES FOR QUITE A QUANDARY, DOESN'T IT?
WHAT IF THIS IS JUST ABOUT SOMEBODY WANTING TO SEE TO IT THAT A VERY NICE AND SPECIAL LADY GETS A RESPECTFUL FUNERAL AND A DECENT BURIAL?
I'M SIGNING THE RELEASE. I'M LEAVING THE DETAILS BLANK, AND IF IT COMES BACK TO ME, I DON'T KNOW ANYTHING...
...AND I WILL DENY THAT I EVER MET YOU.
BUT I AM GLAD I DID.

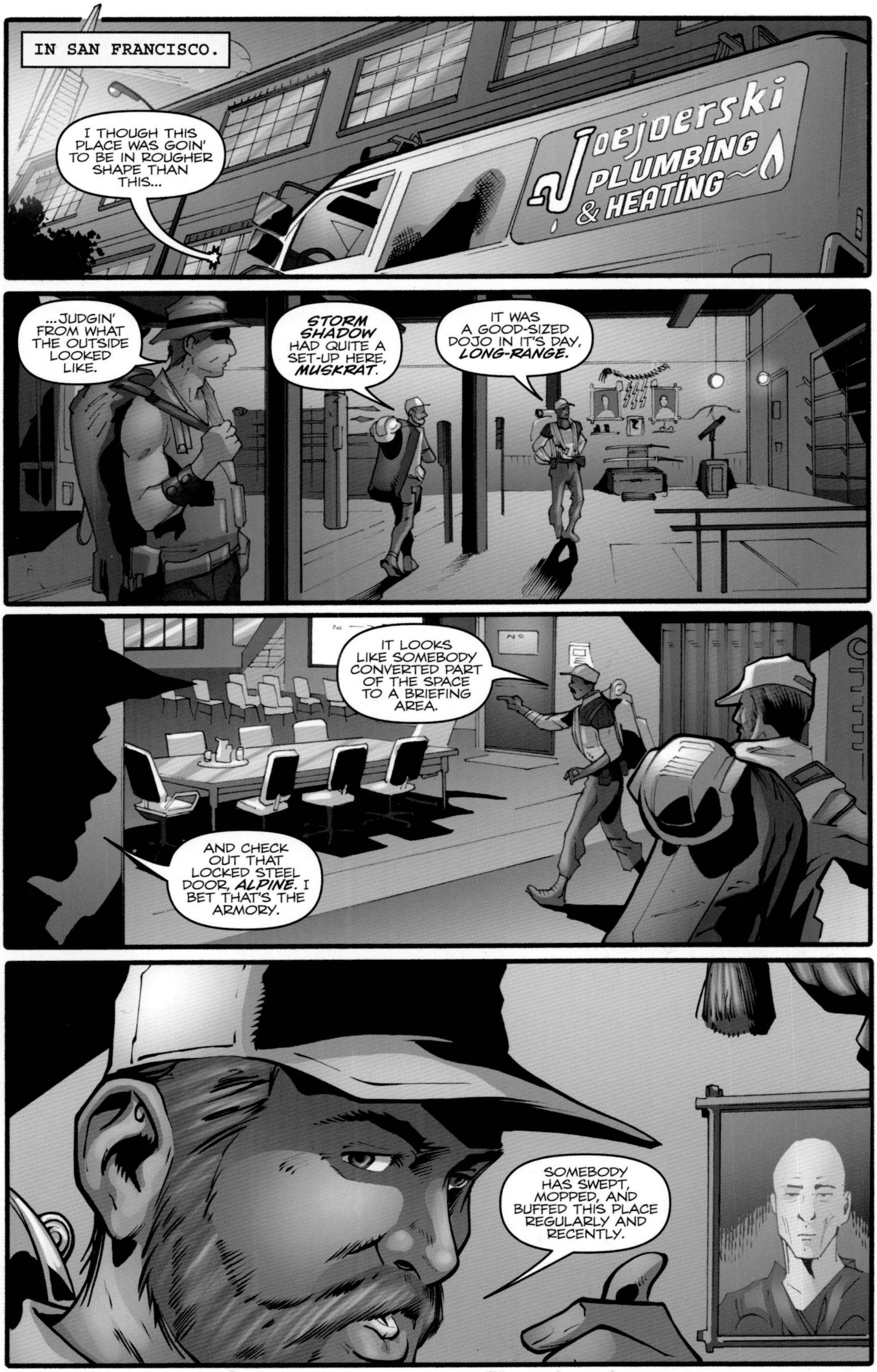
IN SAN FRANCISCO.
I THOUGH THIS PLACE WAS GOIN' TO BE IN ROUGHER SHAPE THAN THIS...
Joejoerski PLUMBING & HEATING
...JUDGIN' FROM WHAT THE OUTSIDE LOOKED LIKE.
STORM SHADOW HAD QUITE A SET-UP HERE, MUSKRAT.
IT WAS A GOOD-SIZED DOJO IN IT'S DAY, LONG-RANGE.
IT LOOKS LIKE SOMEBODY CONVERTED PART OF THE SPACE TO A BRIEFING AREA.
AND CHECK OUT THAT LOCKED STEEL DOOR, ALPINE. I BET THAT'S THE ARMORY.
SOMEBODY HAS SWEPT, MOPPED, AND BUFFED THIS PLACE REGULARLY AND RECENTLY.

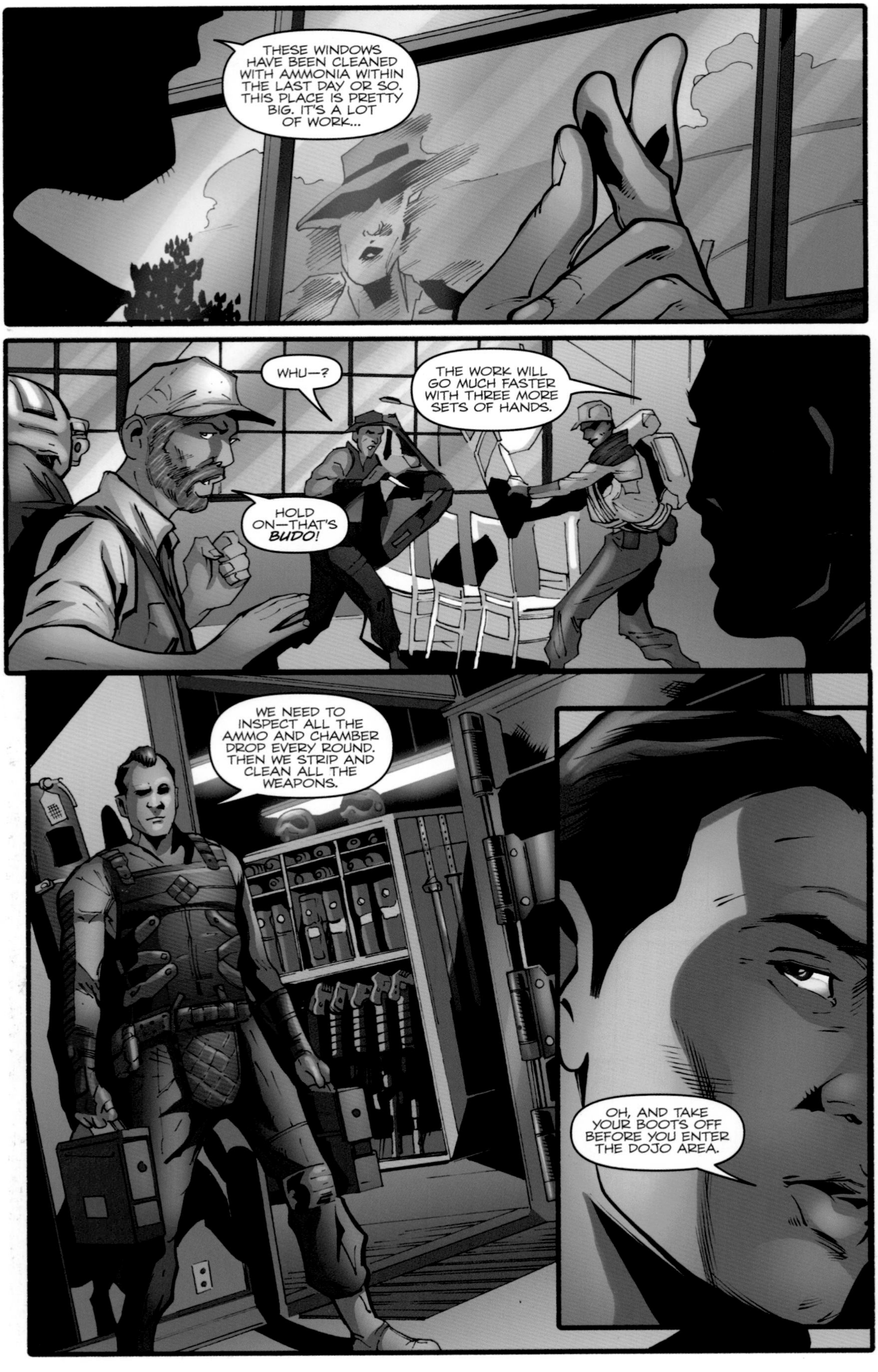
THESE WINDOWS HAVE BEEN CLEANED WITH AMMONIA WITHIN THE LAST DAY OR SO. THIS PLACE IS PRETTY BIG. IT'S A LOT OF WORK...
WHU—?
THE WORK WILL GO MUCH FASTER WITH THREE MORE SETS OF HANDS.
HOLD ON—THAT'S *BUDO*!
WE NEED TO INSPECT ALL THE AMMO AND CHAMBER DROP EVERY ROUND. THEN WE STRIP AND CLEAN ALL THE WEAPONS.
OH, AND TAKE YOUR BOOTS OFF BEFORE YOU ENTER THE DOJO AREA.

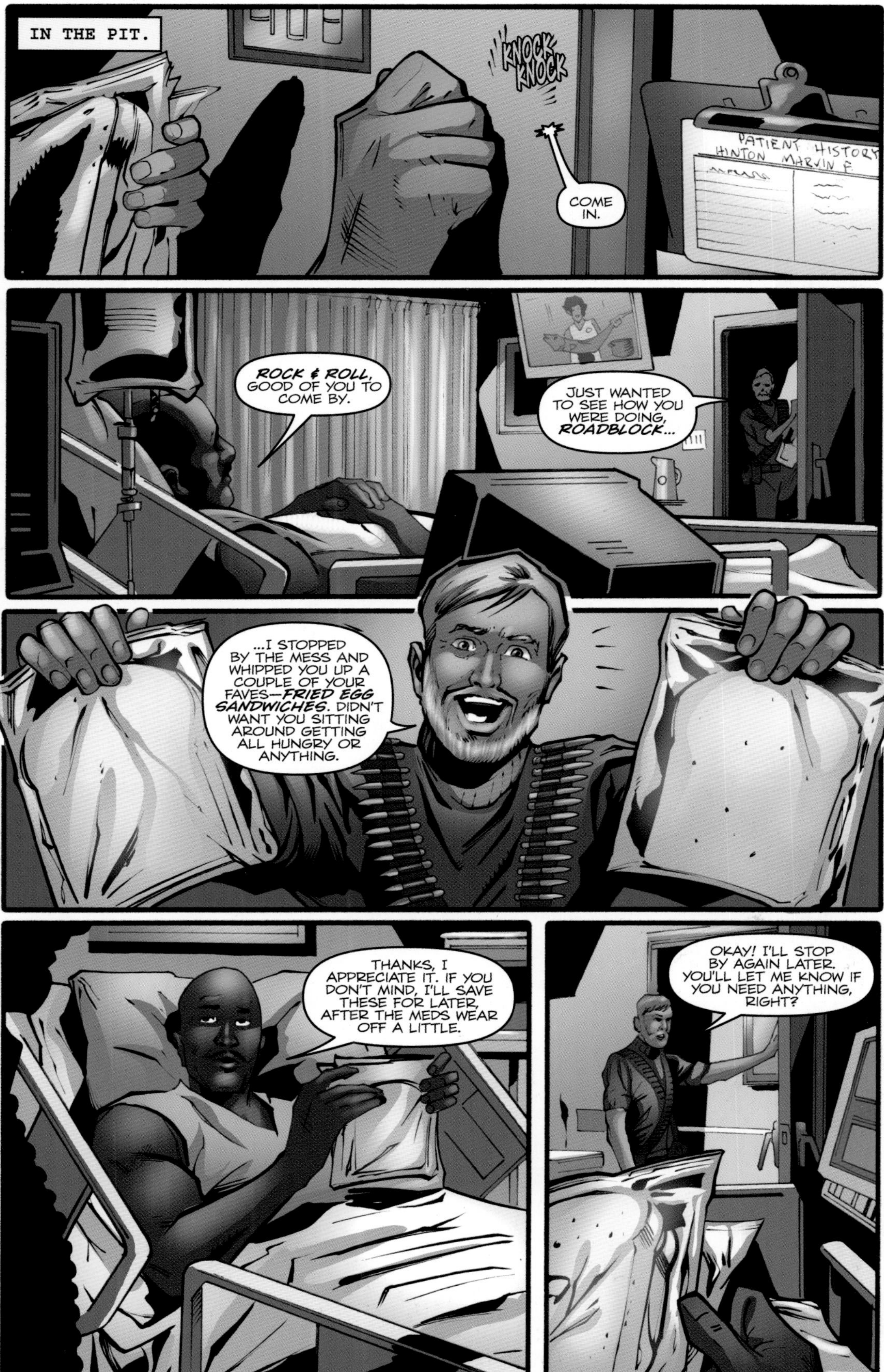

IN THE PIT.
KNOCK KNOCK
PATIENT HISTORY
HINTON MARVIN F.
COME IN.
ROCK & ROLL, GOOD OF YOU TO COME BY.
JUST WANTED TO SEE HOW YOU WERE DOING, ROADBLOCK...
...I STOPPED BY THE MESS AND WHIPPED YOU UP A COUPLE OF YOUR FAVES—FRIED EGG SANDWICHES. DIDN'T WANT YOU SITTING AROUND GETTING ALL HUNGRY OR ANYTHING.
THANKS, I APPRECIATE IT. IF YOU DON'T MIND, I'LL SAVE THESE FOR LATER, AFTER THE MEDS WEAR OFF A LITTLE.
OKAY! I'LL STOP BY AGAIN LATER. YOU'LL LET ME KNOW IF YOU NEED ANYTHING, RIGHT?

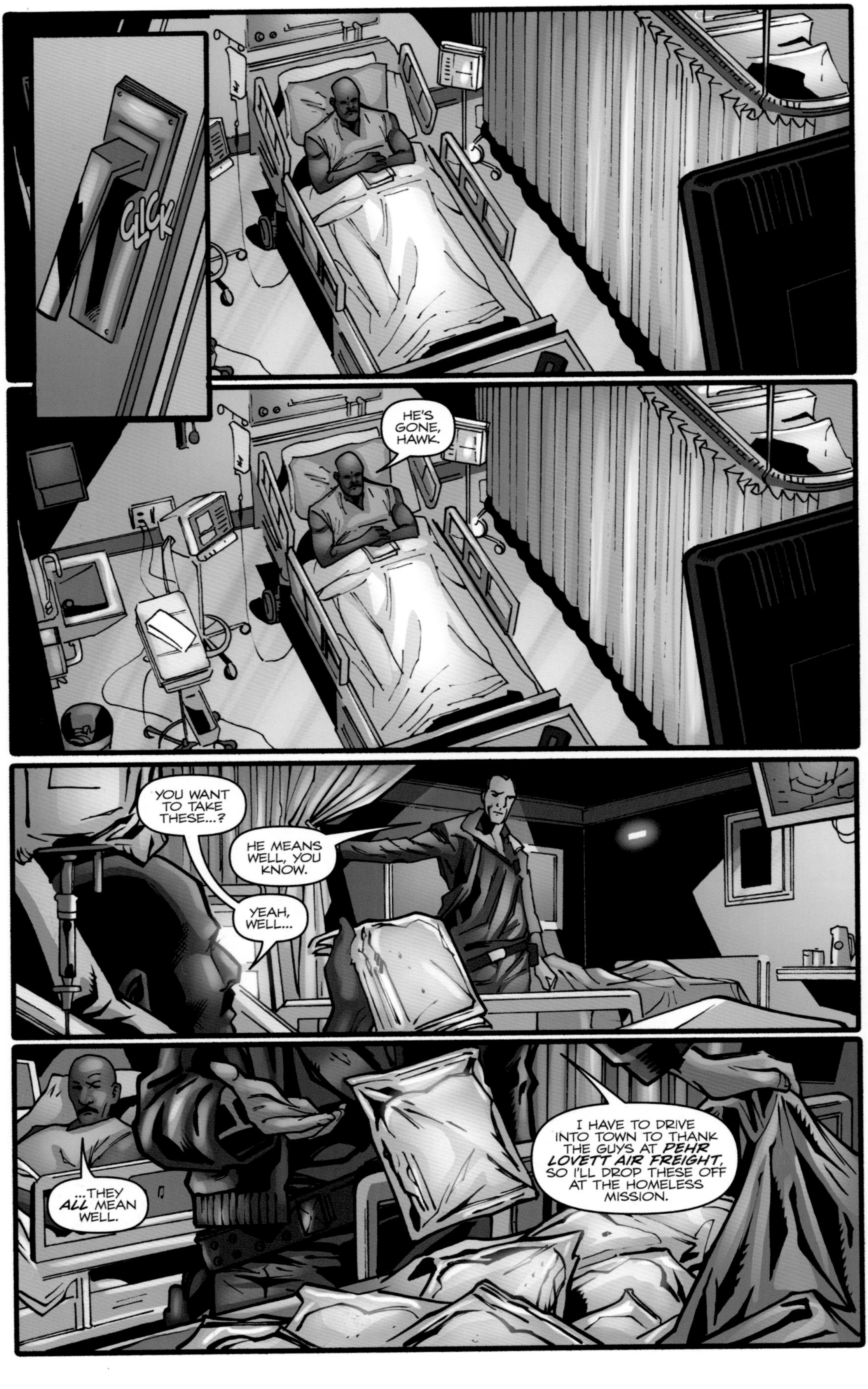
CLICK
HE'S GONE, HAWK.
YOU WANT TO TAKE THESE...?
HE MEANS WELL, YOU KNOW.
YEAH, WELL...
...THEY ALL MEAN WELL.
I HAVE TO DRIVE INTO TOWN TO THANK THE GUYS AT PEHR LOVETT AIR FREIGHT, SO I'LL DROP THESE OFF AT THE HOMELESS MISSION.

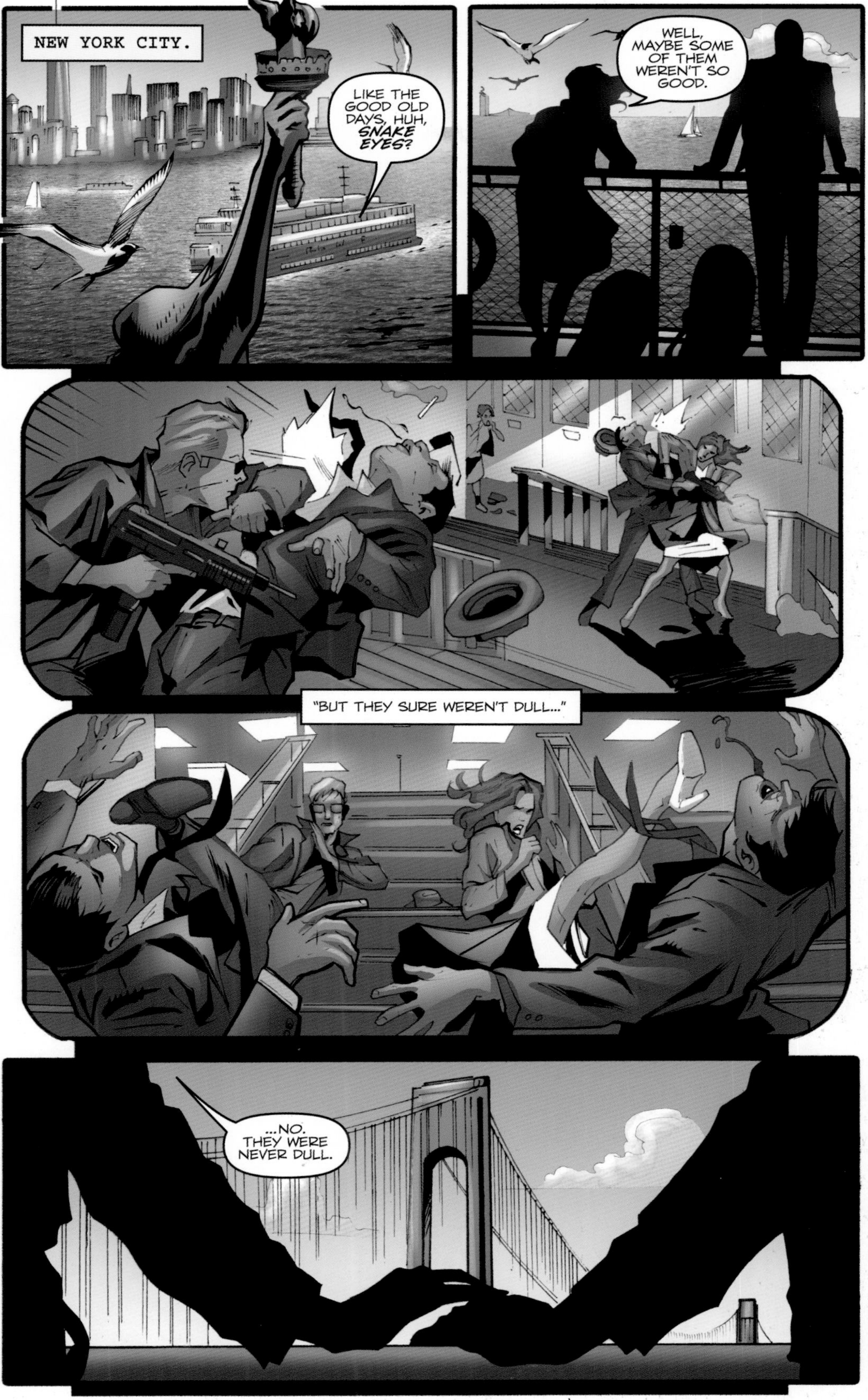
NEW YORK CITY.
LIKE THE GOOD OLD DAYS, HUH, SNAKE EYES?
WELL, MAYBE SOME OF THEM WEREN'T SO GOOD.
"BUT THEY SURE WEREN'T DULL..."
...NO. THEY WERE NEVER DULL.

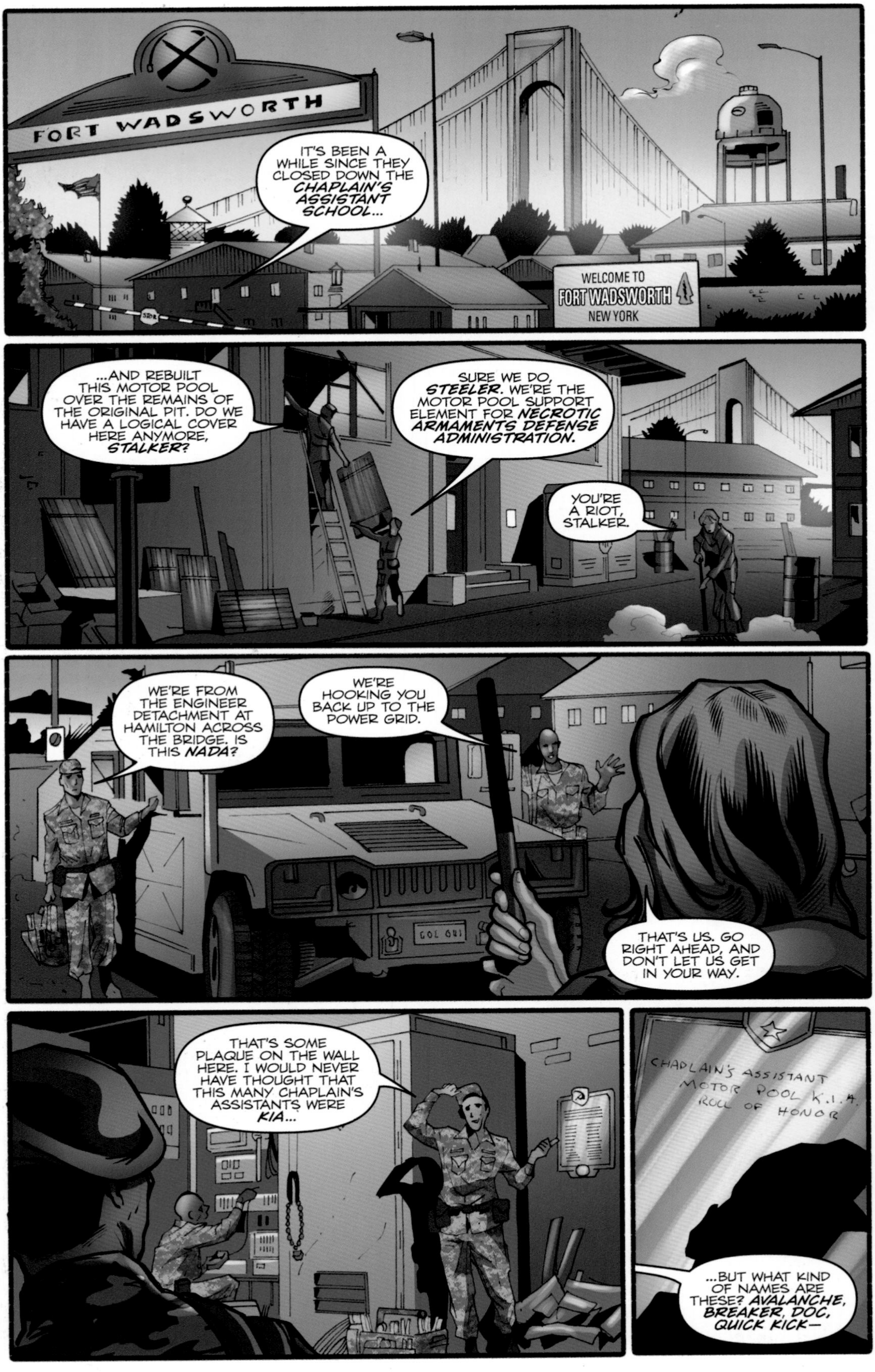
FORT WADSWORTH
IT'S BEEN A WHILE SINCE THEY CLOSED DOWN THE CHAPLAIN'S ASSISTANT SCHOOL...
WELCOME TO FORT WADSWORTH NEW YORK
...AND REBUILT THIS MOTOR POOL OVER THE REMAINS OF THE ORIGINAL PIT. DO WE HAVE A LOGICAL COVER HERE ANYMORE, STALKER?
SURE WE DO, STEELER. WE'RE THE MOTOR POOL SUPPORT ELEMENT FOR NECROTIC ARMAMENTS DEFENSE ADMINISTRATION.
YOU'RE A RIOT, STALKER.
WE'RE FROM THE ENGINEER DETACHMENT AT HAMILTON ACROSS THE BRIDGE. IS THIS NADA?
WE'RE HOOKING YOU BACK UP TO THE POWER GRID.
THAT'S US. GO RIGHT AHEAD, AND DON'T LET US GET IN YOUR WAY.
THAT'S SOME PLAQUE ON THE WALL HERE. I WOULD NEVER HAVE THOUGHT THAT THIS MANY CHAPLAIN'S ASSISTANTS WERE KIA...
CHAPLAIN'S ASSISTANT MOTOR POOL K.I.A. ROLL OF HONOR
...BUT WHAT KIND OF NAMES ARE THESE? AVALANCHE, BREAKER, DOC, QUICK KICK—

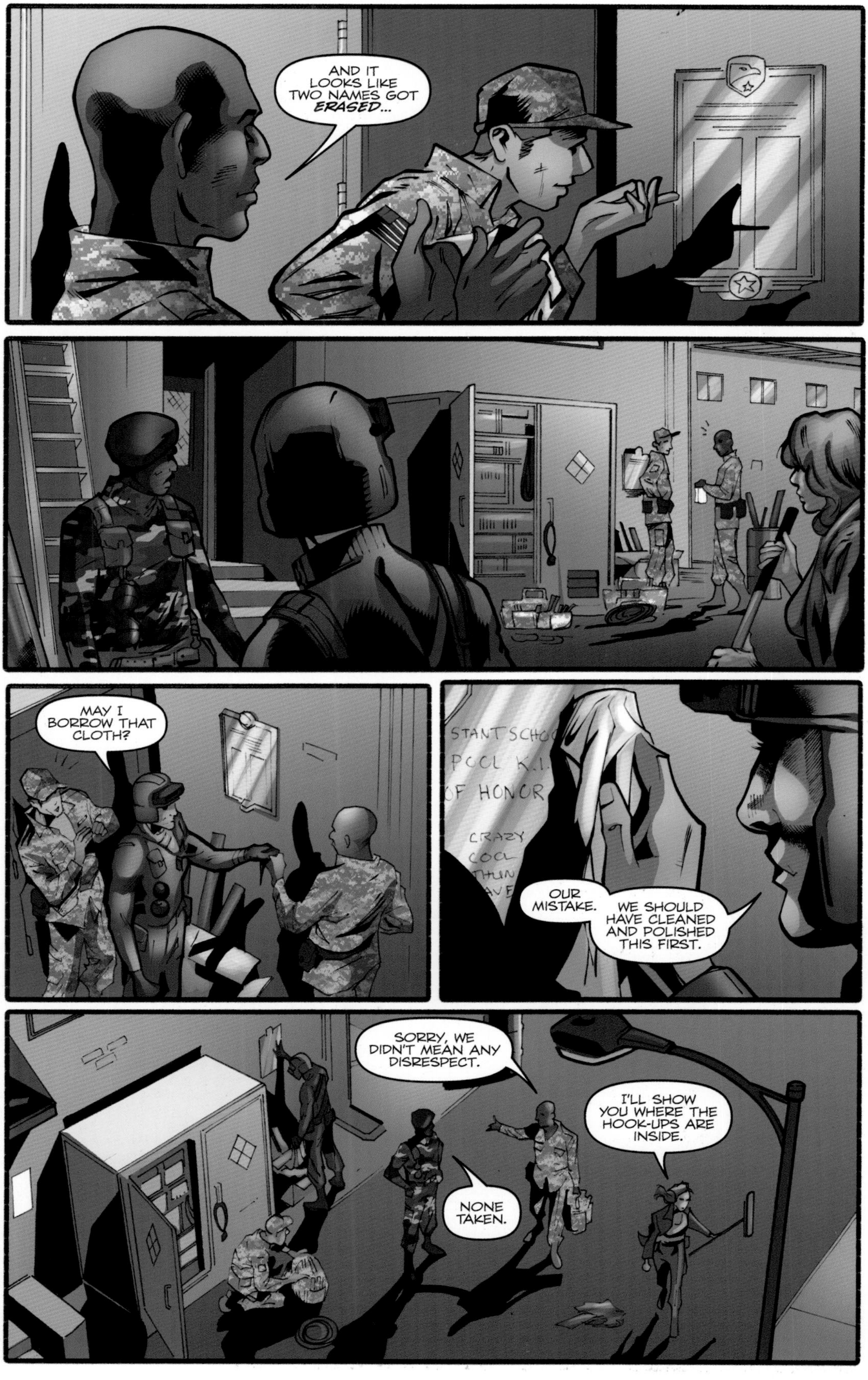
AND IT LOOKS LIKE TWO NAMES GOT *ERASED*...
MAY I BORROW THAT CLOTH?
OUR MISTAKE.
WE SHOULD HAVE CLEANED AND POLISHED THIS FIRST.
SORRY, WE DIDN'T MEAN ANY DISRESPECT.
NONE TAKEN.
I'LL SHOW YOU WHERE THE HOOK-UPS ARE INSIDE.

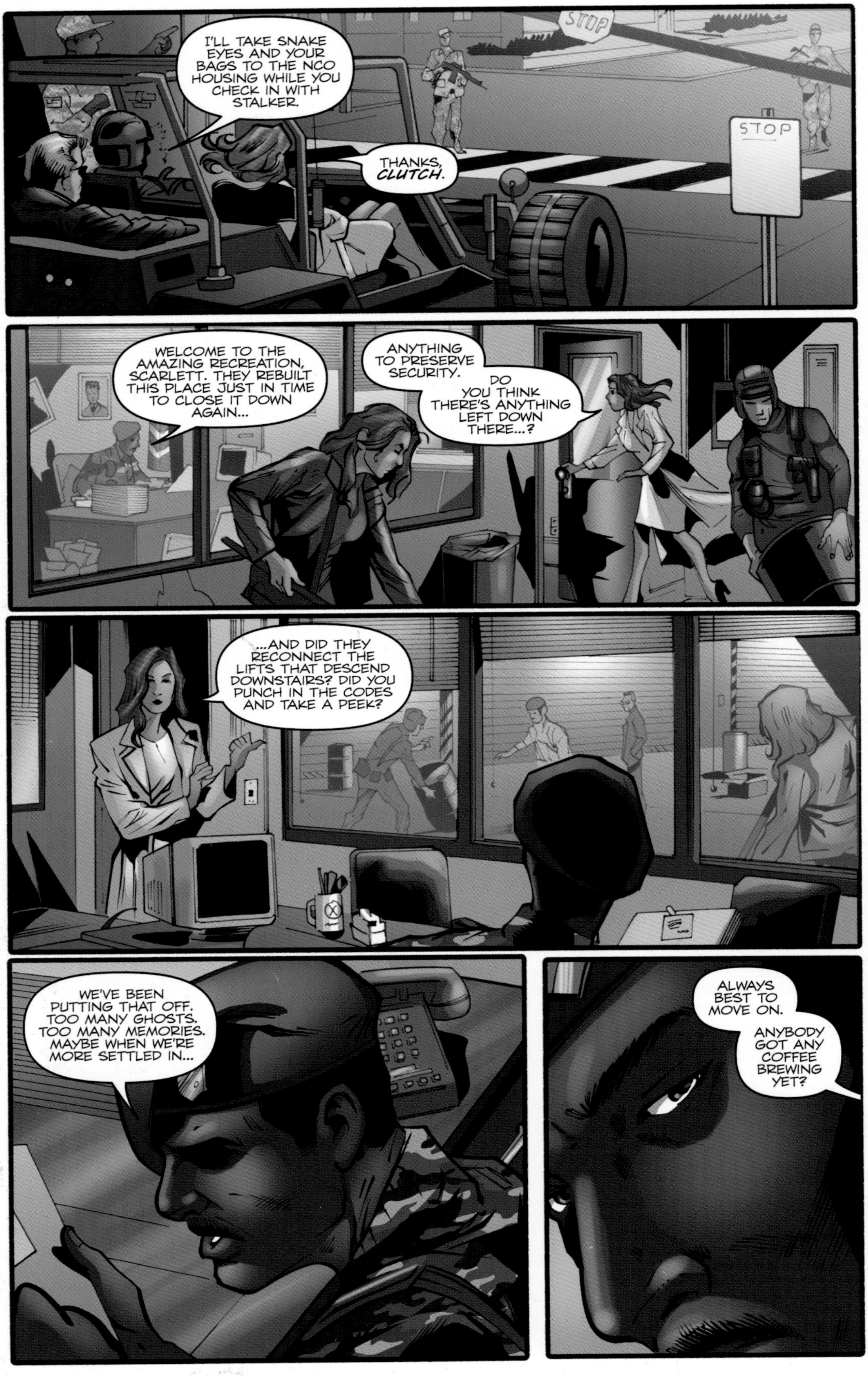
I'LL TAKE SNAKE EYES AND YOUR BAGS TO THE NCO HOUSING WHILE YOU CHECK IN WITH STALKER.
STOP
STOP
THANKS, CLUTCH.
WELCOME TO THE AMAZING RECREATION, SCARLETT. THEY REBUILT THIS PLACE JUST IN TIME TO CLOSE IT DOWN AGAIN...
ANYTHING TO PRESERVE SECURITY.
DO YOU THINK THERE'S ANYTHING LEFT DOWN THERE...?
...AND DID THEY RECONNECT THE LIFTS THAT DESCEND DOWNSTAIRS? DID YOU PUNCH IN THE CODES AND TAKE A PEEK?
WE'VE BEEN PUTTING THAT OFF. TOO MANY GHOSTS. TOO MANY MEMORIES. MAYBE WHEN WE'RE MORE SETTLED IN...
ALWAYS BEST TO MOVE ON.
ANYBODY GOT ANY COFFEE BREWING YET?

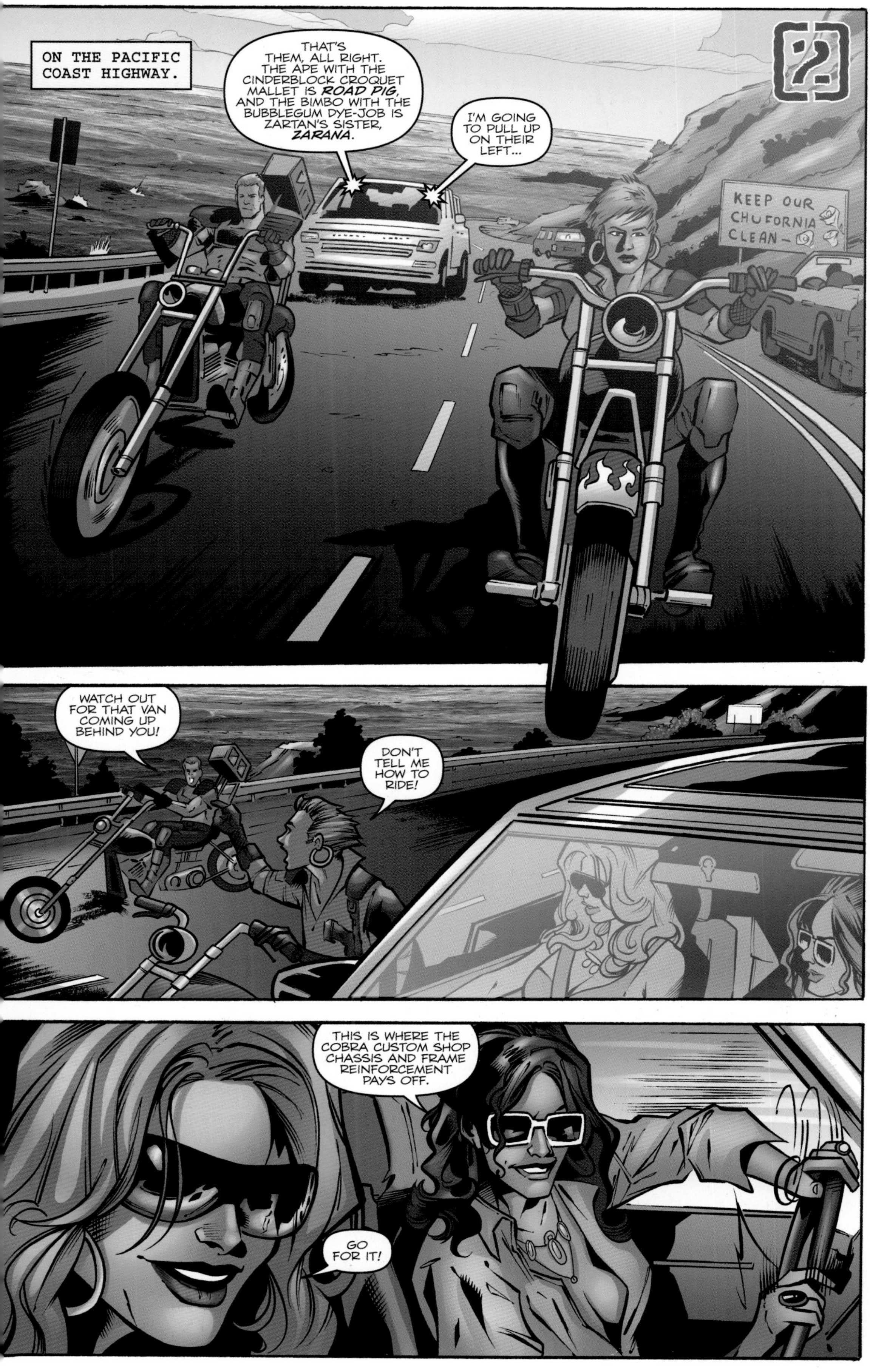

ON THE PACIFIC COAST HIGHWAY.
THAT'S THEM, ALL RIGHT. THE APE WITH THE CINDERBLOCK CROQUET MALLET IS ROAD PIG, AND THE BIMBO WITH THE BUBBLEGUM DYE-JOB IS ZARTAN'S SISTER, ZARANA.
I'M GOING TO PULL UP ON THEIR LEFT...
KEEP OUR CHUFORNIA CLEAN
WATCH OUT FOR THAT VAN COMING UP BEHIND YOU!
DON'T TELL ME HOW TO RIDE!
THIS IS WHERE THE COBRA CUSTOM SHOP CHASSIS AND FRAME REINFORCEMENT PAYS OFF.
GO FOR IT!

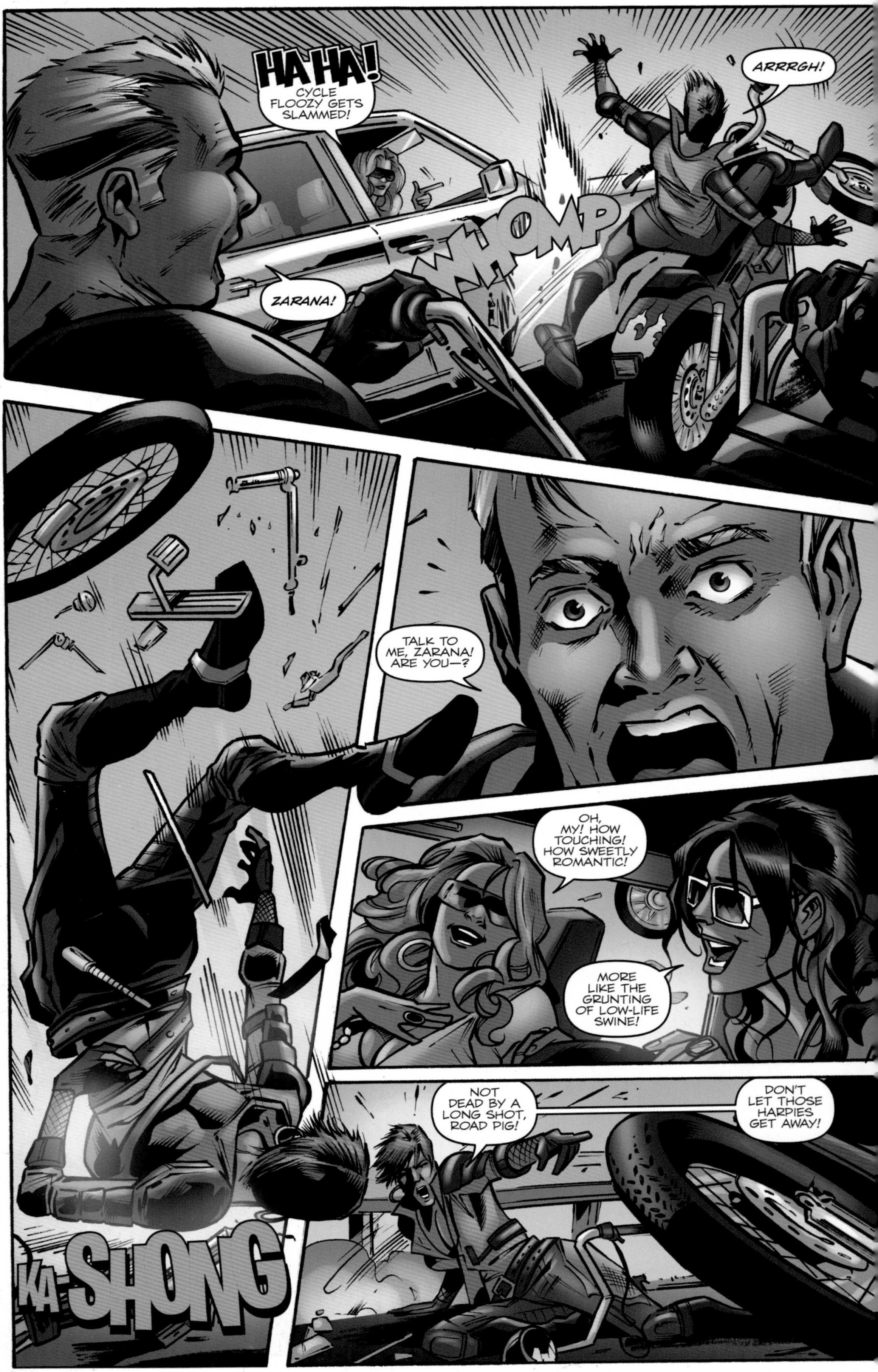
HAHA!
CYCLE FLOOZY GETS SLAMMED!
ARRRGH!
WHOMP
ZARANA!
TALK TO ME, ZARANA! ARE YOU—?
OH, MY! HOW TOUCHING! HOW SWEETLY ROMANTIC!
MORE LIKE THE GRUNTING OF LOW-LIFE SWINE!
NOT DEAD BY A LONG SHOT, ROAD PIG!
DON'T LET THOSE HARPIES GET AWAY!
KA-SHONG

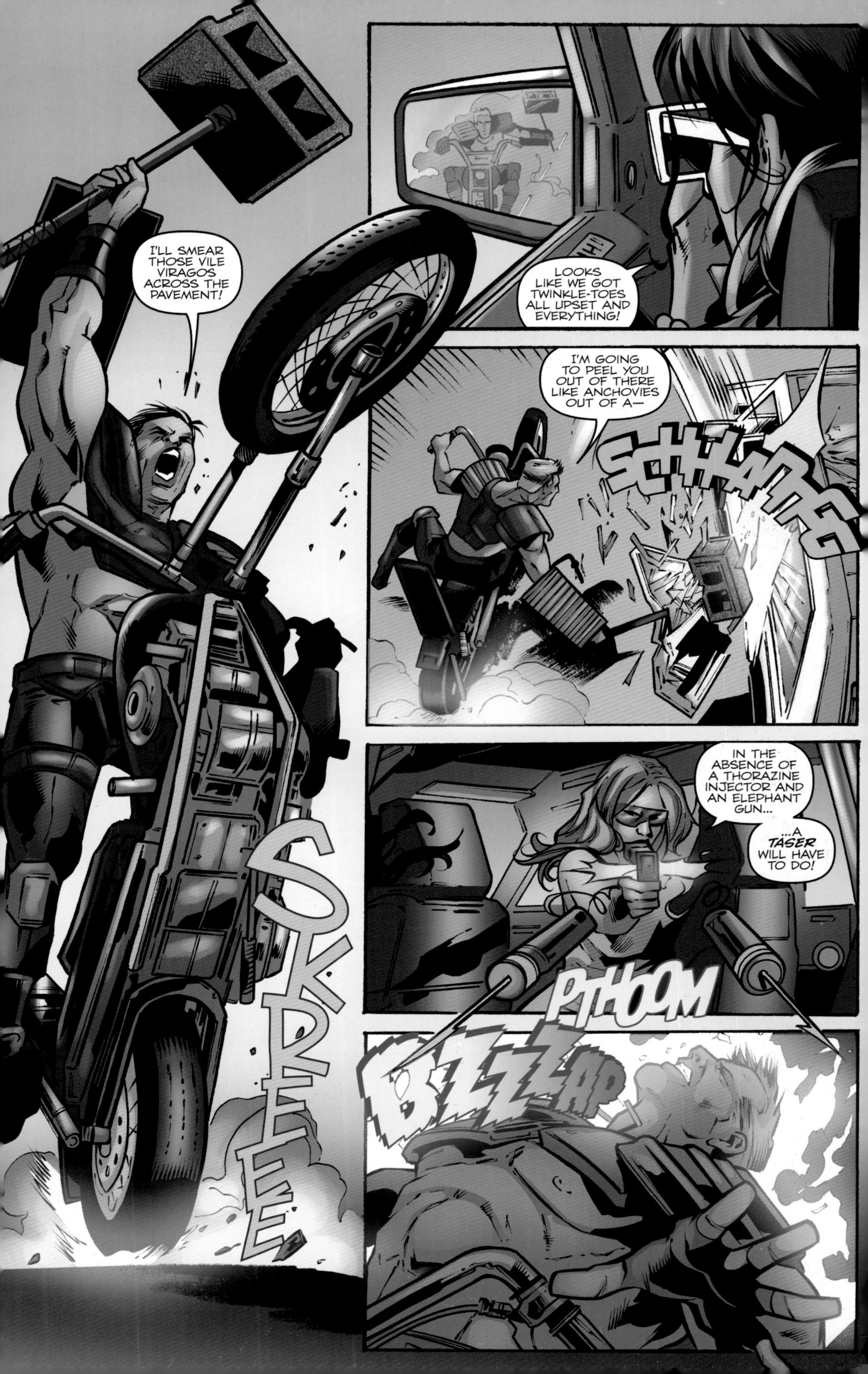
I'LL SMEAR THOSE VILE VIRAGOS ACROSS THE PAVEMENT!
SKREEEE
LOOKS LIKE WE GOT TWINKLE-TOES ALL UPSET AND EVERYTHING!
I'M GOING TO PEEL YOU OUT OF THERE LIKE ANCHOVIES OUT OF A—
SCHLAFFEG
IN THE ABSENCE OF A THORAZINE INJECTOR AND AN ELEPHANT GUN...
...A TASER WILL HAVE TO DO!
PTHOOM
BZZZAP

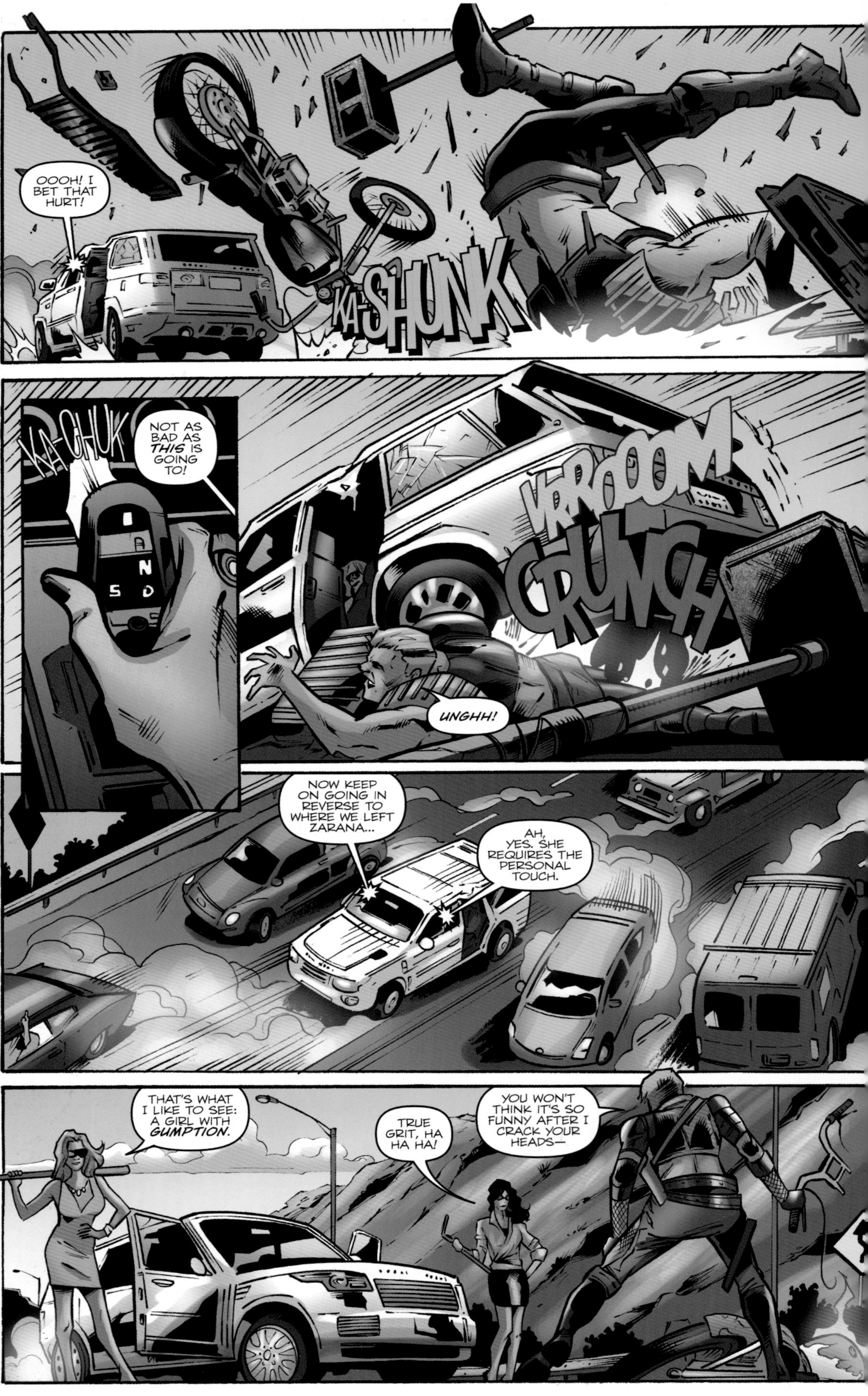
OOOH! I BET THAT HURT!
KA-SHUNK
KA-CHUK
NOT AS BAD AS *THIS* IS GOING TO!
VRROOOM
CRUNCH
UNGHH!
NOW KEEP ON GOING IN REVERSE TO WHERE WE LEFT ZARANA...
AH, YES. SHE REQUIRES THE PERSONAL TOUCH.
THAT'S WHAT I LIKE TO SEE: A GIRL WITH ***GUMPTION***.
TRUE GRIT, HA HA HA!
YOU WON'T THINK IT'S SO FUNNY AFTER I CRACK YOUR HEADS—

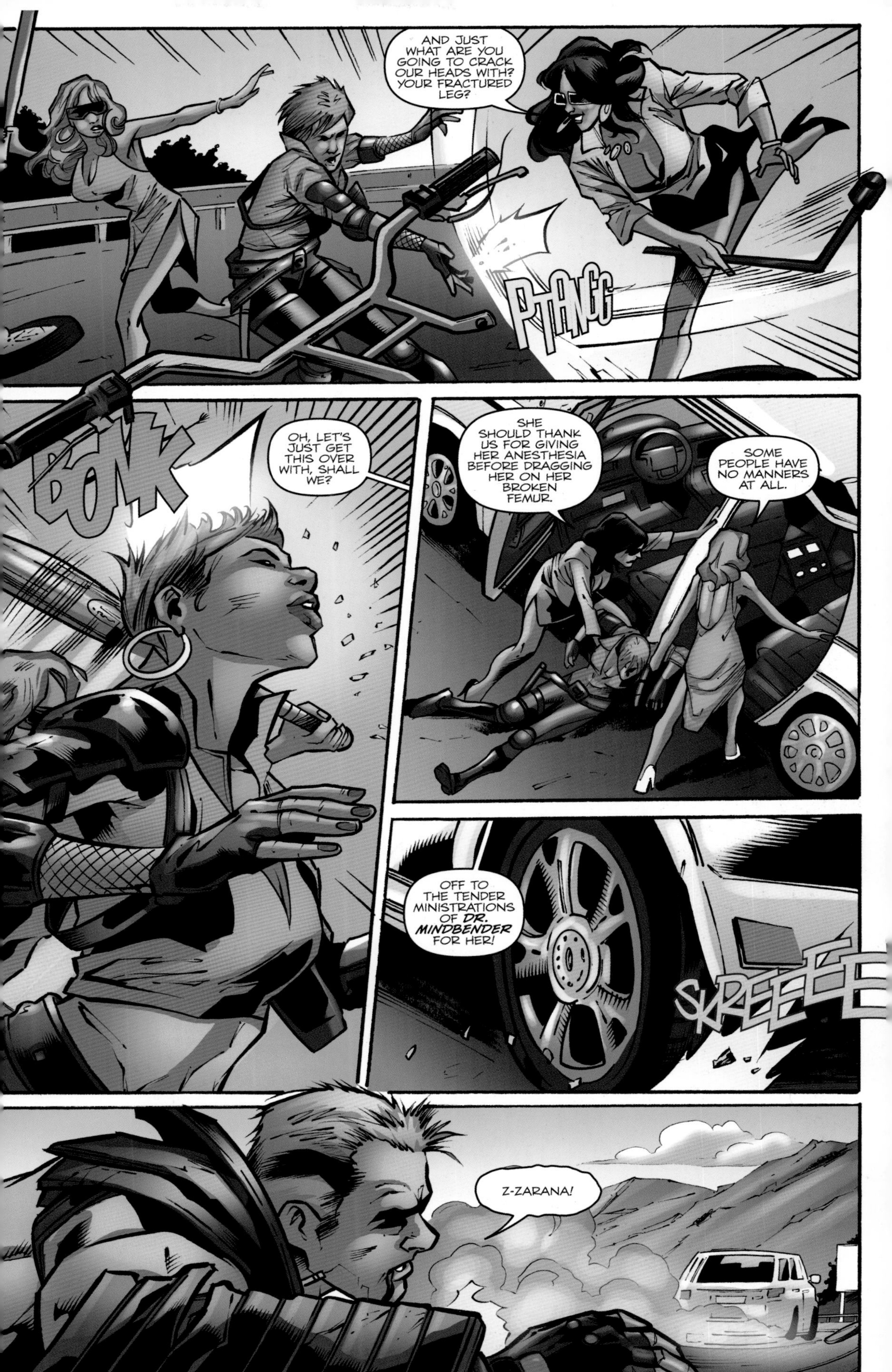

AND JUST WHAT ARE YOU GOING TO CRACK OUR HEADS WITH? YOUR FRACTURED LEG?
PTANGG
BONK
OH, LET'S JUST GET THIS OVER WITH, SHALL WE?
SHE SHOULD THANK US FOR GIVING HER ANESTHESIA BEFORE DRAGGING HER ON HER BROKEN FEMUR.
SOME PEOPLE HAVE NO MANNERS AT ALL.
OFF TO THE TENDER MINISTRATIONS OF DR. MINDBENDER FOR HER!
SKREEEEE
Z-ZARANA!

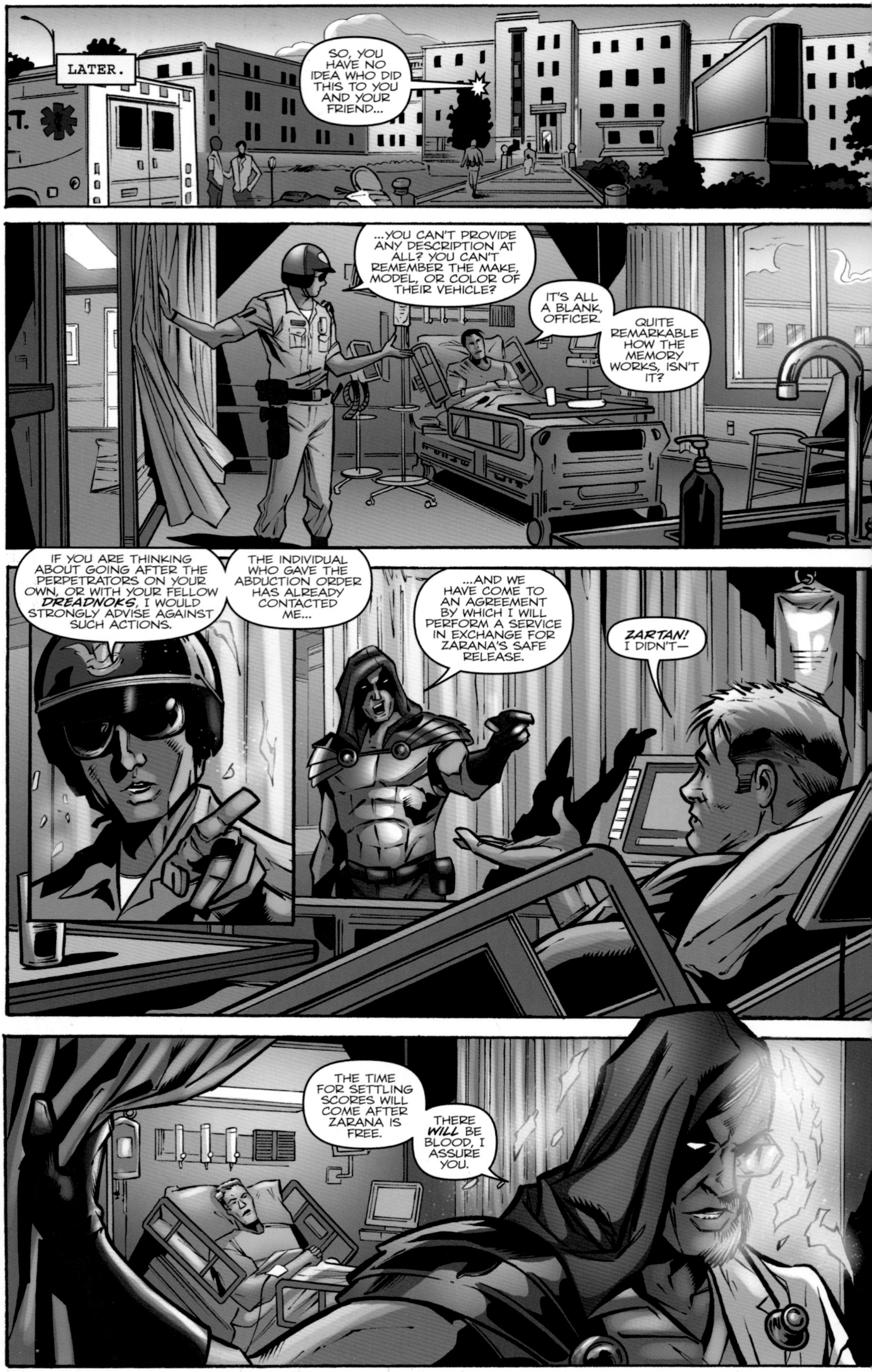
LATER.
SO, YOU HAVE NO IDEA WHO DID THIS TO YOU AND YOUR FRIEND...
...YOU CAN'T PROVIDE ANY DESCRIPTION AT ALL? YOU CAN'T REMEMBER THE MAKE, MODEL, OR COLOR OF THEIR VEHICLE?
IT'S ALL A BLANK, OFFICER.
QUITE REMARKABLE HOW THE MEMORY WORKS, ISN'T IT?
IF YOU ARE THINKING ABOUT GOING AFTER THE PERPETRATORS ON YOUR OWN, OR WITH YOUR FELLOW DREADNOKS, I WOULD STRONGLY ADVISE AGAINST SUCH ACTIONS.
THE INDIVIDUAL WHO GAVE THE ABDUCTION ORDER HAS ALREADY CONTACTED ME...
...AND WE HAVE COME TO AN AGREEMENT BY WHICH I WILL PERFORM A SERVICE IN EXCHANGE FOR ZARANA'S SAFE RELEASE.
ZARTAN! I DIDN'T—
THE TIME FOR SETTLING SCORES WILL COME AFTER ZARANA IS FREE.
THERE WILL BE BLOOD, I ASSURE YOU.

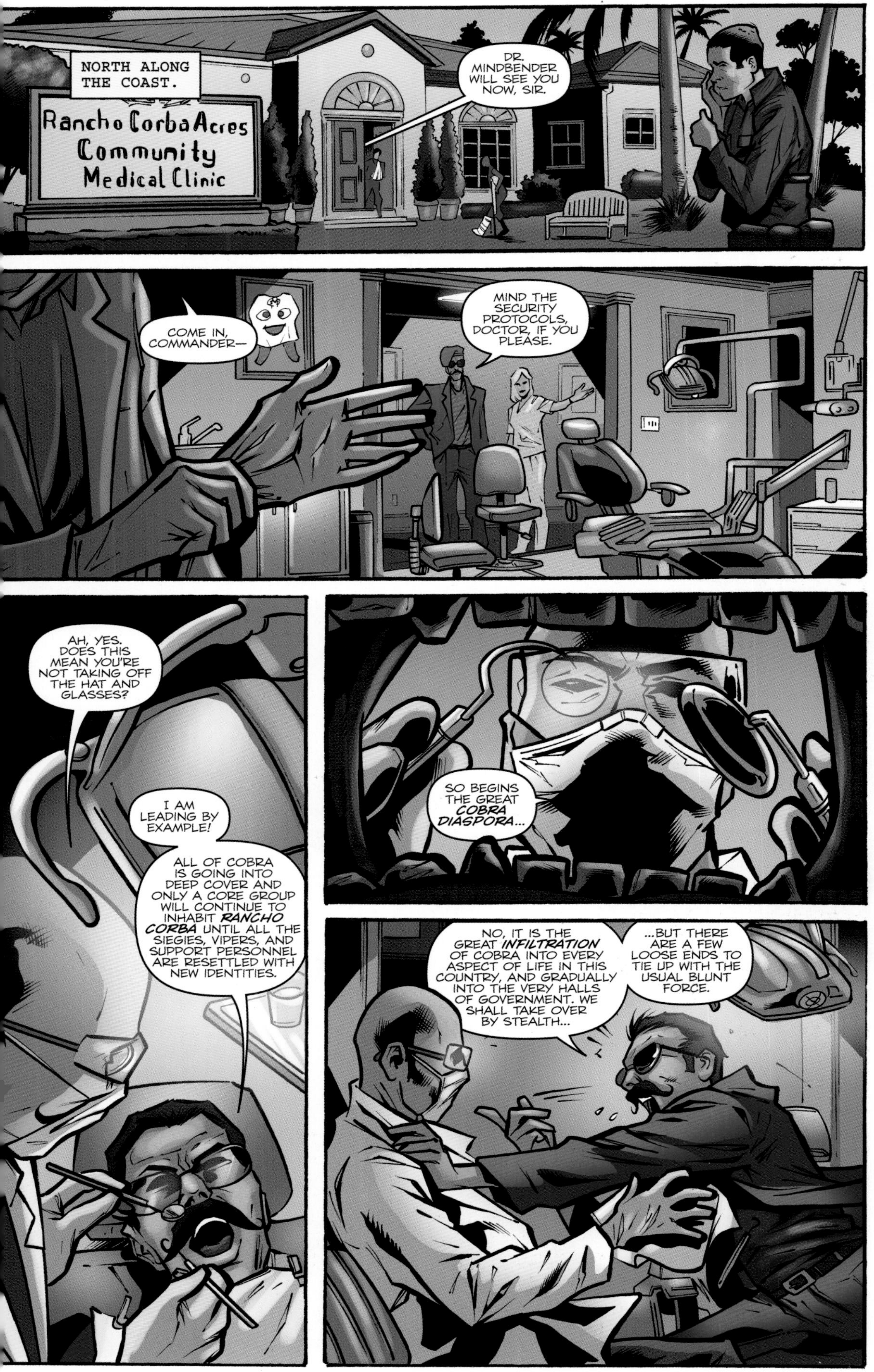
NORTH ALONG THE COAST.
Rancho Corba Acres Community Medical Clinic
DR. MINDBENDER WILL SEE YOU NOW, SIR.
COME IN, COMMANDER—
MIND THE SECURITY PROTOCOLS, DOCTOR, IF YOU PLEASE.
AH, YES. DOES THIS MEAN YOU'RE NOT TAKING OFF THE HAT AND GLASSES?
I AM LEADING BY EXAMPLE!
ALL OF COBRA IS GOING INTO DEEP COVER AND ONLY A CORE GROUP WILL CONTINUE TO INHABIT RANCHO CORBA UNTIL ALL THE SIEGIES, VIPERS, AND SUPPORT PERSONNEL ARE RESETTLED WITH NEW IDENTITIES.
SO BEGINS THE GREAT COBRA DIASPORA...
NO, IT IS THE GREAT INFILTRATION OF COBRA INTO EVERY ASPECT OF LIFE IN THIS COUNTRY, AND GRADUALLY INTO THE VERY HALLS OF GOVERNMENT. WE SHALL TAKE OVER BY STEALTH...
...BUT THERE ARE A FEW LOOSE ENDS TO TIE UP WITH THE USUAL BLUNT FORCE.

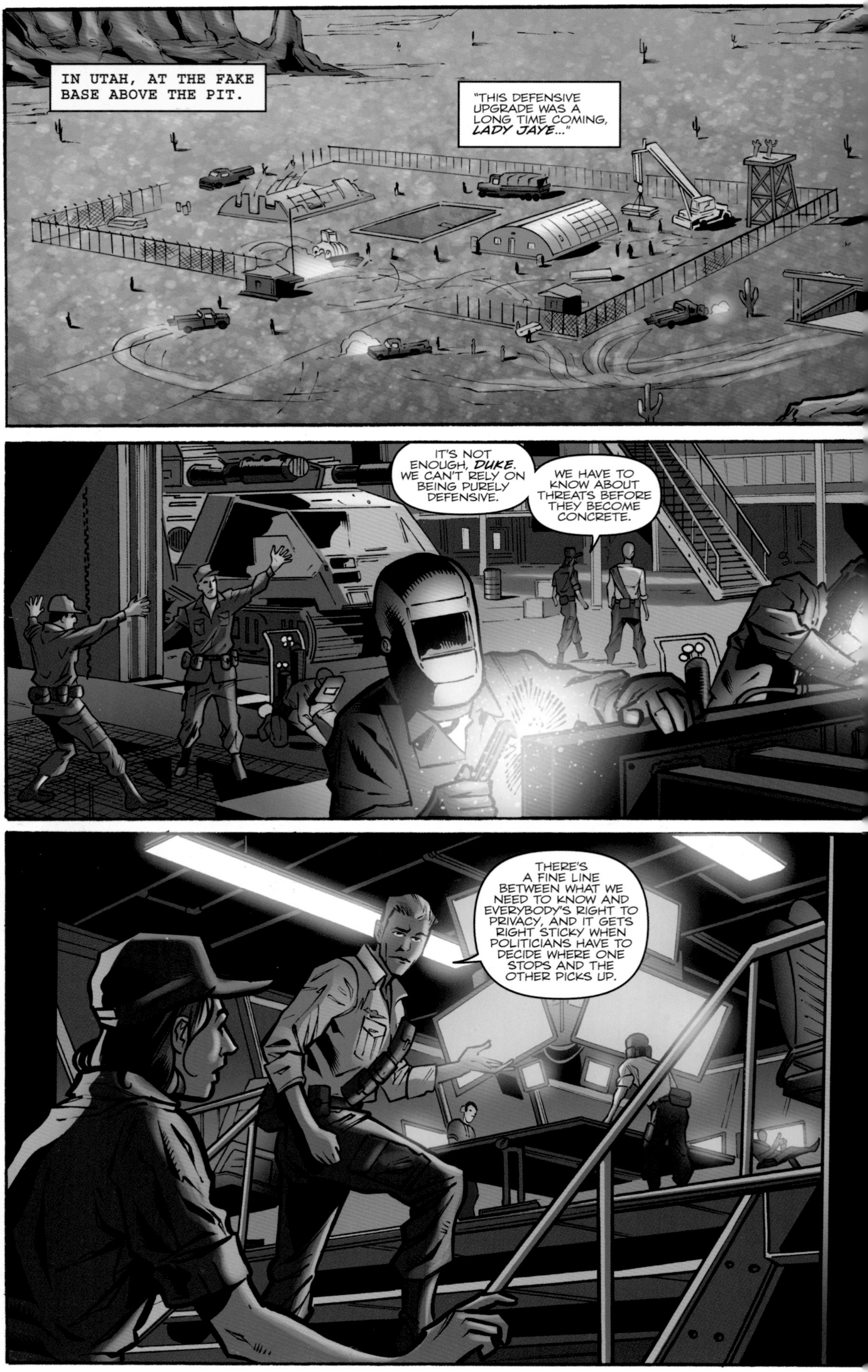
IN UTAH, AT THE FAKE BASE ABOVE THE PIT.
"THIS DEFENSIVE UPGRADE WAS A LONG TIME COMING, LADY JAYE..."
IT'S NOT ENOUGH, DUKE. WE CAN'T RELY ON BEING PURELY DEFENSIVE.
WE HAVE TO KNOW ABOUT THREATS BEFORE THEY BECOME CONCRETE.
THERE'S A FINE LINE BETWEEN WHAT WE NEED TO KNOW AND EVERYBODY'S RIGHT TO PRIVACY, AND IT GETS RIGHT STICKY WHEN POLITICIANS HAVE TO DECIDE WHERE ONE STOPS AND THE OTHER PICKS UP.

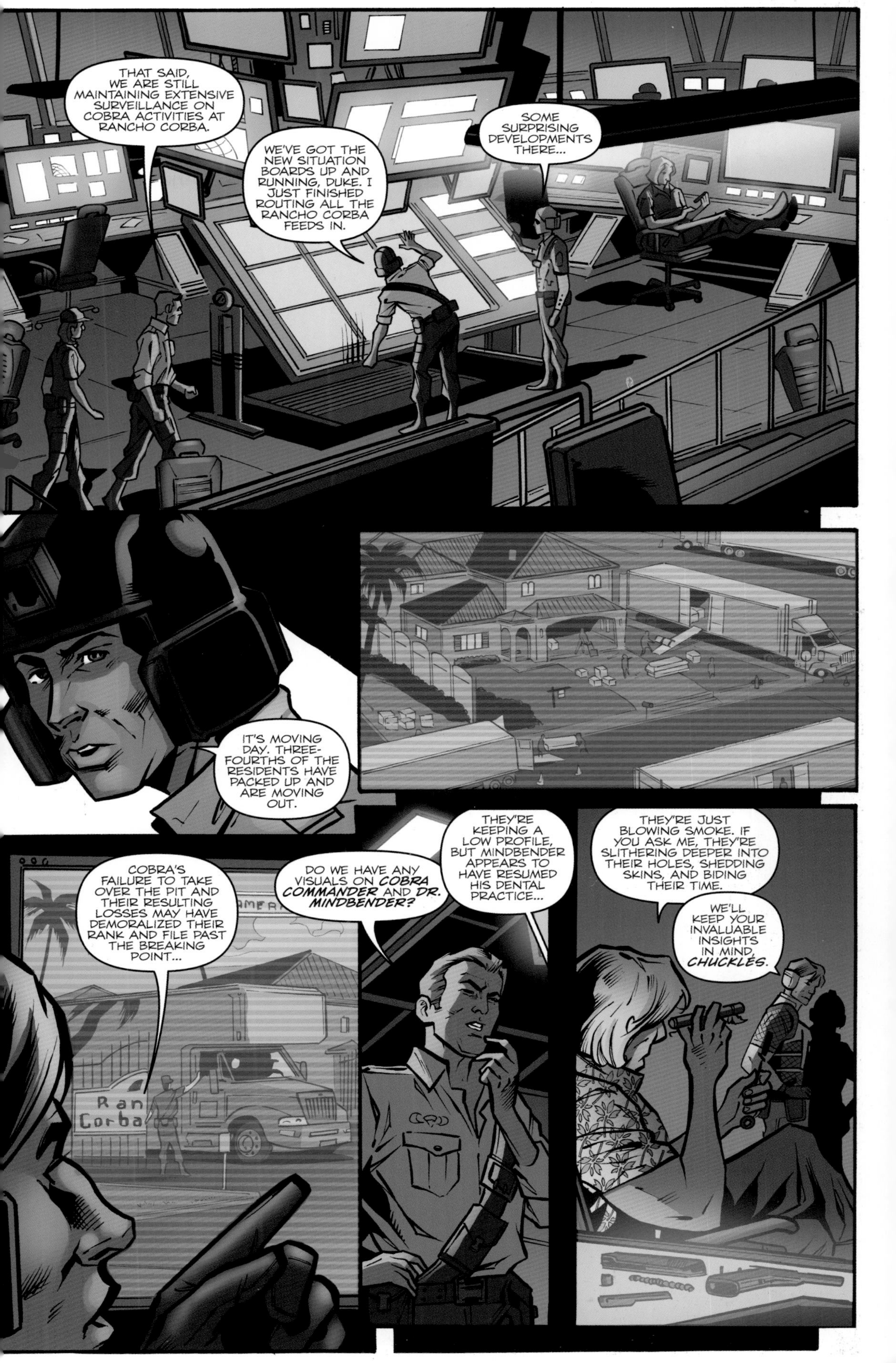
THAT SAID, WE ARE STILL MAINTAINING EXTENSIVE SURVEILLANCE ON COBRA ACTIVITIES AT RANCHO CORBA.
WE'VE GOT THE NEW SITUATION BOARDS UP AND RUNNING, DUKE. I JUST FINISHED ROUTING ALL THE RANCHO CORBA FEEDS IN.
SOME SURPRISING DEVELOPMENTS THERE...
IT'S MOVING DAY. THREE-FOURTHS OF THE RESIDENTS HAVE PACKED UP AND ARE MOVING OUT.
COBRA'S FAILURE TO TAKE OVER THE PIT AND THEIR RESULTING LOSSES MAY HAVE DEMORALIZED THEIR RANK AND FILE PAST THE BREAKING POINT...
Ran
Corba
DO WE HAVE ANY VISUALS ON ***COBRA COMMANDER*** AND ***DR. MINDBENDER?***
THEY'RE KEEPING A LOW PROFILE, BUT MINDBENDER APPEARS TO HAVE RESUMED HIS DENTAL PRACTICE...
THEY'RE JUST BLOWING SMOKE. IF YOU ASK ME, THEY'RE SLITHERING DEEPER INTO THEIR HOLES, SHEDDING SKINS, AND BIDING THEIR TIME.
WE'LL KEEP YOUR INVALUABLE INSIGHTS IN MIND, ***CHUCKLES***.

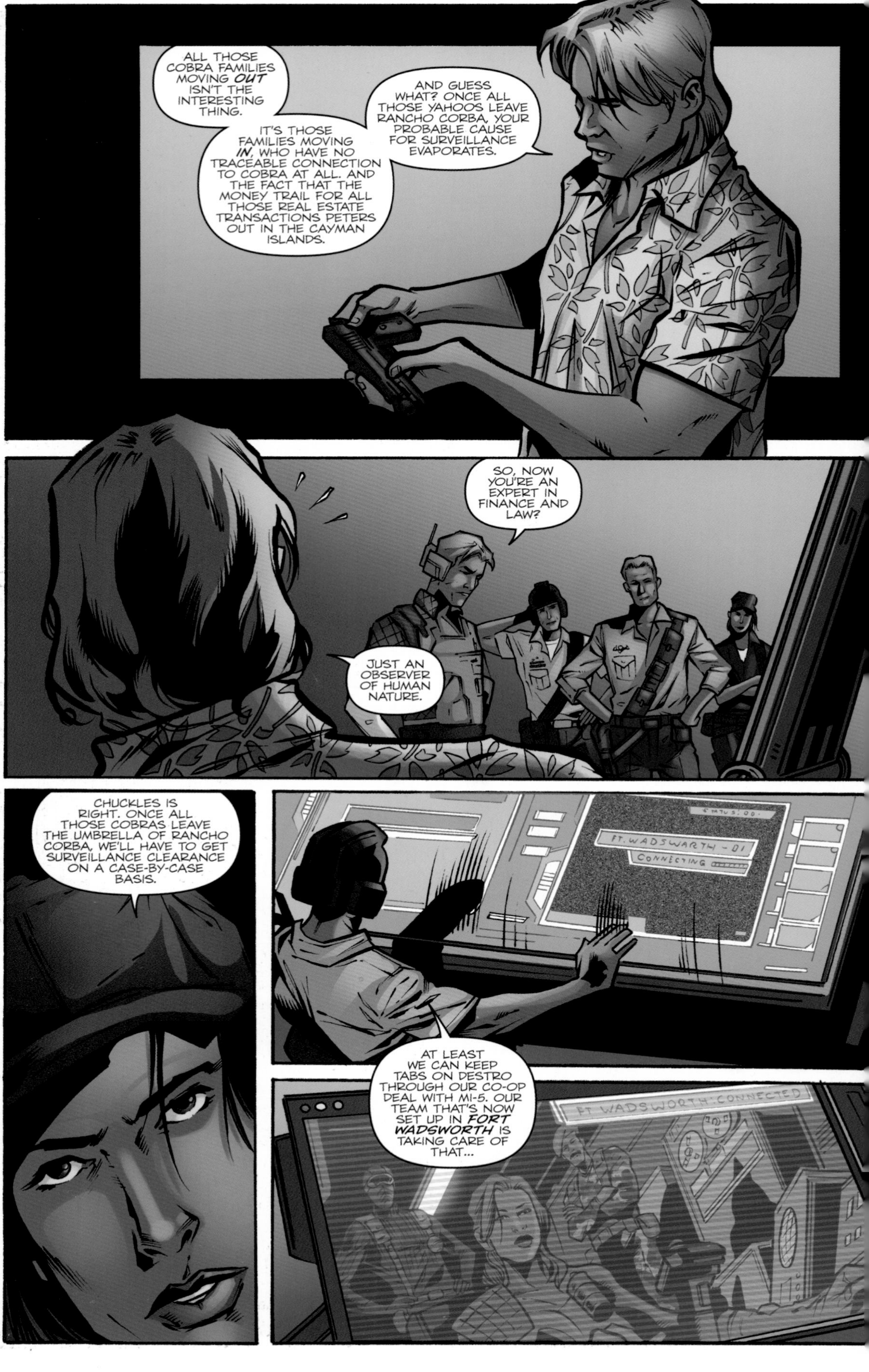

ALL THOSE COBRA FAMILIES MOVING OUT ISN'T THE INTERESTING THING.
IT'S THOSE FAMILIES MOVING IN, WHO HAVE NO TRACEABLE CONNECTION TO COBRA AT ALL. AND THE FACT THAT THE MONEY TRAIL FOR ALL THOSE REAL ESTATE TRANSACTIONS PETERS OUT IN THE CAYMAN ISLANDS.
AND GUESS WHAT? ONCE ALL THOSE YAHOOS LEAVE RANCHO CORBA, YOUR PROBABLE CAUSE FOR SURVEILLANCE EVAPORATES.
SO, NOW YOU'RE AN EXPERT IN FINANCE AND LAW?
JUST AN OBSERVER OF HUMAN NATURE.
CHUCKLES IS RIGHT. ONCE ALL THOSE COBRAS LEAVE THE UMBRELLA OF RANCHO CORBA, WE'LL HAVE TO GET SURVEILLANCE CLEARANCE ON A CASE-BY-CASE BASIS.
FT. WADSWORTH - 01
CONNECTING
AT LEAST WE CAN KEEP TABS ON DESTRO THROUGH OUR CO-OP DEAL WITH MI-5. OUR TEAM THAT'S NOW SET UP IN FORT WADSWORTH IS TAKING CARE OF THAT...
FT. WADSWORTH: CONNECTED

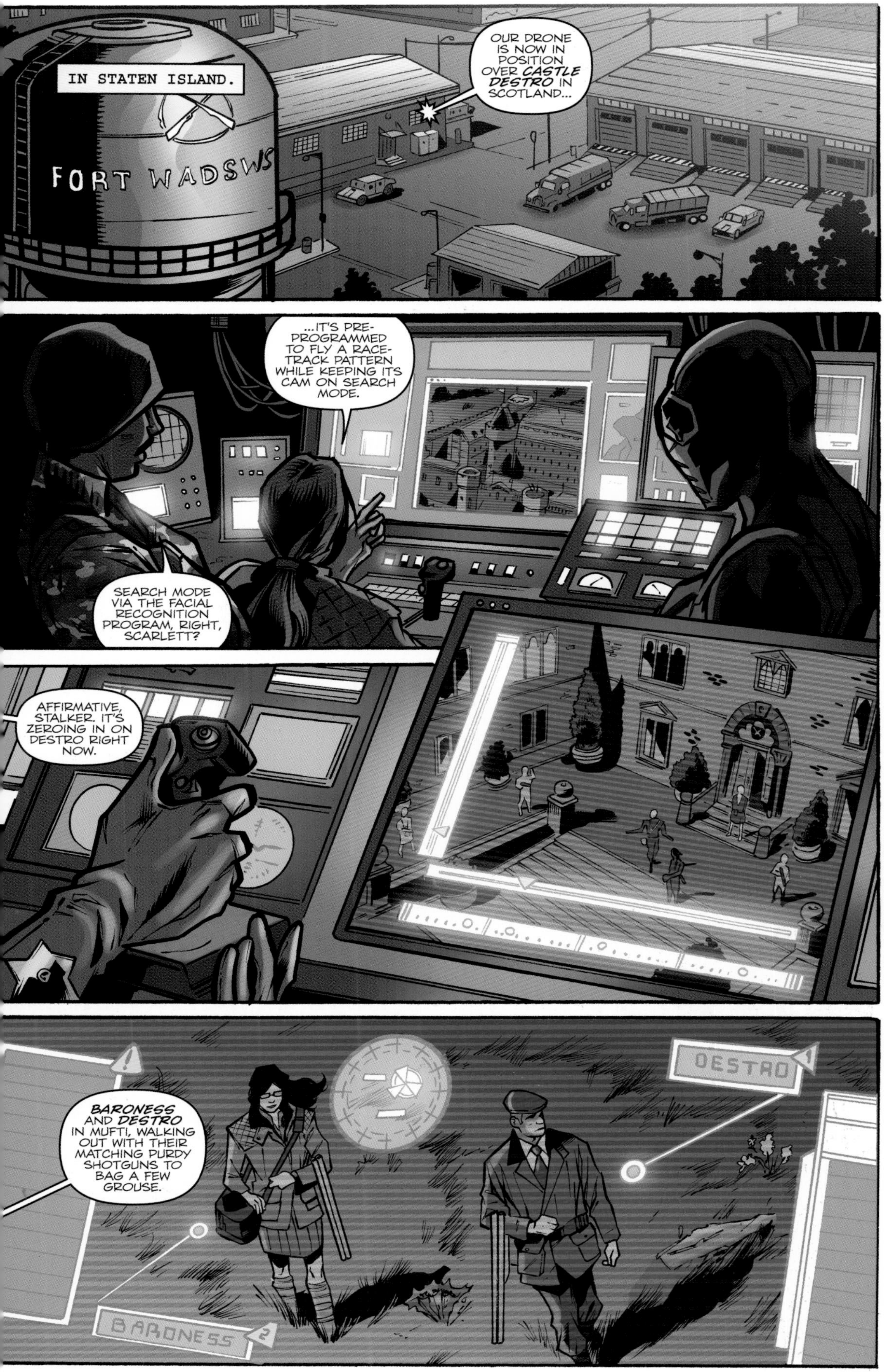
IN STATEN ISLAND.
FORT WADSWS
OUR DRONE IS NOW IN POSITION OVER CASTLE DESTRO IN SCOTLAND...
...IT'S PRE-PROGRAMMED TO FLY A RACE-TRACK PATTERN WHILE KEEPING ITS CAM ON SEARCH MODE.
SEARCH MODE VIA THE FACIAL RECOGNITION PROGRAM, RIGHT, SCARLETT?
AFFIRMATIVE, STALKER. IT'S ZEROING IN ON DESTRO RIGHT NOW.
DESTRO
BARONESS AND DESTRO IN MUFTI, WALKING OUT WITH THEIR MATCHING PURDY SHOTGUNS TO BAG A FEW GROUSE.
BARONESS

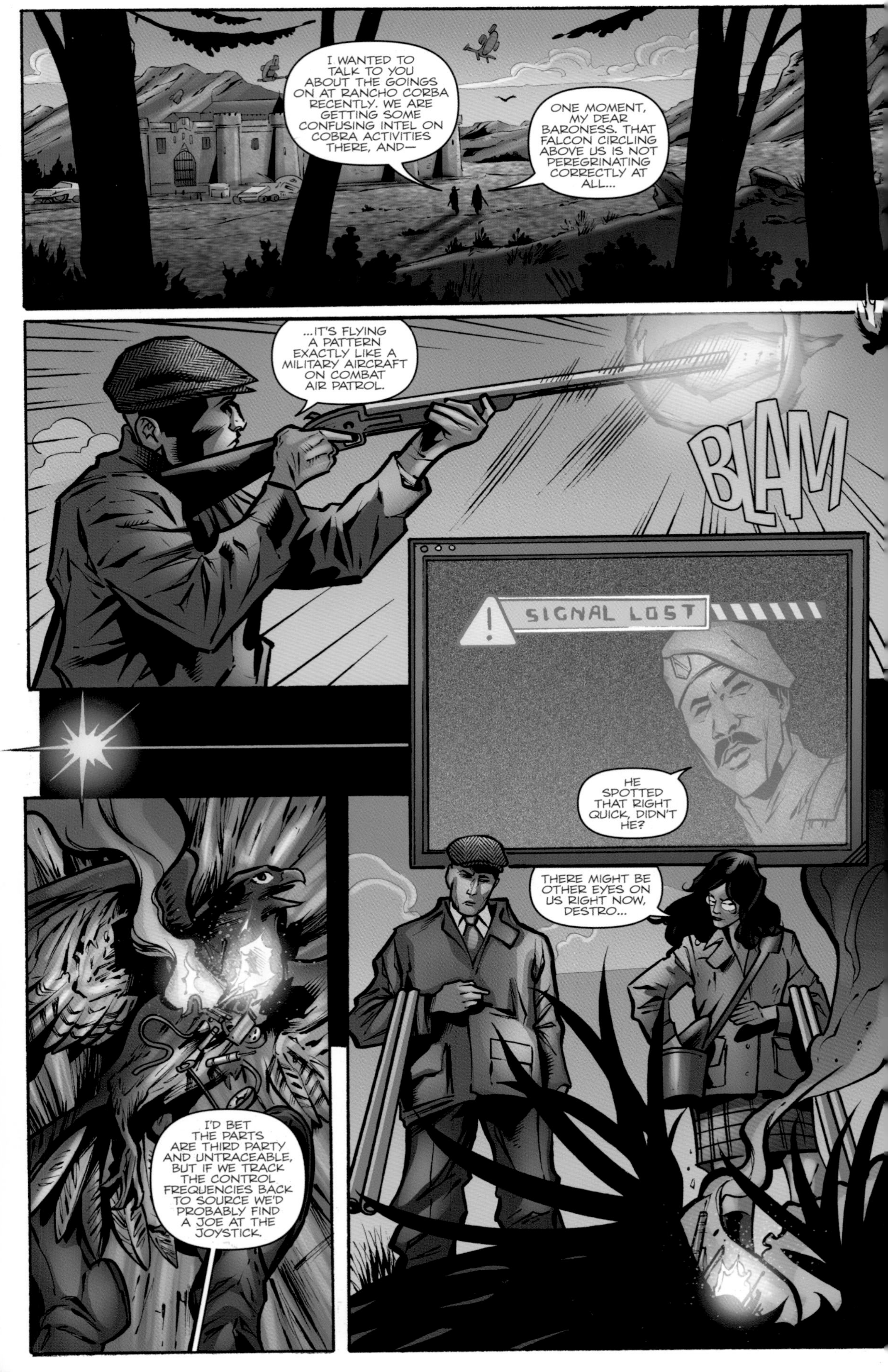
I WANTED TO TALK TO YOU ABOUT THE GOINGS ON AT RANCHO CORBA RECENTLY. WE ARE GETTING SOME CONFUSING INTEL ON COBRA ACTIVITIES THERE, AND—
ONE MOMENT, MY DEAR BARONESS. THAT FALCON CIRCLING ABOVE US IS NOT PEREGRINATING CORRECTLY AT ALL...
...IT'S FLYING A PATTERN EXACTLY LIKE A MILITARY AIRCRAFT ON COMBAT AIR PATROL.
BLAM
SIGNAL LOST
HE SPOTTED THAT RIGHT QUICK, DIDN'T HE?
I'D BET THE PARTS ARE THIRD PARTY AND UNTRACEABLE, BUT IF WE TRACK THE CONTROL FREQUENCIES BACK TO SOURCE WE'D PROBABLY FIND A JOE AT THE JOYSTICK.
THERE MIGHT BE OTHER EYES ON US RIGHT NOW, DESTRO...

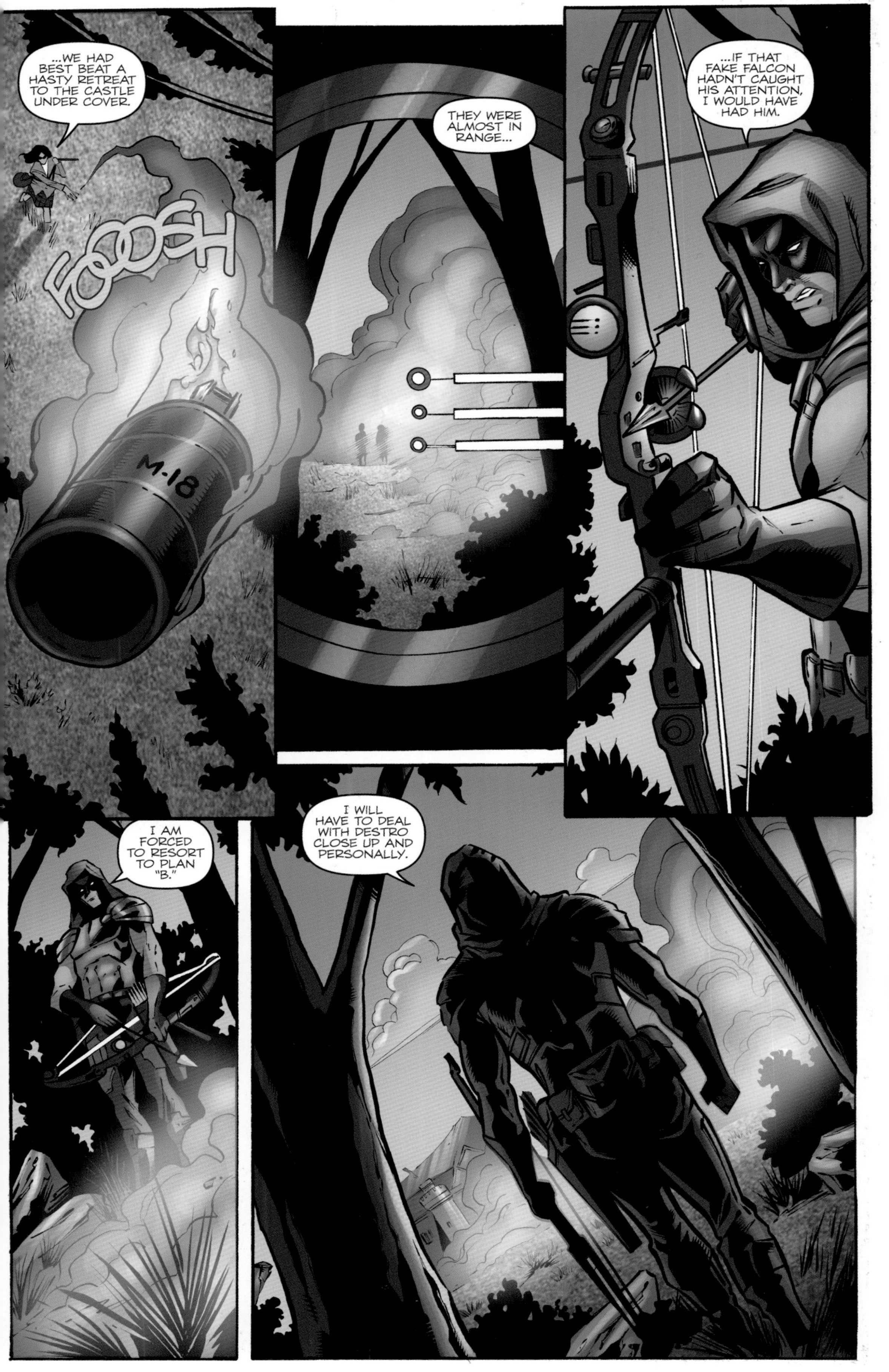

...WE HAD BEST BEAT A HASTY RETREAT TO THE CASTLE UNDER COVER.
FOOOSH
M-18
THEY WERE ALMOST IN RANGE...
...IF THAT FAKE FALCON HADN'T CAUGHT HIS ATTENTION, I WOULD HAVE HAD HIM.
I AM FORCED TO RESORT TO PLAN "B."
I WILL HAVE TO DEAL WITH DESTRO CLOSE UP AND PERSONALLY.

SOMEWHERE ELSE IN AMERICA.

WOW! YOUR CREDENTIALS ARE QUITE IMPRESSIVE! YALE, POLI-SCI, HARVARD BUSINESS SCHOOL—I'M SURE WENDY WOULD LOVE TO HAVE YOU ON BOARD...

OUT OF BUSINESS

ELECT W.L. TORRES FOR AN ALL AMERICAN FUTURE TODAY

MONTY'S CAFE

STORE CLOSING

WENDY LING TORRES CAMPAIGN HEADQUARTERS

ELECT

VOTE FOR WENDY

VOTE FOR WEND FOR AN A AMERIC

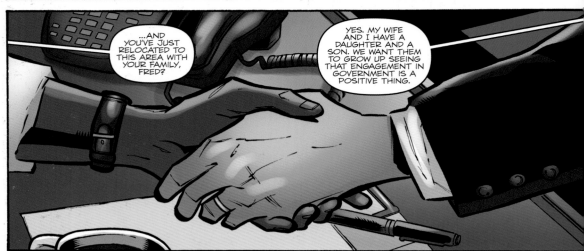

...AND YOU'VE JUST RELOCATED TO THIS AREA WITH YOUR FAMILY, FRED?

YES. MY WIFE AND I HAVE A DAUGHTER AND A SON. WE WANT THEM TO GROW UP SEEING THAT ENGAGEMENT IN GOVERNMENT IS A POSITIVE THING.

I THINK THIS IS A DONE DEAL... GEE, YOUR MONIKER IS A REAL MOUTHFUL— FREDERICK SEVERIN NEUNDREISS—AM I PRONOUNCING THAT RIGHT?

IT'S PRONOUNCED "SEVEN NINE DRY." IT'S EASIER TO REMEMBER AS SEVEN NINE THREE. HA HA. OLD FAMILY JOKE...

...BUT EVERYBODY CALLS ME FRED.

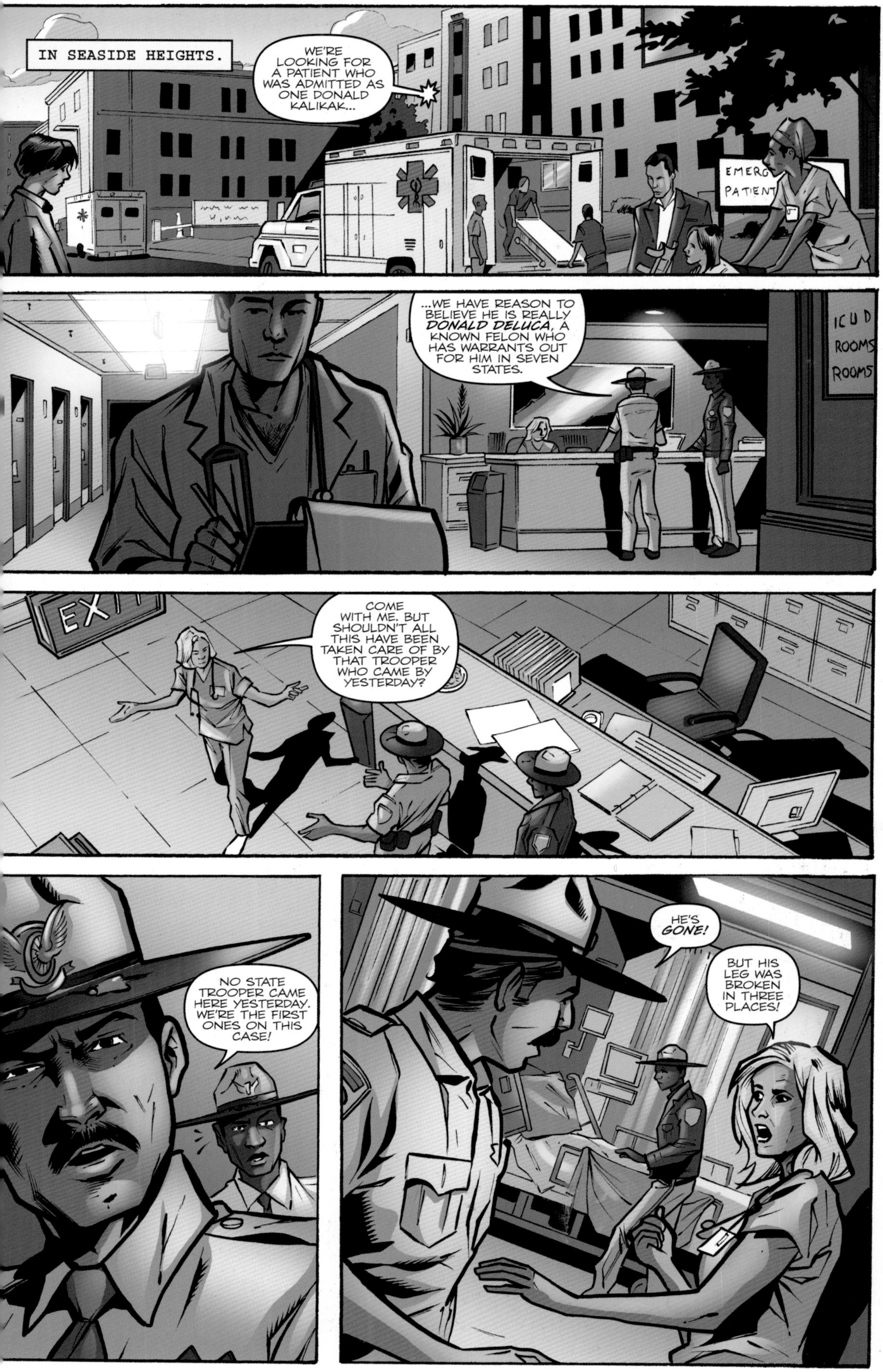
IN SEASIDE HEIGHTS.
WE'RE LOOKING FOR A PATIENT WHO WAS ADMITTED AS ONE DONALD KALIKAK...
EMERG
PATIENT
...WE HAVE REASON TO BELIEVE HE IS REALLY DONALD DELUCA, A KNOWN FELON WHO HAS WARRANTS OUT FOR HIM IN SEVEN STATES.
ICU D
ROOMS
ROOMS
EXIT
COME WITH ME. BUT SHOULDN'T ALL THIS HAVE BEEN TAKEN CARE OF BY THAT TROOPER WHO CAME BY YESTERDAY?
NO STATE TROOPER CAME HERE YESTERDAY. WE'RE THE FIRST ONES ON THIS CASE!
HE'S GONE!
BUT HIS LEG WAS BROKEN IN THREE PLACES!

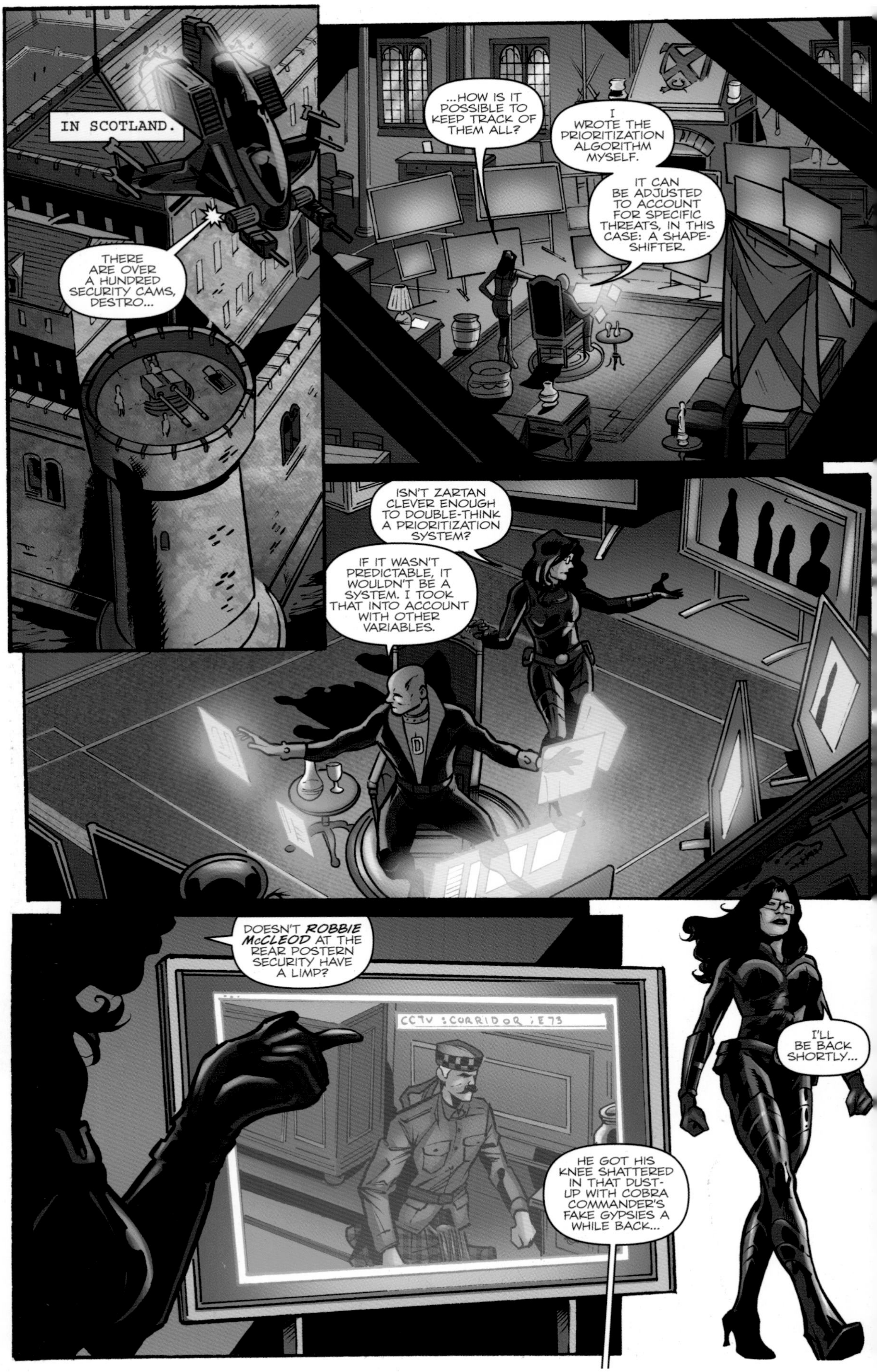

IN SCOTLAND.
THERE ARE OVER A HUNDRED SECURITY CAMS, DESTRO...
...HOW IS IT POSSIBLE TO KEEP TRACK OF THEM ALL?
I WROTE THE PRIORITIZATION ALGORITHM MYSELF.
IT CAN BE ADJUSTED TO ACCOUNT FOR SPECIFIC THREATS, IN THIS CASE: A SHAPE-SHIFTER.
ISN'T ZARTAN CLEVER ENOUGH TO DOUBLE-THINK A PRIORITIZATION SYSTEM?
IF IT WASN'T PREDICTABLE, IT WOULDN'T BE A SYSTEM. I TOOK THAT INTO ACCOUNT WITH OTHER VARIABLES.
DOESN'T ROBBIE McCLEOD AT THE REAR POSTERN SECURITY HAVE A LIMP?
CCTV :CORRIDOR ;E73
HE GOT HIS KNEE SHATTERED IN THAT DUST-UP WITH COBRA COMMANDER'S FAKE GYPSIES A WHILE BACK...
I'LL BE BACK SHORTLY...

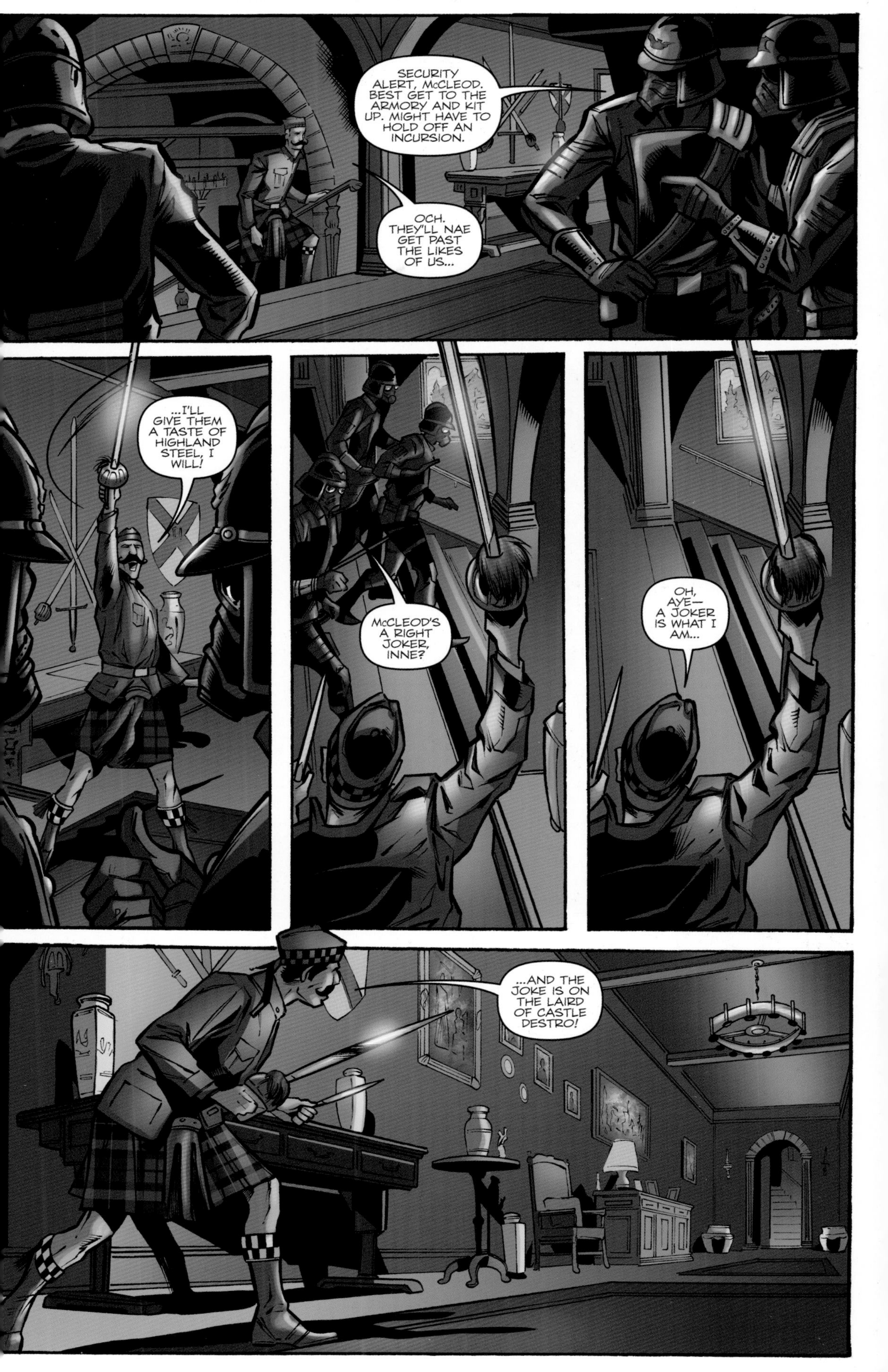
SECURITY ALERT, McCLEOD. BEST GET TO THE ARMORY AND KIT UP. MIGHT HAVE TO HOLD OFF AN INCURSION.
OCH. THEY'LL NAE GET PAST THE LIKES OF US...
...I'LL GIVE THEM A TASTE OF HIGHLAND STEEL, I WILL!
McCLEOD'S A RIGHT JOKER, INNE?
OH, AYE— A JOKER IS WHAT I AM...
...AND THE JOKE IS ON THE LAIRD OF CASTLE DESTRO!

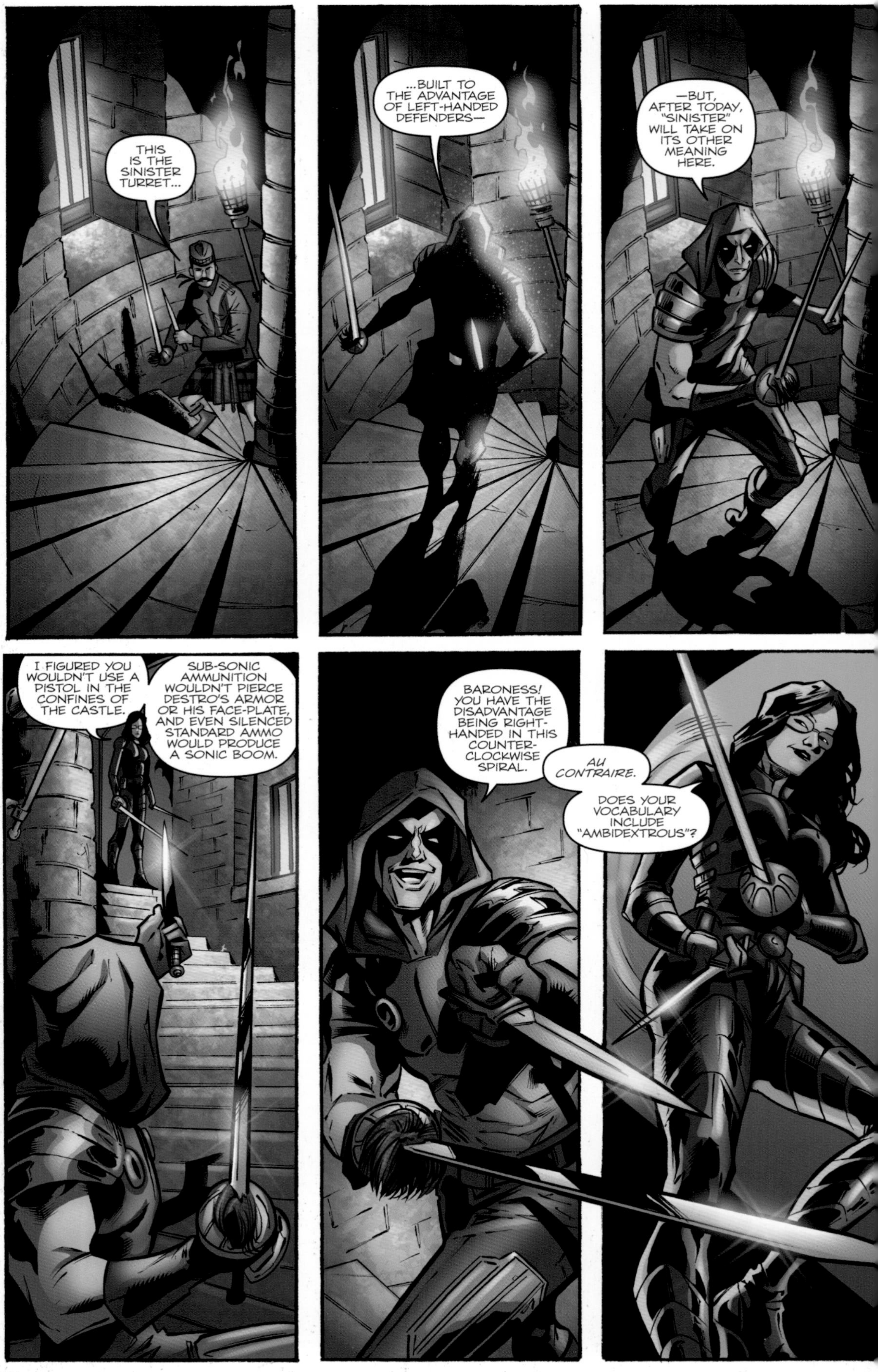
THIS IS THE SINISTER TURRET...
...BUILT TO THE ADVANTAGE OF LEFT-HANDED DEFENDERS—
—BUT, AFTER TODAY, "SINISTER" WILL TAKE ON ITS OTHER MEANING HERE.
I FIGURED YOU WOULDN'T USE A PISTOL IN THE CONFINES OF THE CASTLE.
SUB-SONIC AMMUNITION WOULDN'T PIERCE DESTRO'S ARMOR OR HIS FACE-PLATE, AND EVEN SILENCED STANDARD AMMO WOULD PRODUCE A SONIC BOOM.
BARONESS! YOU HAVE THE DISADVANTAGE BEING RIGHT-HANDED IN THIS COUNTER-CLOCKWISE SPIRAL.
AU CONTRAIRE.
DOES YOUR VOCABULARY INCLUDE "AMBIDEXTROUS"?

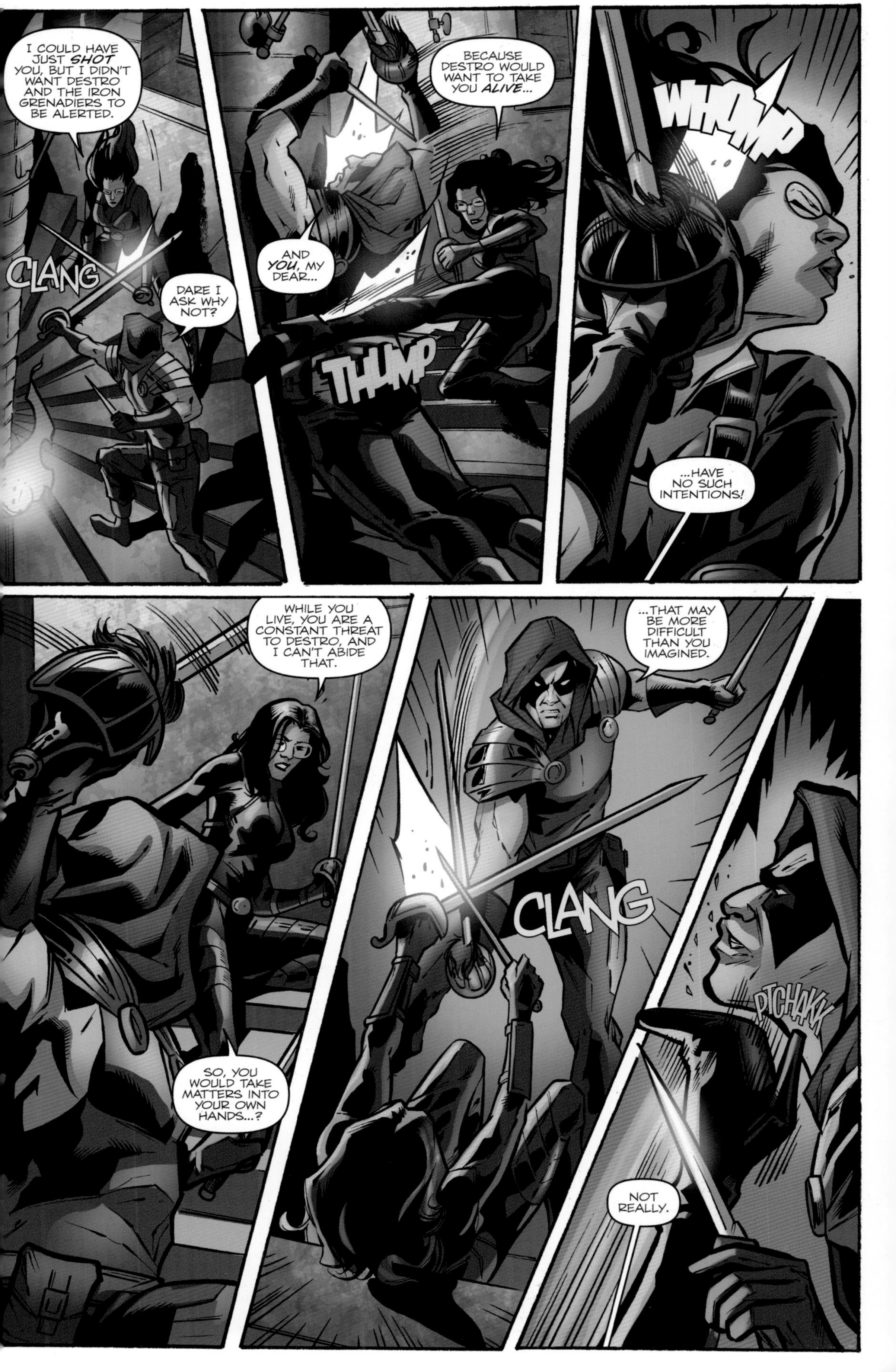
I COULD HAVE JUST SHOT YOU, BUT I DIDN'T WANT DESTRO AND THE IRON GRENADIERS TO BE ALERTED.
CLANG
DARE I ASK WHY NOT?
BECAUSE DESTRO WOULD WANT TO TAKE YOU ALIVE...
AND YOU, MY DEAR...
THUMP
WHOMP
...HAVE NO SUCH INTENTIONS!
WHILE YOU LIVE, YOU ARE A CONSTANT THREAT TO DESTRO, AND I CAN'T ABIDE THAT.
SO, YOU WOULD TAKE MATTERS INTO YOUR OWN HANDS...?
...THAT MAY BE MORE DIFFICULT THAN YOU IMAGINED.
CLANG
PTCHAKK
NOT REALLY.

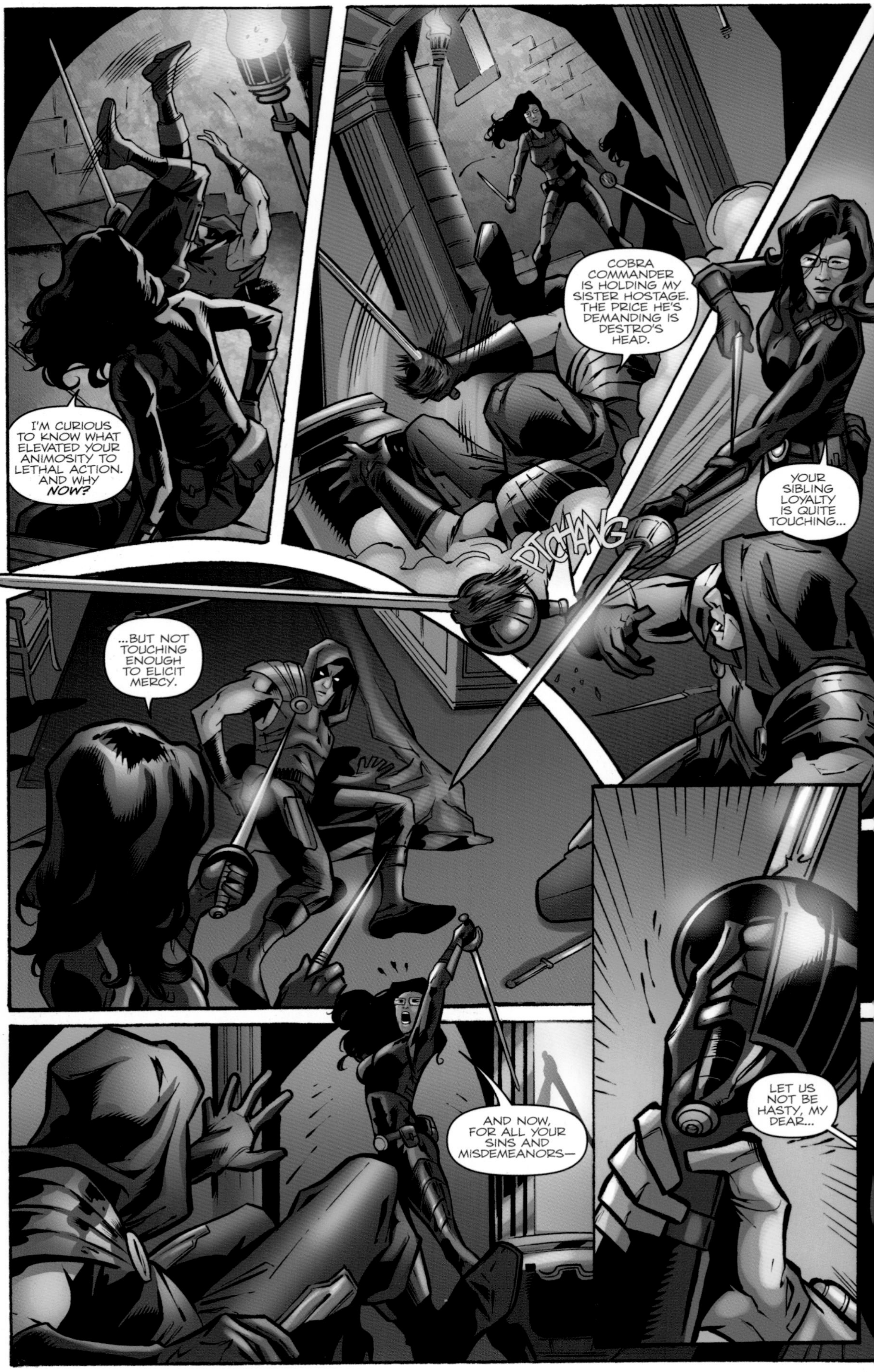

I'M CURIOUS TO KNOW WHAT ELEVATED YOUR ANIMOSITY TO LETHAL ACTION. AND WHY *NOW?*
COBRA COMMANDER IS HOLDING MY SISTER HOSTAGE. THE PRICE HE'S DEMANDING IS DESTRO'S HEAD.
YOUR SIBLING LOYALTY IS QUITE TOUCHING...
PTCHANG
...BUT NOT TOUCHING ENOUGH TO ELICIT MERCY.
AND NOW, FOR ALL YOUR SINS AND MISDEMEANORS—
LET US NOT BE HASTY, MY DEAR...

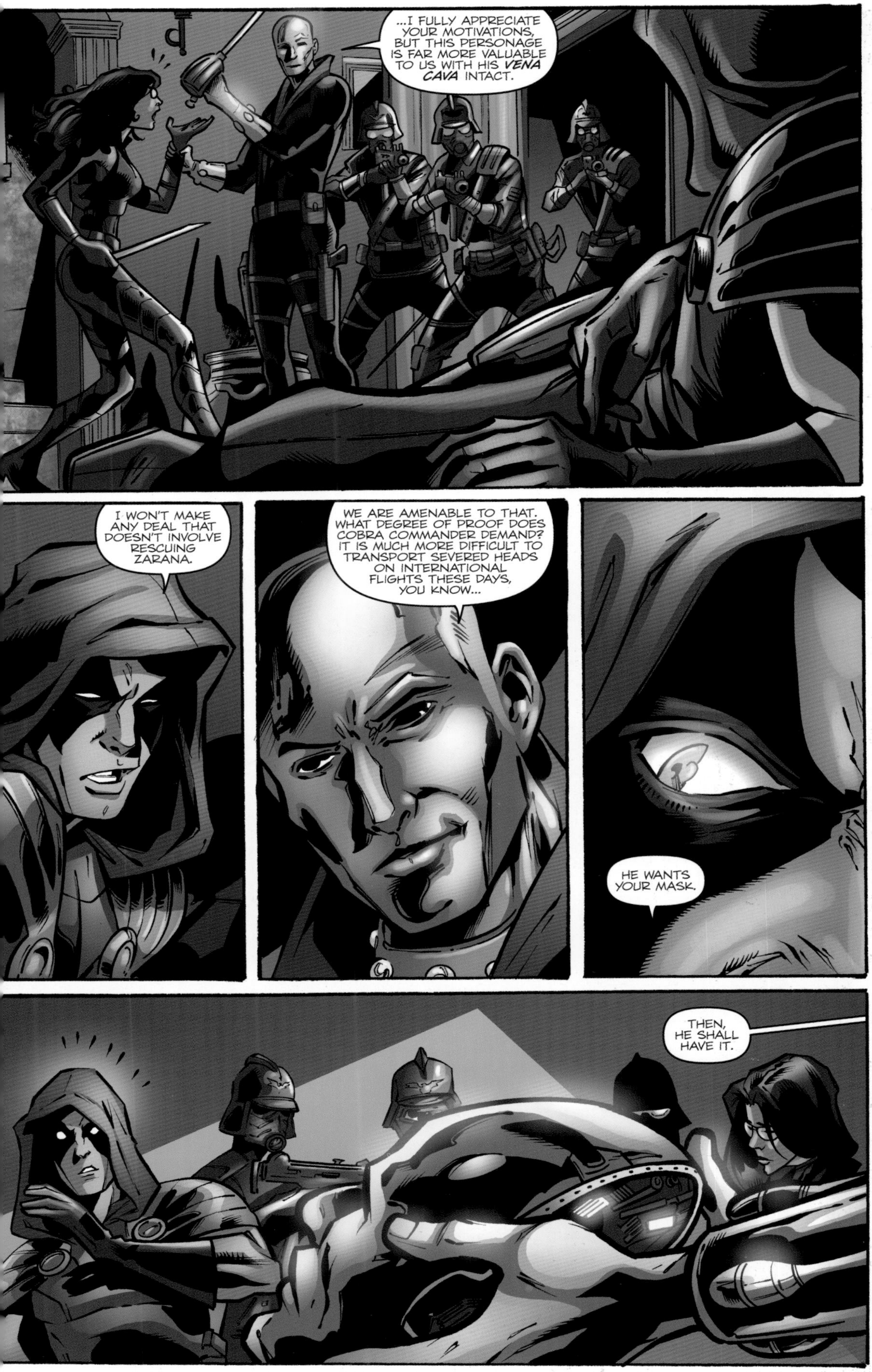
...I FULLY APPRECIATE YOUR MOTIVATIONS, BUT THIS PERSONAGE IS FAR MORE VALUABLE TO US WITH HIS *VENA CAVA* INTACT.
I WON'T MAKE ANY DEAL THAT DOESN'T INVOLVE RESCUING ZARANA.
WE ARE AMENABLE TO THAT. WHAT DEGREE OF PROOF DOES COBRA COMMANDER DEMAND? IT IS MUCH MORE DIFFICULT TO TRANSPORT SEVERED HEADS ON INTERNATIONAL FLIGHTS THESE DAYS, YOU KNOW...
HE WANTS YOUR MASK.
THEN, HE SHALL HAVE IT.

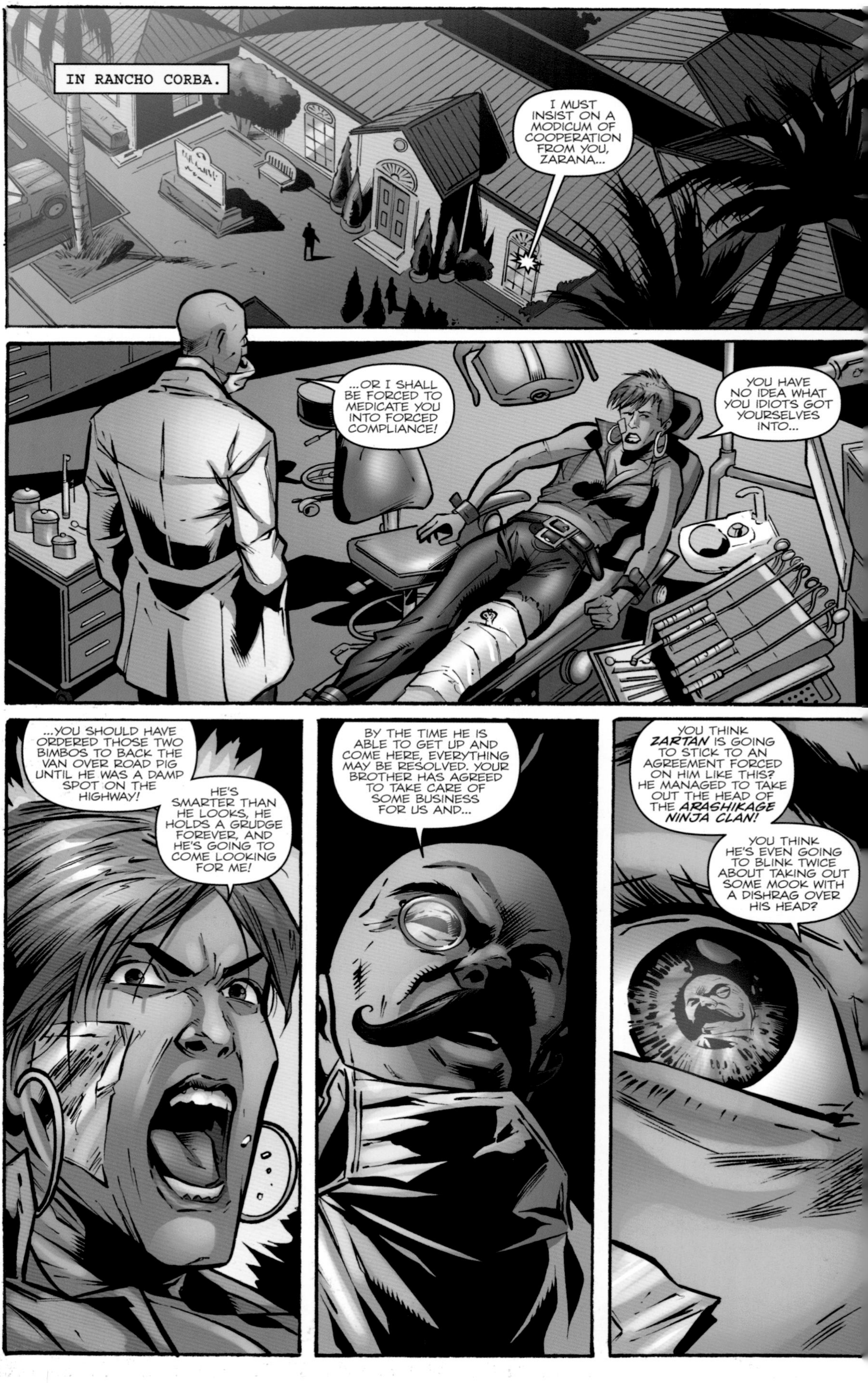
IN RANCHO CORBA.
I MUST INSIST ON A MODICUM OF COOPERATION FROM YOU, ZARANA...
...OR I SHALL BE FORCED TO MEDICATE YOU INTO FORCED COMPLIANCE!
YOU HAVE NO IDEA WHAT YOU IDIOTS GOT YOURSELVES INTO...
...YOU SHOULD HAVE ORDERED THOSE TWO BIMBOS TO BACK THE VAN OVER ROAD PIG UNTIL HE WAS A DAMP SPOT ON THE HIGHWAY!
HE'S SMARTER THAN HE LOOKS, HE HOLDS A GRUDGE FOREVER, AND HE'S GOING TO COME LOOKING FOR ME!
BY THE TIME HE IS ABLE TO GET UP AND COME HERE, EVERYTHING MAY BE RESOLVED. YOUR BROTHER HAS AGREED TO TAKE CARE OF SOME BUSINESS FOR US AND...
YOU THINK ZARTAN IS GOING TO STICK TO AN AGREEMENT FORCED ON HIM LIKE THIS? HE MANAGED TO TAKE OUT THE HEAD OF THE ARASHIKAGE NINJA CLAN!
YOU THINK HE'S EVEN GOING TO BLINK TWICE ABOUT TAKING OUT SOME MOOK WITH A DISHRAG OVER HIS HEAD?

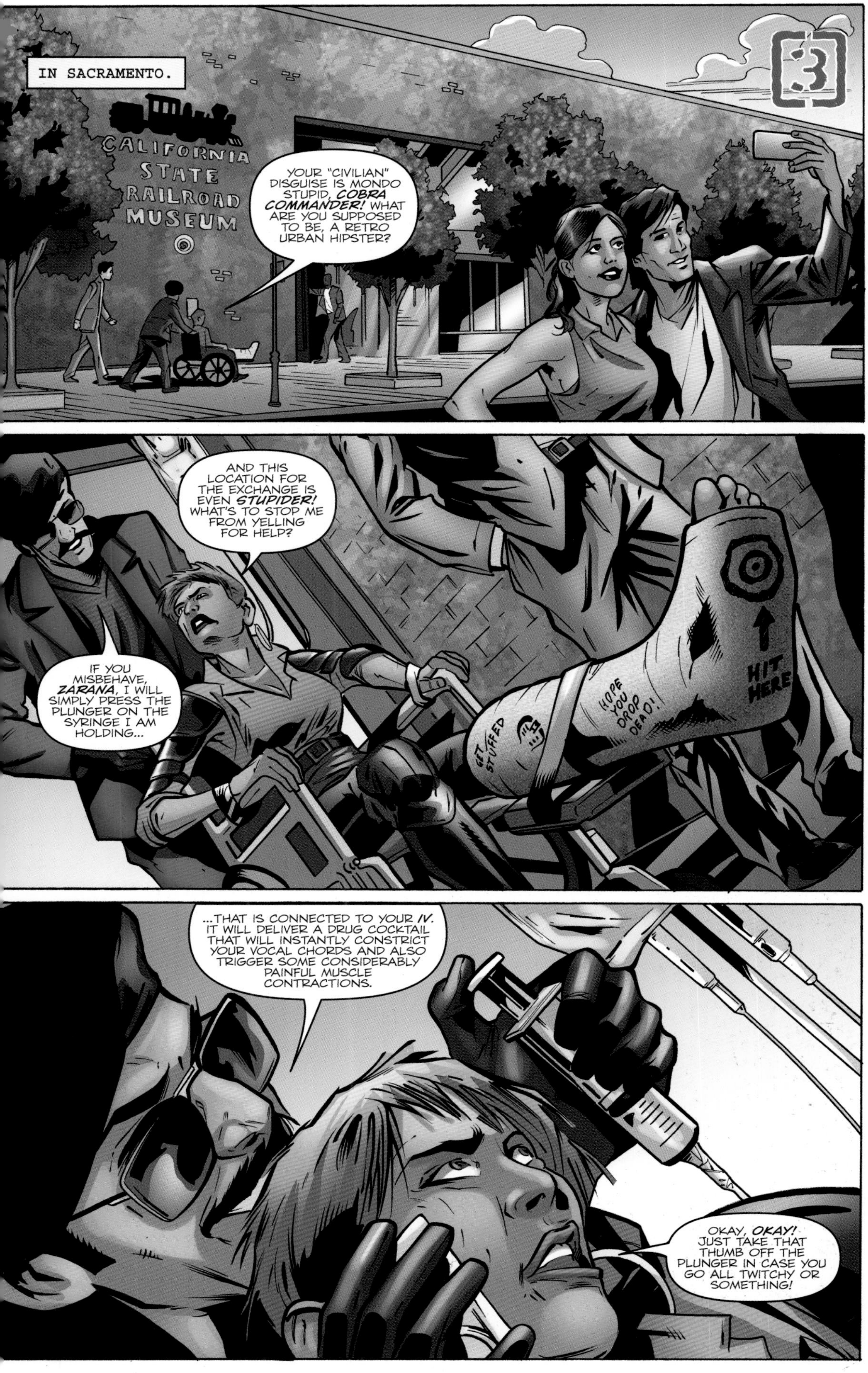
IN SACRAMENTO.
3
CALIFORNIA STATE RAILROAD MUSEUM
YOUR "CIVILIAN" DISGUISE IS MONDO STUPID, COBRA COMMANDER! WHAT ARE YOU SUPPOSED TO BE, A RETRO URBAN HIPSTER?
AND THIS LOCATION FOR THE EXCHANGE IS EVEN STUPIDER! WHAT'S TO STOP ME FROM YELLING FOR HELP?
IF YOU MISBEHAVE, ZARANA, I WILL SIMPLY PRESS THE PLUNGER ON THE SYRINGE I AM HOLDING...
HIT HERE
HOPE YOU DROP DEAD!
GET STUFFED
...THAT IS CONNECTED TO YOUR IV. IT WILL DELIVER A DRUG COCKTAIL THAT WILL INSTANTLY CONSTRICT YOUR VOCAL CHORDS AND ALSO TRIGGER SOME CONSIDERABLY PAINFUL MUSCLE CONTRACTIONS.
OKAY, OKAY! JUST TAKE THAT THUMB OFF THE PLUNGER IN CASE YOU GO ALL TWITCHY OR SOMETHING!

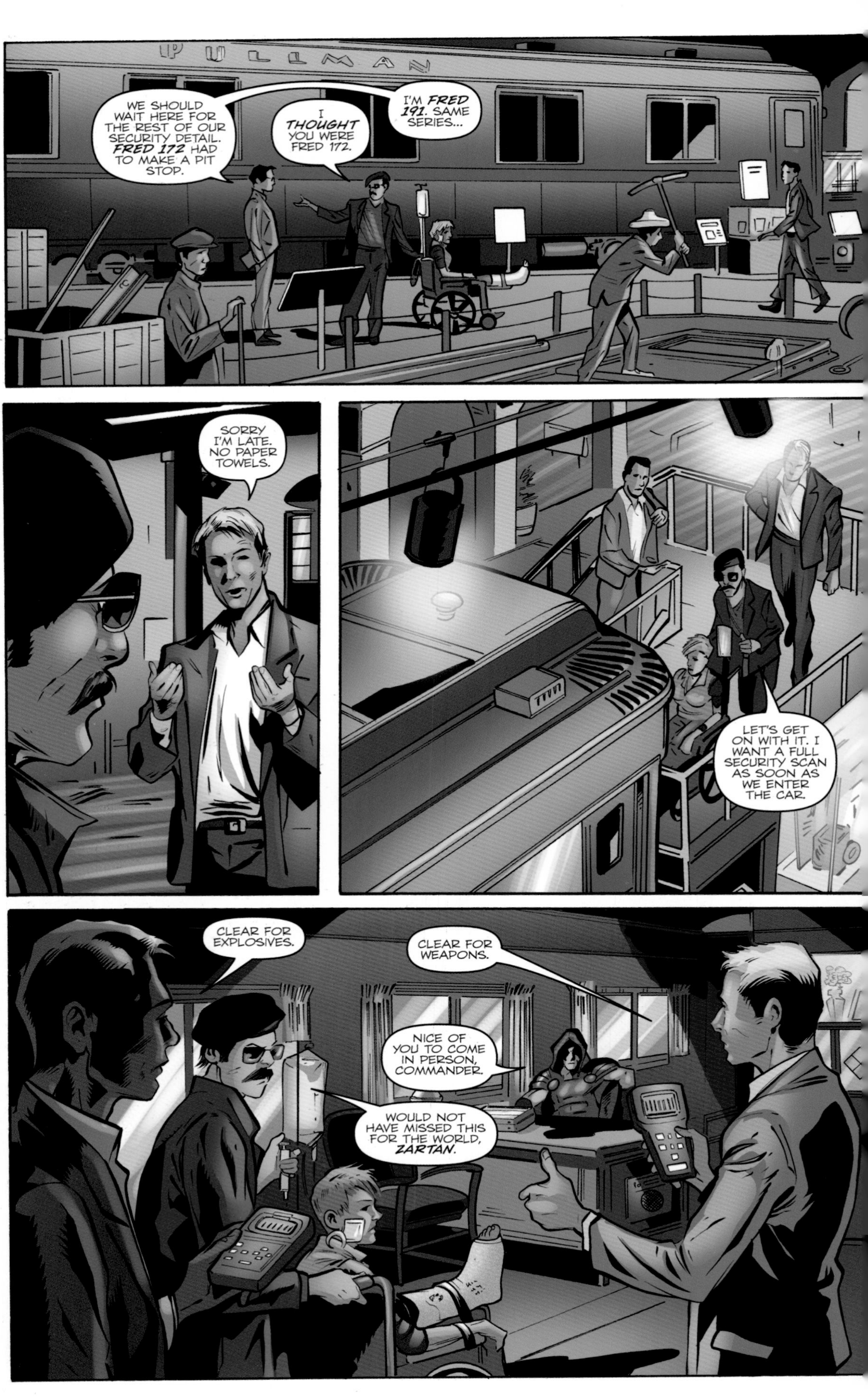
PULLMAN
WE SHOULD WAIT HERE FOR THE REST OF OUR SECURITY DETAIL. FRED 172 HAD TO MAKE A PIT STOP.
I THOUGHT YOU WERE FRED 172.
I'M FRED 191. SAME SERIES...
SORRY I'M LATE. NO PAPER TOWELS.
LET'S GET ON WITH IT. I WANT A FULL SECURITY SCAN AS SOON AS WE ENTER THE CAR.
CLEAR FOR EXPLOSIVES.
CLEAR FOR WEAPONS.
NICE OF YOU TO COME IN PERSON, COMMANDER.
WOULD NOT HAVE MISSED THIS FOR THE WORLD, ZARTAN.

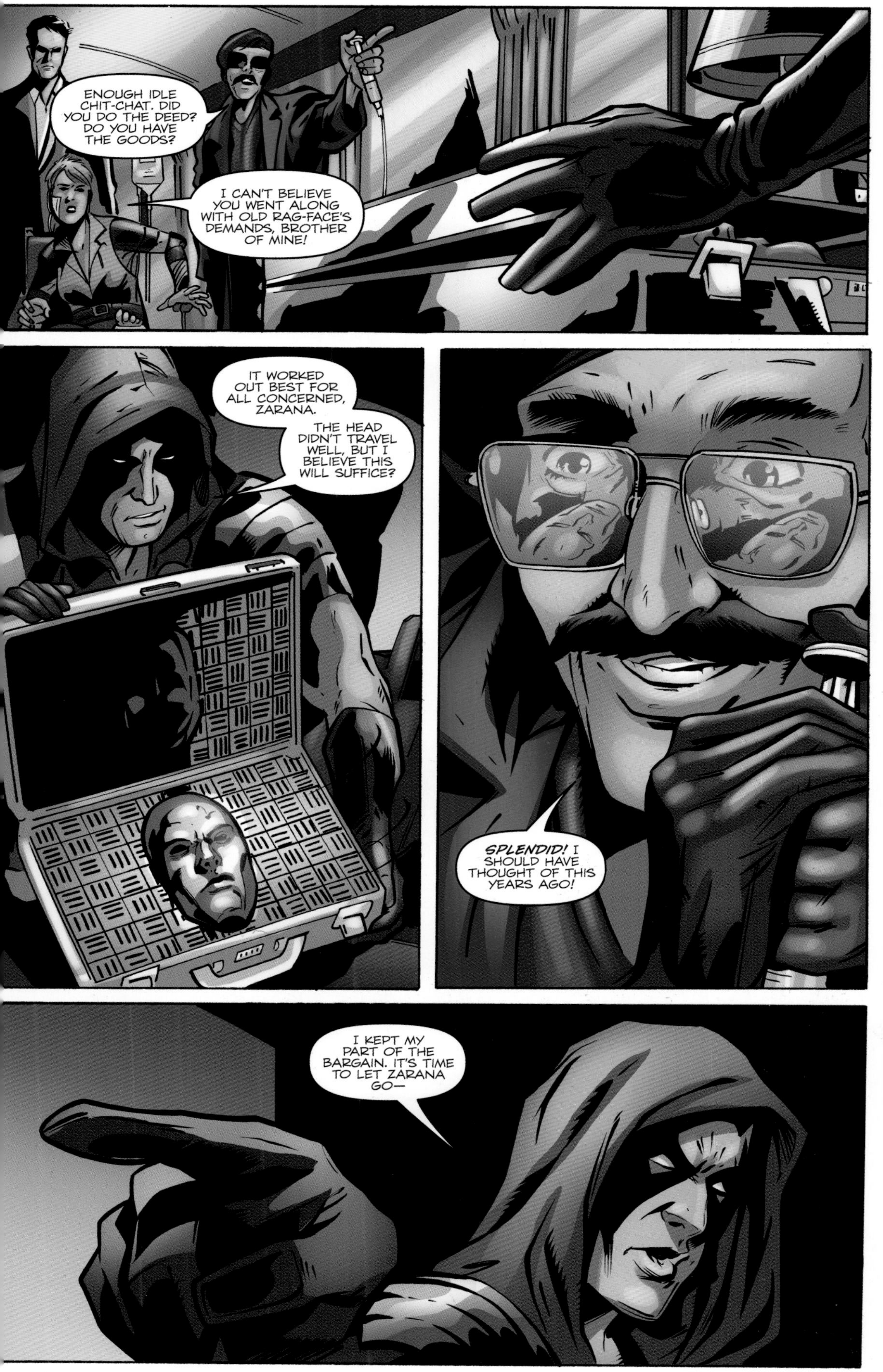
ENOUGH IDLE CHIT-CHAT. DID YOU DO THE DEED? DO YOU HAVE THE GOODS?
I CAN'T BELIEVE YOU WENT ALONG WITH OLD RAG-FACE'S DEMANDS, BROTHER OF MINE!
IT WORKED OUT BEST FOR ALL CONCERNED, ZARANA.
THE HEAD DIDN'T TRAVEL WELL, BUT I BELIEVE THIS WILL SUFFICE?
SPLENDID! I SHOULD HAVE THOUGHT OF THIS YEARS AGO!
I KEPT MY PART OF THE BARGAIN. IT'S TIME TO LET ZARANA GO—

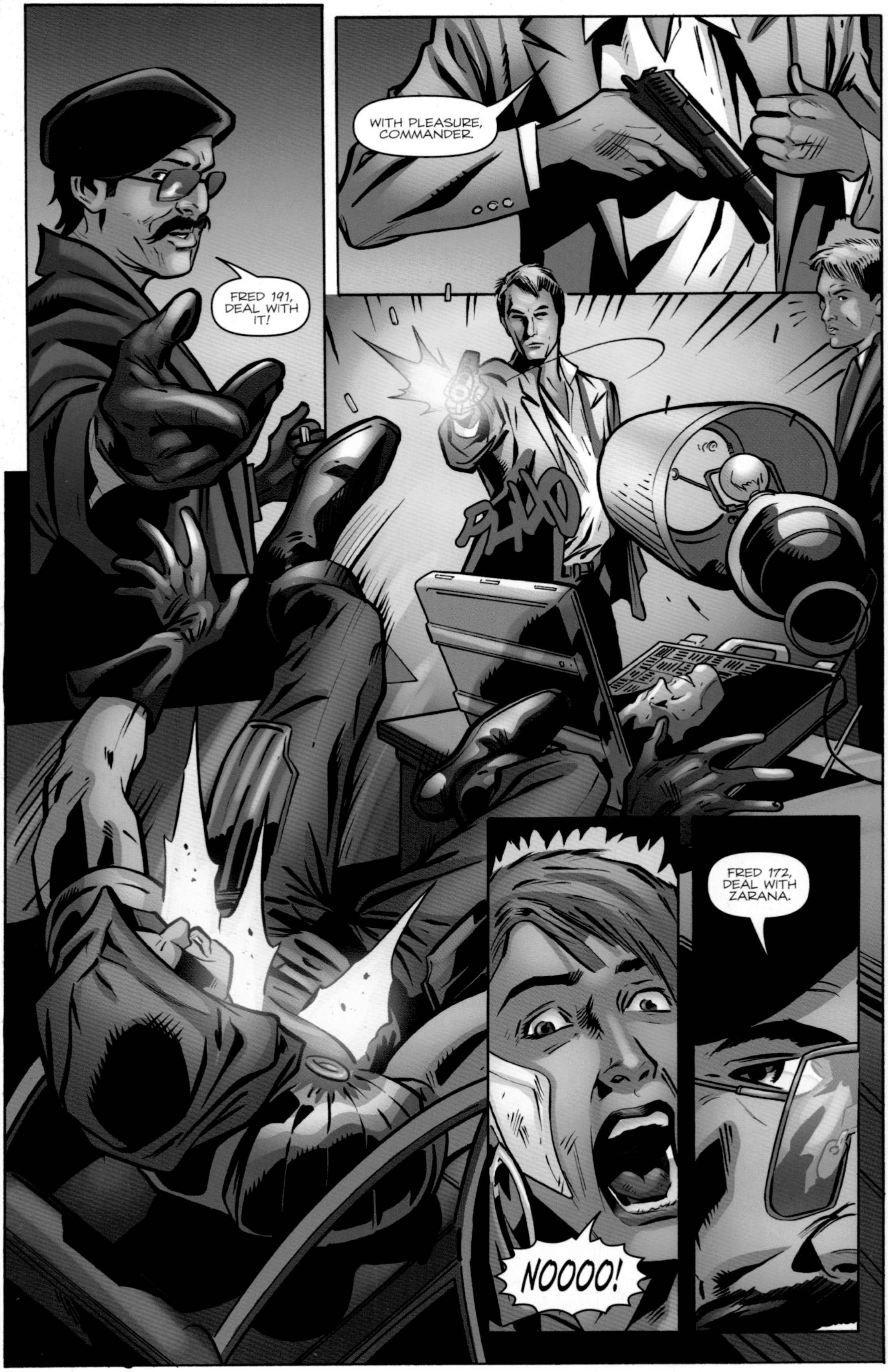
WITH PLEASURE, COMMANDER.
FRED 191, DEAL WITH IT!
PLUD
FRED 172, DEAL WITH ZARANA.
NOOOO!

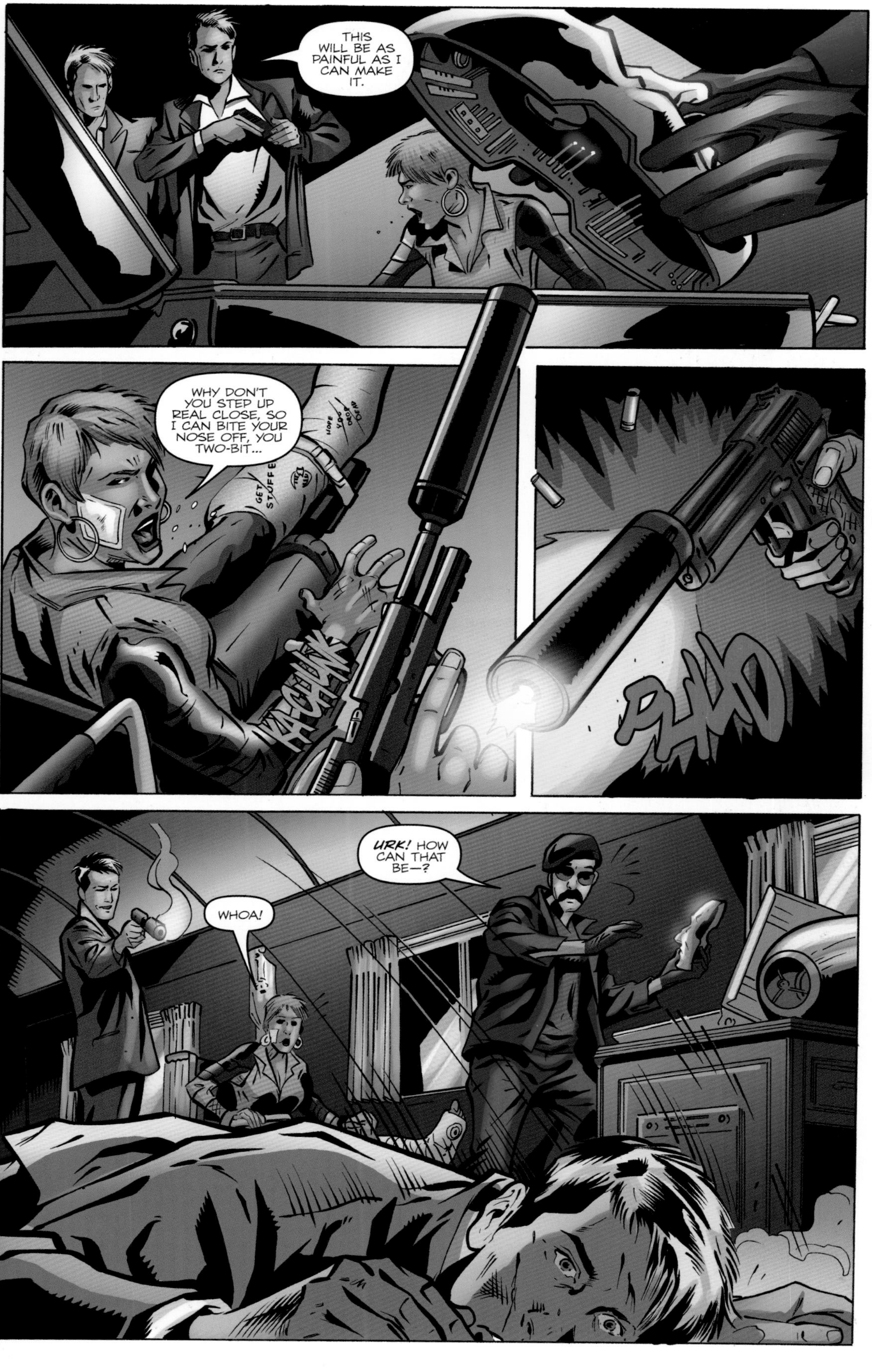
THIS WILL BE AS PAINFUL AS I CAN MAKE IT.
WHY DON'T YOU STEP UP REAL CLOSE, SO I CAN BITE YOUR NOSE OFF, YOU TWO-BIT...
KA-CHUNK
URK! HOW CAN THAT BE—?
WHOA!

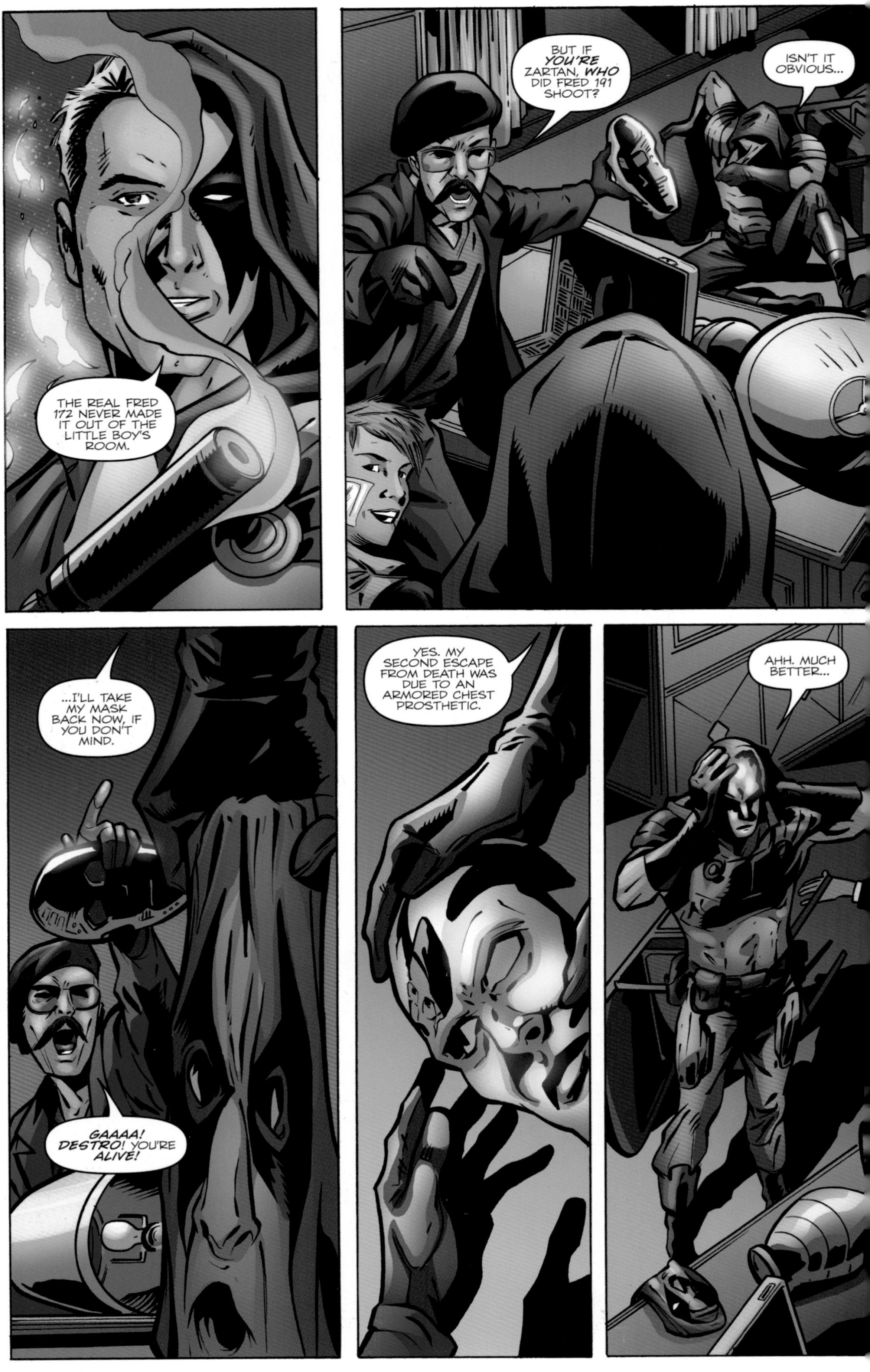
THE REAL FRED 172 NEVER MADE IT OUT OF THE LITTLE BOY'S ROOM.
BUT IF *YOU'RE* ZARTAN, *WHO* DID FRED 191 SHOOT?
ISN'T IT OBVIOUS...
...I'LL TAKE MY MASK BACK NOW, IF YOU DON'T MIND.
GAAAA! DESTRO! YOU'RE *ALIVE!*
YES. MY SECOND ESCAPE FROM DEATH WAS DUE TO AN ARMORED CHEST PROSTHETIC.
AHH. MUCH BETTER...

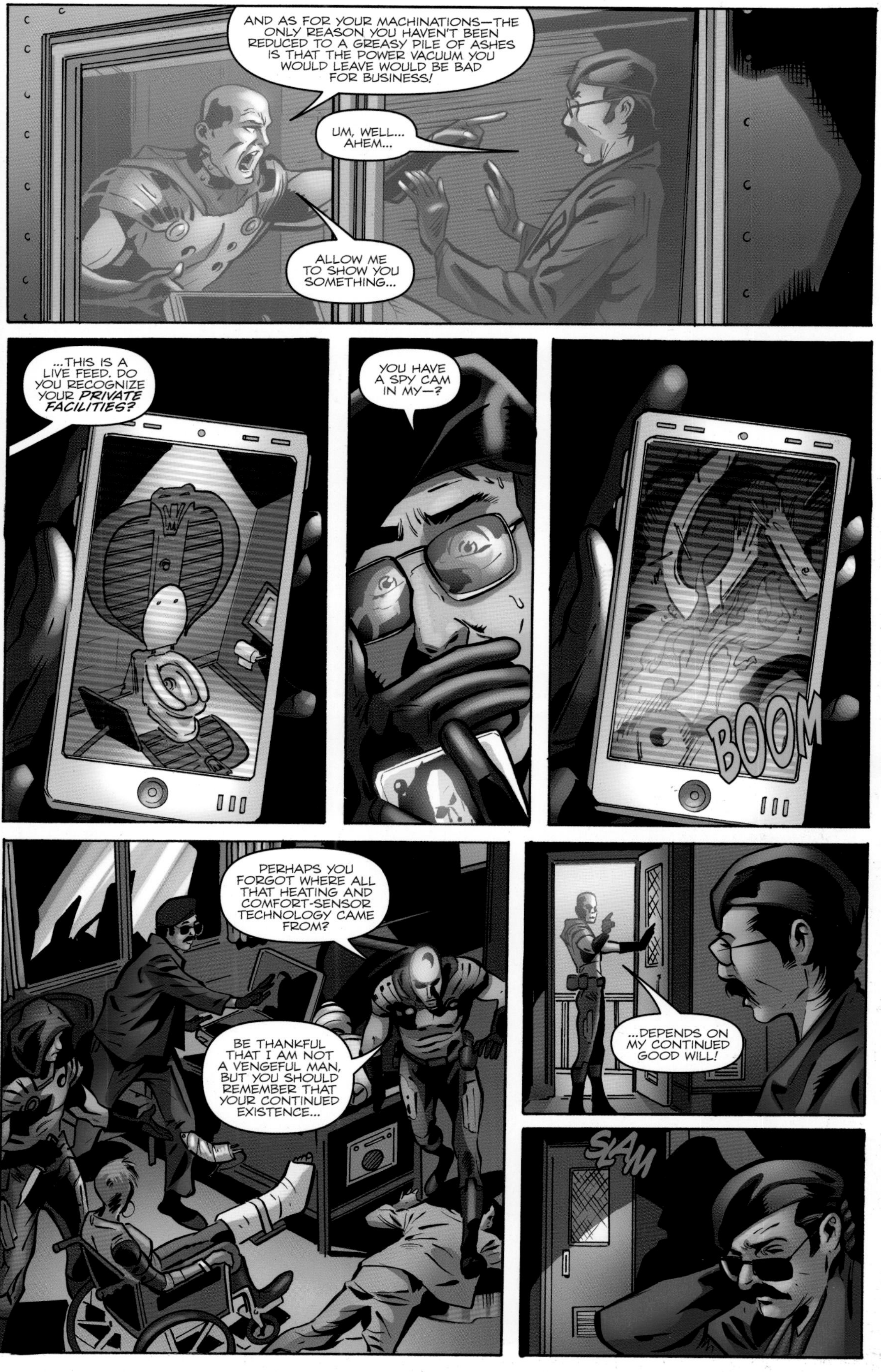
AND AS FOR YOUR MACHINATIONS—THE ONLY REASON YOU HAVEN'T BEEN REDUCED TO A GREASY PILE OF ASHES IS THAT THE POWER VACUUM YOU WOULD LEAVE WOULD BE BAD FOR BUSINESS!
UM, WELL... AHEM...
ALLOW ME TO SHOW YOU SOMETHING...
...THIS IS A LIVE FEED. DO YOU RECOGNIZE YOUR PRIVATE FACILITIES?
YOU HAVE A SPY CAM IN MY—?
BOOM
PERHAPS YOU FORGOT WHERE ALL THAT HEATING AND COMFORT-SENSOR TECHNOLOGY CAME FROM?
BE THANKFUL THAT I AM NOT A VENGEFUL MAN, BUT YOU SHOULD REMEMBER THAT YOUR CONTINUED EXISTENCE...
...DEPENDS ON MY CONTINUED GOOD WILL!
SLAM

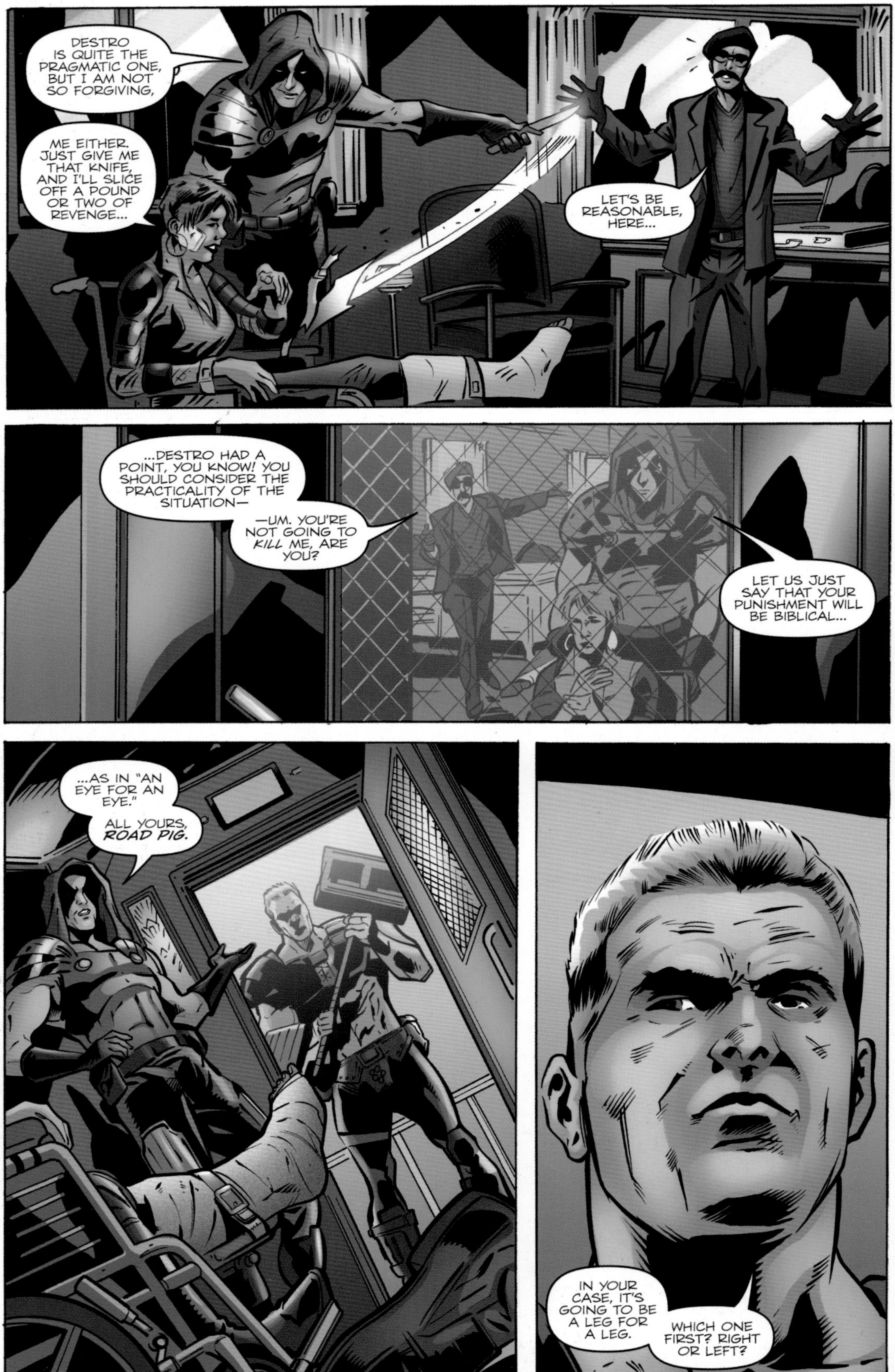
DESTRO IS QUITE THE PRAGMATIC ONE, BUT I AM NOT SO FORGIVING,
ME EITHER. JUST GIVE ME THAT KNIFE, AND I'LL SLICE OFF A POUND OR TWO OF REVENGE...
LET'S BE REASONABLE, HERE...
...DESTRO HAD A POINT, YOU KNOW! YOU SHOULD CONSIDER THE PRACTICALITY OF THE SITUATION—
—UM. YOU'RE NOT GOING TO *KILL* ME, ARE YOU?
LET US JUST SAY THAT YOUR PUNISHMENT WILL BE BIBLICAL...
...AS IN "AN EYE FOR AN EYE."
ALL YOURS, ***ROAD PIG***.
IN YOUR CASE, IT'S GOING TO BE A LEG FOR A LEG.
WHICH ONE FIRST? RIGHT OR LEFT?

IN THE PIT.

SECURITY CCTV : 07

SECURITY CCTV : 07

MAINFRAME, YOU HACKED THE MUSEUM SECURITY CAMS, WASN'T THERE A CAM INSIDE THE PULLMAN?

THAT SURE IS AN INTERESTING PARADE OF CHARACTERS GOING IN AND OUT OF THAT PULLMAN CAR...

THERE WAS, BUT IT'S BEEN DISABLED...

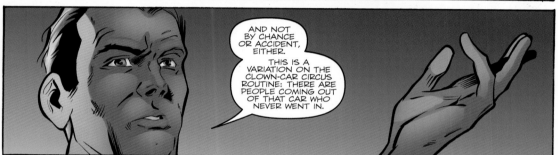

AND NOT BY CHANCE OR ACCIDENT, EITHER.

THIS IS A VARIATION ON THE CLOWN-CAR CIRCUS ROUTINE: THERE ARE PEOPLE COMING OUT OF THAT CAR WHO NEVER WENT IN.

SECURITY CCTV

LOOK! THERE'S THE **BARONESS** PICKING UP DESTRO IN THE PARKING LOT! WE NEVER SAW DESTRO GO IN...

AND THE TWO **FRED SERIES SIEGIES** WHO WERE GUARDING COBRA COMMANDER NEVER CAME OUT.

IF THEY AREN'T ALREADY MEAT, ROAD PIG WILL LAY THEM OUT BEFORE HE DOES A NUMBER ON THE HEAD SNAKE.

LOOKS LIKE COBRA COMMANDER TOOK ZARANA HOSTAGE TO FORCE ZARTAN TO TAKE OUT DESTRO—BUT OL' METAL-FACE TURNED THE TABLES.

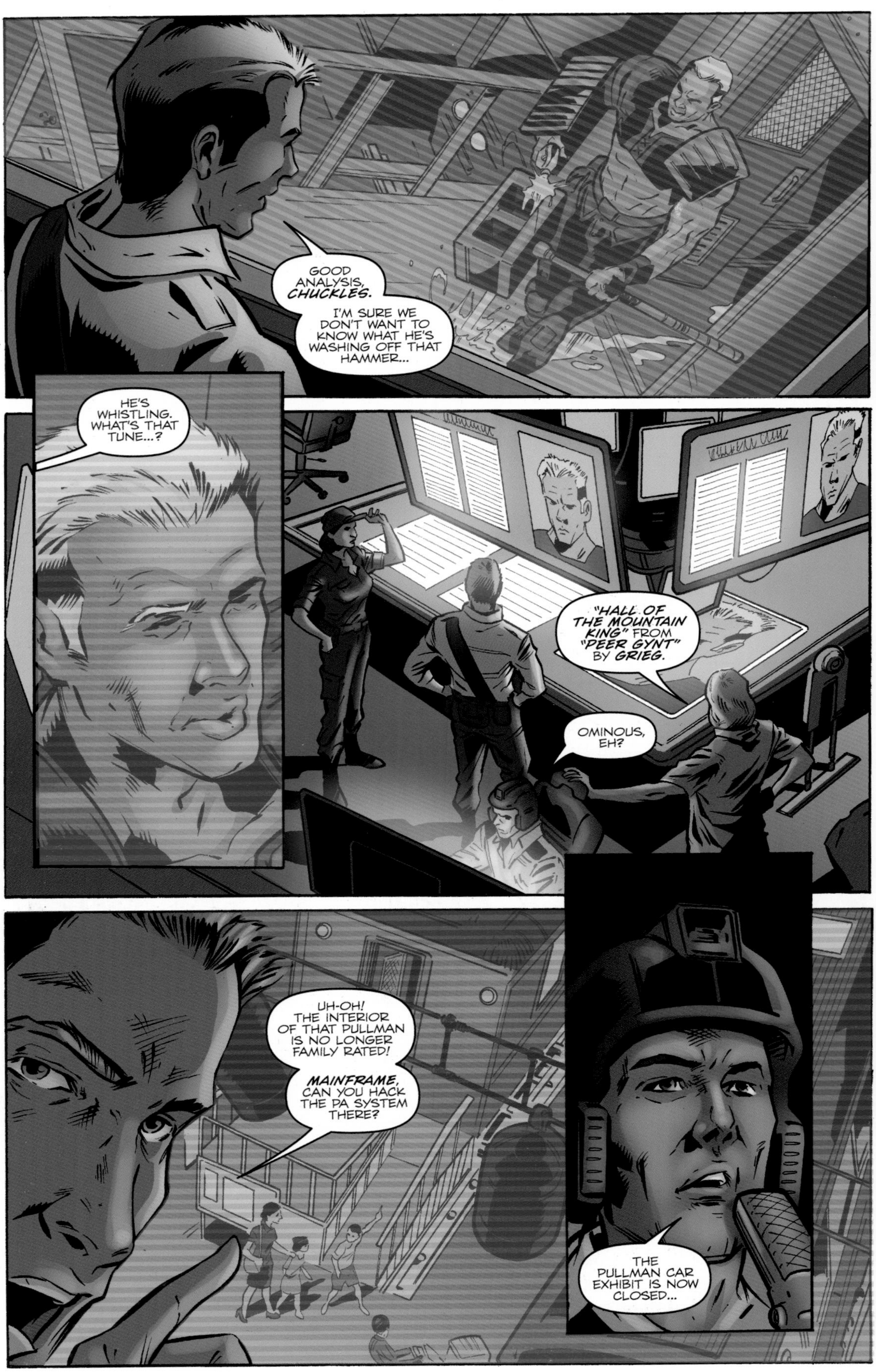
GOOD ANALYSIS, CHUCKLES.
I'M SURE WE DON'T WANT TO KNOW WHAT HE'S WASHING OFF THAT HAMMER...
HE'S WHISTLING. WHAT'S THAT TUNE...?
"HALL OF THE MOUNTAIN KING" FROM "PEER GYNT" BY GRIEG.
OMINOUS, EH?
UH-OH! THE INTERIOR OF THAT PULLMAN IS NO LONGER FAMILY RATED!
MAINFRAME, CAN YOU HACK THE PA SYSTEM THERE?
THE PULLMAN CAR EXHIBIT IS NOW CLOSED...

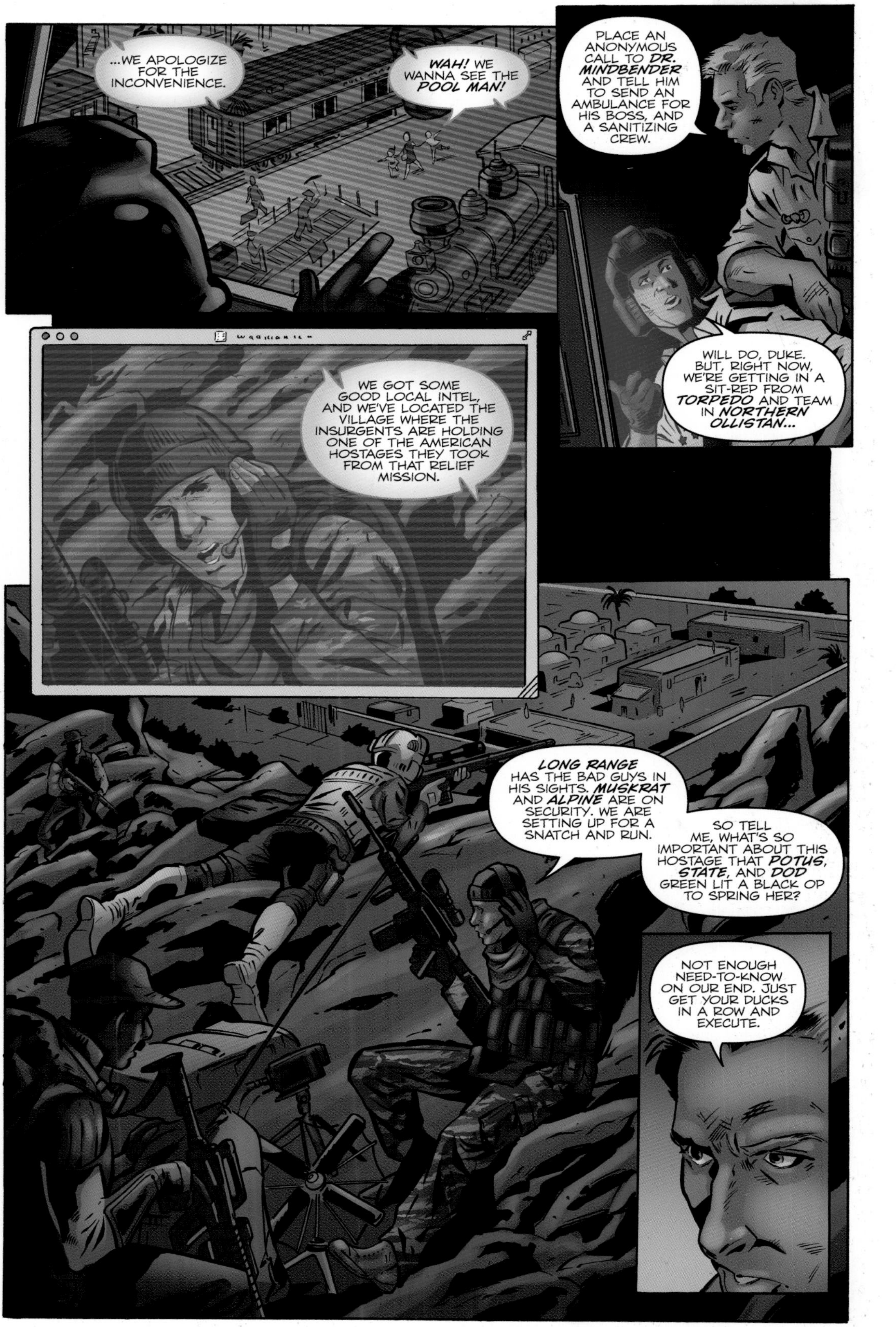
...WE APOLOGIZE FOR THE INCONVENIENCE.
WAH! WE WANNA SEE THE POOL MAN!
PLACE AN ANONYMOUS CALL TO DR. MINDBENDER AND TELL HIM TO SEND AN AMBULANCE FOR HIS BOSS, AND A SANITIZING CREW.
WILL DO, DUKE. BUT, RIGHT NOW, WE'RE GETTING IN A SIT-REP FROM TORPEDO AND TEAM IN NORTHERN OLLISTAN...
WE GOT SOME GOOD LOCAL INTEL, AND WE'VE LOCATED THE VILLAGE WHERE THE INSURGENTS ARE HOLDING ONE OF THE AMERICAN HOSTAGES THEY TOOK FROM THAT RELIEF MISSION.
LONG RANGE HAS THE BAD GUYS IN HIS SIGHTS. MUSKRAT AND ALPINE ARE ON SECURITY. WE ARE SETTING UP FOR A SNATCH AND RUN.
SO TELL ME, WHAT'S SO IMPORTANT ABOUT THIS HOSTAGE THAT POTUS, STATE, AND DOD GREEN LIT A BLACK OP TO SPRING HER?
NOT ENOUGH NEED-TO-KNOW ON OUR END. JUST GET YOUR DUCKS IN A ROW AND EXECUTE.

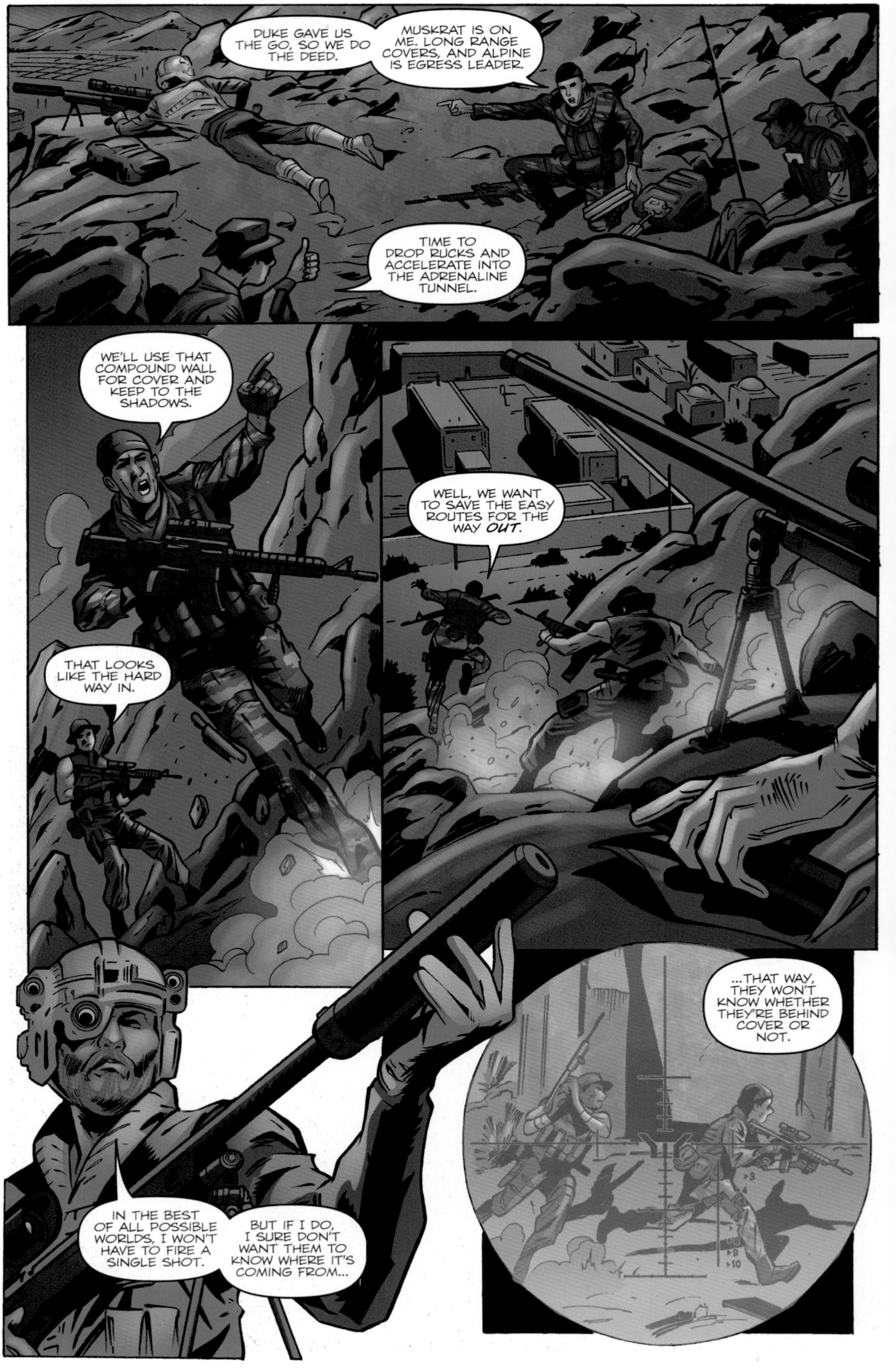
DUKE GAVE US THE GO, SO WE DO THE DEED.
MUSKRAT IS ON ME. LONG RANGE COVERS, AND ALPINE IS EGRESS LEADER.
TIME TO DROP RUCKS AND ACCELERATE INTO THE ADRENALINE TUNNEL.
WE'LL USE THAT COMPOUND WALL FOR COVER AND KEEP TO THE SHADOWS.
THAT LOOKS LIKE THE HARD WAY IN.
WELL, WE WANT TO SAVE THE EASY ROUTES FOR THE WAY *OUT*.
IN THE BEST OF ALL POSSIBLE WORLDS, I WON'T HAVE TO FIRE A SINGLE SHOT.
BUT IF I DO, I SURE DON'T WANT THEM TO KNOW WHERE IT'S COMING FROM...
...THAT WAY, THEY WON'T KNOW WHETHER THEY'RE BEHIND COVER OR NOT.

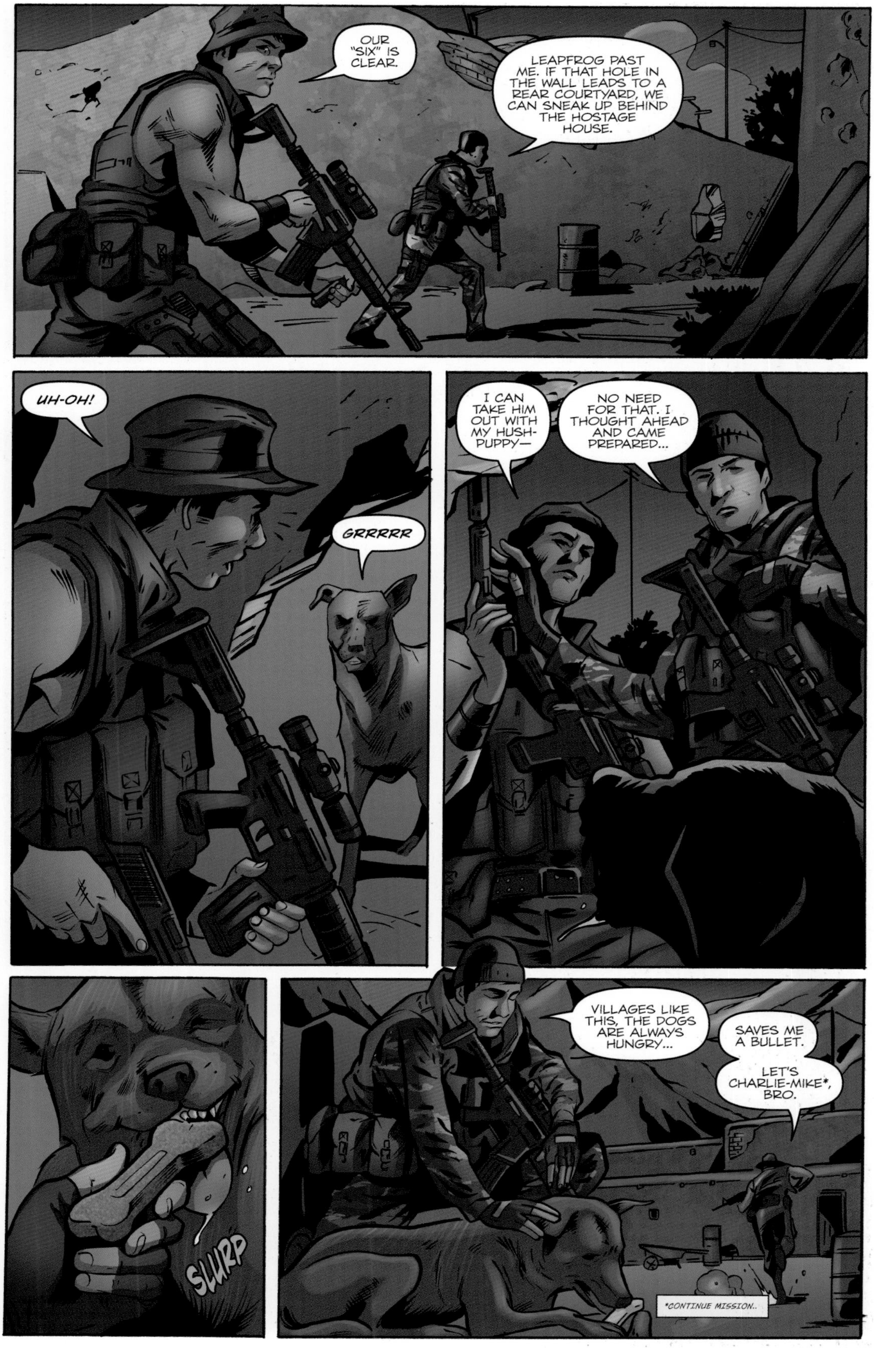
OUR "SIX" IS CLEAR.
LEAPFROG PAST ME. IF THAT HOLE IN THE WALL LEADS TO A REAR COURTYARD, WE CAN SNEAK UP BEHIND THE HOSTAGE HOUSE.
UH-OH!
GRRRRR
I CAN TAKE HIM OUT WITH MY HUSH-PUPPY—
NO NEED FOR THAT. I THOUGHT AHEAD AND CAME PREPARED...
SLURP
VILLAGES LIKE THIS, THE DOGS ARE ALWAYS HUNGRY...
SAVES ME A BULLET.
LET'S CHARLIE-MIKE*, BRO.
*CONTINUE MISSION..

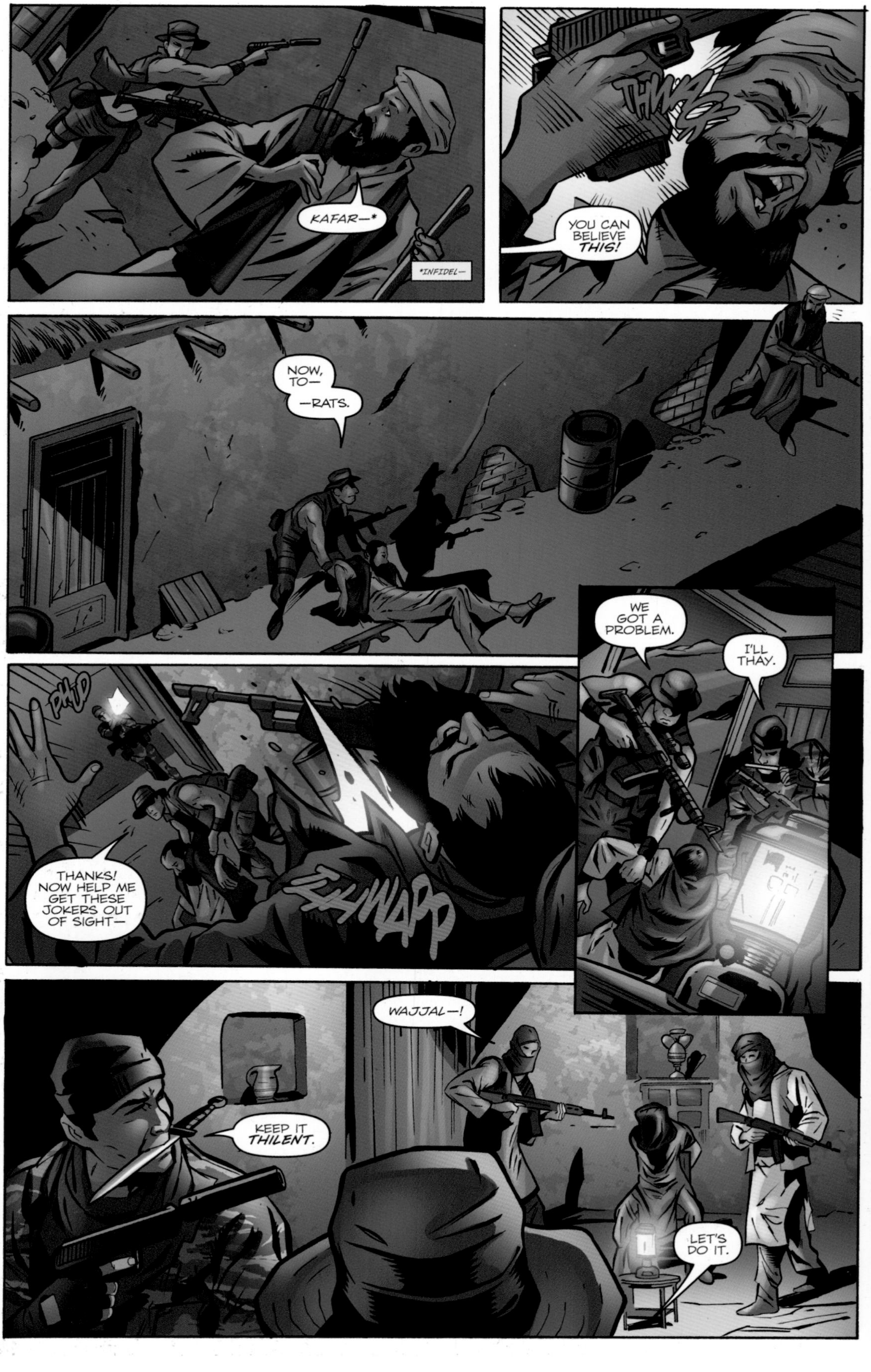
KAFAR—*
*INFIDEL—
THWACK
YOU CAN BELIEVE THIS!
NOW, TO—
—RATS.
WE GOT A PROBLEM.
I'LL THAY.
THUD
THANKS! NOW HELP ME GET THESE JOKERS OUT OF SIGHT—
THWAPP
WAJJAL—!
KEEP IT THILENT.
LET'S DO IT.

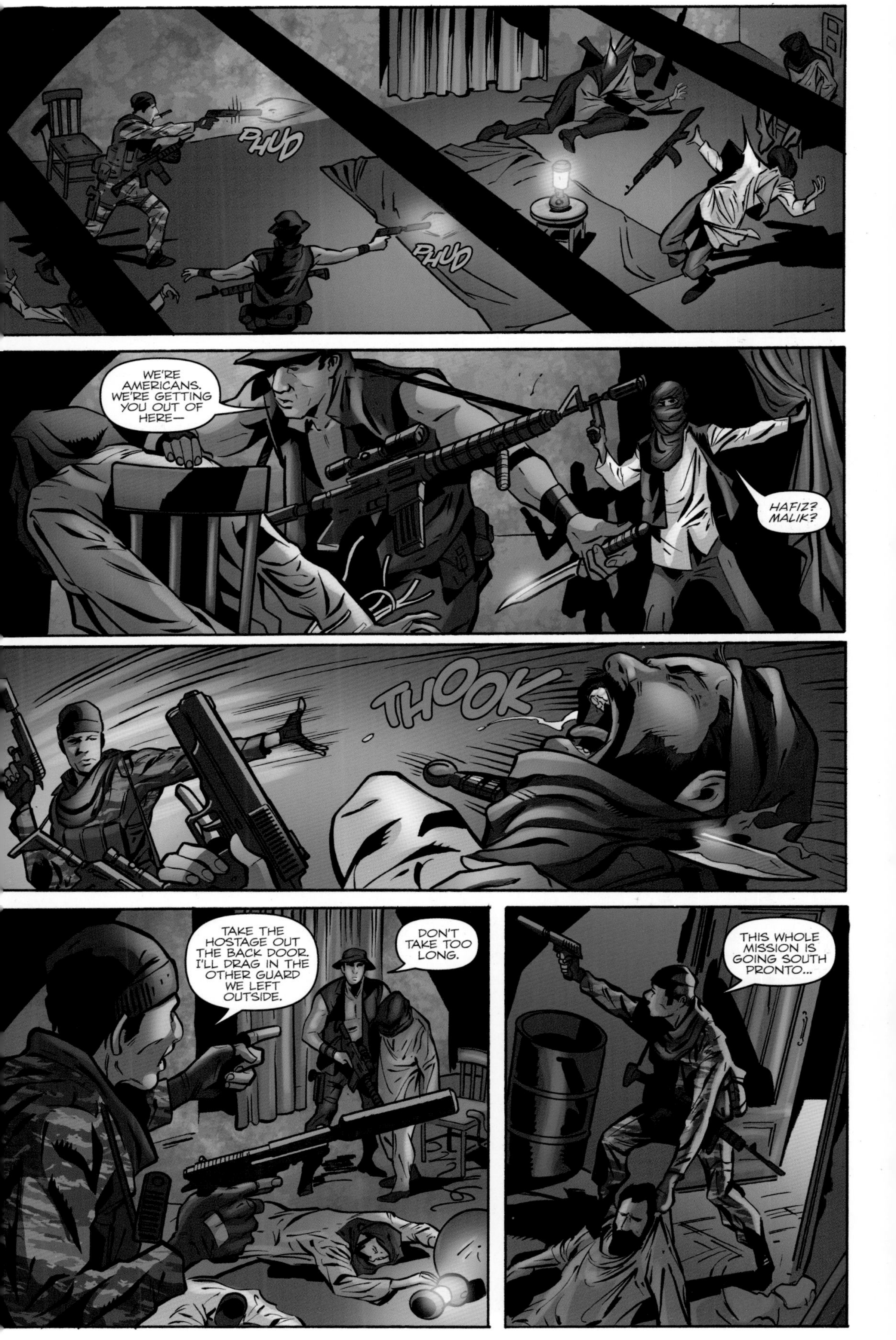
PHUD
PHUD
WE'RE AMERICANS. WE'RE GETTING YOU OUT OF HERE—
HAFIZ? MALIK?
THOOK
TAKE THE HOSTAGE OUT THE BACK DOOR. I'LL DRAG IN THE OTHER GUARD WE LEFT OUTSIDE.
DON'T TAKE TOO LONG.
THIS WHOLE MISSION IS GOING SOUTH PRONTO...

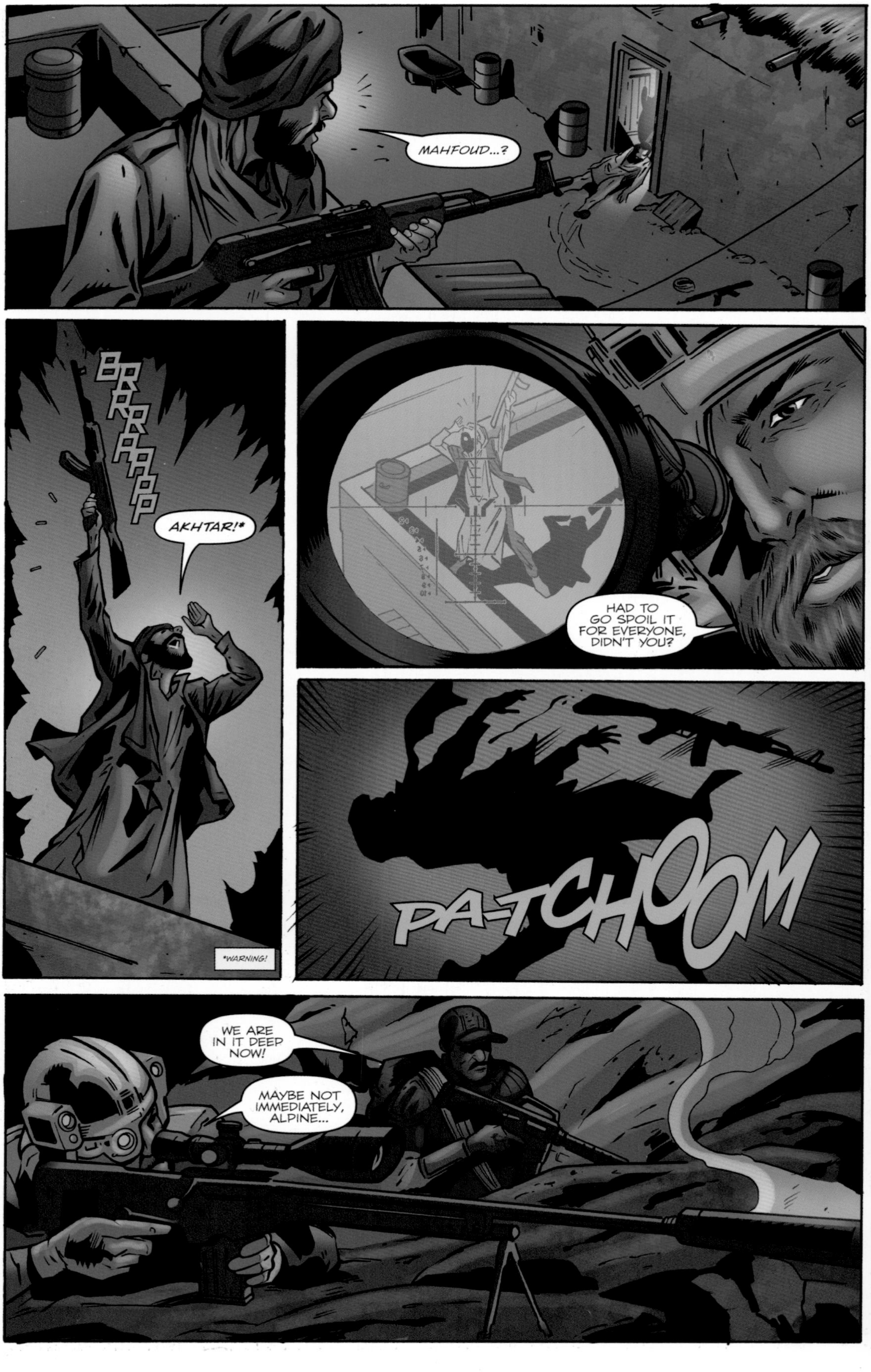
MAHFOUD...?
BRRRRAPP
AKHTAR!*
*WARNING!
HAD TO GO SPOIL IT FOR EVERYONE, DIDN'T YOU?
PA-TCHOOM
WE ARE IN IT DEEP NOW!
MAYBE NOT IMMEDIATELY, ALPINE...

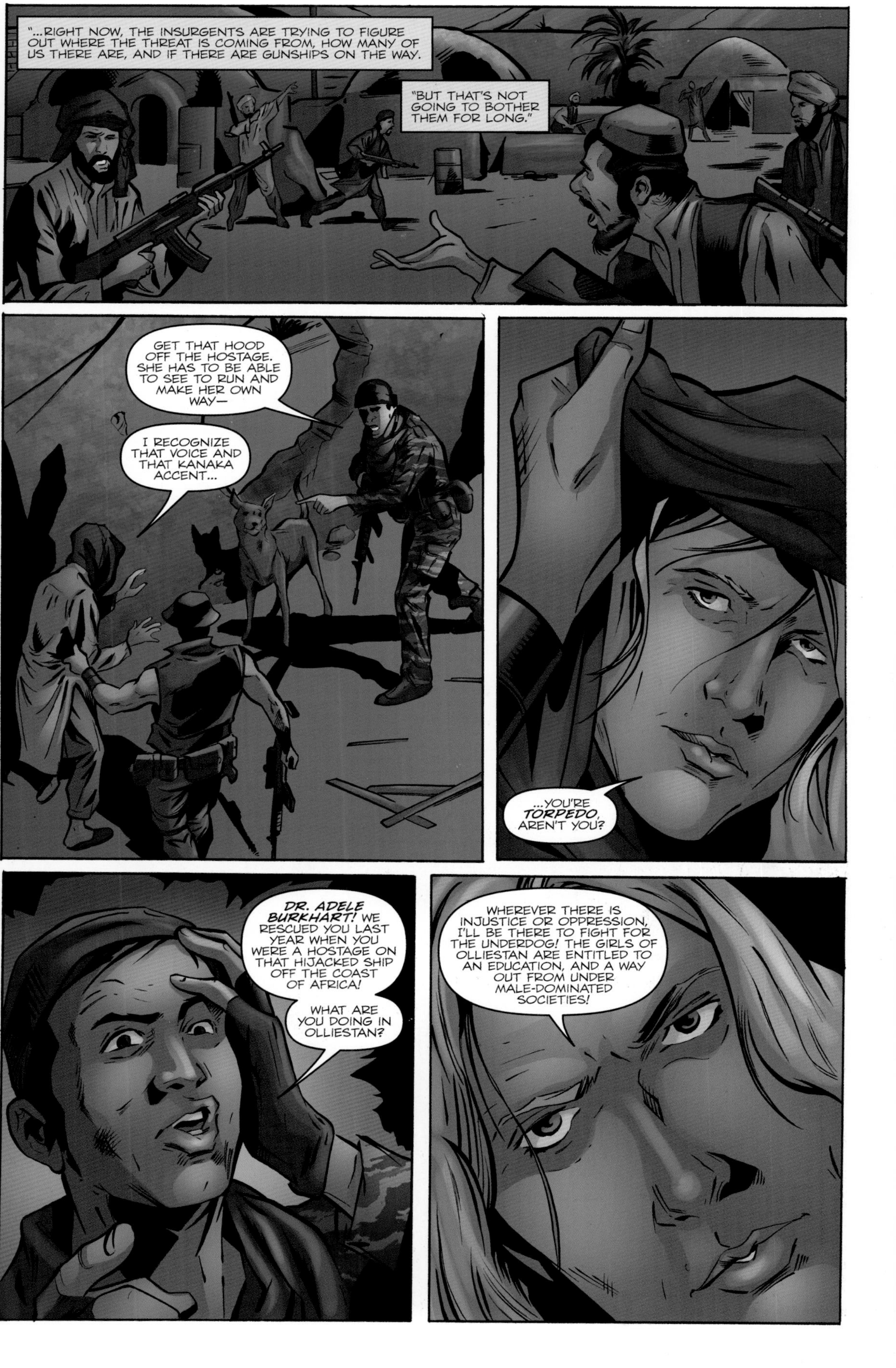
"...RIGHT NOW, THE INSURGENTS ARE TRYING TO FIGURE OUT WHERE THE THREAT IS COMING FROM, HOW MANY OF US THERE ARE, AND IF THERE ARE GUNSHIPS ON THE WAY.
"BUT THAT'S NOT GOING TO BOTHER THEM FOR LONG."
GET THAT HOOD OFF THE HOSTAGE. SHE HAS TO BE ABLE TO SEE TO RUN AND MAKE HER OWN WAY—
I RECOGNIZE THAT VOICE AND THAT KANAKA ACCENT...
...YOU'RE TORPEDO, AREN'T YOU?
DR. ADELE BURKHART! WE RESCUED YOU LAST YEAR WHEN YOU WERE A HOSTAGE ON THAT HIJACKED SHIP OFF THE COAST OF AFRICA!
WHAT ARE YOU DOING IN OLLIESTAN?
WHEREVER THERE IS INJUSTICE OR OPPRESSION, I'LL BE THERE TO FIGHT FOR THE UNDERDOG! THE GIRLS OF OLLIESTAN ARE ENTITLED TO AN EDUCATION, AND A WAY OUT FROM UNDER MALE-DOMINATED SOCIETIES!

PA-TCHOOM PA-TCHOOM

BRRAAAPP BRRAAAAP

THEY FIGURED OUT WHERE WE ARE—

THAT POOR DOG!

MOVE IT OUT, PEOPLE!

THIS SHOULD DISCOURAGE THEM SOME.

VROOOOOM

BE PILOTA ALWATAKA!*

*DRONE!

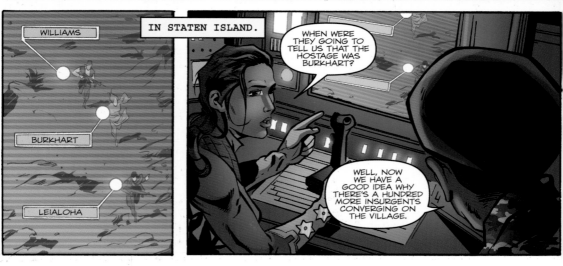

WILLIAMS

BURKHART

LEIALOHA

IN STATEN ISLAND.

WHEN WERE THEY GOING TO TELL US THAT THE HOSTAGE WAS BURKHART?

WELL, NOW WE HAVE A GOOD IDEA WHY THERE'S A HUNDRED MORE INSURGENTS CONVERGING ON THE VILLAGE.

IN SEATTLE.

IT SHOULD BE ON THIS BLOCK...

...THERE IT IS. NICE STREET. NICE BUILDING.

SECOND FLOOR, ABOVE THE COFFEE SHOP.

THIS WILL TAKE SOME GETTING USED TO.

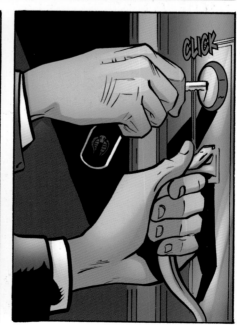

CLICK

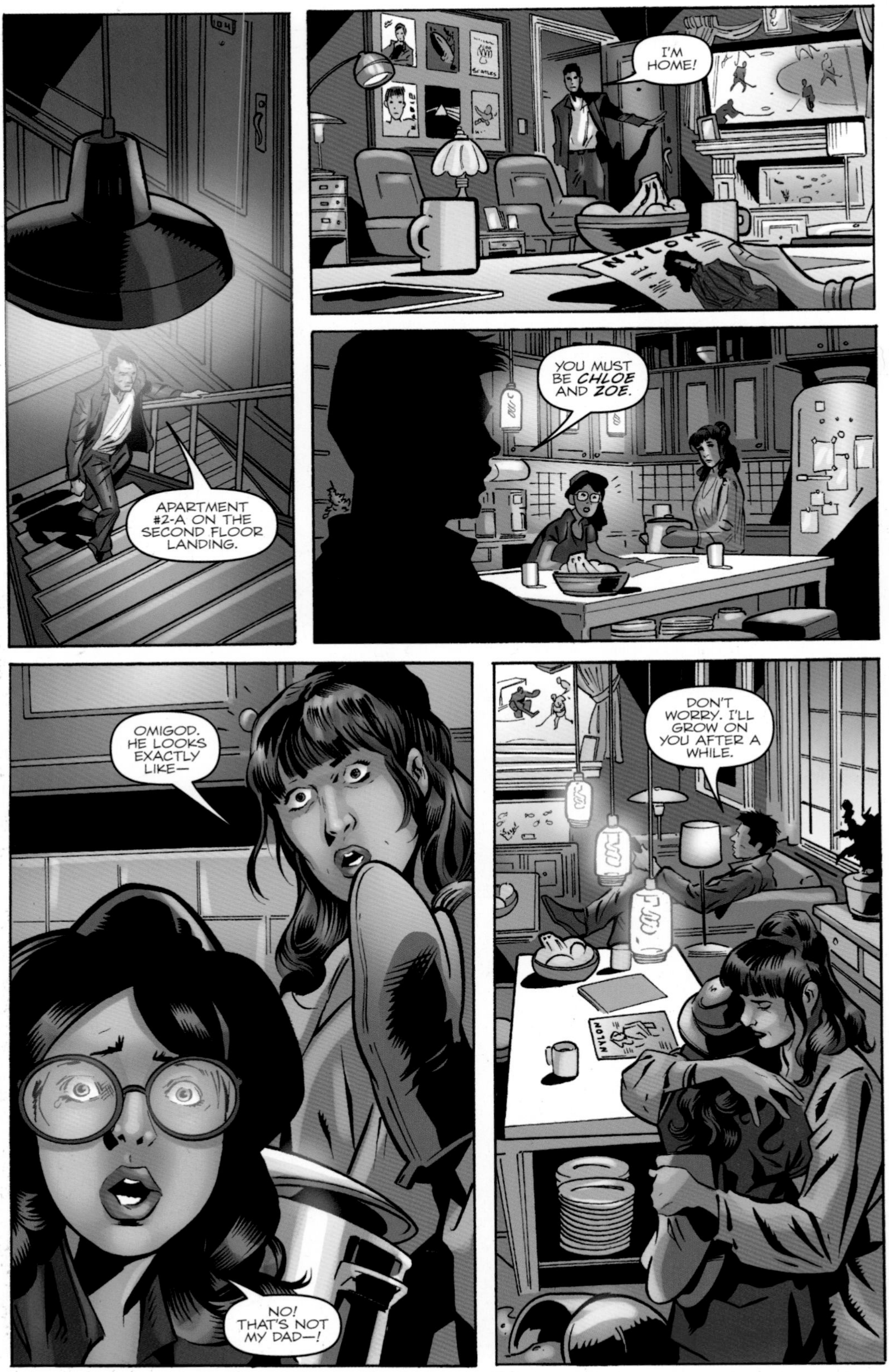
APARTMENT #2-A ON THE SECOND FLOOR LANDING.
I'M HOME!
NYLON
YOU MUST BE CHLOE AND ZOE.
OMIGOD. HE LOOKS EXACTLY LIKE—
NO! THAT'S NOT MY DAD—!
DON'T WORRY. I'LL GROW ON YOU AFTER A WHILE.

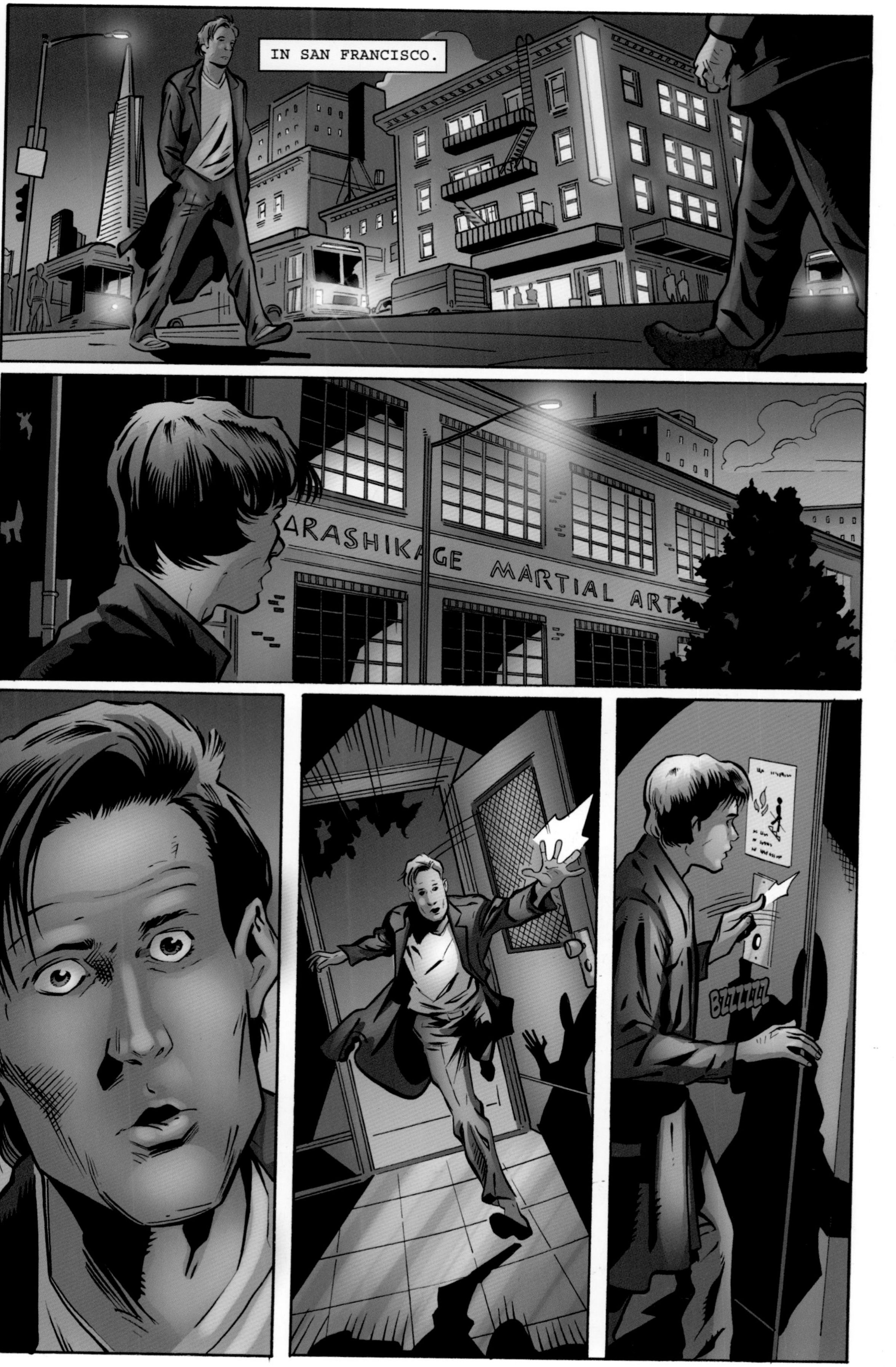
IN SAN FRANCISCO.
ARASHIKAGE MARTIAL ART
BZZZZZZ

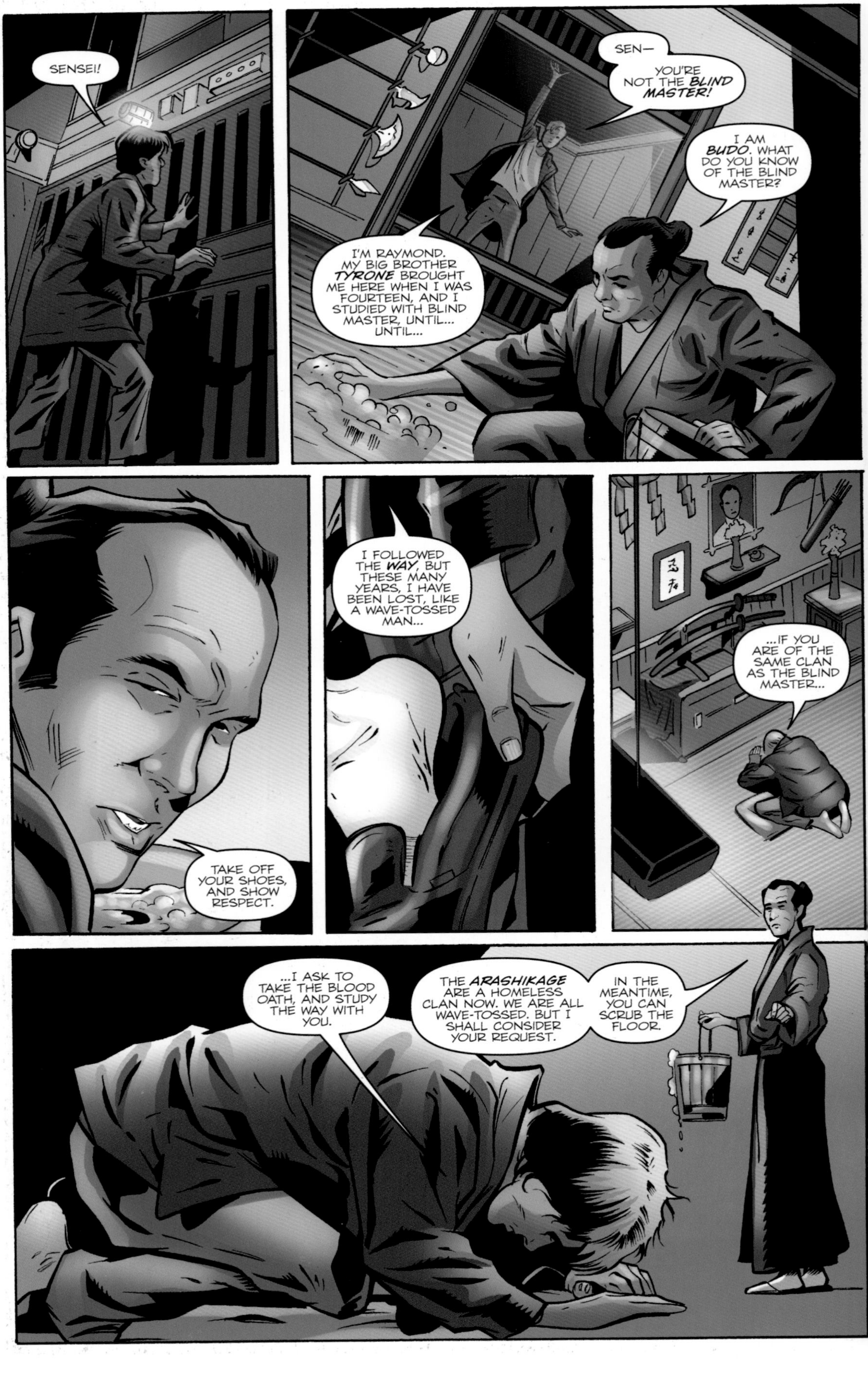
SENSEI!
SEN—
YOU'RE NOT THE BLIND MASTER!
I AM BUDO. WHAT DO YOU KNOW OF THE BLIND MASTER?
I'M RAYMOND. MY BIG BROTHER TYRONE BROUGHT ME HERE WHEN I WAS FOURTEEN, AND I STUDIED WITH BLIND MASTER, UNTIL... UNTIL...
TAKE OFF YOUR SHOES, AND SHOW RESPECT.
I FOLLOWED THE WAY, BUT THESE MANY YEARS, I HAVE BEEN LOST, LIKE A WAVE-TOSSED MAN...
...IF YOU ARE OF THE SAME CLAN AS THE BLIND MASTER...
...I ASK TO TAKE THE BLOOD OATH, AND STUDY THE WAY WITH YOU.
THE ARASHIKAGE ARE A HOMELESS CLAN NOW. WE ARE ALL WAVE-TOSSED. BUT I SHALL CONSIDER YOUR REQUEST.
IN THE MEANTIME, YOU CAN SCRUB THE FLOOR.

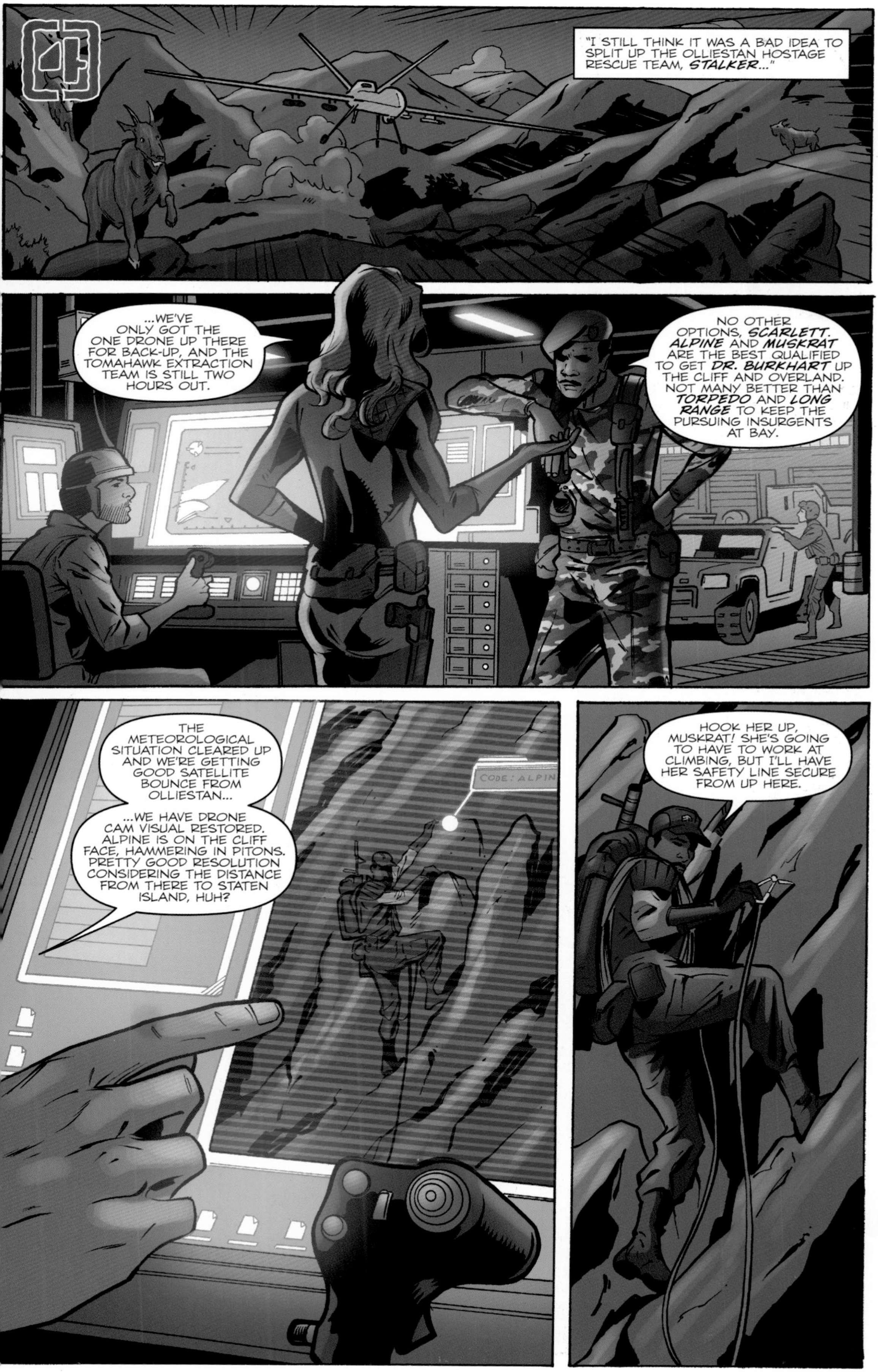
"I STILL THINK IT WAS A BAD IDEA TO SPLIT UP THE OLLIESTAN HOSTAGE RESCUE TEAM, STALKER..."
...WE'VE ONLY GOT THE ONE DRONE UP THERE FOR BACK-UP, AND THE TOMAHAWK EXTRACTION TEAM IS STILL TWO HOURS OUT.
NO OTHER OPTIONS, SCARLETT. ALPINE AND MUSKRAT ARE THE BEST QUALIFIED TO GET DR. BURKHART UP THE CLIFF AND OVERLAND. NOT MANY BETTER THAN TORPEDO AND LONG RANGE TO KEEP THE PURSUING INSURGENTS AT BAY.
THE METEOROLOGICAL SITUATION CLEARED UP AND WE'RE GETTING GOOD SATELLITE BOUNCE FROM OLLIESTAN...
...WE HAVE DRONE CAM VISUAL RESTORED. ALPINE IS ON THE CLIFF FACE, HAMMERING IN PITONS. PRETTY GOOD RESOLUTION CONSIDERING THE DISTANCE FROM THERE TO STATEN ISLAND, HUH?
CODE: ALPIN
HOOK HER UP, MUSKRAT! SHE'S GOING TO HAVE TO WORK AT CLIMBING, BUT I'LL HAVE HER SAFETY LINE SECURE FROM UP HERE.

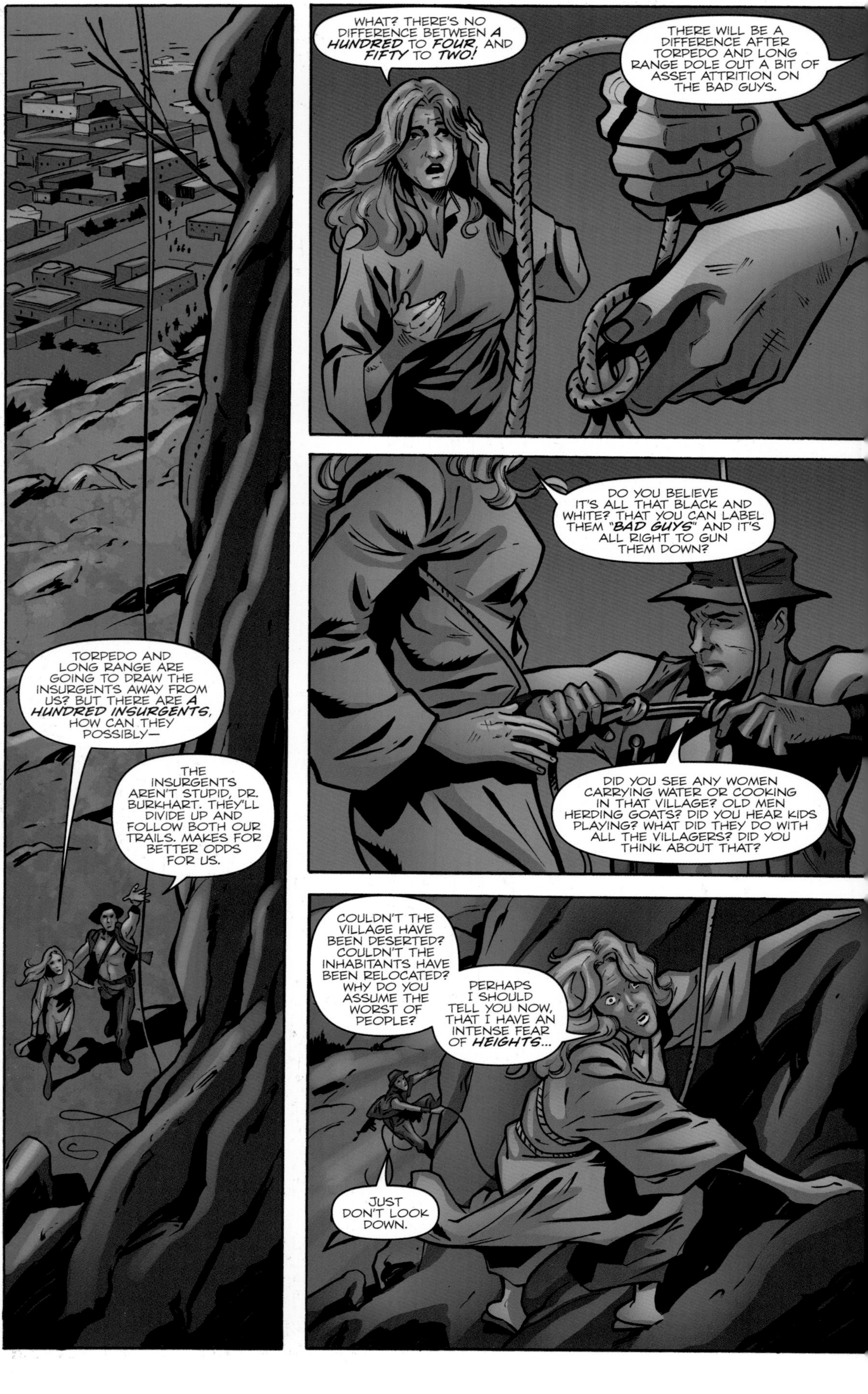
TORPEDO AND LONG RANGE ARE GOING TO DRAW THE INSURGENTS AWAY FROM US? BUT THERE ARE A HUNDRED INSURGENTS, HOW CAN THEY POSSIBLY—
THE INSURGENTS AREN'T STUPID, DR. BURKHART. THEY'LL DIVIDE UP AND FOLLOW BOTH OUR TRAILS. MAKES FOR BETTER ODDS FOR US.
WHAT? THERE'S NO DIFFERENCE BETWEEN A HUNDRED TO FOUR, AND FIFTY TO TWO!
THERE WILL BE A DIFFERENCE AFTER TORPEDO AND LONG RANGE DOLE OUT A BIT OF ASSET ATTRITION ON THE BAD GUYS.
DO YOU BELIEVE IT'S ALL THAT BLACK AND WHITE? THAT YOU CAN LABEL THEM "BAD GUYS" AND IT'S ALL RIGHT TO GUN THEM DOWN?
DID YOU SEE ANY WOMEN CARRYING WATER OR COOKING IN THAT VILLAGE? OLD MEN HERDING GOATS? DID YOU HEAR KIDS PLAYING? WHAT DID THEY DO WITH ALL THE VILLAGERS? DID YOU THINK ABOUT THAT?
COULDN'T THE VILLAGE HAVE BEEN DESERTED? COULDN'T THE INHABITANTS HAVE BEEN RELOCATED? WHY DO YOU ASSUME THE WORST OF PEOPLE?
PERHAPS I SHOULD TELL YOU NOW, THAT I HAVE AN INTENSE FEAR OF HEIGHTS...
JUST DON'T LOOK DOWN.

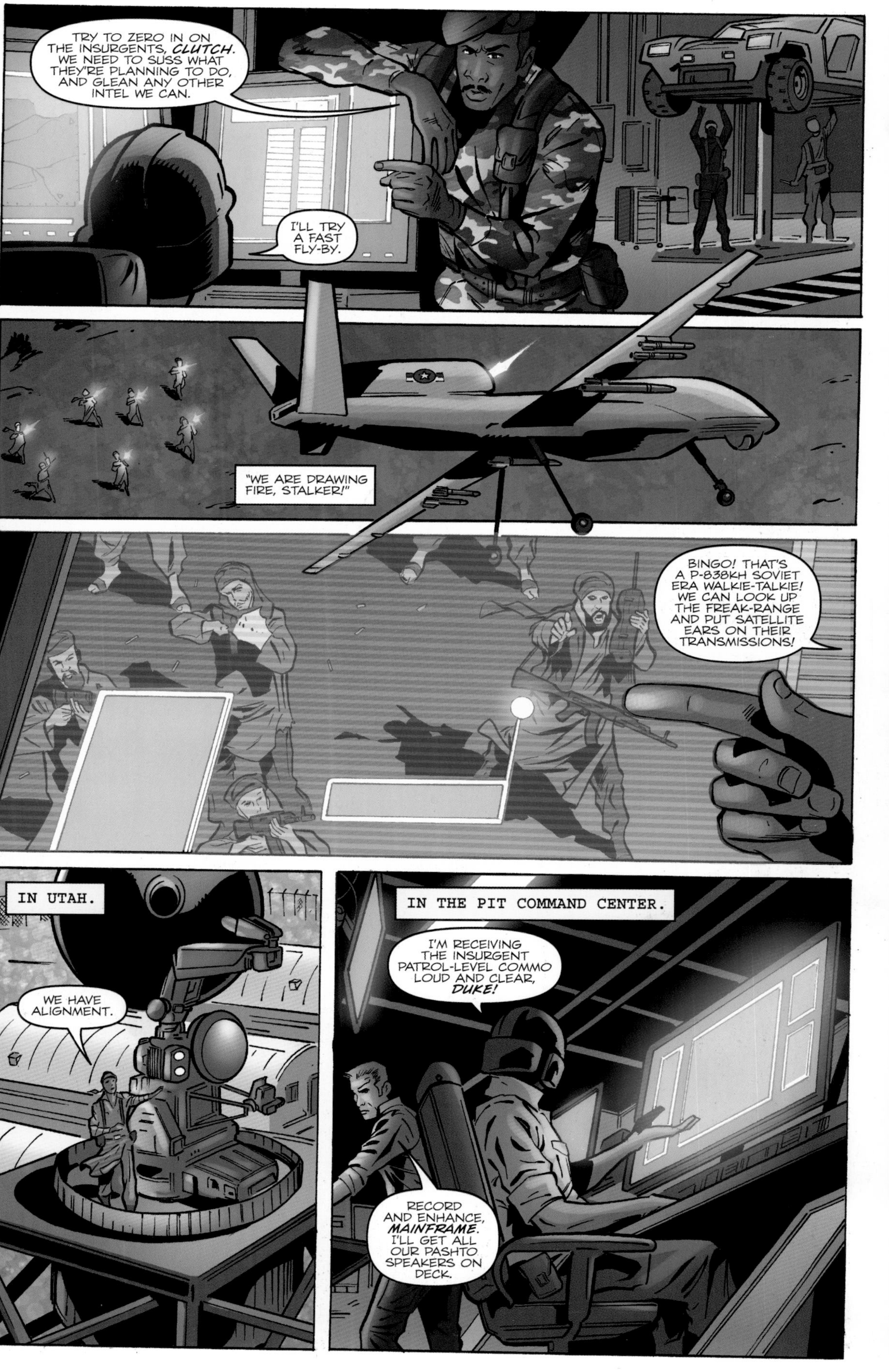

TRY TO ZERO IN ON THE INSURGENTS, CLUTCH. WE NEED TO SUSS WHAT THEY'RE PLANNING TO DO, AND GLEAN ANY OTHER INTEL WE CAN.
I'LL TRY A FAST FLY-BY.
"WE ARE DRAWING FIRE, STALKER!"
BINGO! THAT'S A P-838KH SOVIET ERA WALKIE-TALKIE! WE CAN LOOK UP THE FREAK-RANGE AND PUT SATELLITE EARS ON THEIR TRANSMISSIONS!
IN UTAH.
WE HAVE ALIGNMENT.
IN THE PIT COMMAND CENTER.
I'M RECEIVING THE INSURGENT PATROL-LEVEL COMMO LOUD AND CLEAR, DUKE!
RECORD AND ENHANCE, MAINFRAME. I'LL GET ALL OUR PASHTO SPEAKERS ON DECK.

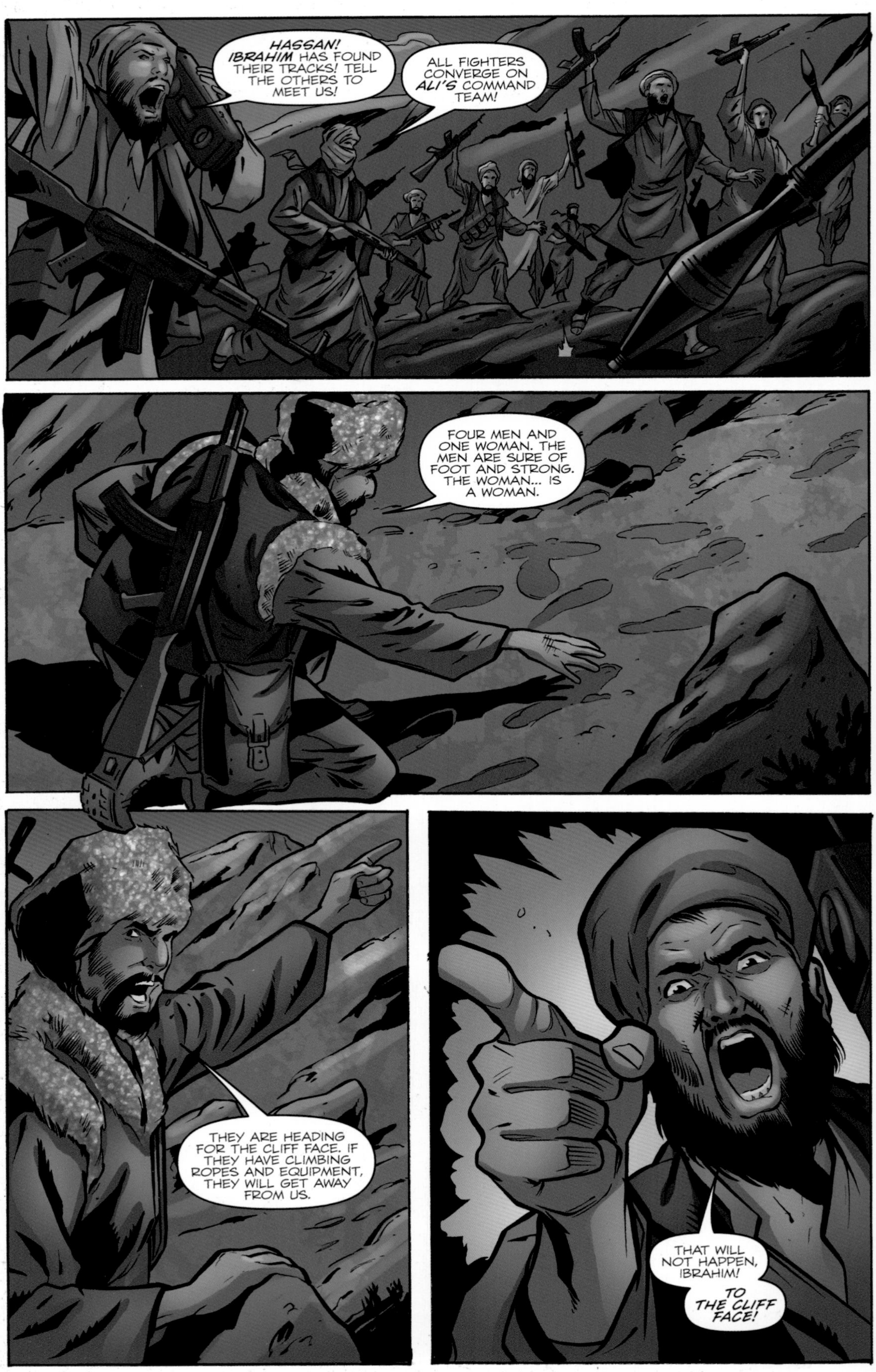
HASSAN! IBRAHIM HAS FOUND THEIR TRACKS! TELL THE OTHERS TO MEET US!
ALL FIGHTERS CONVERGE ON ALI'S COMMAND TEAM!
FOUR MEN AND ONE WOMAN. THE MEN ARE SURE OF FOOT AND STRONG. THE WOMAN... IS A WOMAN.
THEY ARE HEADING FOR THE CLIFF FACE. IF THEY HAVE CLIMBING ROPES AND EQUIPMENT, THEY WILL GET AWAY FROM US.
THAT WILL NOT HAPPEN, IBRAHIM!
TO THE CLIFF FACE!

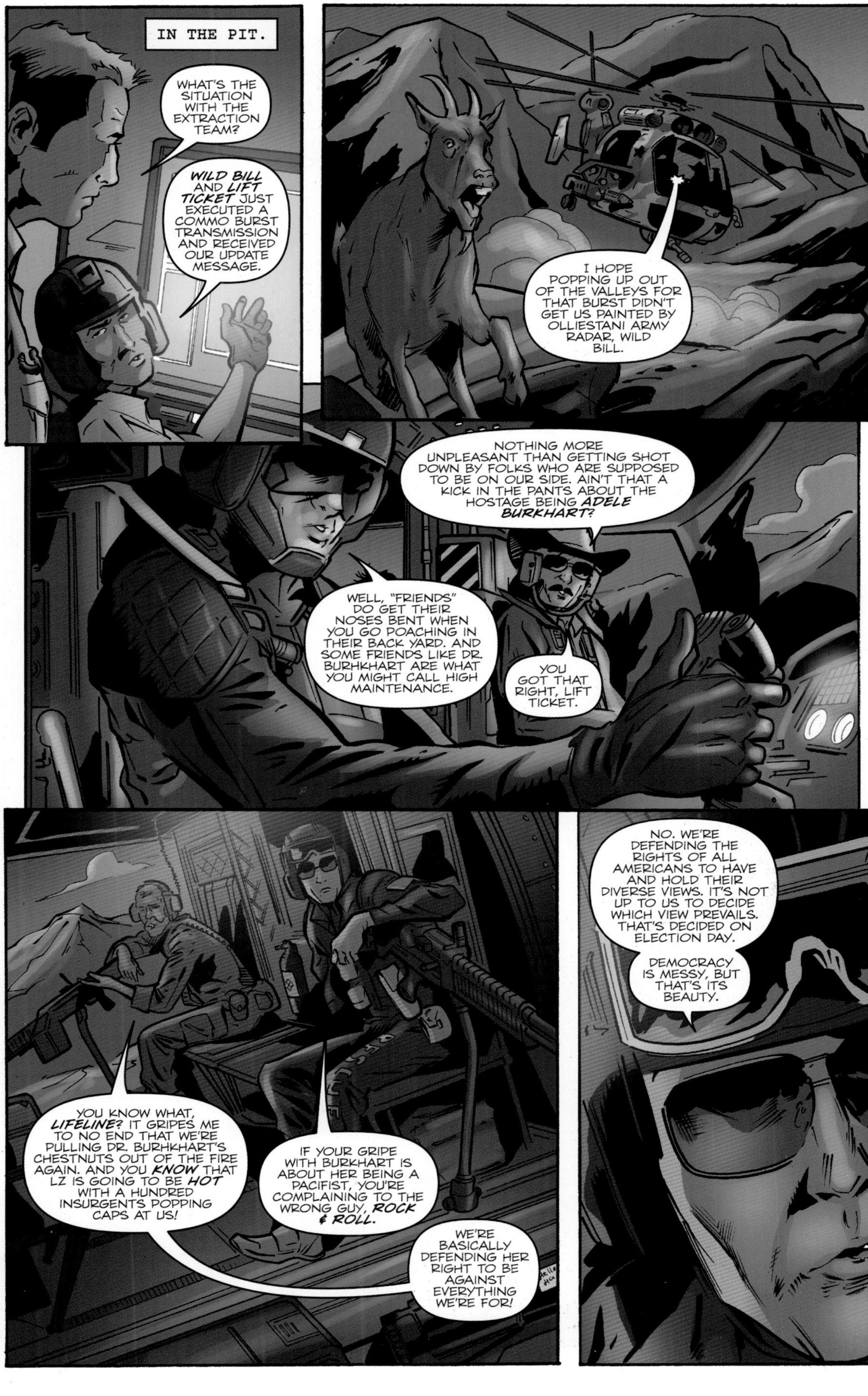
IN THE PIT.
WHAT'S THE SITUATION WITH THE EXTRACTION TEAM?
WILD BILL AND LIFT TICKET JUST EXECUTED A COMMO BURST TRANSMISSION AND RECEIVED OUR UPDATE MESSAGE.
I HOPE POPPING UP OUT OF THE VALLEYS FOR THAT BURST DIDN'T GET US PAINTED BY OLLIESTANI ARMY RADAR, WILD BILL.
NOTHING MORE UNPLEASANT THAN GETTING SHOT DOWN BY FOLKS WHO ARE SUPPOSED TO BE ON OUR SIDE. AIN'T THAT A KICK IN THE PANTS ABOUT THE HOSTAGE BEING ADELE BURKHART?
WELL, "FRIENDS" DO GET THEIR NOSES BENT WHEN YOU GO POACHING IN THEIR BACK YARD. AND SOME FRIENDS LIKE DR. BURHKHART ARE WHAT YOU MIGHT CALL HIGH MAINTENANCE.
YOU GOT THAT RIGHT, LIFT TICKET.
YOU KNOW WHAT, LIFELINE? IT GRIPES ME TO NO END THAT WE'RE PULLING DR. BURHKHART'S CHESTNUTS OUT OF THE FIRE AGAIN. AND YOU KNOW THAT LZ IS GOING TO BE HOT WITH A HUNDRED INSURGENTS POPPING CAPS AT US!
IF YOUR GRIPE WITH BURKHART IS ABOUT HER BEING A PACIFIST, YOU'RE COMPLAINING TO THE WRONG GUY, ROCK & ROLL.
WE'RE BASICALLY DEFENDING HER RIGHT TO BE AGAINST EVERYTHING WE'RE FOR!
NO. WE'RE DEFENDING THE RIGHTS OF ALL AMERICANS TO HAVE AND HOLD THEIR DIVERSE VIEWS. IT'S NOT UP TO US TO DECIDE WHICH VIEW PREVAILS. THAT'S DECIDED ON ELECTION DAY.
DEMOCRACY IS MESSY, BUT THAT'S ITS BEAUTY.

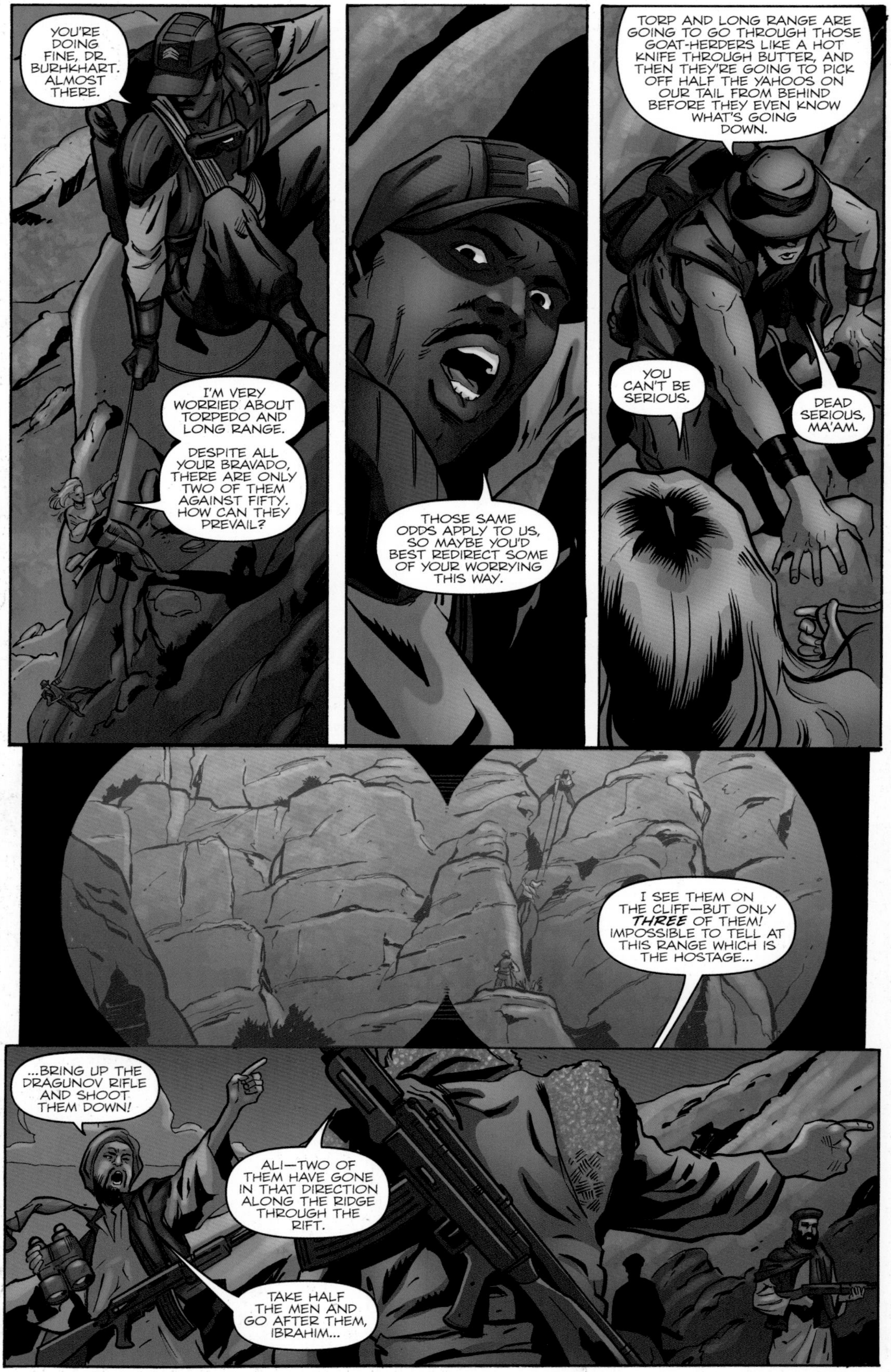
YOU'RE DOING FINE, DR. BURHKHART. ALMOST THERE.
I'M VERY WORRIED ABOUT TORPEDO AND LONG RANGE.
DESPITE ALL YOUR BRAVADO, THERE ARE ONLY TWO OF THEM AGAINST FIFTY. HOW CAN THEY PREVAIL?
THOSE SAME ODDS APPLY TO US, SO MAYBE YOU'D BEST REDIRECT SOME OF YOUR WORRYING THIS WAY.
TORP AND LONG RANGE ARE GOING TO GO THROUGH THOSE GOAT-HERDERS LIKE A HOT KNIFE THROUGH BUTTER, AND THEN THEY'RE GOING TO PICK OFF HALF THE YAHOOS ON OUR TAIL FROM BEHIND BEFORE THEY EVEN KNOW WHAT'S GOING DOWN.
YOU CAN'T BE SERIOUS.
DEAD SERIOUS, MA'AM.
I SEE THEM ON THE CLIFF—BUT ONLY *THREE* OF THEM! IMPOSSIBLE TO TELL AT THIS RANGE WHICH IS THE HOSTAGE...
...BRING UP THE DRAGUNOV RIFLE AND SHOOT THEM DOWN!
ALI—TWO OF THEM HAVE GONE IN THAT DIRECTION ALONG THE RIDGE THROUGH THE RIFT.
TAKE HALF THE MEN AND GO AFTER THEM, IBRAHIM...

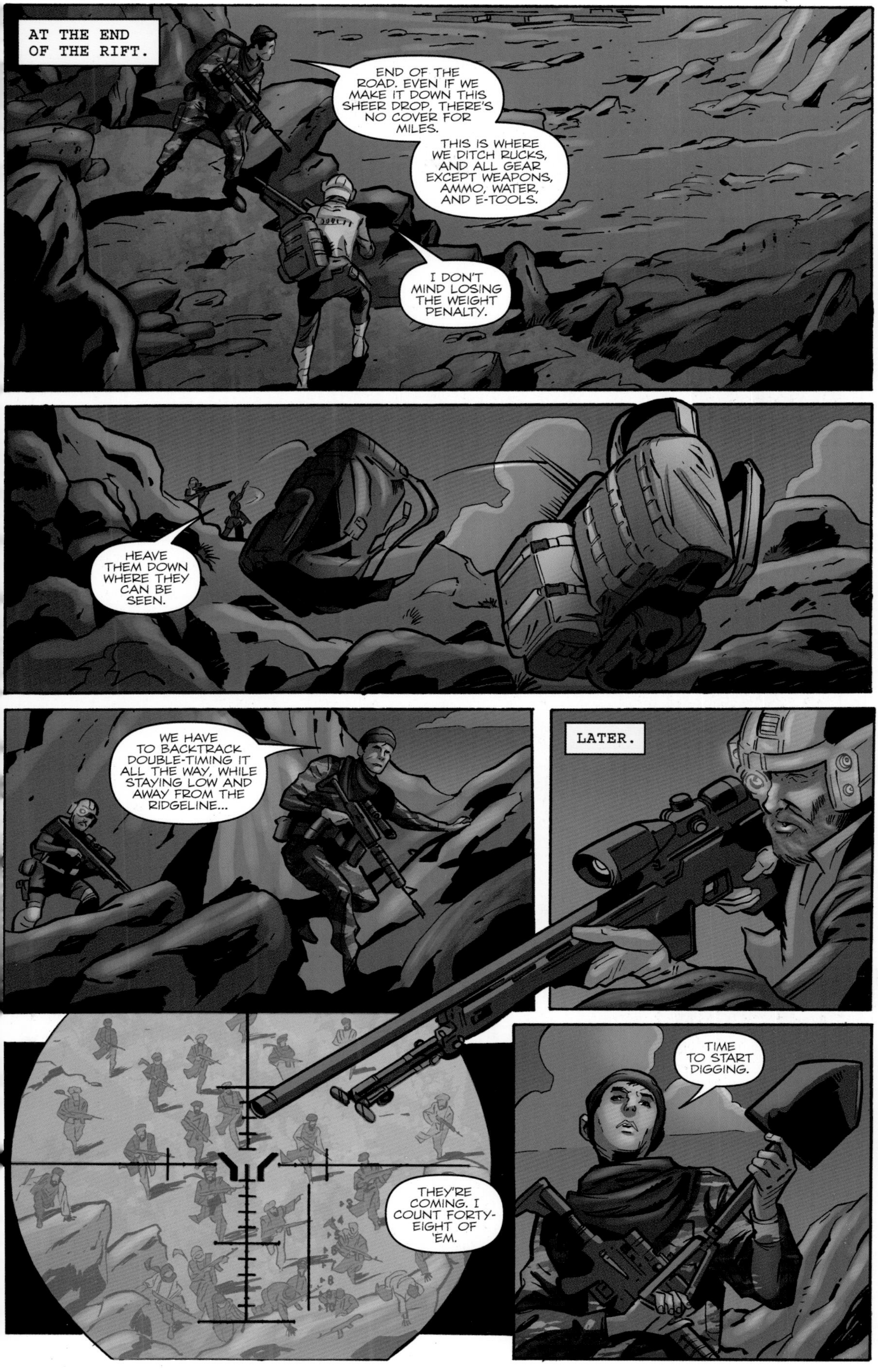
AT THE END OF THE RIFT.
END OF THE ROAD. EVEN IF WE MAKE IT DOWN THIS SHEER DROP, THERE'S NO COVER FOR MILES.
THIS IS WHERE WE DITCH RUCKS, AND ALL GEAR EXCEPT WEAPONS, AMMO, WATER, AND E-TOOLS.
I DON'T MIND LOSING THE WEIGHT PENALTY.
HEAVE THEM DOWN WHERE THEY CAN BE SEEN.
WE HAVE TO BACKTRACK DOUBLE-TIMING IT ALL THE WAY, WHILE STAYING LOW AND AWAY FROM THE RIDGELINE...
LATER.
THEY'RE COMING. I COUNT FORTY-EIGHT OF 'EM.
TIME TO START DIGGING.

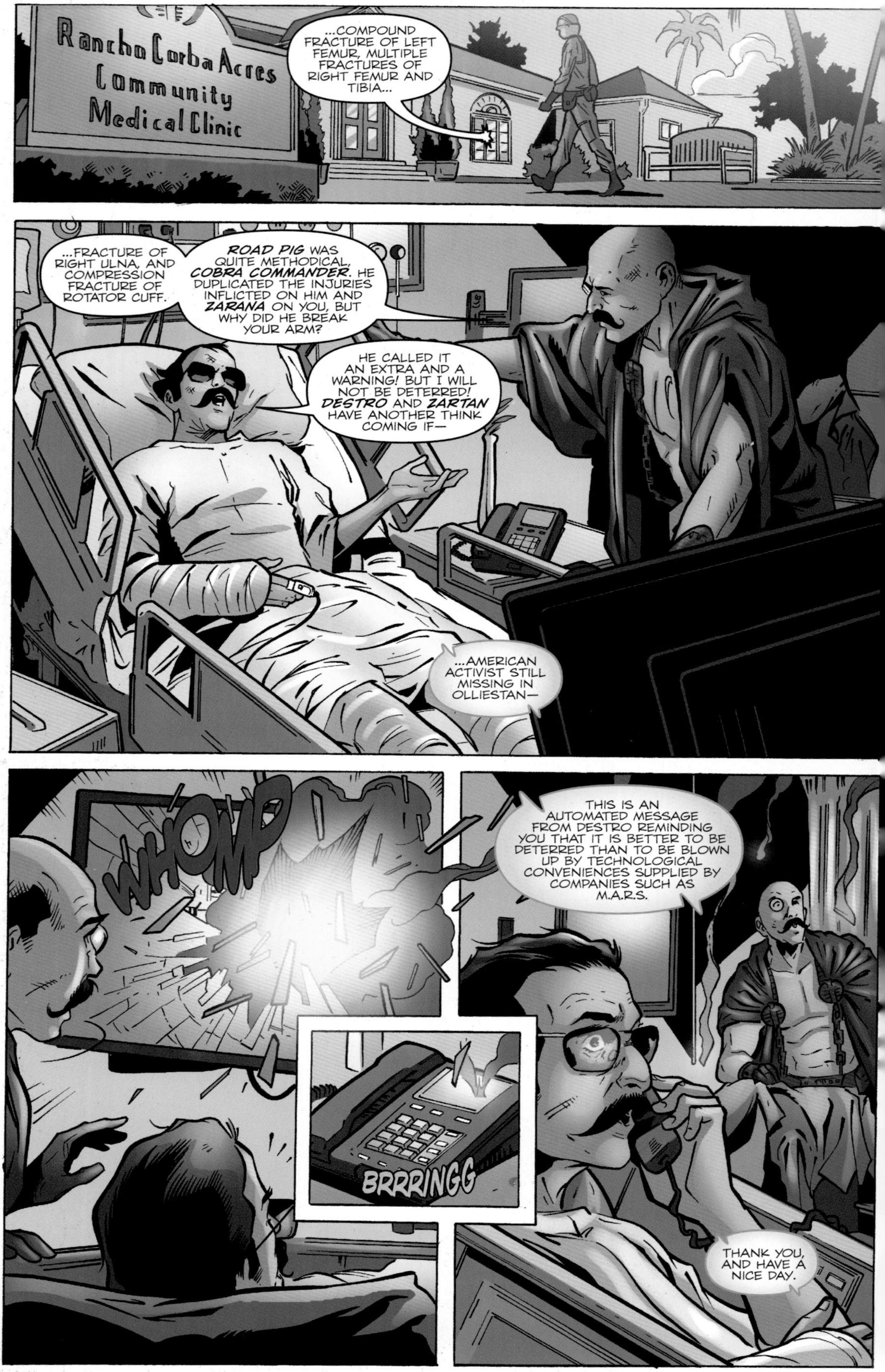
Rancho Corba Acres
Community
Medical Clinic
...COMPOUND FRACTURE OF LEFT FEMUR, MULTIPLE FRACTURES OF RIGHT FEMUR AND TIBIA...
...FRACTURE OF RIGHT ULNA, AND COMPRESSION FRACTURE OF ROTATOR CUFF.
ROAD PIG WAS QUITE METHODICAL, COBRA COMMANDER. HE DUPLICATED THE INJURIES INFLICTED ON HIM AND ZARANA ON YOU, BUT WHY DID HE BREAK YOUR ARM?
HE CALLED IT AN EXTRA AND A WARNING! BUT I WILL NOT BE DETERRED! DESTRO AND ZARTAN HAVE ANOTHER THINK COMING IF—
...AMERICAN ACTIVIST STILL MISSING IN OLLIESTAN—
WHOMP
BRRRINGG
THIS IS AN AUTOMATED MESSAGE FROM DESTRO REMINDING YOU THAT IT IS BETTER TO BE DETERRED THAN TO BE BLOWN UP BY TECHNOLOGICAL CONVENIENCES SUPPLIED BY COMPANIES SUCH AS M.A.R.S.
THANK YOU, AND HAVE A NICE DAY.

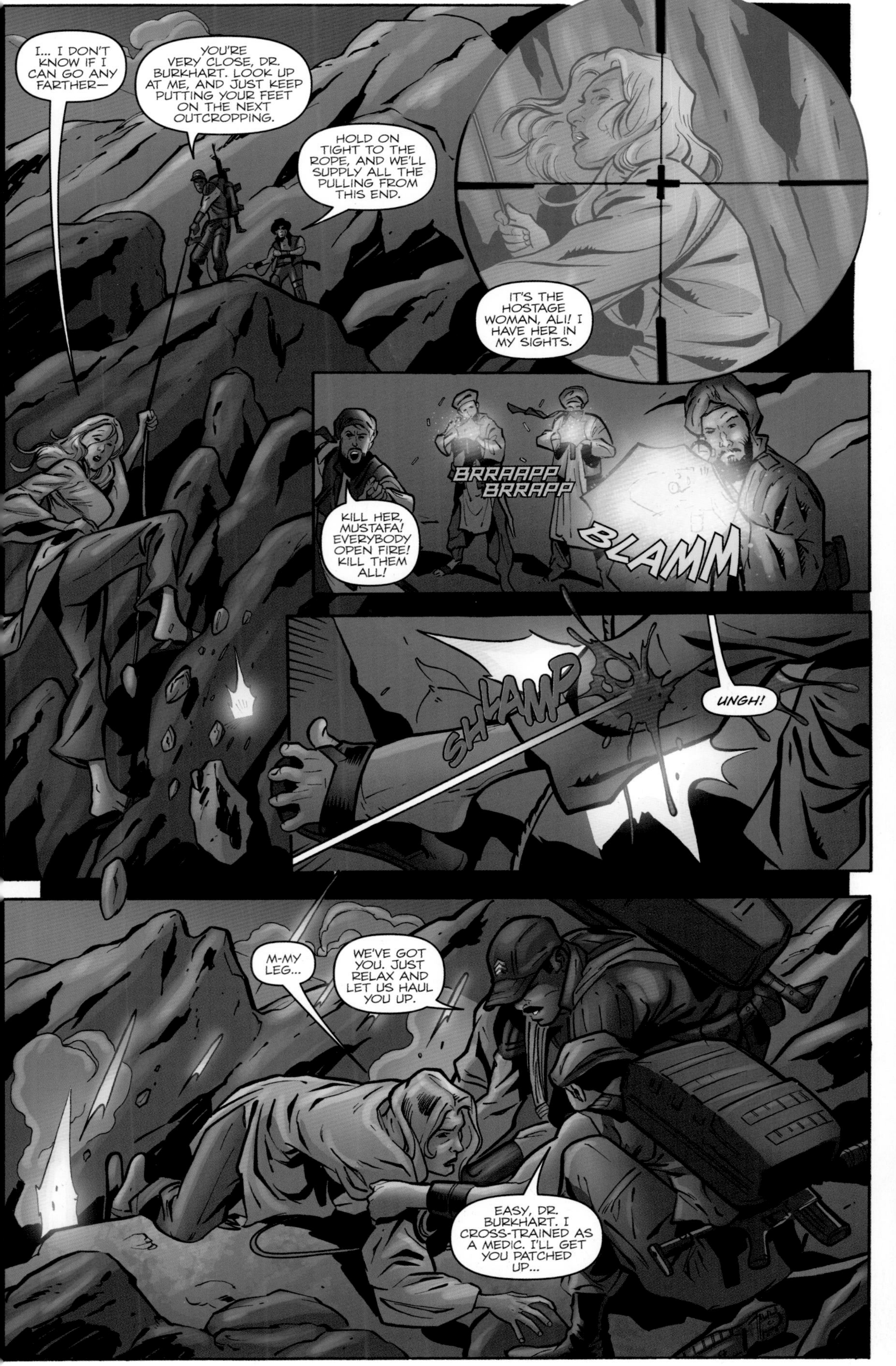

I... I DON'T KNOW IF I CAN GO ANY FARTHER—
YOU'RE VERY CLOSE, DR. BURKHART. LOOK UP AT ME, AND JUST KEEP PUTTING YOUR FEET ON THE NEXT OUTCROPPING.
HOLD ON TIGHT TO THE ROPE, AND WE'LL SUPPLY ALL THE PULLING FROM THIS END.
IT'S THE HOSTAGE WOMAN, ALI! I HAVE HER IN MY SIGHTS.
KILL HER, MUSTAFA! EVERYBODY OPEN FIRE! KILL THEM ALL!
BRRAAPP
BRRAPP
BLAMM
SHLAMP
UNGH!
M-MY LEG...
WE'VE GOT YOU. JUST RELAX AND LET US HAUL YOU UP.
EASY, DR. BURKHART. I CROSS-TRAINED AS A MEDIC. I'LL GET YOU PATCHED UP...

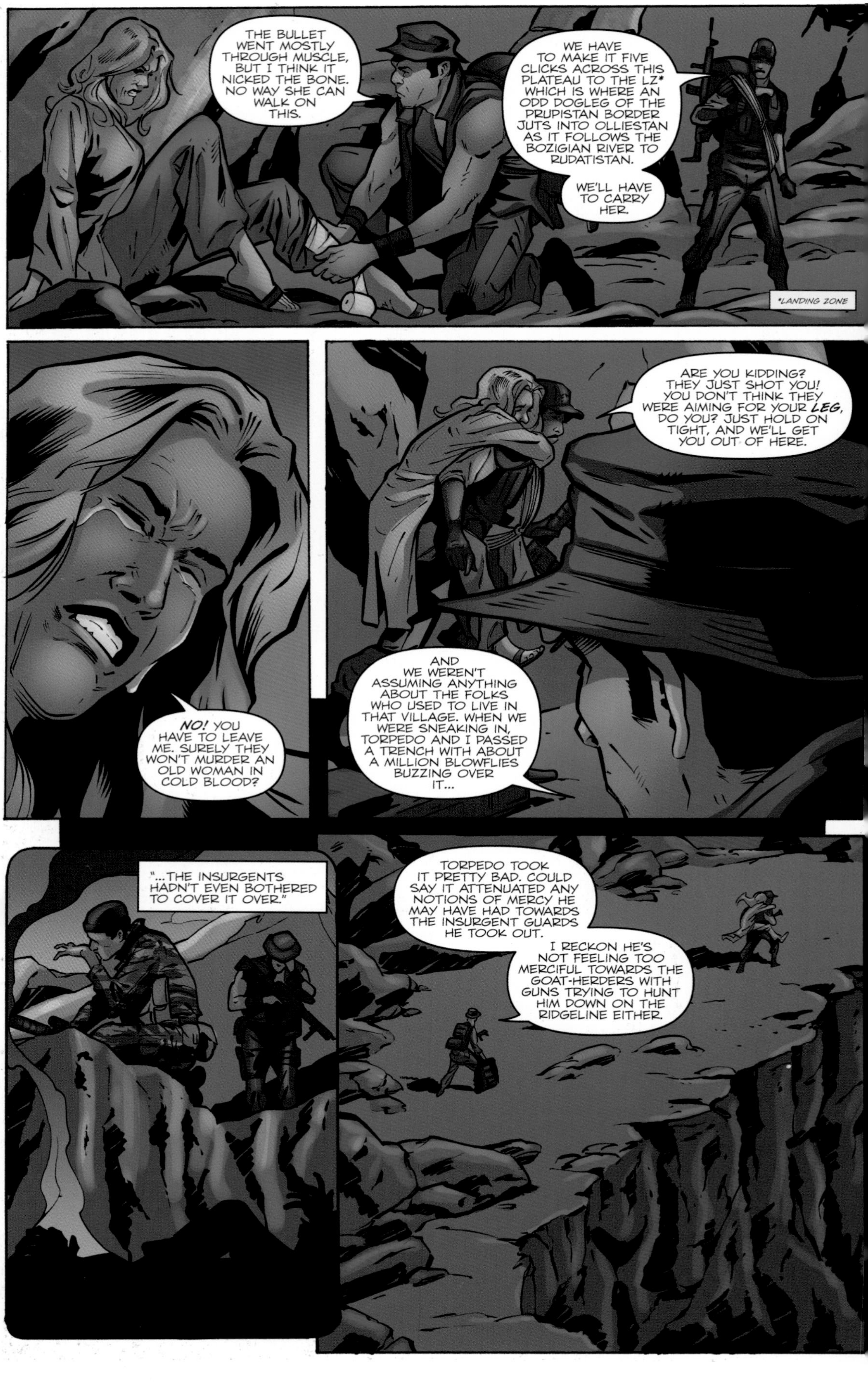
THE BULLET WENT MOSTLY THROUGH MUSCLE, BUT I THINK IT NICKED THE BONE. NO WAY SHE CAN WALK ON THIS.
WE HAVE TO MAKE IT FIVE CLICKS ACROSS THIS PLATEAU TO THE LZ* WHICH IS WHERE AN ODD DOGLEG OF THE PRUPISTAN BORDER JUTS INTO OLLIESTAN AS IT FOLLOWS THE BOZIGIAN RIVER TO RUDATISTAN.
WE'LL HAVE TO CARRY HER.
*LANDING ZONE
NO! YOU HAVE TO LEAVE ME. SURELY THEY WON'T MURDER AN OLD WOMAN IN COLD BLOOD?
ARE YOU KIDDING? THEY JUST SHOT YOU! YOU DON'T THINK THEY WERE AIMING FOR YOUR LEG, DO YOU? JUST HOLD ON TIGHT, AND WE'LL GET YOU OUT OF HERE.
AND WE WEREN'T ASSUMING ANYTHING ABOUT THE FOLKS WHO USED TO LIVE IN THAT VILLAGE. WHEN WE WERE SNEAKING IN, TORPEDO AND I PASSED A TRENCH WITH ABOUT A MILLION BLOWFLIES BUZZING OVER IT...
"...THE INSURGENTS HADN'T EVEN BOTHERED TO COVER IT OVER."
TORPEDO TOOK IT PRETTY BAD. COULD SAY IT ATTENUATED ANY NOTIONS OF MERCY HE MAY HAVE HAD TOWARDS THE INSURGENT GUARDS HE TOOK OUT.
I RECKON HE'S NOT FEELING TOO MERCIFUL TOWARDS THE GOAT-HERDERS WITH GUNS TRYING TO HUNT HIM DOWN ON THE RIDGELINE EITHER.

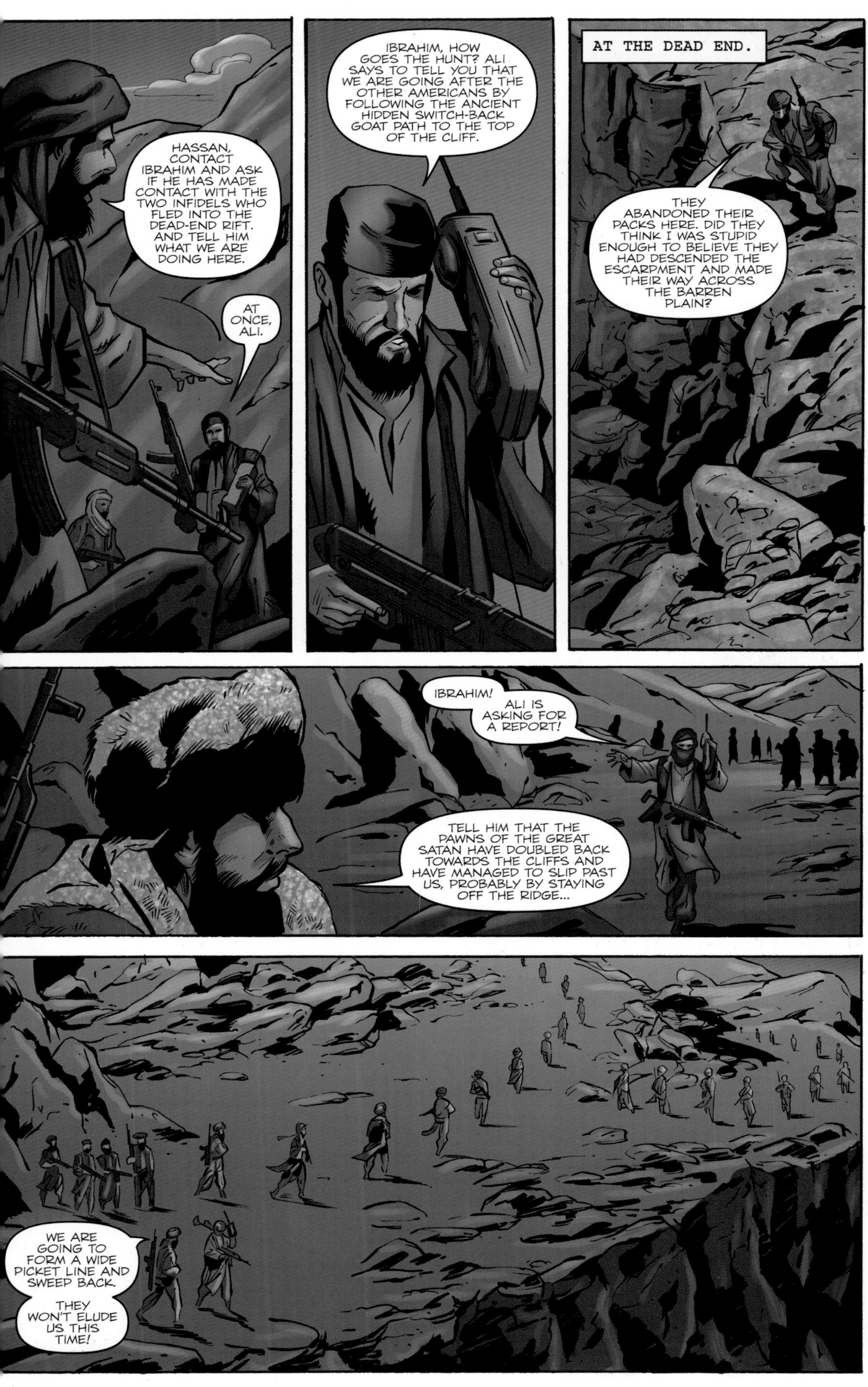
HASSAN, CONTACT IBRAHIM AND ASK IF HE HAS MADE CONTACT WITH THE TWO INFIDELS WHO FLED INTO THE DEAD-END RIFT. AND TELL HIM WHAT WE ARE DOING HERE.
AT ONCE, ALI.
IBRAHIM, HOW GOES THE HUNT? ALI SAYS TO TELL YOU THAT WE ARE GOING AFTER THE OTHER AMERICANS BY FOLLOWING THE ANCIENT HIDDEN SWITCH-BACK GOAT PATH TO THE TOP OF THE CLIFF.
AT THE DEAD END.
THEY ABANDONED THEIR PACKS HERE. DID THEY THINK I WAS STUPID ENOUGH TO BELIEVE THEY HAD DESCENDED THE ESCARPMENT AND MADE THEIR WAY ACROSS THE BARREN PLAIN?
IBRAHIM!
ALI IS ASKING FOR A REPORT!
TELL HIM THAT THE PAWNS OF THE GREAT SATAN HAVE DOUBLED BACK TOWARDS THE CLIFFS AND HAVE MANAGED TO SLIP PAST US, PROBABLY BY STAYING OFF THE RIDGE...
WE ARE GOING TO FORM A WIDE PICKET LINE AND SWEEP BACK.
THEY WON'T ELUDE US THIS TIME!

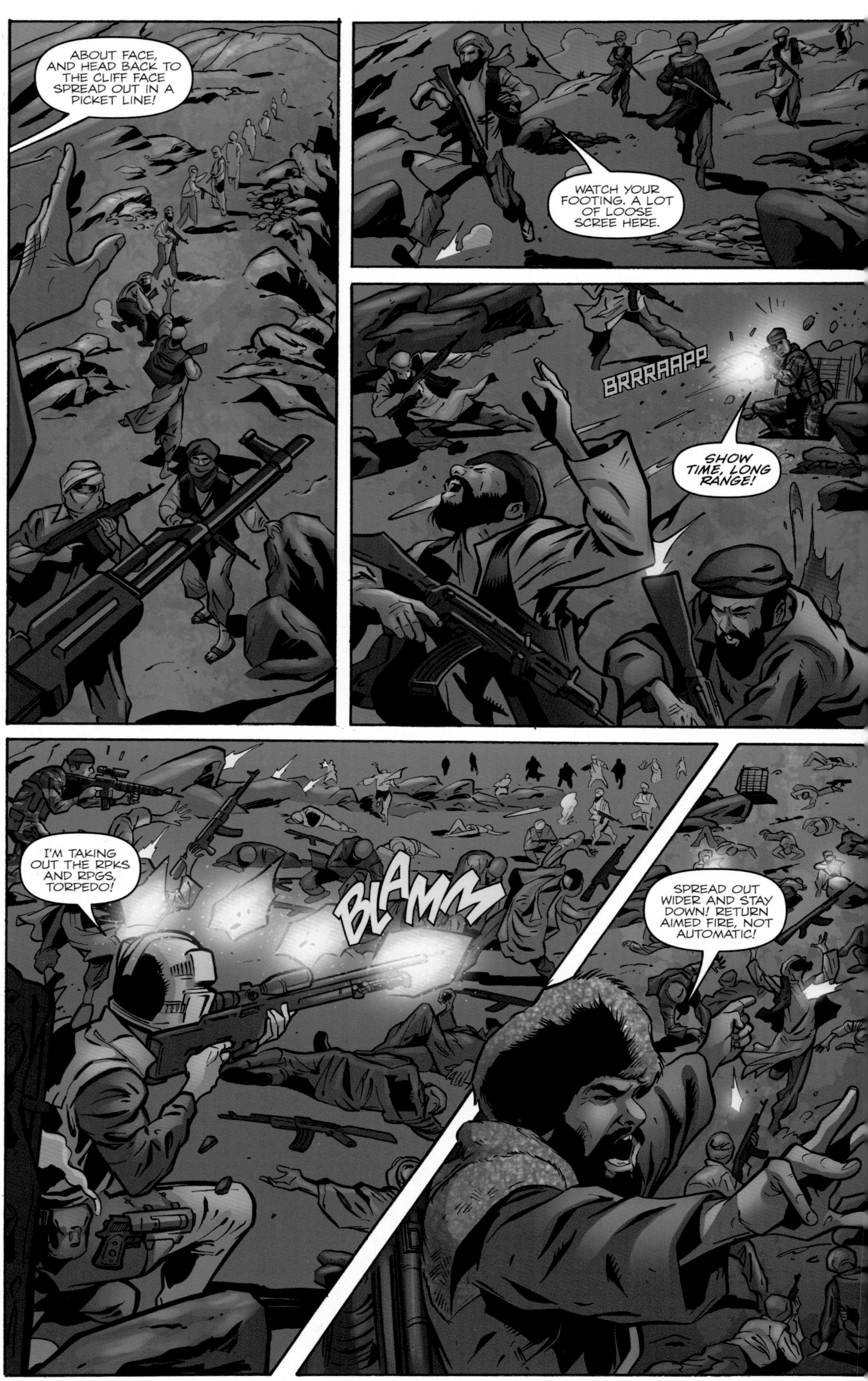
ABOUT FACE, AND HEAD BACK TO THE CLIFF FACE SPREAD OUT IN A PICKET LINE!
WATCH YOUR FOOTING. A LOT OF LOOSE SCREE HERE.
BRRRAAPP
SHOW TIME, LONG RANGE!
I'M TAKING OUT THE RPKS AND RPGS, TORPEDO!
BLAMM
SPREAD OUT WIDER AND STAY DOWN! RETURN AIMED FIRE, NOT AUTOMATIC!

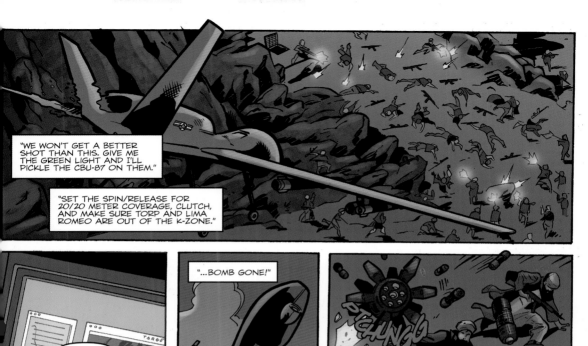

"WE WON'T GET A BETTER SHOT THAN THIS. GIVE ME THE GREEN LIGHT AND I'LL PICKLE THE CBU-87 ON THEM."

"SET THE SPIN/RELEASE FOR 20/20 METER COVERAGE, CLUTCH, AND MAKE SURE TORP AND LIMA ROMEO ARE OUT OF THE K-ZONE."

THAT'S A RODGE, STALKER...

"...BOMB GONE!"

DCHUNGG

WHAM

WHAM

WHAM

WHAM

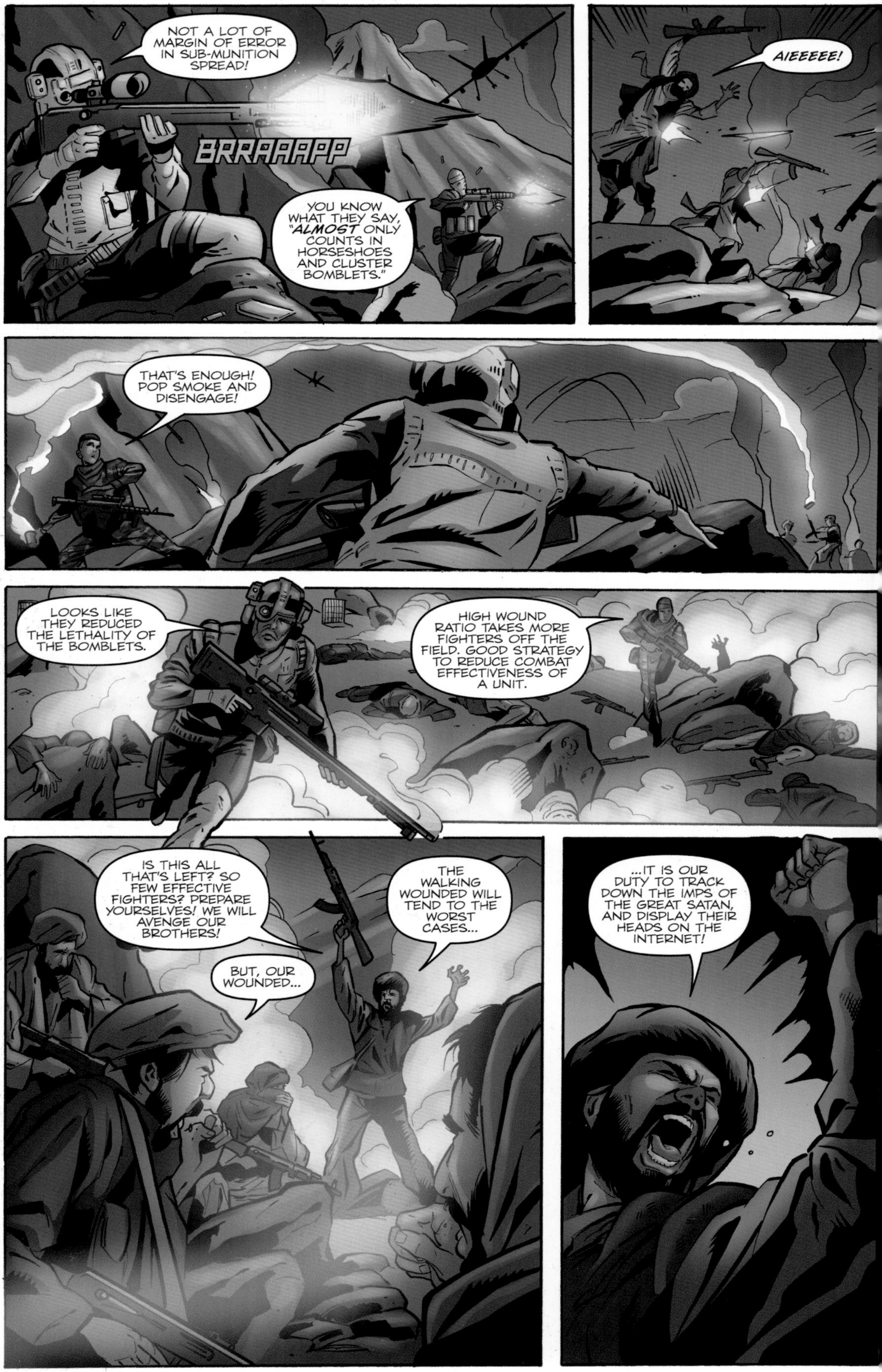
NOT A LOT OF MARGIN OF ERROR IN SUB-MUNITION SPREAD!
BRRAAAAPP
YOU KNOW WHAT THEY SAY, "ALMOST ONLY COUNTS IN HORSESHOES AND CLUSTER BOMBLETS."
AIEEEEE!
THAT'S ENOUGH! POP SMOKE AND DISENGAGE!
LOOKS LIKE THEY REDUCED THE LETHALITY OF THE BOMBLETS.
HIGH WOUND RATIO TAKES MORE FIGHTERS OFF THE FIELD. GOOD STRATEGY TO REDUCE COMBAT EFFECTIVENESS OF A UNIT.
IS THIS ALL THAT'S LEFT? SO FEW EFFECTIVE FIGHTERS? PREPARE YOURSELVES! WE WILL AVENGE OUR BROTHERS!
BUT, OUR WOUNDED...
THE WALKING WOUNDED WILL TEND TO THE WORST CASES...
...IT IS OUR DUTY TO TRACK DOWN THE IMPS OF THE GREAT SATAN, AND DISPLAY THEIR HEADS ON THE INTERNET!

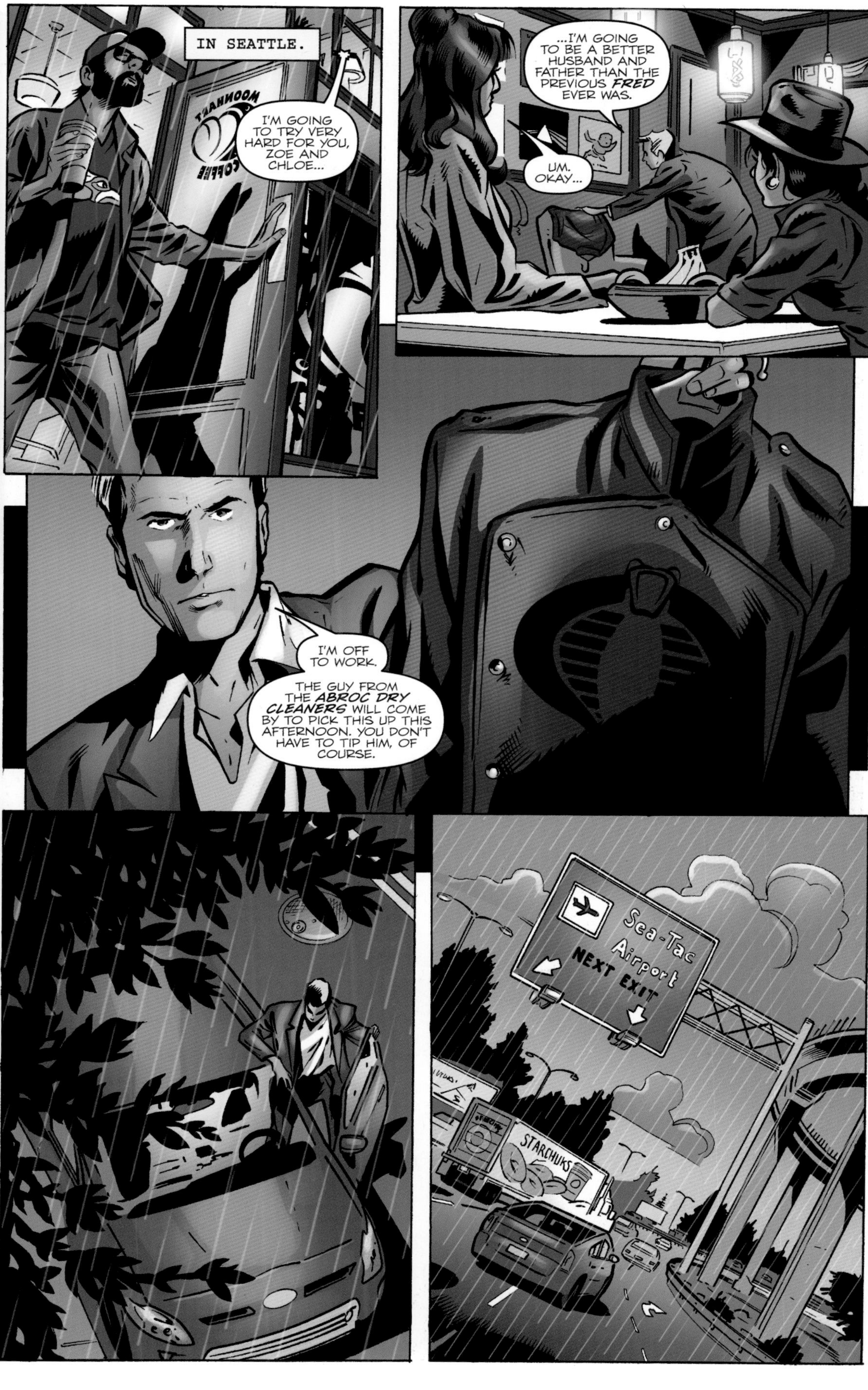
IN SEATTLE.
MOONHAN'T COFFEE
I'M GOING TO TRY VERY HARD FOR YOU, ZOE AND CHLOE...
...I'M GOING TO BE A BETTER HUSBAND AND FATHER THAN THE PREVIOUS FRED EVER WAS.
UM. OKAY...
I'M OFF TO WORK.
THE GUY FROM THE ABROC DRY CLEANERS WILL COME BY TO PICK THIS UP THIS AFTERNOON. YOU DON'T HAVE TO TIP HIM, OF COURSE.
Sea-Tac Airport NEXT EXIT
STARCHUKS

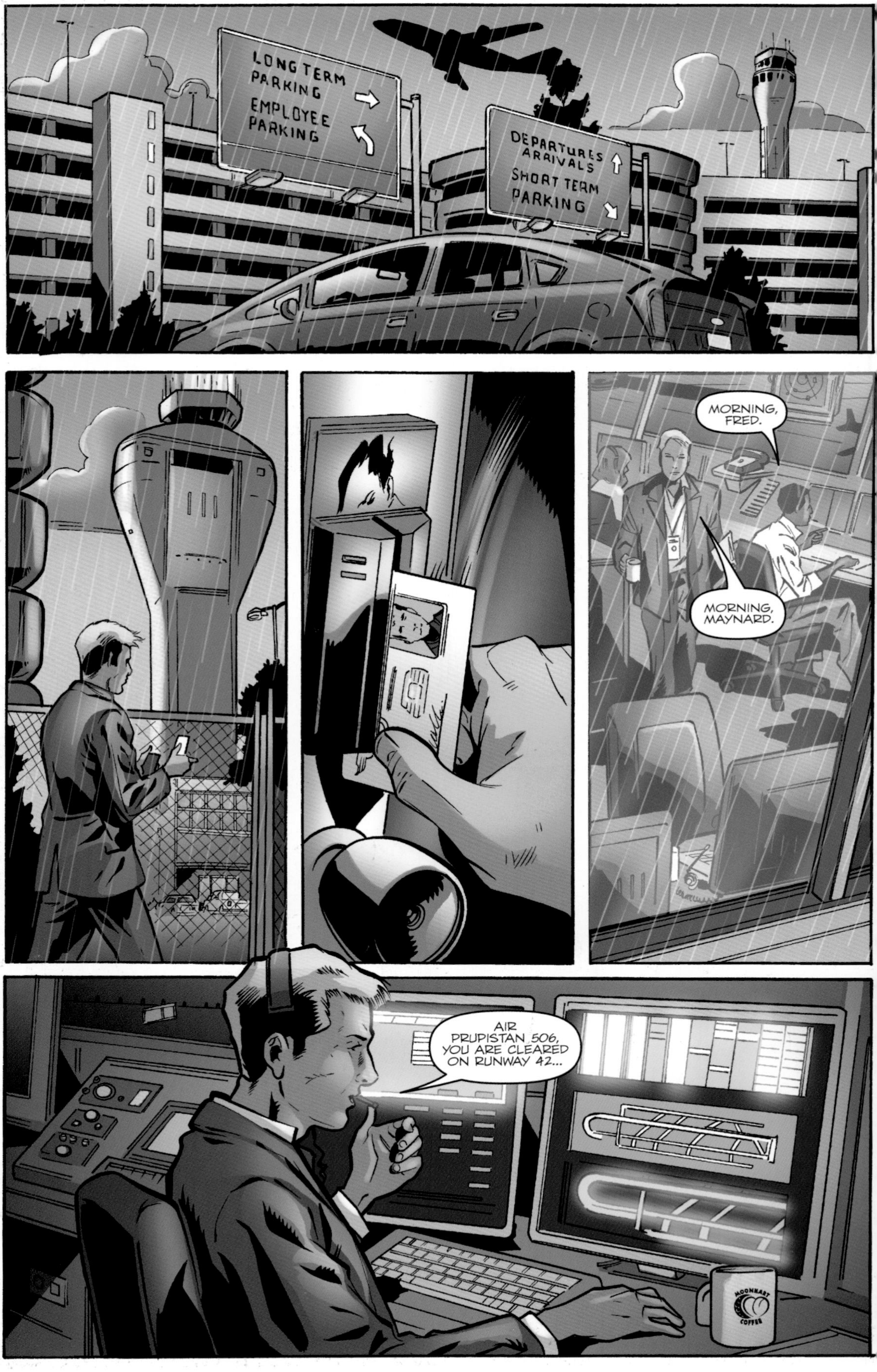
LONG TERM PARKING
EMPLOYEE PARKING
DEPARTURES ARAIVALS
SHORT TERM PARKING
MORNING, FRED.
MORNING, MAYNARD.
AIR PRUPISTAN 506, YOU ARE CLEARED ON RUNWAY 42...
MOONKART COFFEE

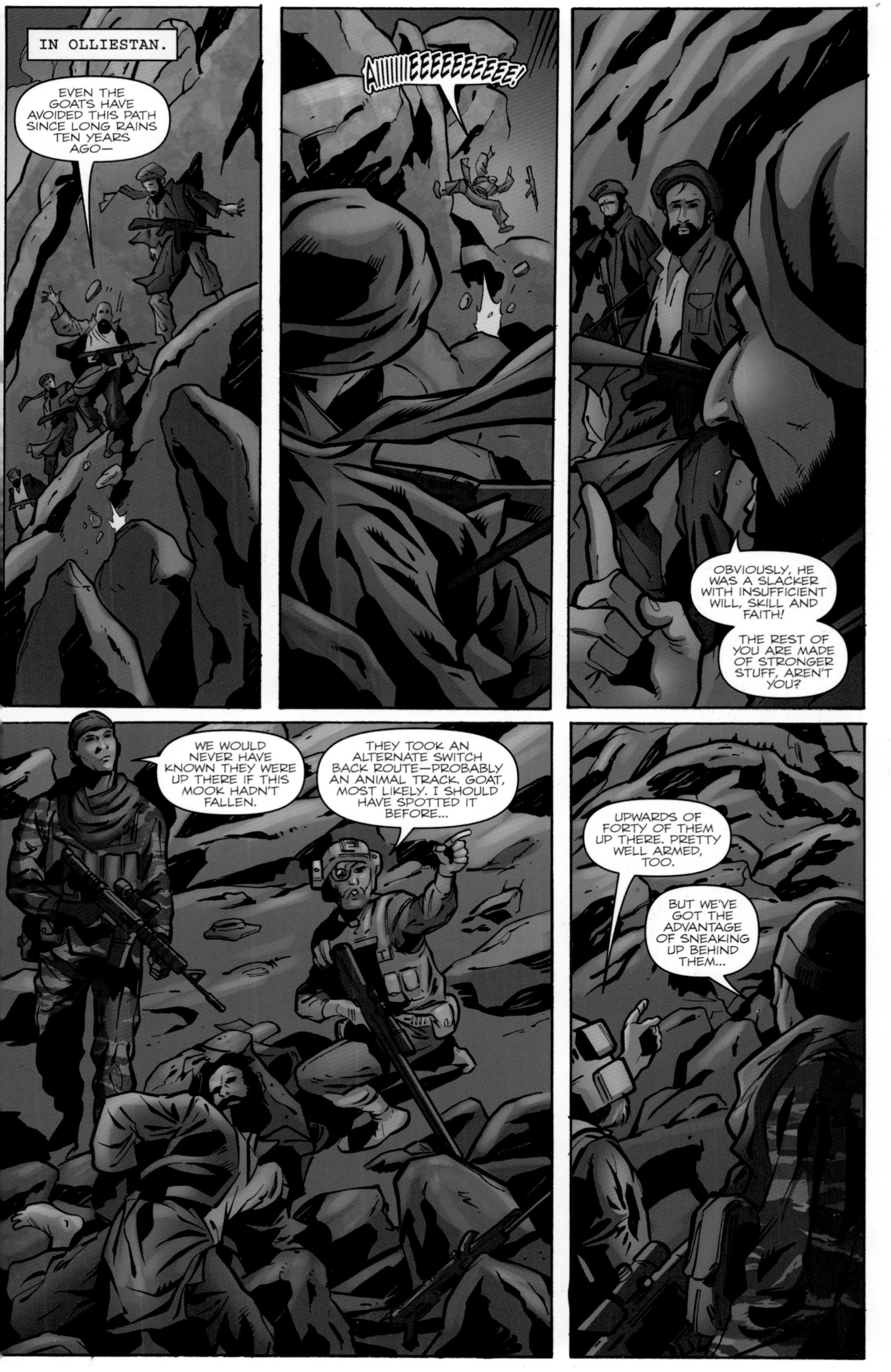

IN OLLIESTAN.
EVEN THE GOATS HAVE AVOIDED THIS PATH SINCE LONG RAINS TEN YEARS AGO—
AIIIIIIEEEEEEEEEE!
OBVIOUSLY, HE WAS A SLACKER WITH INSUFFICIENT WILL, SKILL AND FAITH!
THE REST OF YOU ARE MADE OF STRONGER STUFF, AREN'T YOU?
WE WOULD NEVER HAVE KNOWN THEY WERE UP THERE IF THIS MOOK HADN'T FALLEN.
THEY TOOK AN ALTERNATE SWITCH BACK ROUTE—PROBABLY AN ANIMAL TRACK. GOAT, MOST LIKELY. I SHOULD HAVE SPOTTED IT BEFORE...
UPWARDS OF FORTY OF THEM UP THERE. PRETTY WELL ARMED, TOO.
BUT WE'VE GOT THE ADVANTAGE OF SNEAKING UP BEHIND THEM...

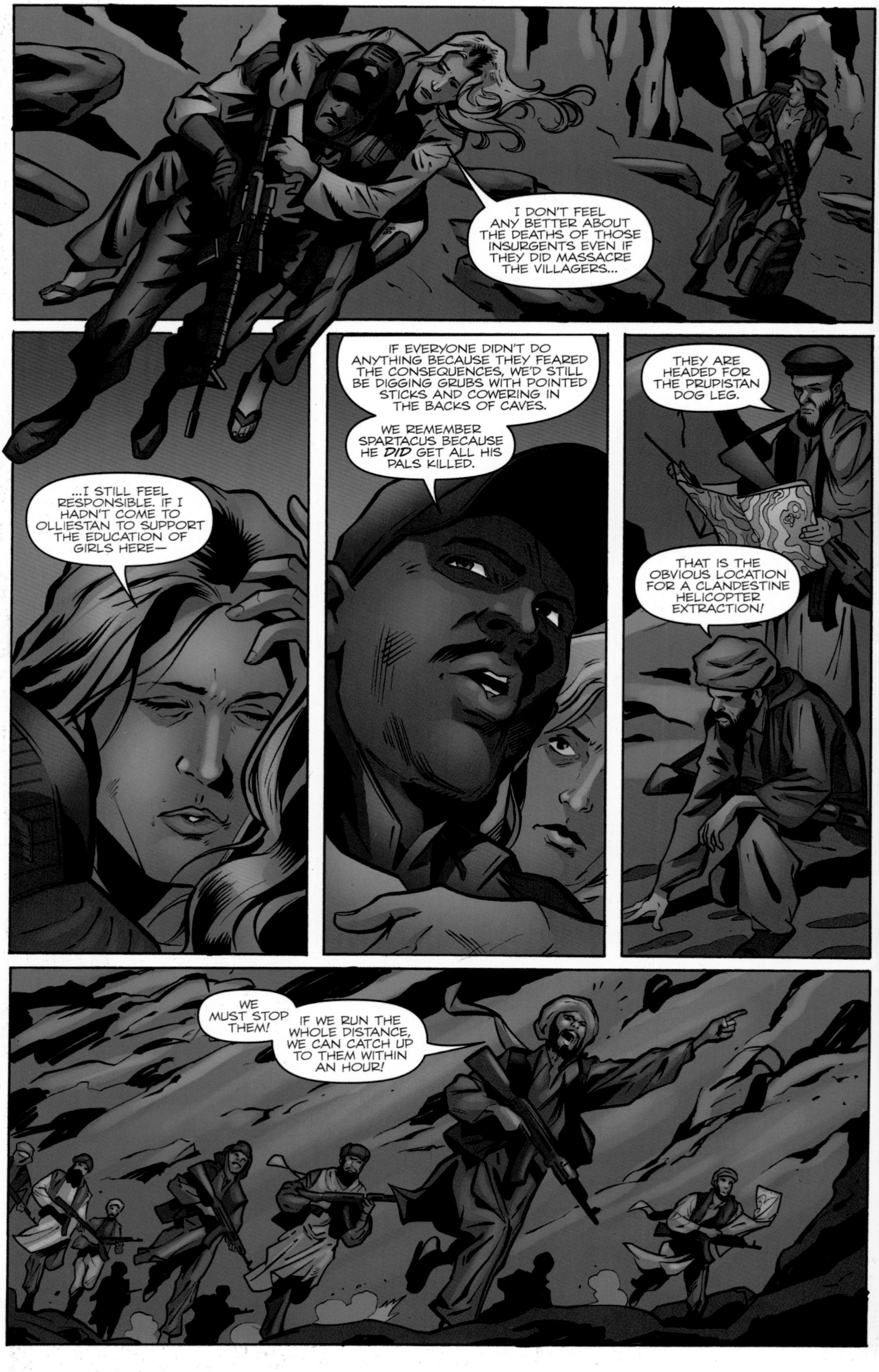
I DON'T FEEL ANY BETTER ABOUT THE DEATHS OF THOSE INSURGENTS EVEN IF THEY DID MASSACRE THE VILLAGERS...
...I STILL FEEL RESPONSIBLE. IF I HADN'T COME TO OLLIESTAN TO SUPPORT THE EDUCATION OF GIRLS HERE—
IF EVERYONE DIDN'T DO ANYTHING BECAUSE THEY FEARED THE CONSEQUENCES, WE'D STILL BE DIGGING GRUBS WITH POINTED STICKS AND COWERING IN THE BACKS OF CAVES.
WE REMEMBER SPARTACUS BECAUSE HE *DID* GET ALL HIS PALS KILLED.
THEY ARE HEADED FOR THE PRUPISTAN DOG LEG.
THAT IS THE OBVIOUS LOCATION FOR A CLANDESTINE HELICOPTER EXTRACTION!
WE MUST STOP THEM!
IF WE RUN THE WHOLE DISTANCE, WE CAN CATCH UP TO THEM WITHIN AN HOUR!

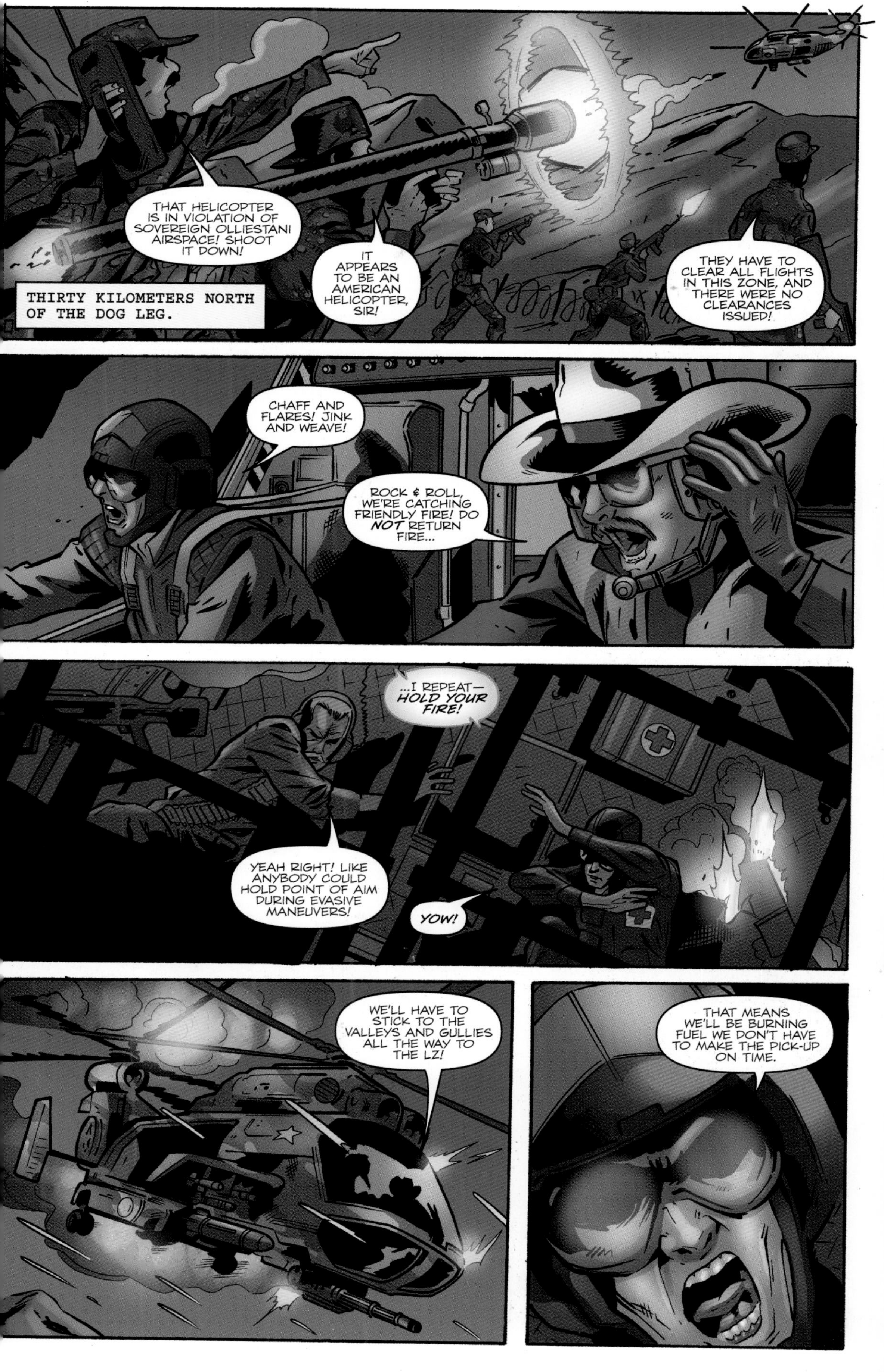
THAT HELICOPTER IS IN VIOLATION OF SOVEREIGN OLLIESTANI AIRSPACE! SHOOT IT DOWN!
IT APPEARS TO BE AN AMERICAN HELICOPTER, SIR!
THEY HAVE TO CLEAR ALL FLIGHTS IN THIS ZONE, AND THERE WERE NO CLEARANCES ISSUED!
THIRTY KILOMETERS NORTH OF THE DOG LEG.
CHAFF AND FLARES! JINK AND WEAVE!
ROCK & ROLL, WE'RE CATCHING FRIENDLY FIRE! DO NOT RETURN FIRE...
...I REPEAT— HOLD YOUR FIRE!
YEAH RIGHT! LIKE ANYBODY COULD HOLD POINT OF AIM DURING EVASIVE MANEUVERS!
YOW!
WE'LL HAVE TO STICK TO THE VALLEYS AND GULLIES ALL THE WAY TO THE LZ!
THAT MEANS WE'LL BE BURNING FUEL WE DON'T HAVE TO MAKE THE PICK-UP ON TIME.

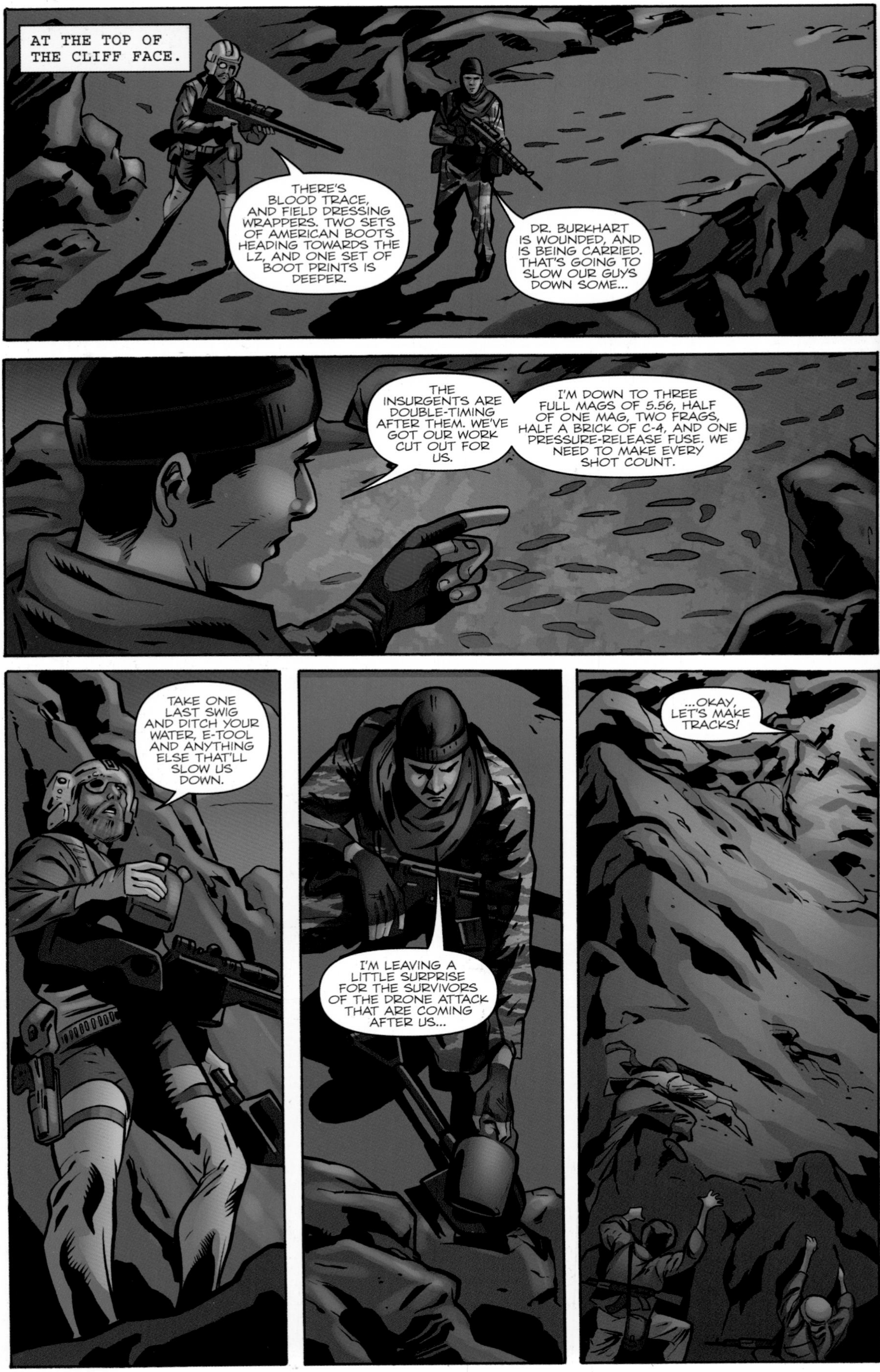
AT THE TOP OF THE CLIFF FACE.
THERE'S BLOOD TRACE, AND FIELD DRESSING WRAPPERS. TWO SETS OF AMERICAN BOOTS HEADING TOWARDS THE LZ, AND ONE SET OF BOOT PRINTS IS DEEPER.
DR. BURKHART IS WOUNDED, AND IS BEING CARRIED. THAT'S GOING TO SLOW OUR GUYS DOWN SOME...
THE INSURGENTS ARE DOUBLE-TIMING AFTER THEM. WE'VE GOT OUR WORK CUT OUT FOR US.
I'M DOWN TO THREE FULL MAGS OF 5.56, HALF OF ONE MAG, TWO FRAGS, HALF A BRICK OF C-4, AND ONE PRESSURE-RELEASE FUSE. WE NEED TO MAKE EVERY SHOT COUNT.
TAKE ONE LAST SWIG AND DITCH YOUR WATER, E-TOOL AND ANYTHING ELSE THAT'LL SLOW US DOWN.
I'M LEAVING A LITTLE SURPRISE FOR THE SURVIVORS OF THE DRONE ATTACK THAT ARE COMING AFTER US...
...OKAY, LET'S MAKE TRACKS!

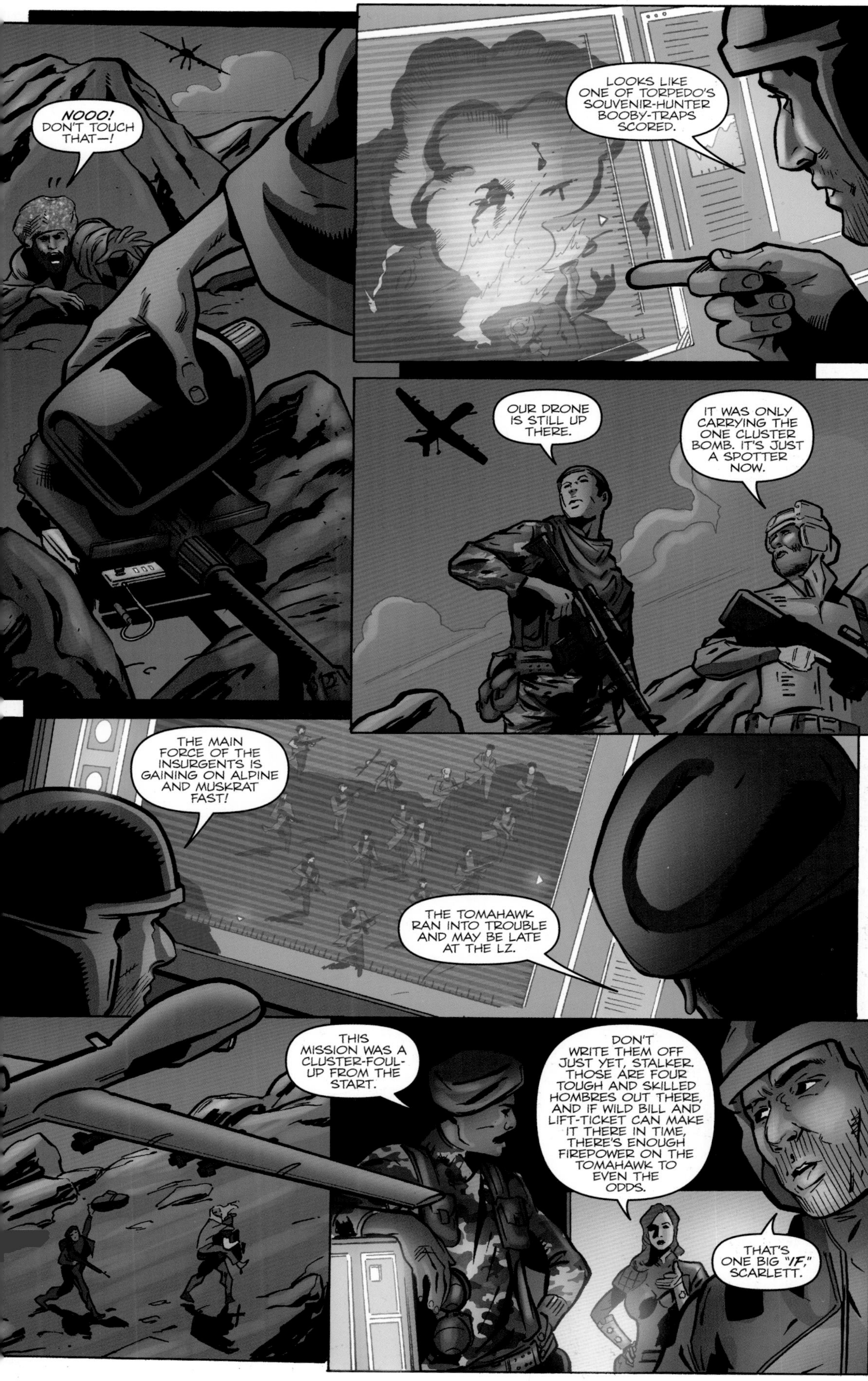
NOOO! DON'T TOUCH THAT—!
LOOKS LIKE ONE OF TORPEDO'S SOUVENIR-HUNTER BOOBY-TRAPS SCORED.
OUR DRONE IS STILL UP THERE.
IT WAS ONLY CARRYING THE ONE CLUSTER BOMB. IT'S JUST A SPOTTER NOW.
THE MAIN FORCE OF THE INSURGENTS IS GAINING ON ALPINE AND MUSKRAT FAST!
THE TOMAHAWK RAN INTO TROUBLE AND MAY BE LATE AT THE LZ.
THIS MISSION WAS A CLUSTER-FOUL-UP FROM THE START.
DON'T WRITE THEM OFF JUST YET, STALKER. THOSE ARE FOUR TOUGH AND SKILLED HOMBRES OUT THERE, AND IF WILD BILL AND LIFT-TICKET CAN MAKE IT THERE IN TIME, THERE'S ENOUGH FIREPOWER ON THE TOMAHAWK TO EVEN THE ODDS.
THAT'S ONE BIG "*IF*," SCARLETT.

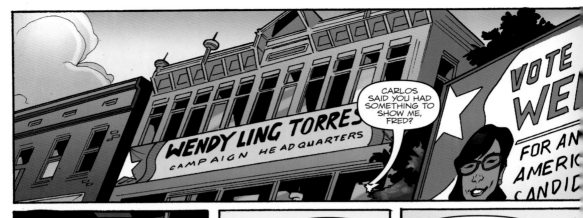

CARLOS SAID YOU HAD SOMETHING TO SHOW ME, FRED?

VOTE WE... FOR AN AMERIC... CANDI...

I JUST WANTED TO SHOW YOU THIS SPREAD SHEET. I ACCESSED ALL COLLATED MINED DATA TO ZERO-IN ON POTENTIAL SUPPORTERS AND MAXIMIZE DIRECT CALL RESULTS.

THAT'S AMAZING! YOU'RE GOING TO GO VERY FAR IN MY CAMPAIGN, AND YOU WILL DEFINITELY BE REMEMBERED WHEN I'M ELECTED!

THANK YOU, MS. TORRES!

CALL ME WENDY. OH, I SEE BY THIS PHOTO THAT YOU PLAYED HIGH SCHOOL FOOTBALL. IS RANCHO CORBA IN NORTHERN CALIFORNIA?

MY FAMILY MOVED THERE WHEN I WAS A SOPHOMORE. I WAS BORN IN A NICE LITTLE TOWN CALLED SPRINGFIELD, AND MOSTLY RAISED IN BROCA BEACH ON THE JERSEY SHORE.

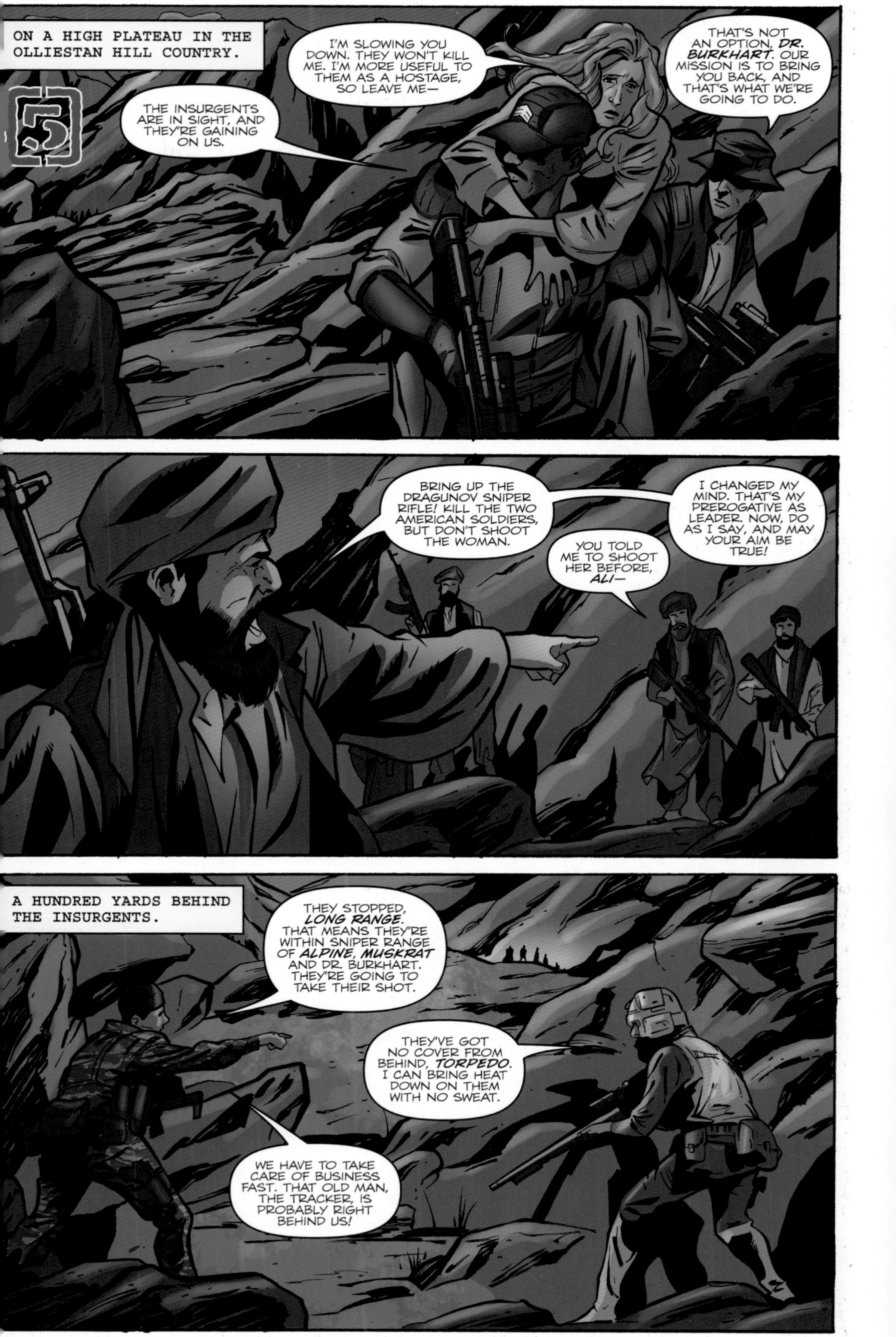
ON A HIGH PLATEAU IN THE OLLIESTAN HILL COUNTRY.
5
THE INSURGENTS ARE IN SIGHT, AND THEY'RE GAINING ON US.
I'M SLOWING YOU DOWN. THEY WON'T KILL ME. I'M MORE USEFUL TO THEM AS A HOSTAGE, SO LEAVE ME—
THAT'S NOT AN OPTION, DR. BURKHART. OUR MISSION IS TO BRING YOU BACK, AND THAT'S WHAT WE'RE GOING TO DO.
BRING UP THE DRAGUNOV SNIPER RIFLE! KILL THE TWO AMERICAN SOLDIERS, BUT DON'T SHOOT THE WOMAN.
YOU TOLD ME TO SHOOT HER BEFORE, ALI—
I CHANGED MY MIND. THAT'S MY PREROGATIVE AS LEADER. NOW, DO AS I SAY, AND MAY YOUR AIM BE TRUE!
A HUNDRED YARDS BEHIND THE INSURGENTS.
THEY STOPPED, LONG RANGE. THAT MEANS THEY'RE WITHIN SNIPER RANGE OF ALPINE, MUSKRAT AND DR. BURKHART. THEY'RE GOING TO TAKE THEIR SHOT.
THEY'VE GOT NO COVER FROM BEHIND, TORPEDO. I CAN BRING HEAT DOWN ON THEM WITH NO SWEAT.
WE HAVE TO TAKE CARE OF BUSINESS FAST. THAT OLD MAN, THE TRACKER, IS PROBABLY RIGHT BEHIND US!

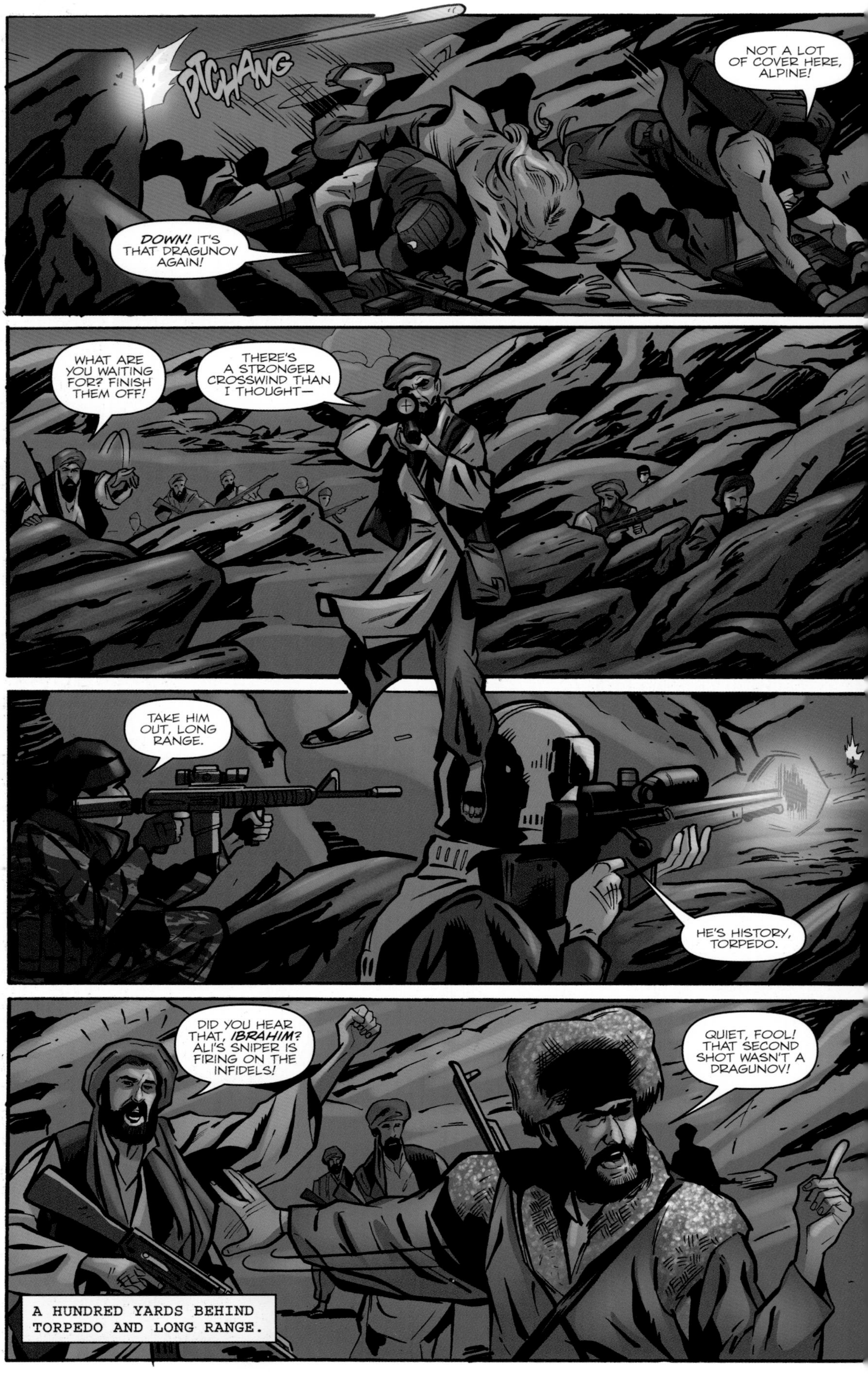
PTCHANG
NOT A LOT OF COVER HERE, ALPINE!
DOWN! IT'S THAT DRAGUNOV AGAIN!
WHAT ARE YOU WAITING FOR? FINISH THEM OFF!
THERE'S A STRONGER CROSSWIND THAN I THOUGHT—
TAKE HIM OUT, LONG RANGE.
HE'S HISTORY, TORPEDO.
DID YOU HEAR THAT, IBRAHIM? ALI'S SNIPER IS FIRING ON THE INFIDELS!
QUIET, FOOL! THAT SECOND SHOT WASN'T A DRAGUNOV!
A HUNDRED YARDS BEHIND TORPEDO AND LONG RANGE.

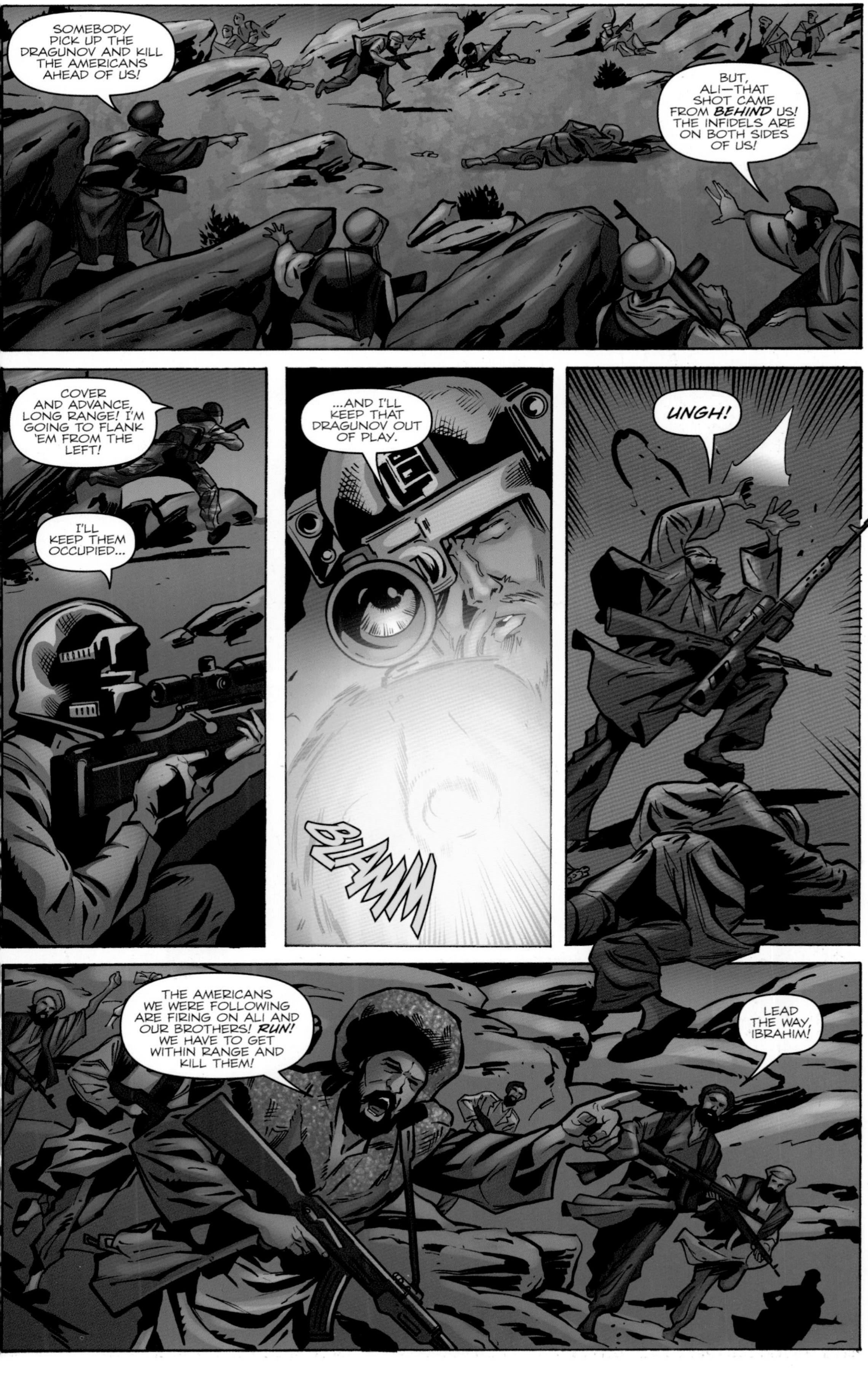
SOMEBODY PICK UP THE DRAGUNOV AND KILL THE AMERICANS AHEAD OF US!
BUT, ALI—THAT SHOT CAME FROM *BEHIND* US! THE INFIDELS ARE ON BOTH SIDES OF US!
COVER AND ADVANCE, LONG RANGE! I'M GOING TO FLANK 'EM FROM THE LEFT!
I'LL KEEP THEM OCCUPIED...
...AND I'LL KEEP THAT DRAGUNOV OUT OF PLAY.
BLAMM
UNGH!
THE AMERICANS WE WERE FOLLOWING ARE FIRING ON ALI AND OUR BROTHERS! *RUN!* WE HAVE TO GET WITHIN RANGE AND KILL THEM!
LEAD THE WAY, IBRAHIM!

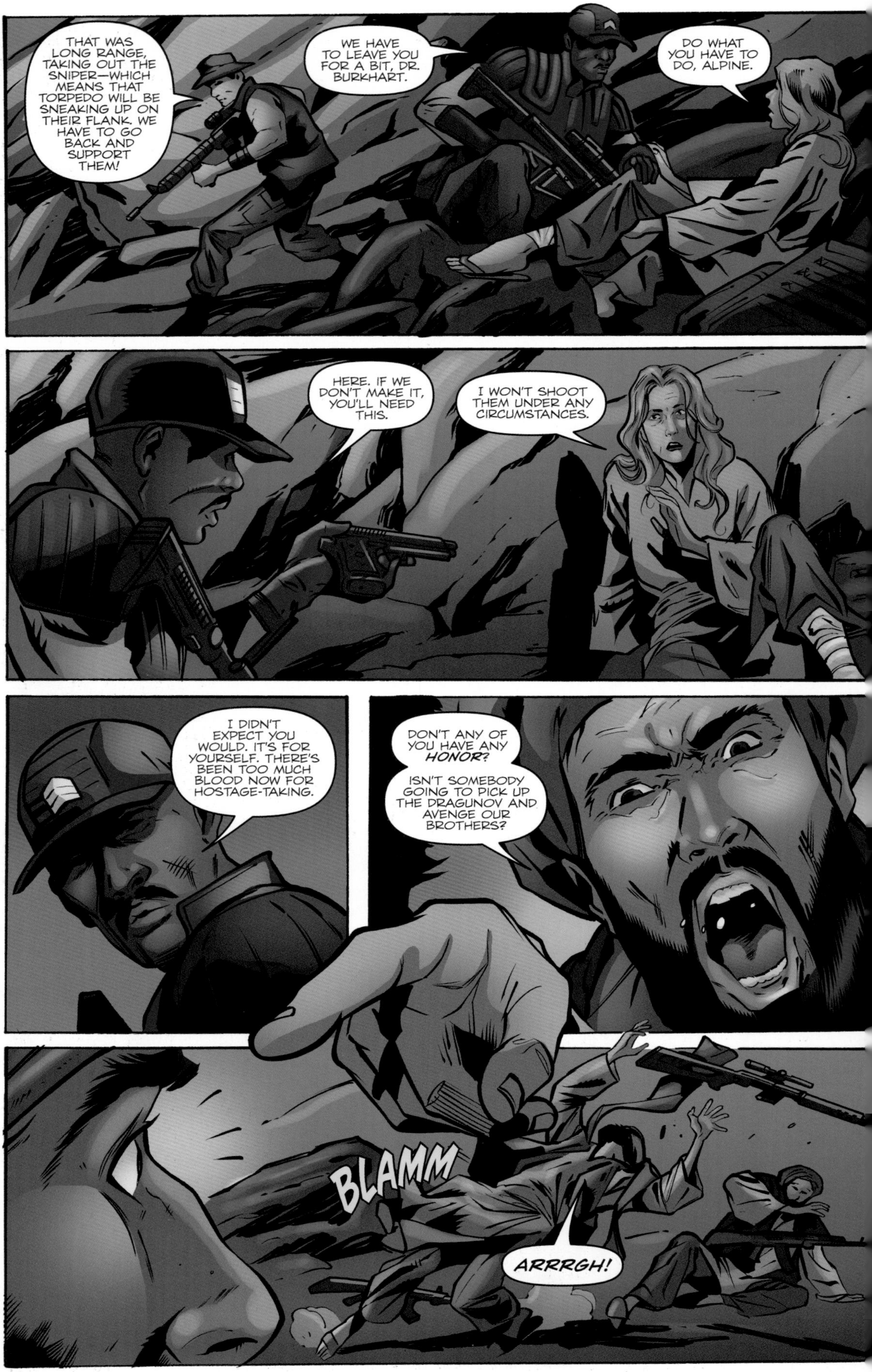
THAT WAS LONG RANGE, TAKING OUT THE SNIPER—WHICH MEANS THAT TORPEDO WILL BE SNEAKING UP ON THEIR FLANK. WE HAVE TO GO BACK AND SUPPORT THEM!
WE HAVE TO LEAVE YOU FOR A BIT, DR. BURKHART.
DO WHAT YOU HAVE TO DO, ALPINE.
HERE. IF WE DON'T MAKE IT, YOU'LL NEED THIS.
I WON'T SHOOT THEM UNDER ANY CIRCUMSTANCES.
I DIDN'T EXPECT YOU WOULD. IT'S FOR YOURSELF. THERE'S BEEN TOO MUCH BLOOD NOW FOR HOSTAGE-TAKING.
DON'T ANY OF YOU HAVE ANY *HONOR?*
ISN'T SOMEBODY GOING TO PICK UP THE DRAGUNOV AND AVENGE OUR BROTHERS?
BLAMM
ARRRGH!

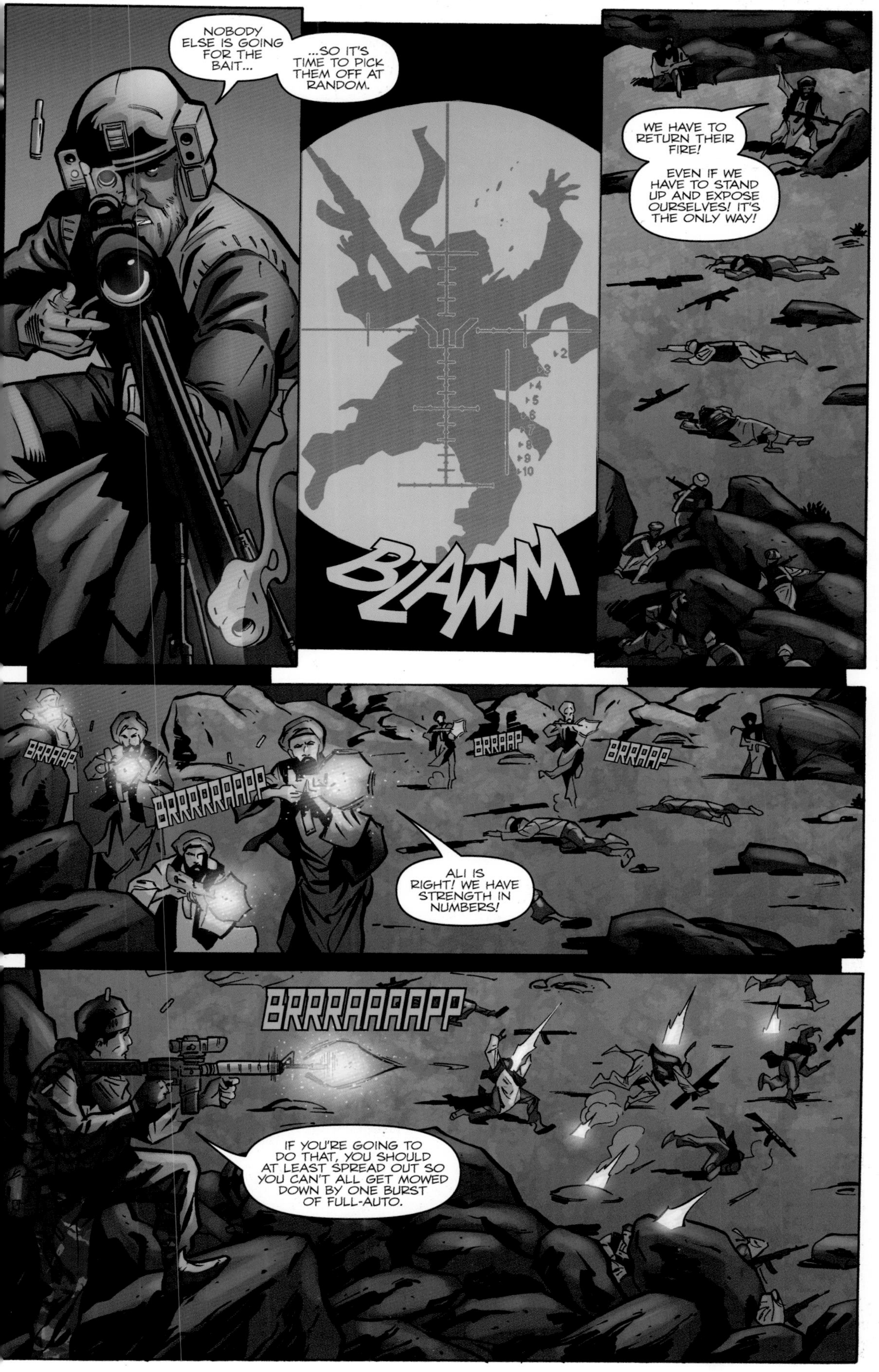
NOBODY ELSE IS GOING FOR THE BAIT...
...SO IT'S TIME TO PICK THEM OFF AT RANDOM.
BLAMM
WE HAVE TO RETURN THEIR FIRE!
EVEN IF WE HAVE TO STAND UP AND EXPOSE OURSELVES! IT'S THE ONLY WAY!
BRRAAP
BRRRRRAAPP
BRRAAP
BRRAAP
ALI IS RIGHT! WE HAVE STRENGTH IN NUMBERS!
BRRRAAAAAPP
IF YOU'RE GOING TO DO THAT, YOU SHOULD AT LEAST SPREAD OUT SO YOU CAN'T ALL GET MOWED DOWN BY ONE BURST OF FULL-AUTO.

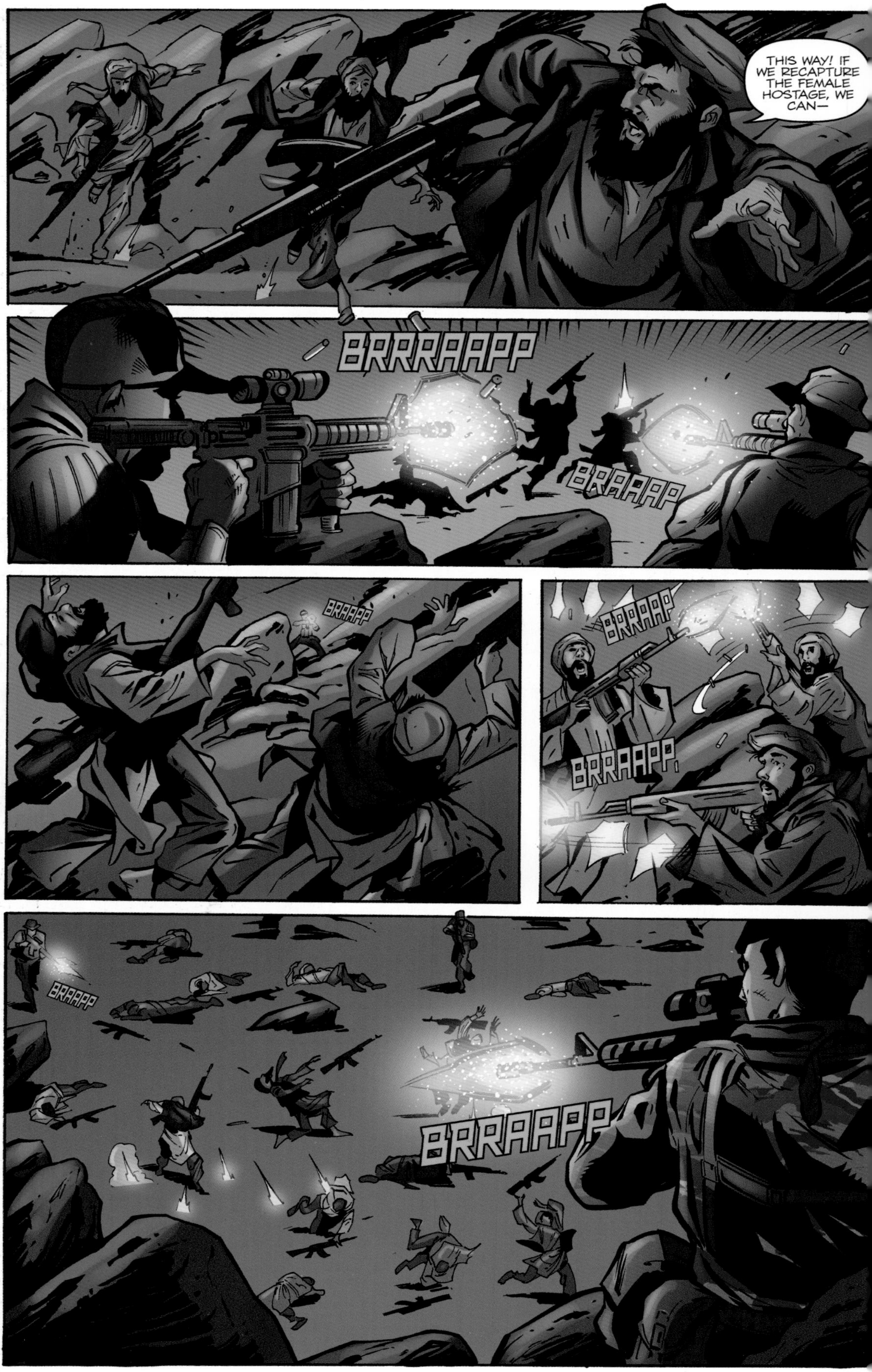
THIS WAY! IF WE RECAPTURE THE FEMALE HOSTAGE, WE CAN—
BRRRAAPP
BRRAAAP
BRAAPP
BRRAAP
BRRAAPP
BRRAAPP
BRRAAPP

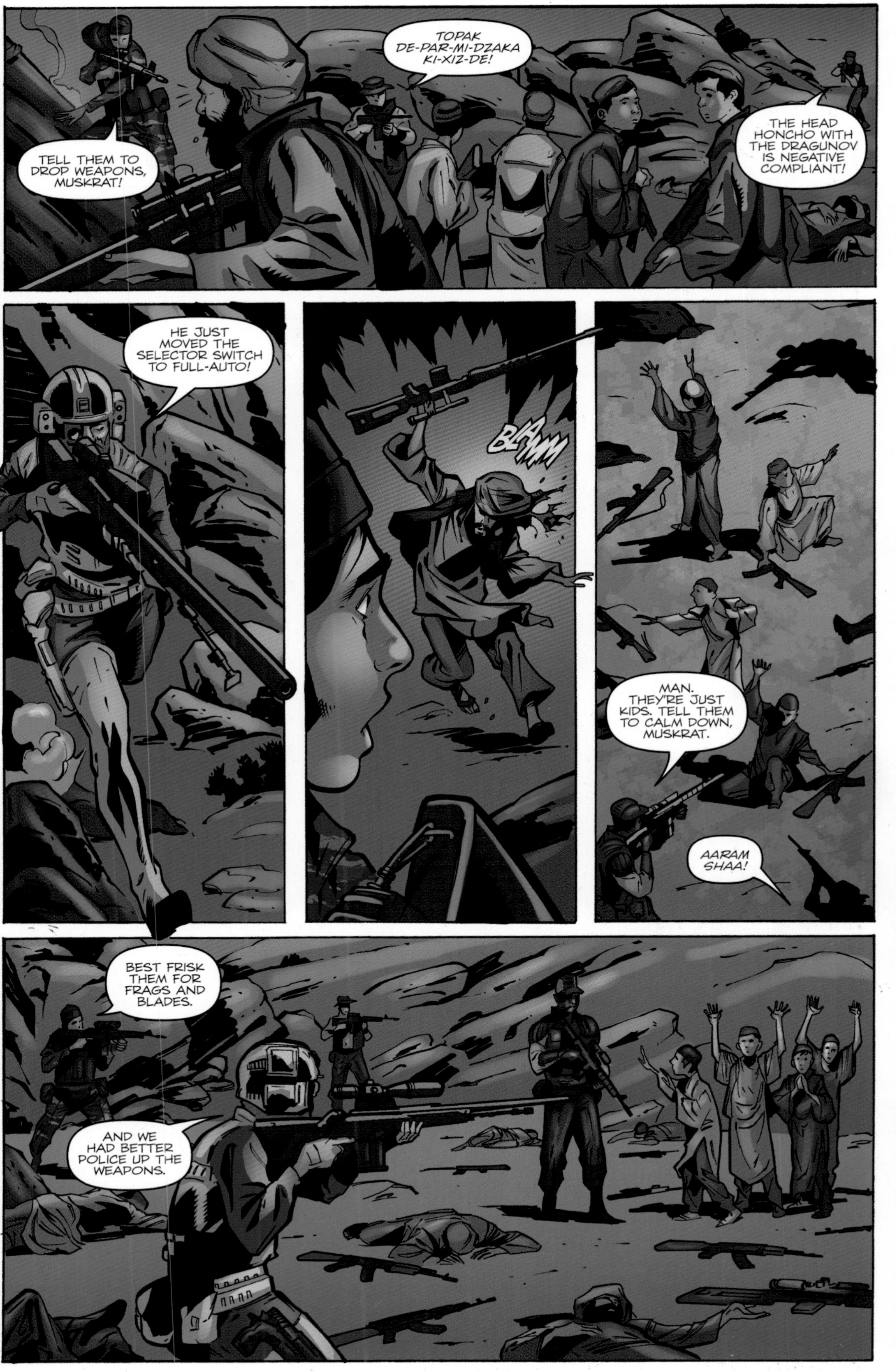
TELL THEM TO DROP WEAPONS, MUSKRAT!
TOPAK DE-PAR-MI-DZAKA KI-XIZ-DE!
THE HEAD HONCHO WITH THE DRAGUNOV IS NEGATIVE COMPLIANT!
HE JUST MOVED THE SELECTOR SWITCH TO FULL-AUTO!
BLAMM
MAN. THEY'RE JUST KIDS. TELL THEM TO CALM DOWN, MUSKRAT.
AARAM SHAA!
BEST FRISK THEM FOR FRAGS AND BLADES.
AND WE HAD BETTER POLICE UP THE WEAPONS.

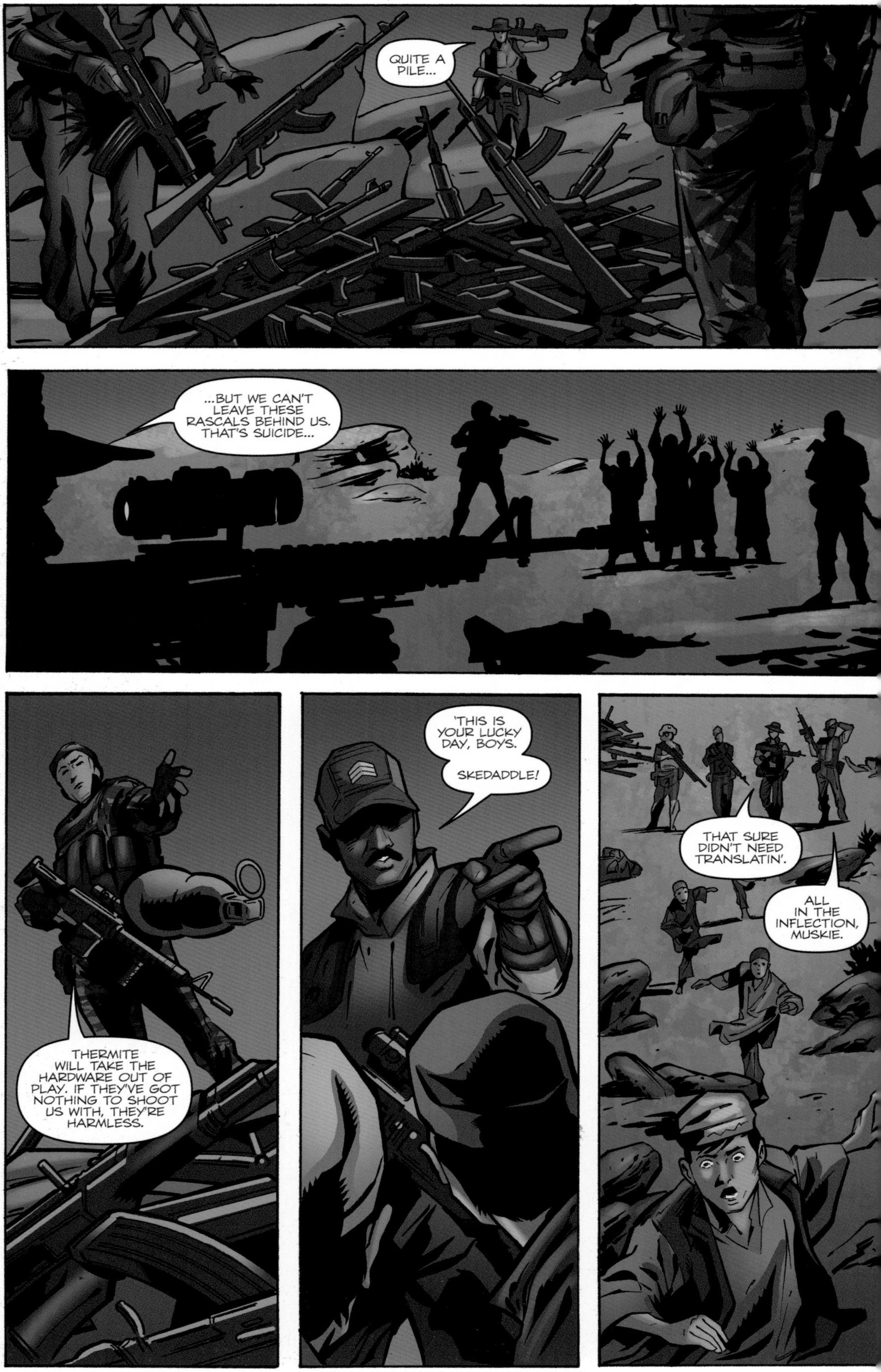
QUITE A PILE...
...BUT WE CAN'T LEAVE THESE RASCALS BEHIND US. THAT'S SUICIDE...
THERMITE WILL TAKE THE HARDWARE OUT OF PLAY. IF THEY'VE GOT NOTHING TO SHOOT US WITH, THEY'RE HARMLESS.
'THIS IS YOUR LUCKY DAY, BOYS.
SKEDADDLE!
THAT SURE DIDN'T NEED TRANSLATIN'.
ALL IN THE INFLECTION, MUSKIE.

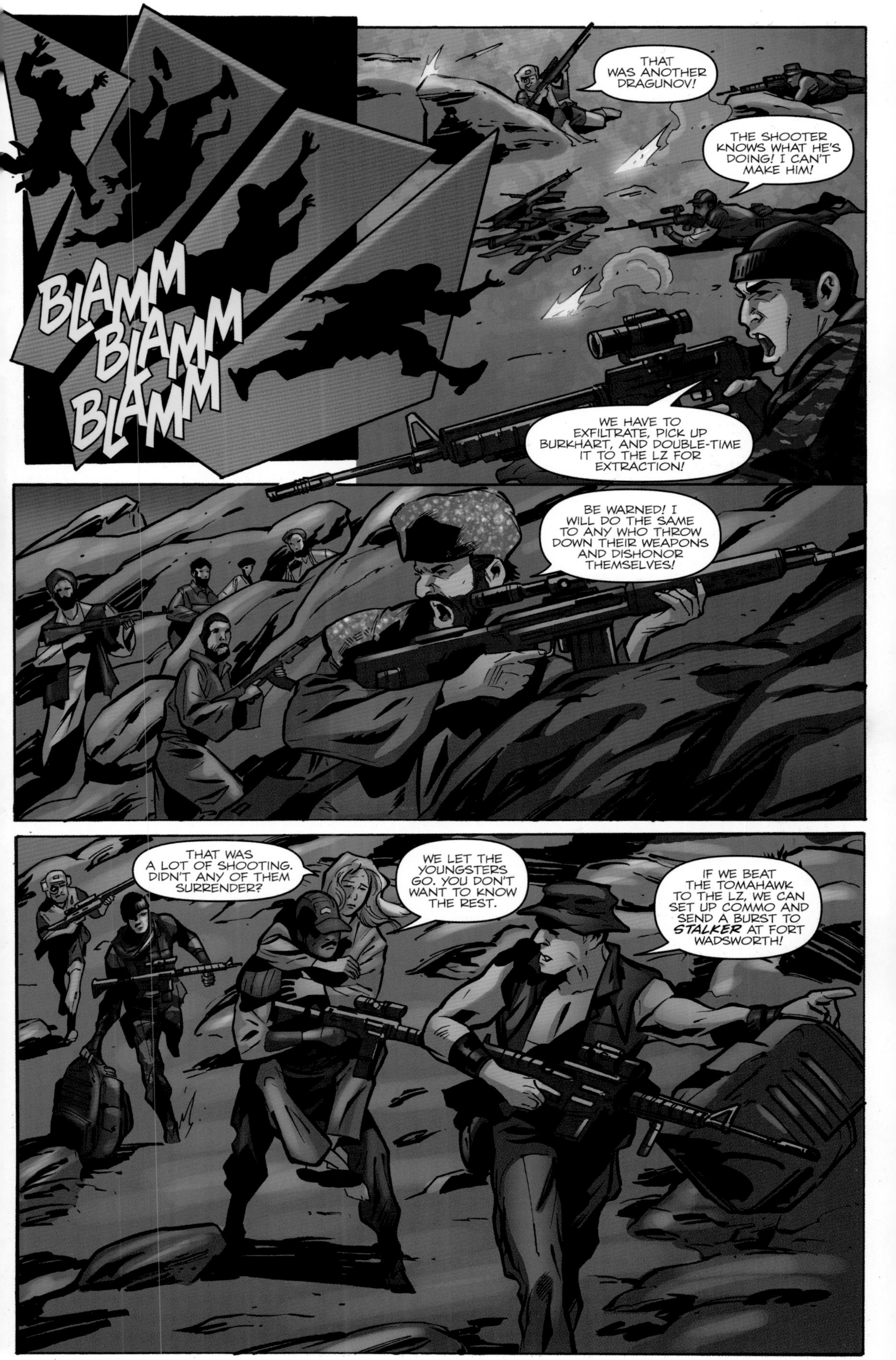

BLAMM BLAMM BLAMM
THAT WAS ANOTHER DRAGUNOV!
THE SHOOTER KNOWS WHAT HE'S DOING! I CAN'T MAKE HIM!
WE HAVE TO EXFILTRATE, PICK UP BURKHART, AND DOUBLE-TIME IT TO THE LZ FOR EXTRACTION!
BE WARNED! I WILL DO THE SAME TO ANY WHO THROW DOWN THEIR WEAPONS AND DISHONOR THEMSELVES!
THAT WAS A LOT OF SHOOTING. DIDN'T ANY OF THEM SURRENDER?
WE LET THE YOUNGSTERS GO. YOU DON'T WANT TO KNOW THE REST.
IF WE BEAT THE TOMAHAWK TO THE LZ, WE CAN SET UP COMMO AND SEND A BURST TO STALKER AT FORT WADSWORTH!

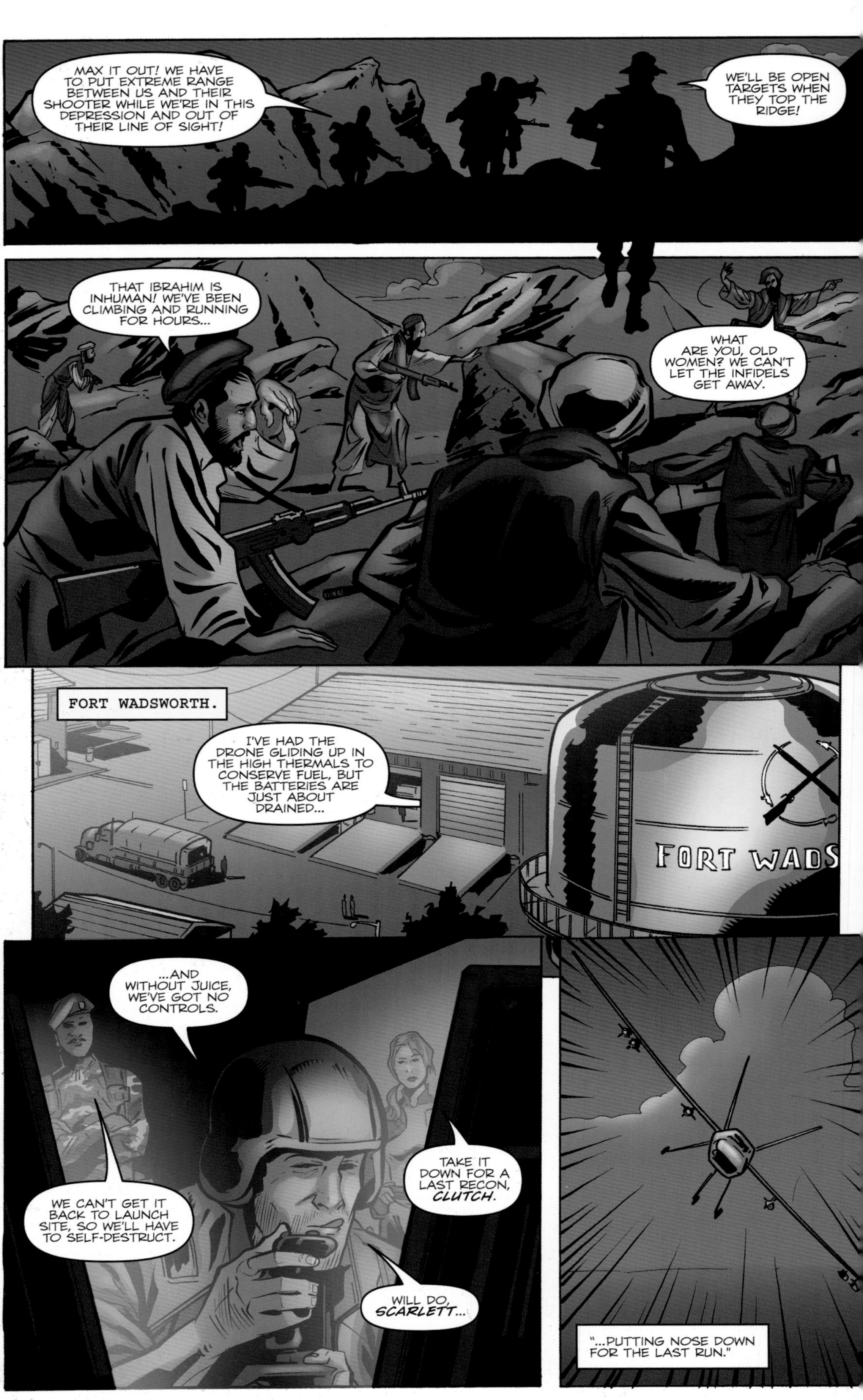
MAX IT OUT! WE HAVE TO PUT EXTREME RANGE BETWEEN US AND THEIR SHOOTER WHILE WE'RE IN THIS DEPRESSION AND OUT OF THEIR LINE OF SIGHT!
WE'LL BE OPEN TARGETS WHEN THEY TOP THE RIDGE!
THAT IBRAHIM IS INHUMAN! WE'VE BEEN CLIMBING AND RUNNING FOR HOURS...
WHAT ARE YOU, OLD WOMEN? WE CAN'T LET THE INFIDELS GET AWAY.
FORT WADSWORTH.
I'VE HAD THE DRONE GLIDING UP IN THE HIGH THERMALS TO CONSERVE FUEL, BUT THE BATTERIES ARE JUST ABOUT DRAINED...
FORT WADS
...AND WITHOUT JUICE, WE'VE GOT NO CONTROLS.
WE CAN'T GET IT BACK TO LAUNCH SITE, SO WE'LL HAVE TO SELF-DESTRUCT.
TAKE IT DOWN FOR A LAST RECON, *CLUTCH*.
WILL DO, *SCARLETT*...
"...PUTTING NOSE DOWN FOR THE LAST RUN."

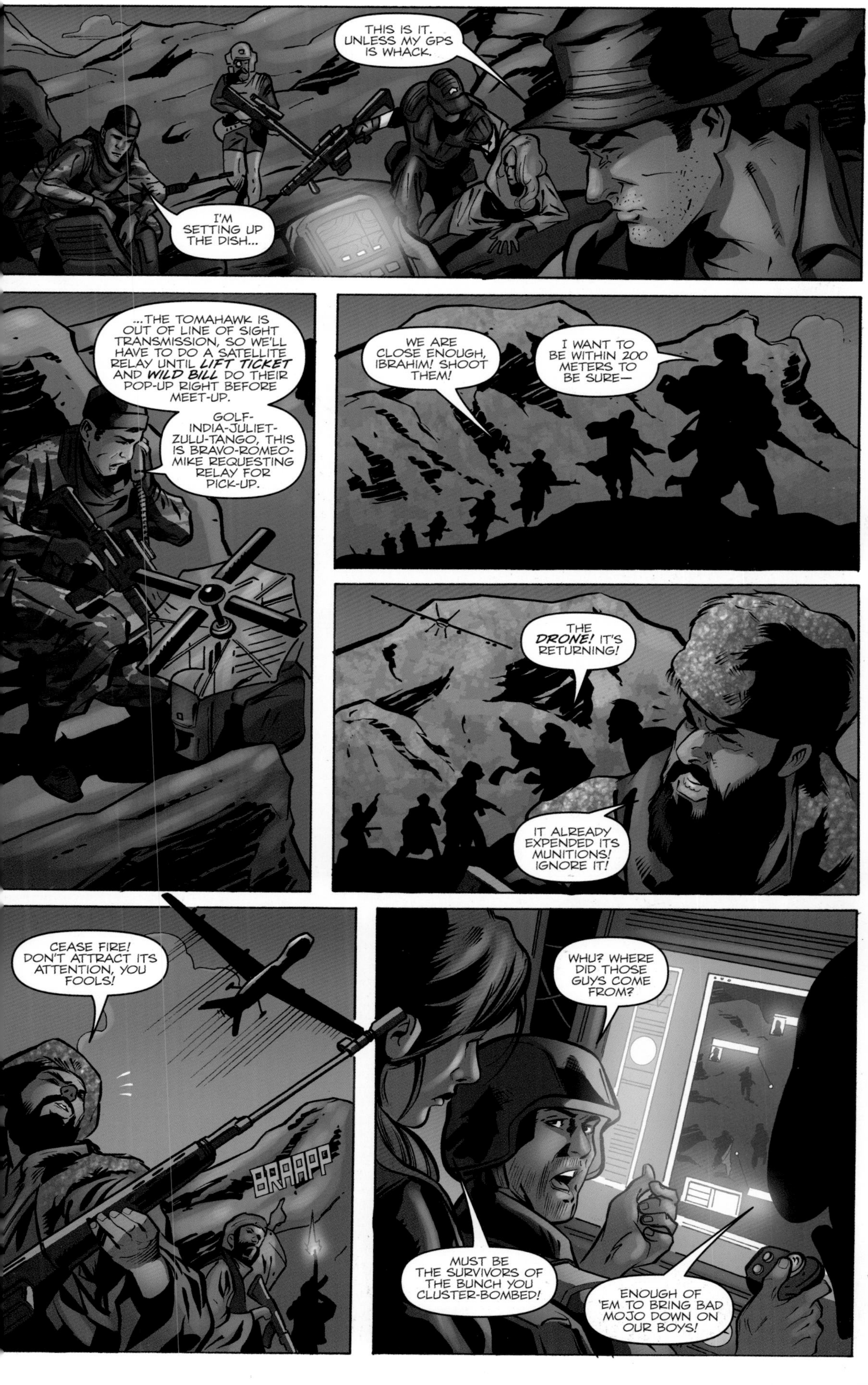
THIS IS IT. UNLESS MY GPS IS WHACK.
I'M SETTING UP THE DISH...
...THE TOMAHAWK IS OUT OF LINE OF SIGHT TRANSMISSION, SO WE'LL HAVE TO DO A SATELLITE RELAY UNTIL LIFT TICKET AND WILD BILL DO THEIR POP-UP RIGHT BEFORE MEET-UP.
GOLF-INDIA-JULIET-ZULU-TANGO, THIS IS BRAVO-ROMEO-MIKE REQUESTING RELAY FOR PICK-UP.
WE ARE CLOSE ENOUGH, IBRAHIM! SHOOT THEM!
I WANT TO BE WITHIN 200 METERS TO BE SURE—
THE DRONE! IT'S RETURNING!
IT ALREADY EXPENDED ITS MUNITIONS! IGNORE IT!
CEASE FIRE! DON'T ATTRACT ITS ATTENTION, YOU FOOLS!
BRAAPP
WHU? WHERE DID THOSE GUYS COME FROM?
MUST BE THE SURVIVORS OF THE BUNCH YOU CLUSTER-BOMBED!
ENOUGH OF 'EM TO BRING BAD MOJO DOWN ON OUR BOYS!

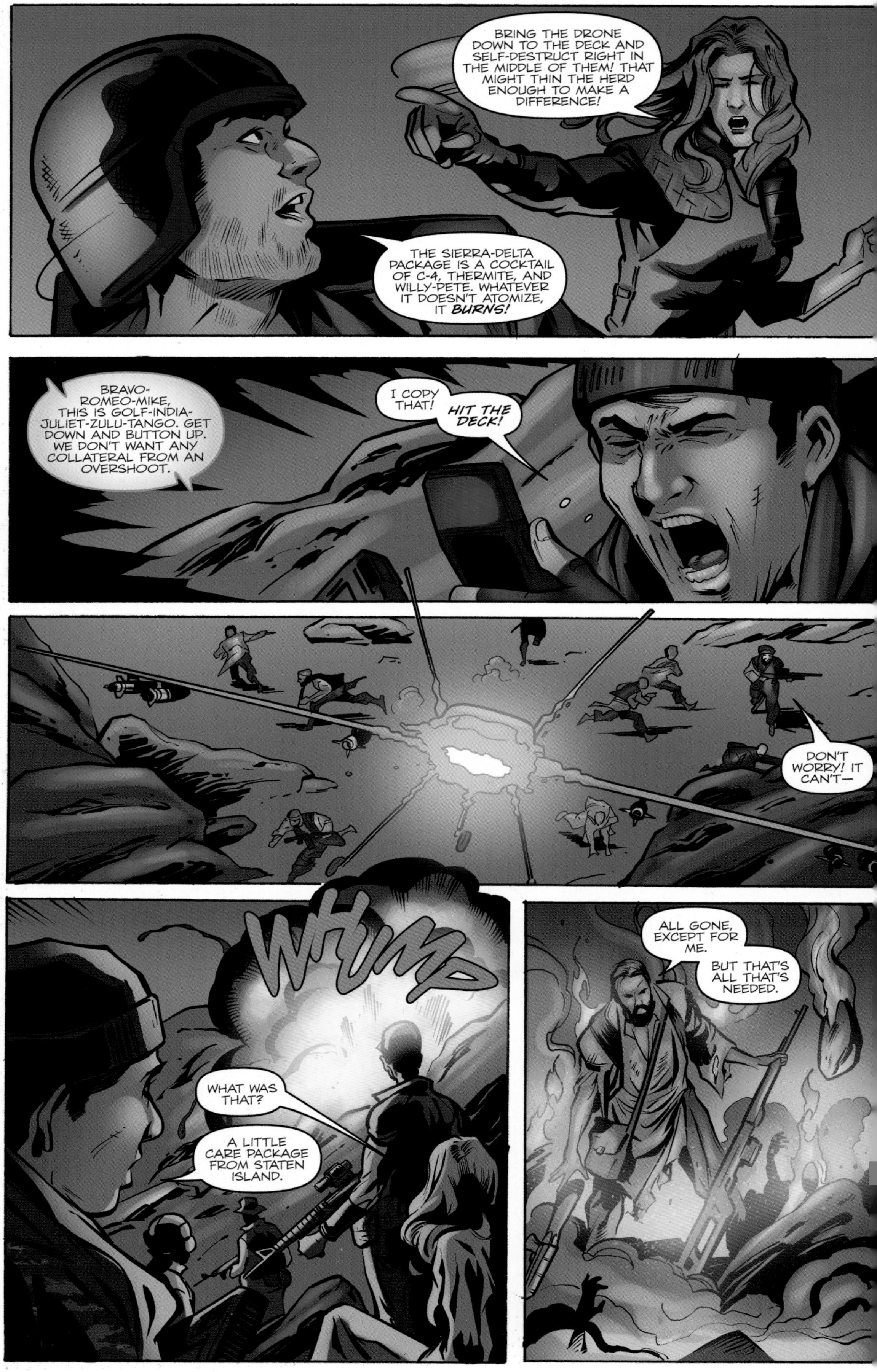
BRING THE DRONE DOWN TO THE DECK AND SELF-DESTRUCT RIGHT IN THE MIDDLE OF THEM! THAT MIGHT THIN THE HERD ENOUGH TO MAKE A DIFFERENCE!
THE SIERRA-DELTA PACKAGE IS A COCKTAIL OF C-4, THERMITE, AND WILLY-PETE. WHATEVER IT DOESN'T ATOMIZE, IT *BURNS!*
BRAVO-ROMEO-MIKE, THIS IS GOLF-INDIA-JULIET-ZULU-TANGO. GET DOWN AND BUTTON UP. WE DON'T WANT ANY COLLATERAL FROM AN OVERSHOOT.
I COPY THAT!
HIT THE DECK!
DON'T WORRY! IT CAN'T—
WHUMP
WHAT WAS THAT?
A LITTLE CARE PACKAGE FROM STATEN ISLAND.
ALL GONE, EXCEPT FOR ME.
BUT THAT'S ALL THAT'S NEEDED.

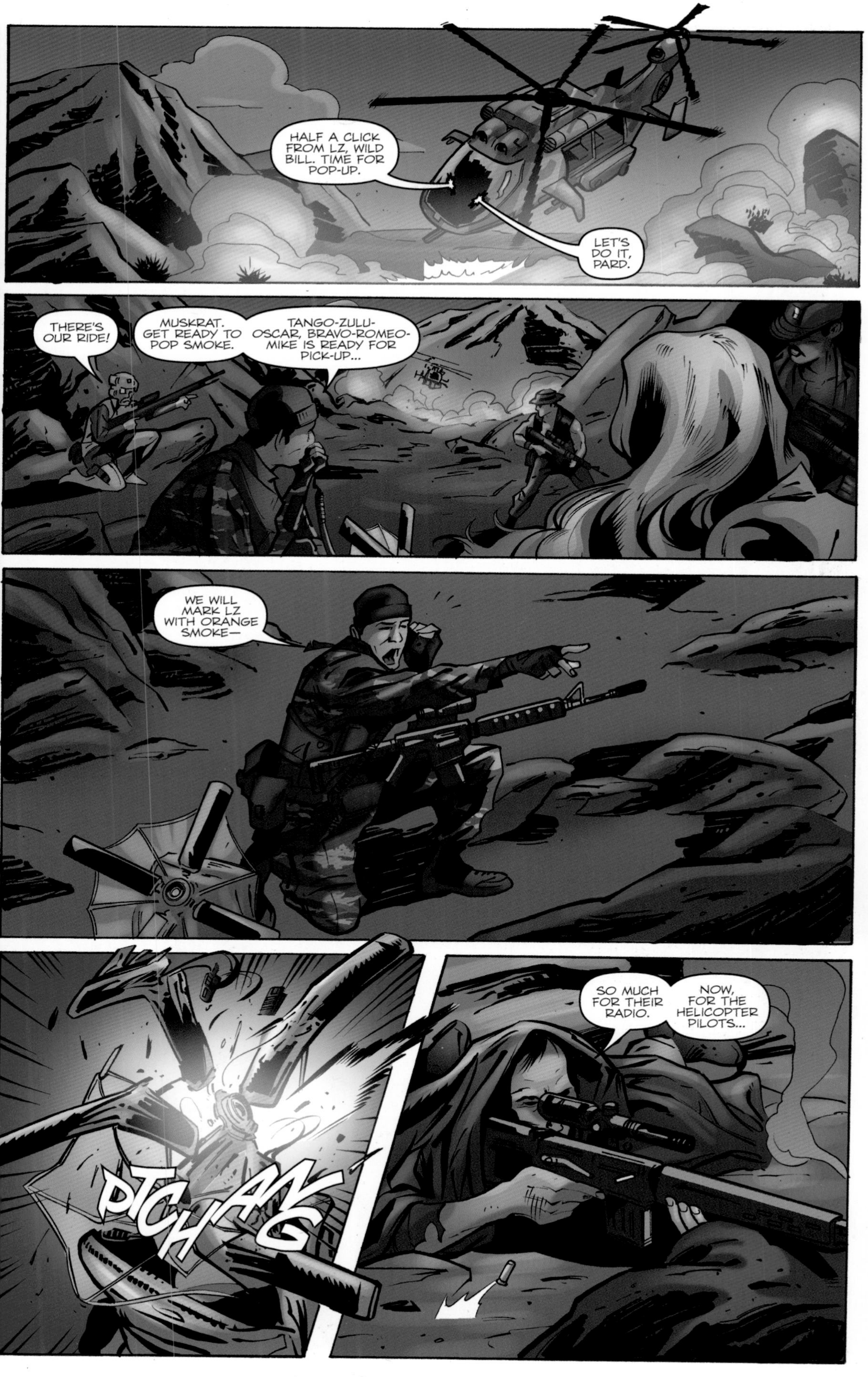
HALF A CLICK FROM LZ, WILD BILL. TIME FOR POP-UP.
LET'S DO IT, PARD.
THERE'S OUR RIDE!
MUSKRAT. GET READY TO POP SMOKE.
TANGO-ZULU-OSCAR, BRAVO-ROMEO-MIKE IS READY FOR PICK-UP...
WE WILL MARK LZ WITH ORANGE SMOKE—
PTCHANG
SO MUCH FOR THEIR RADIO.
NOW, FOR THE HELICOPTER PILOTS...

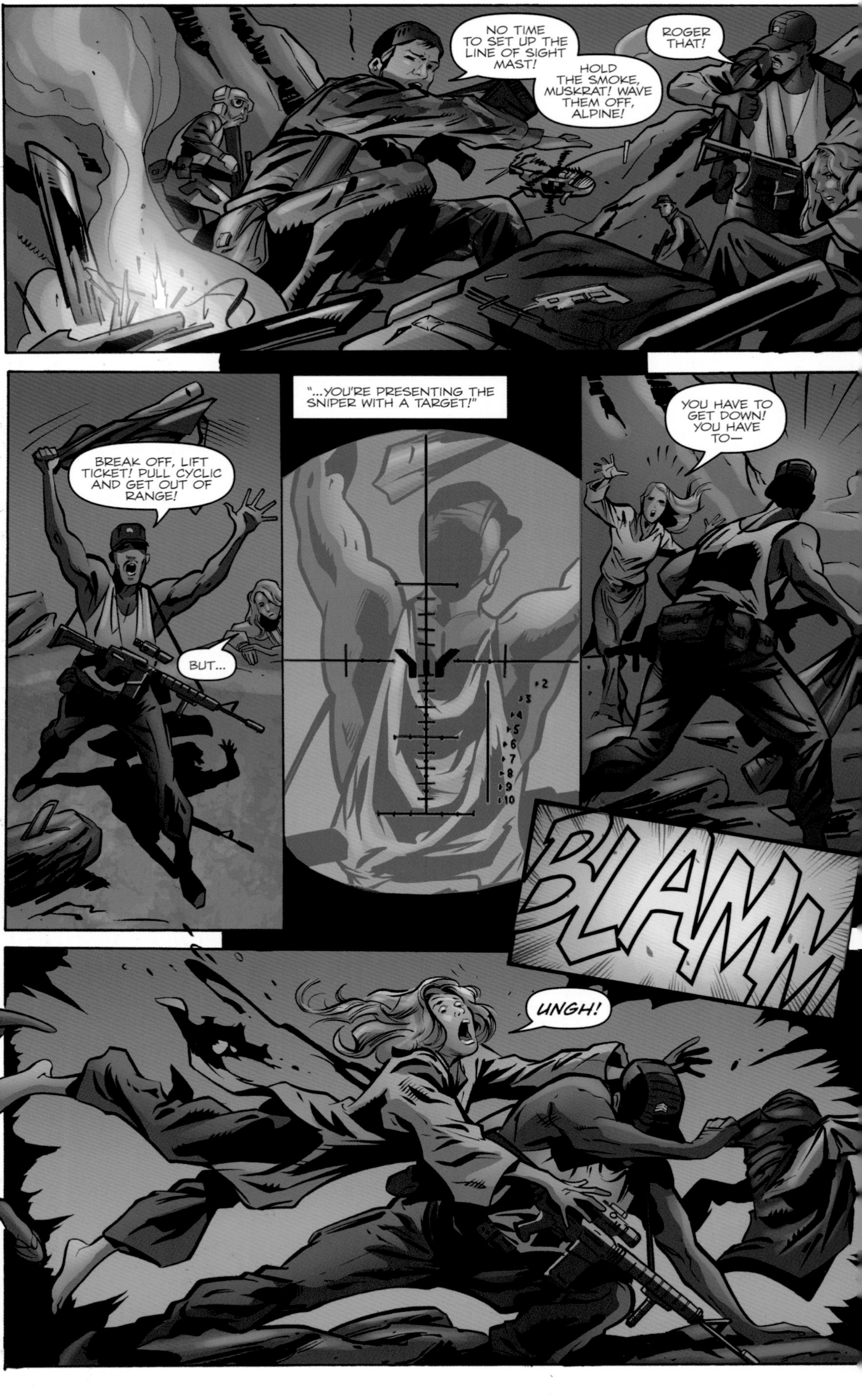
NO TIME TO SET UP THE LINE OF SIGHT MAST!
HOLD THE SMOKE, MUSKRAT! WAVE THEM OFF, ALPINE!
ROGER THAT!
BREAK OFF, LIFT TICKET! PULL CYCLIC AND GET OUT OF RANGE!
BUT...
"...YOU'RE PRESENTING THE SNIPER WITH A TARGET!"
YOU HAVE TO GET DOWN! YOU HAVE TO—
BLAMM
UNGH!

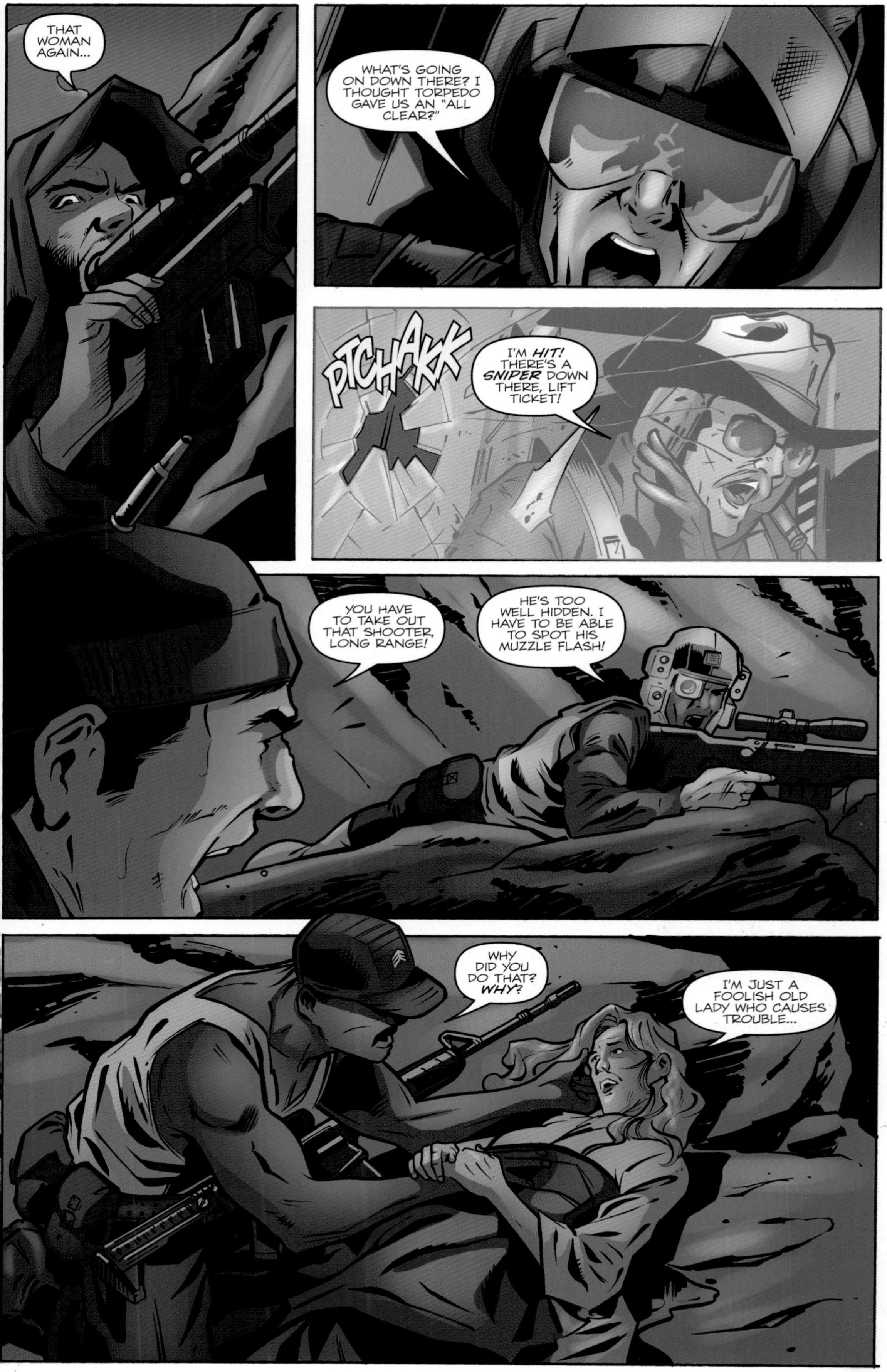
THAT WOMAN AGAIN...
WHAT'S GOING ON DOWN THERE? I THOUGHT TORPEDO GAVE US AN "ALL CLEAR?"
PTCHAKK
I'M HIT! THERE'S A SNIPER DOWN THERE, LIFT TICKET!
YOU HAVE TO TAKE OUT THAT SHOOTER, LONG RANGE!
HE'S TOO WELL HIDDEN. I HAVE TO BE ABLE TO SPOT HIS MUZZLE FLASH!
WHY DID YOU DO THAT? WHY?
I'M JUST A FOOLISH OLD LADY WHO CAUSES TROUBLE...

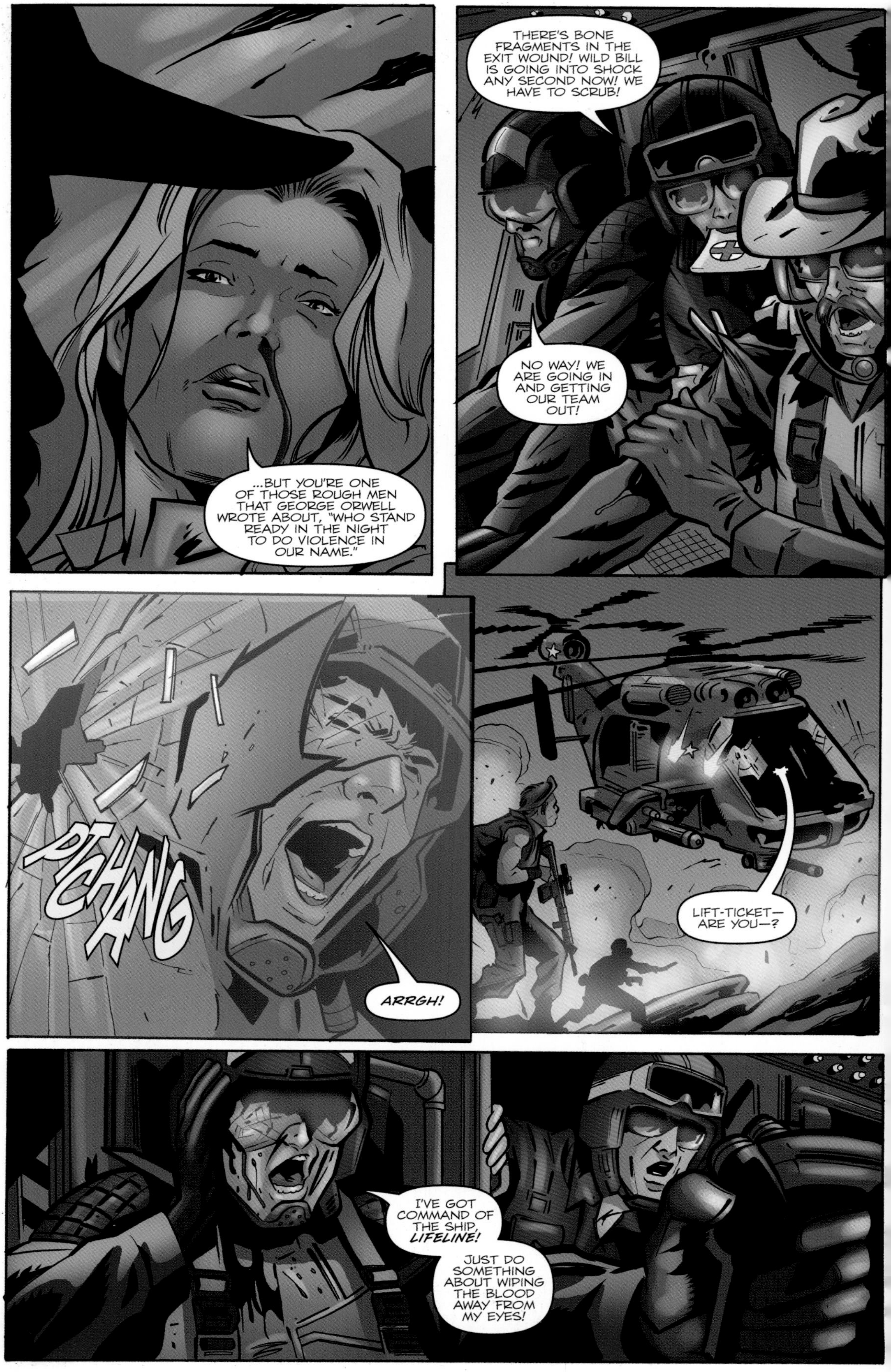
...BUT YOU'RE ONE OF THOSE ROUGH MEN THAT GEORGE ORWELL WROTE ABOUT, "WHO STAND READY IN THE NIGHT TO DO VIOLENCE IN OUR NAME."
THERE'S BONE FRAGMENTS IN THE EXIT WOUND! WILD BILL IS GOING INTO SHOCK ANY SECOND NOW! WE HAVE TO SCRUB!
NO WAY! WE ARE GOING IN AND GETTING OUR TEAM OUT!
PTCHANG
ARRGH!
LIFT-TICKET— ARE YOU—?
I'VE GOT COMMAND OF THE SHIP, LIFELINE!
JUST DO SOMETHING ABOUT WIPING THE BLOOD AWAY FROM MY EYES!

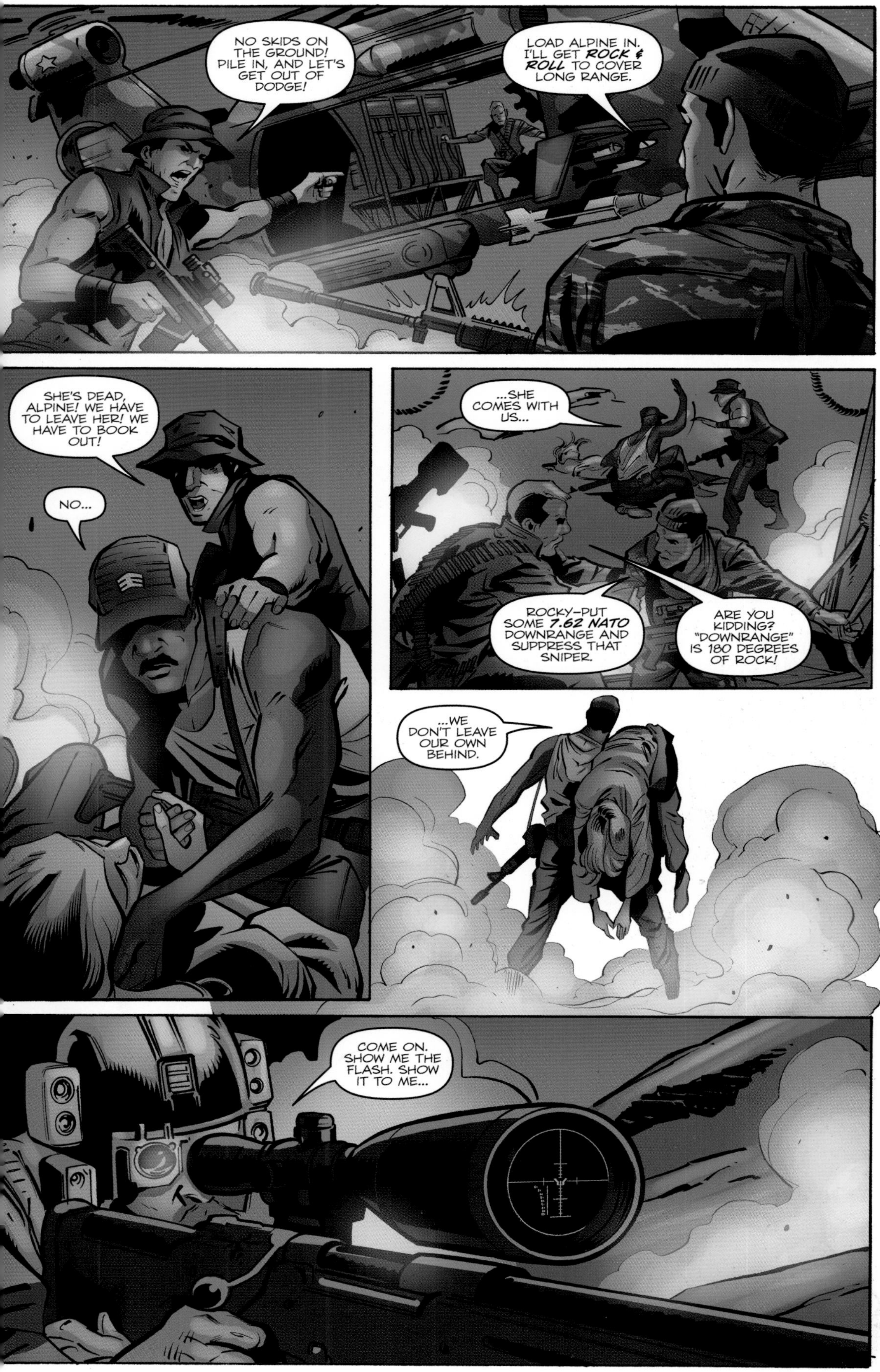
NO SKIDS ON THE GROUND! PILE IN, AND LET'S GET OUT OF DODGE!
LOAD ALPINE IN. I'LL GET ROCK & ROLL TO COVER LONG RANGE.
SHE'S DEAD, ALPINE! WE HAVE TO LEAVE HER! WE HAVE TO BOOK OUT!
NO...
...SHE COMES WITH US...
ROCKY–PUT SOME 7.62 NATO DOWNRANGE AND SUPPRESS THAT SNIPER.
ARE YOU KIDDING? "DOWNRANGE" IS 180 DEGREES OF ROCK!
...WE DON'T LEAVE OUR OWN BEHIND.
COME ON. SHOW ME THE FLASH. SHOW IT TO ME...

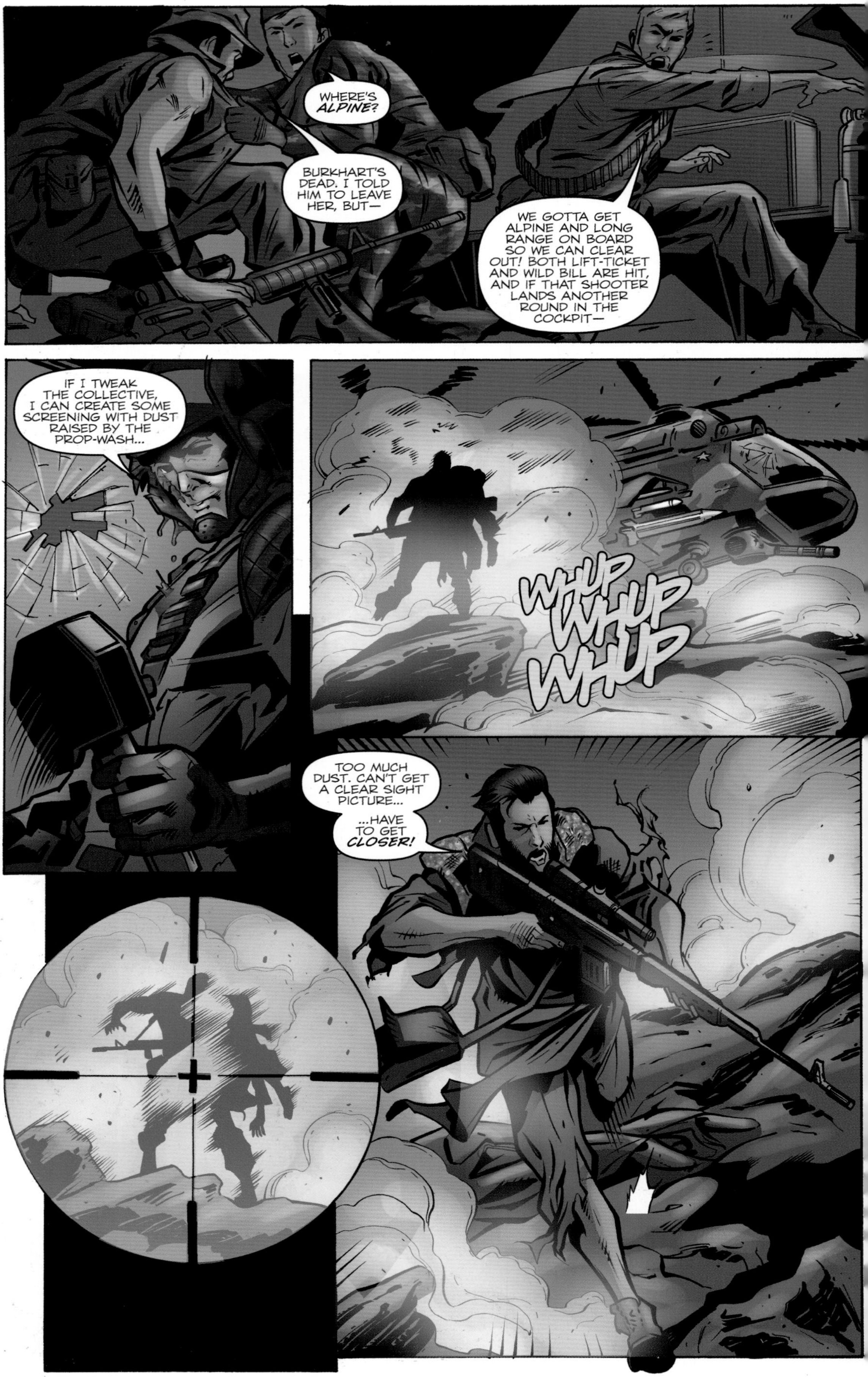
WHERE'S ALPINE?
BURKHART'S DEAD. I TOLD HIM TO LEAVE HER, BUT—
WE GOTTA GET ALPINE AND LONG RANGE ON BOARD SO WE CAN CLEAR OUT! BOTH LIFT-TICKET AND WILD BILL ARE HIT, AND IF THAT SHOOTER LANDS ANOTHER ROUND IN THE COCKPIT—
IF I TWEAK THE COLLECTIVE, I CAN CREATE SOME SCREENING WITH DUST RAISED BY THE PROP-WASH...
WHUP WHUP WHUP
TOO MUCH DUST. CAN'T GET A CLEAR SIGHT PICTURE...
...HAVE TO GET CLOSER!

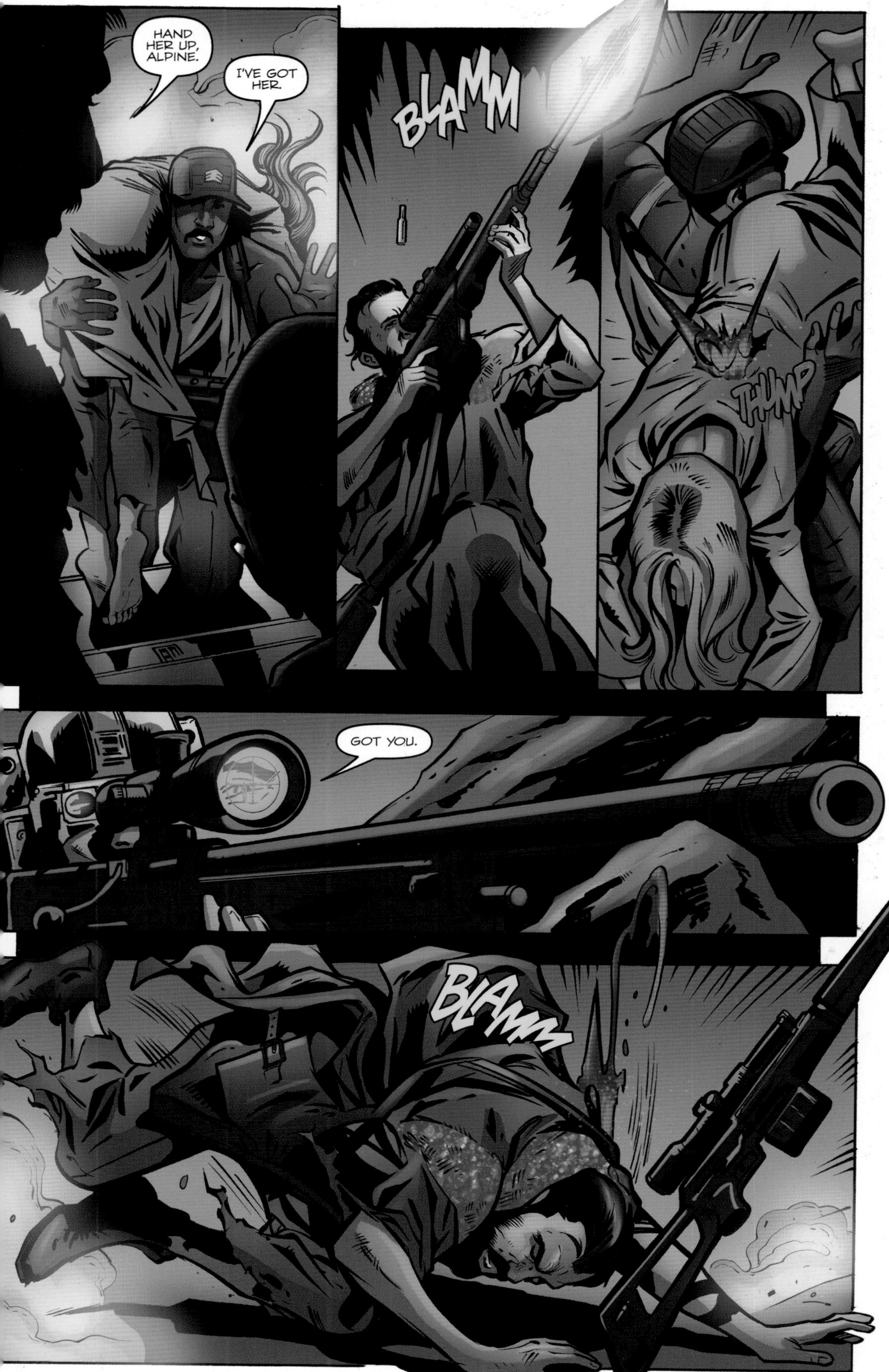
HAND HER UP, ALPINE.
I'VE GOT HER.
BLAMM
THUMP
GOT YOU.
BLAMM

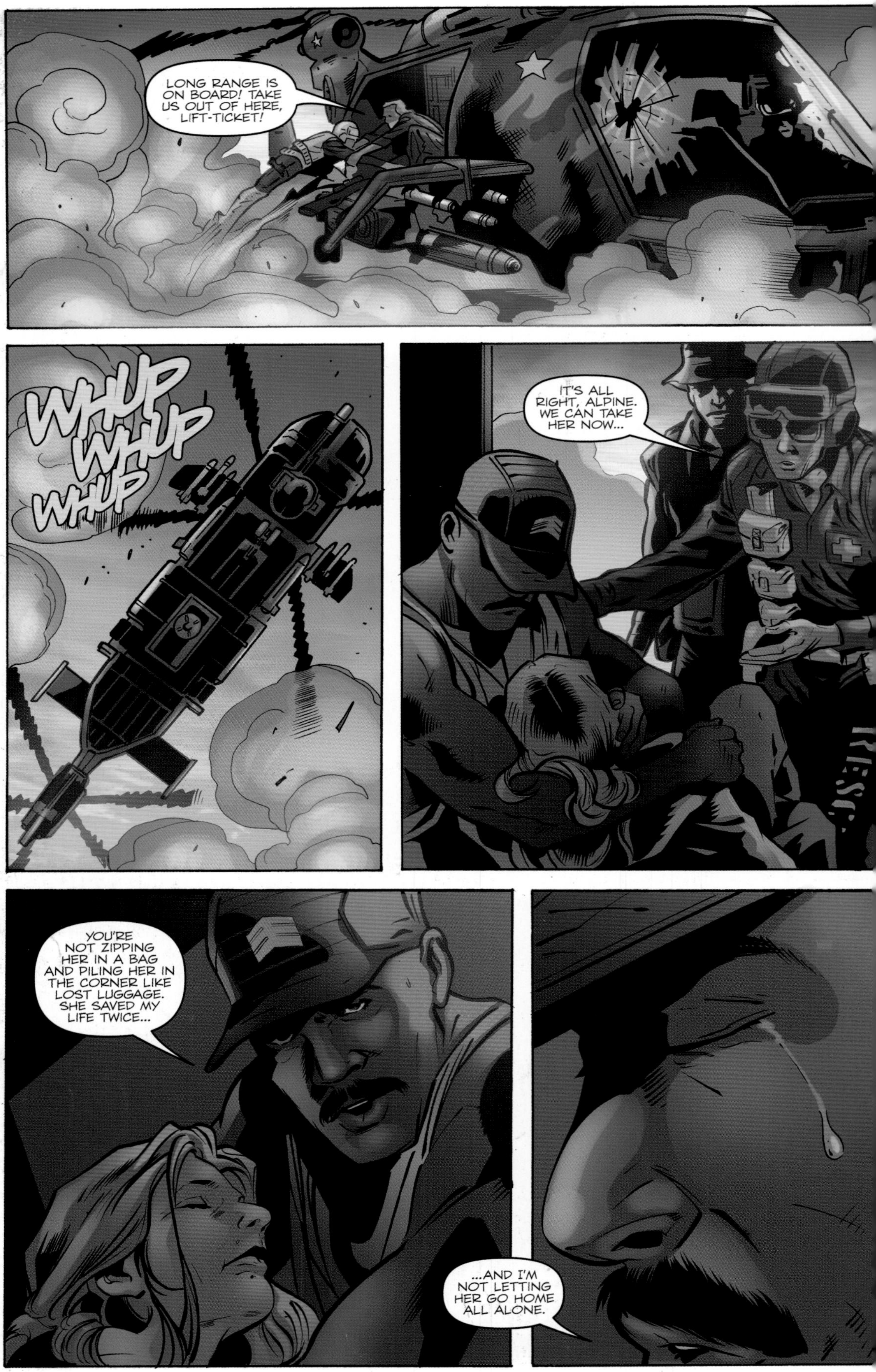
LONG RANGE IS ON BOARD! TAKE US OUT OF HERE, LIFT-TICKET!
WHUP WHUP WHUP
IT'S ALL RIGHT, ALPINE. WE CAN TAKE HER NOW...
YOU'RE NOT ZIPPING HER IN A BAG AND PILING HER IN THE CORNER LIKE LOST LUGGAGE. SHE SAVED MY LIFE TWICE...
...AND I'M NOT LETTING HER GO HOME ALL ALONE.

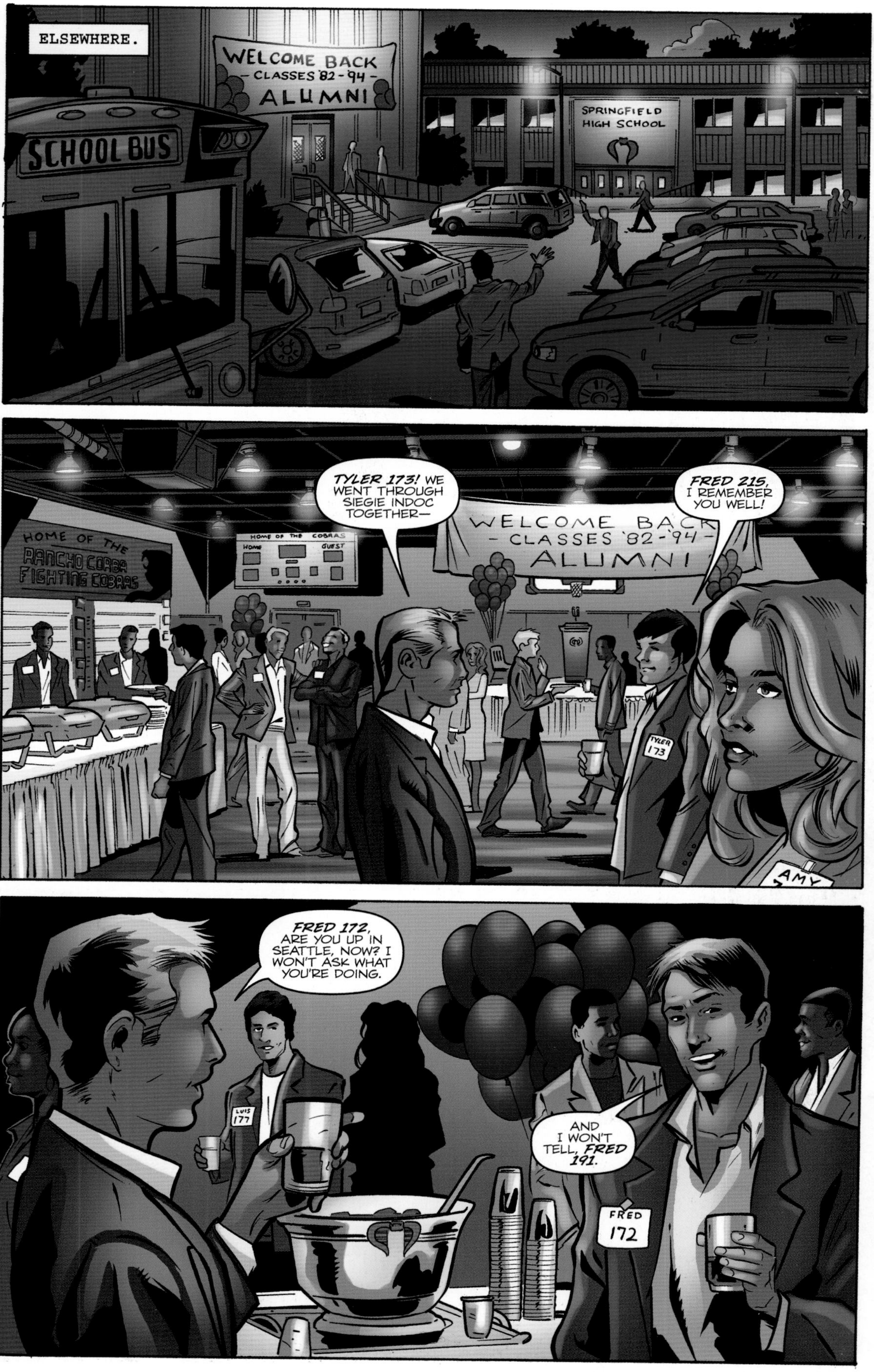
ELSEWHERE.
WELCOME BACK
-CLASSES '82-'94-
ALUMNI
SCHOOL BUS
SPRINGFIELD HIGH SCHOOL
TYLER 173! WE WENT THROUGH SIEGIE INDOC TOGETHER—
FRED 215, I REMEMBER YOU WELL!
HOME OF THE RANCHO COBRA FIGHTING COBRAS
HOME OF THE COBRAS
HOME GUEST
WELCOME BACK
-CLASSES '82-'94-
ALUMNI
TYLER 173
AMY
FRED 172, ARE YOU UP IN SEATTLE, NOW? I WON'T ASK WHAT YOU'RE DOING.
LUIS 177
AND I WON'T TELL, FRED 191.
FRED 172

MAY I INTRODUCE TO YOU, THE MAN WHO NEEDS NO INTRODUCTION!

PUT YOUR HANDS TOGETHER FOR THE BIG KAHUNA, THE TOP DOG, SUPREME SNAKE!

AND LET'S HEAR IT FOR DR. MINDBENDER AS WELL!

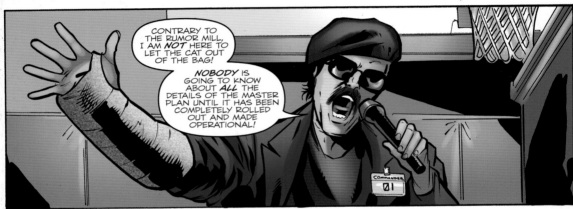

CONTRARY TO THE RUMOR MILL, I AM NOT HERE TO LET THE CAT OUT OF THE BAG!

NOBODY IS GOING TO KNOW ABOUT ALL THE DETAILS OF THE MASTER PLAN UNTIL IT HAS BEEN COMPLETELY ROLLED OUT AND MADE OPERATIONAL!

BUT EVERY SINGLE CRIMSON GUARD HERE IS PLAYING AN INTEGRAL PART IN THAT PLAN, AND EVERY PARTICIPANT IS JUST AS IMPORTANT AS ANY OTHER!

NOBODY KNOWS ANY MORE THAN THEIR OWN PART, AND NOBODY IS DIVULGING WHAT THEY ARE DOING TO ANYBODY ELSE. THAT MAKES OUR SECURITY IMPENETRABLE!

JUST KNOW THAT WHEN IT ALL COMES TOGETHER, THE WORLD WILL BE CHANGED FOREVER...

...AND ALL OF YOU WILL HAVE HAD A HAND IN IT!

COBRAAAAA!

TO BE CONTINUED!

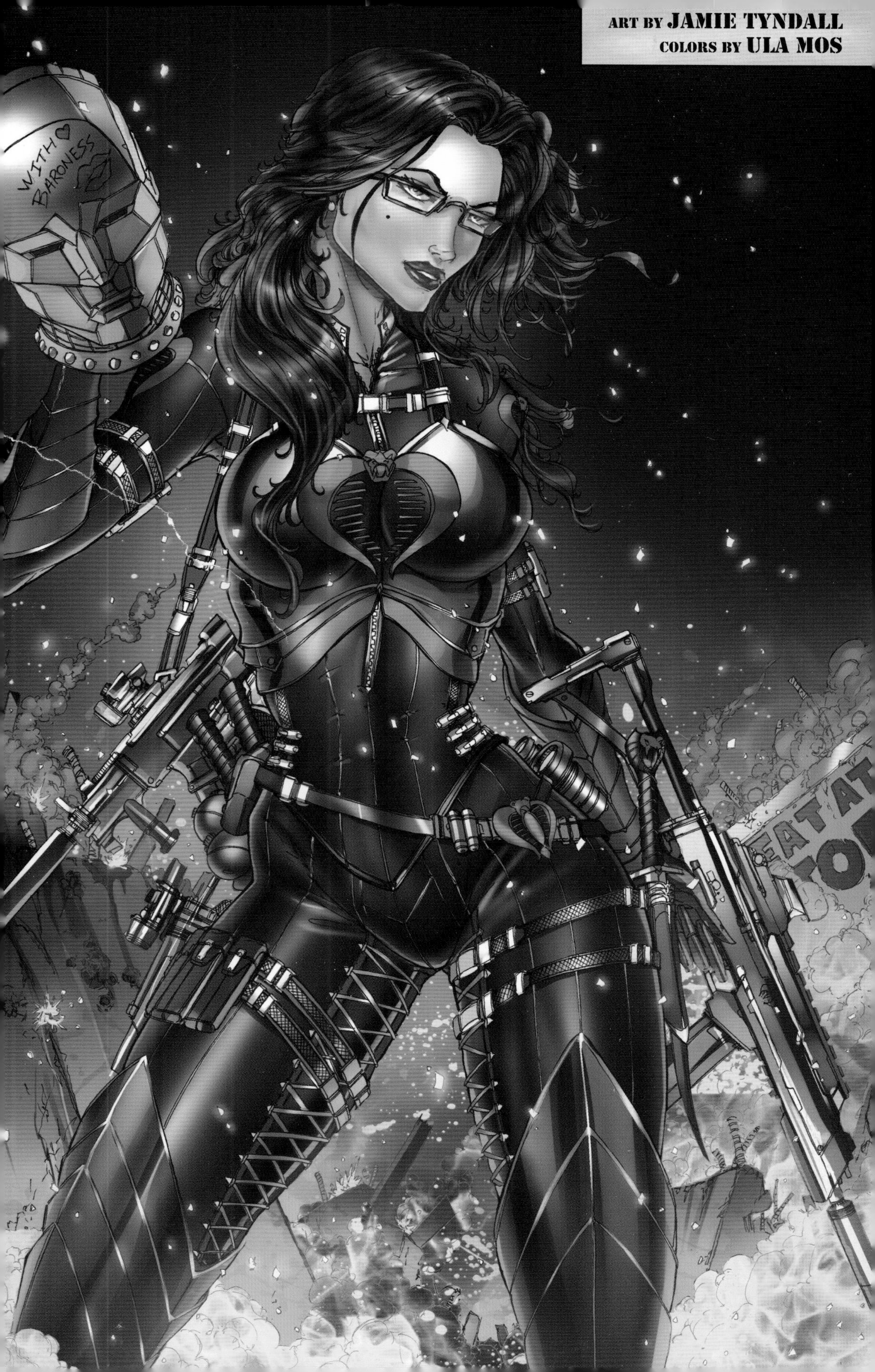
WITH ♡
BARONESS

ART BY JAMIE TYNDALL
COLORS BY ULA MOS

SKETCH BY LARRY HAMA

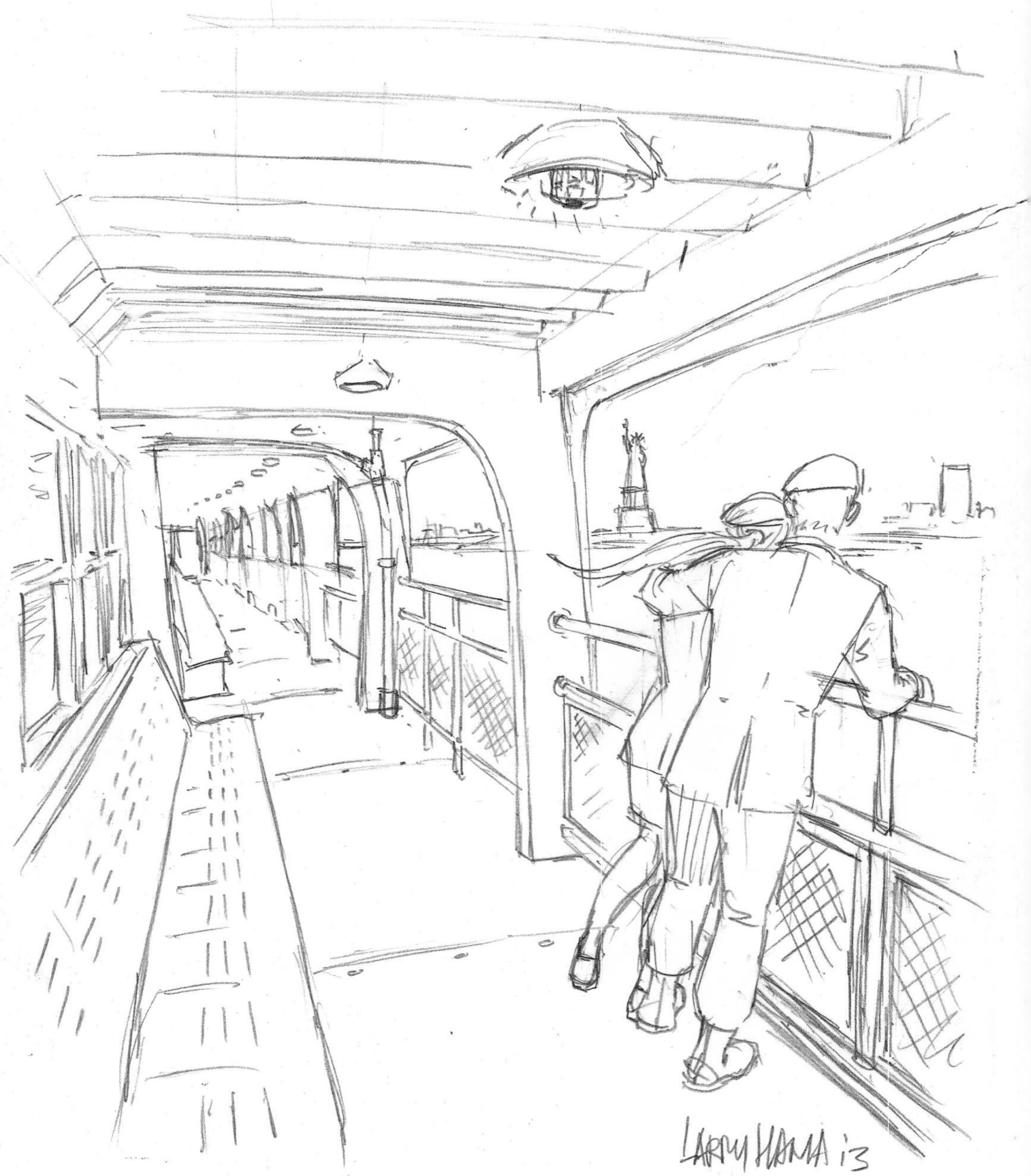
LARRY HAMA '13

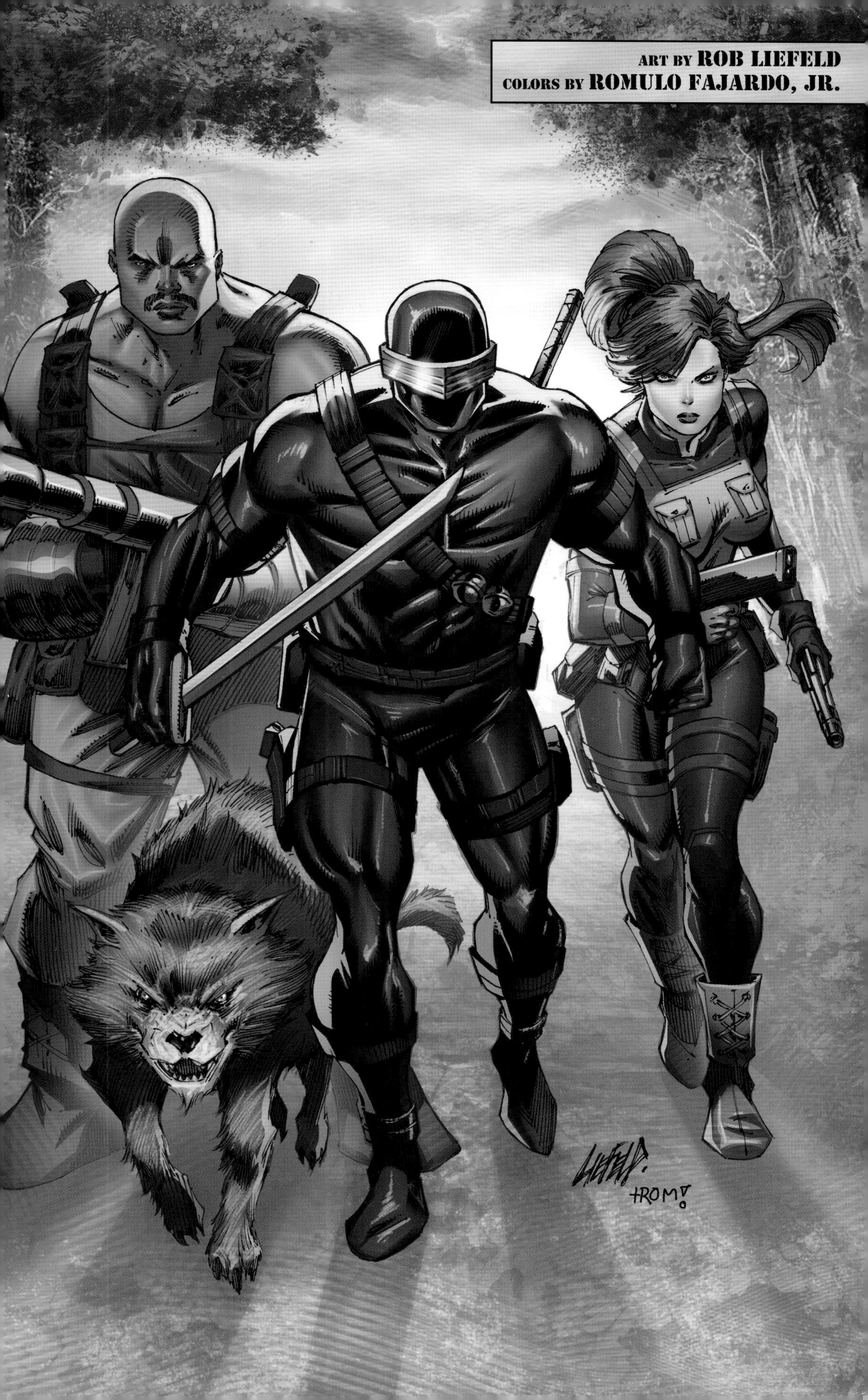

ART BY ROB LIEFELD
COLORS BY ROMULO FAJARDO, JR.

SKETCH BY LARRY HAMA

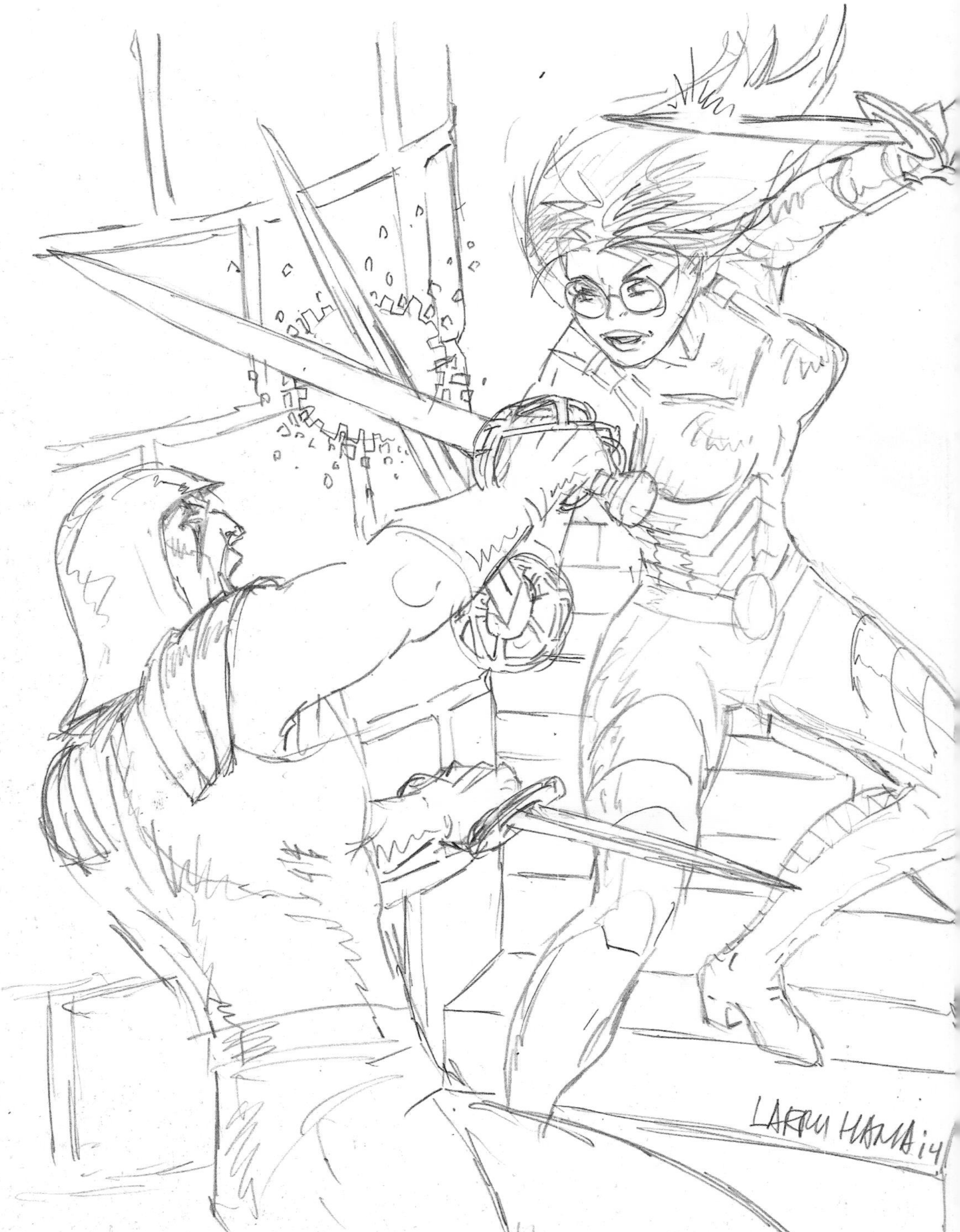
LARRY HAMA '14

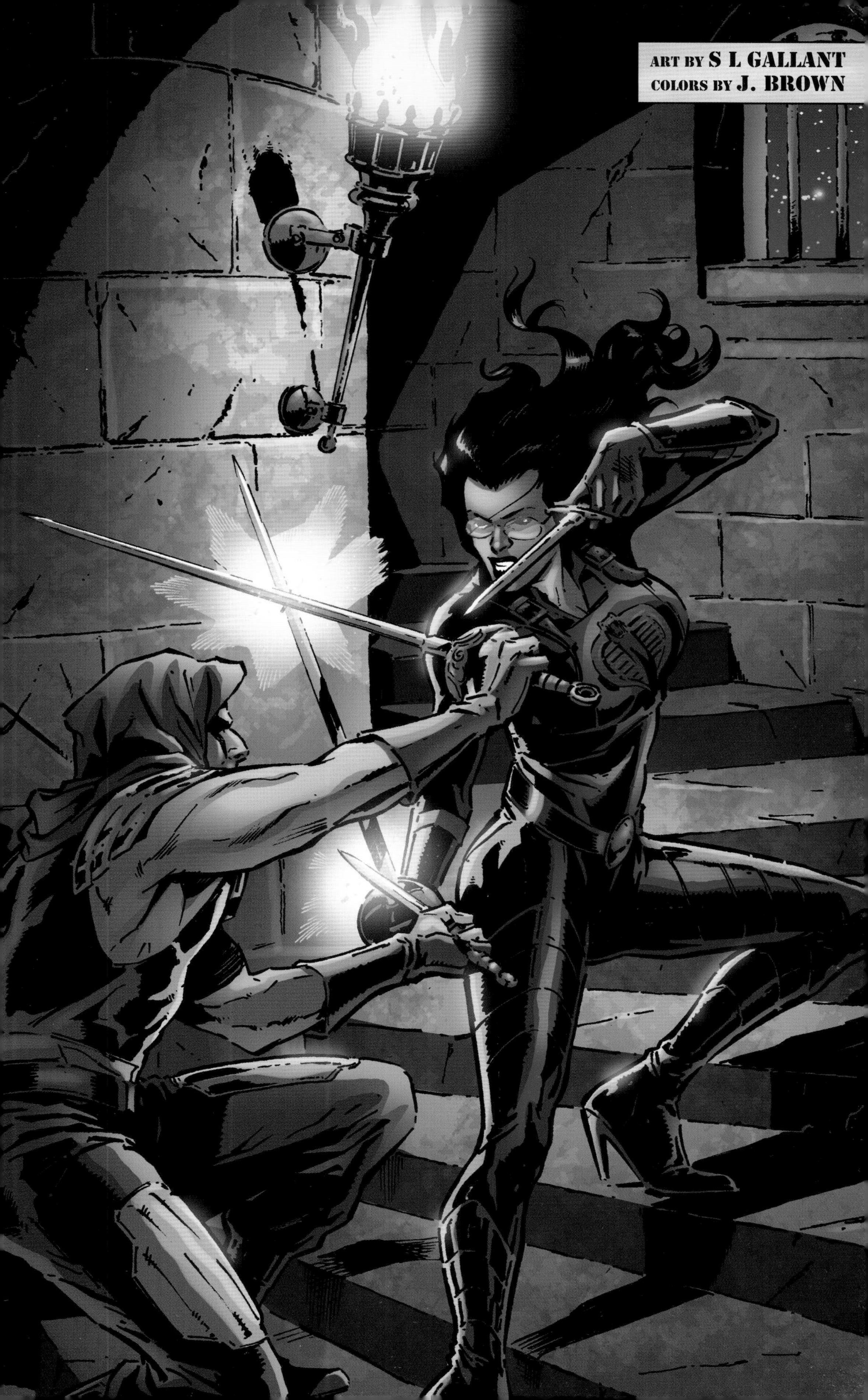
ART BY S L GALLANT
COLORS BY J. BROWN

SKETCH BY **LARRY HAMA**

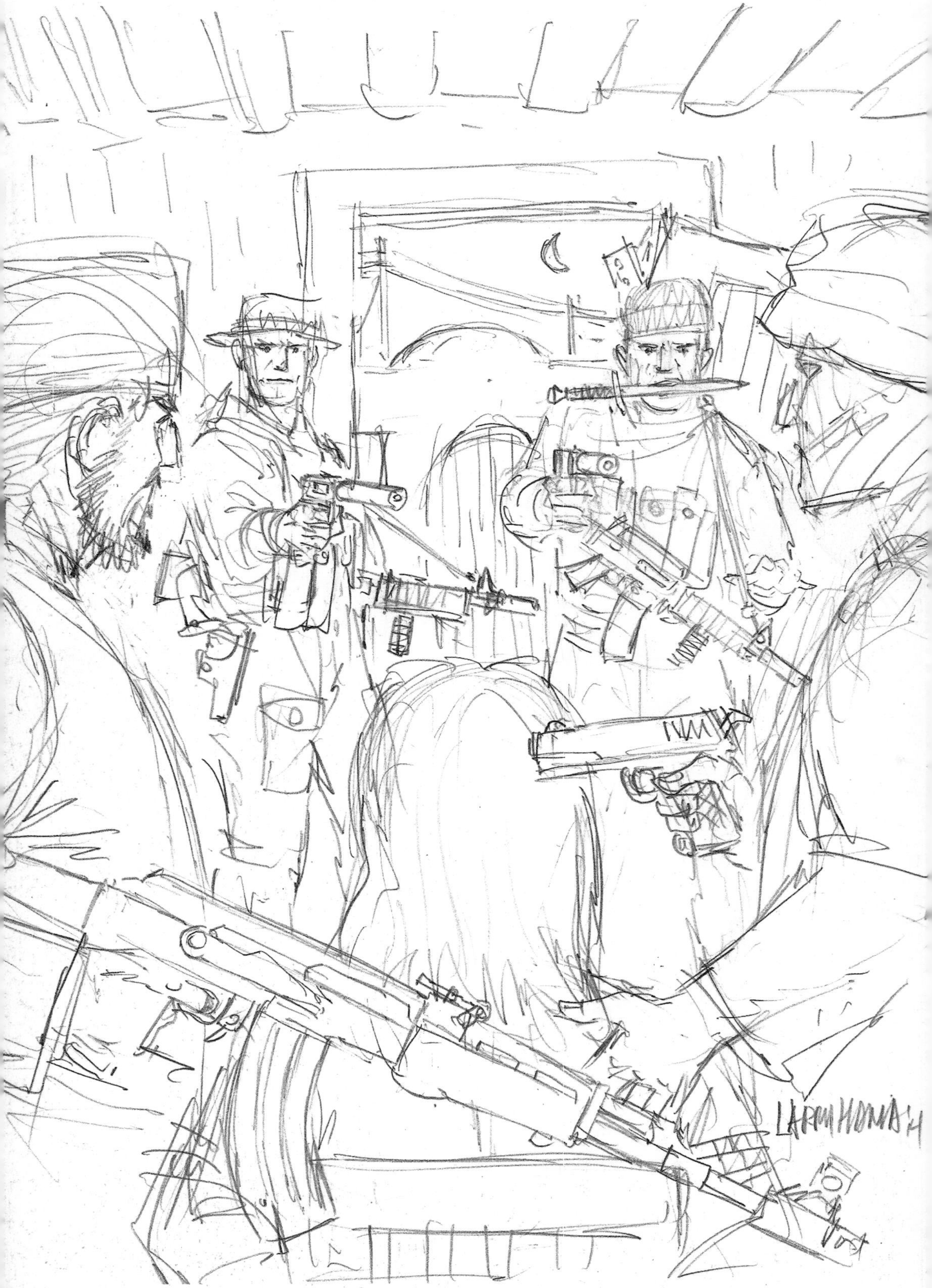
LARRY HAMA '14

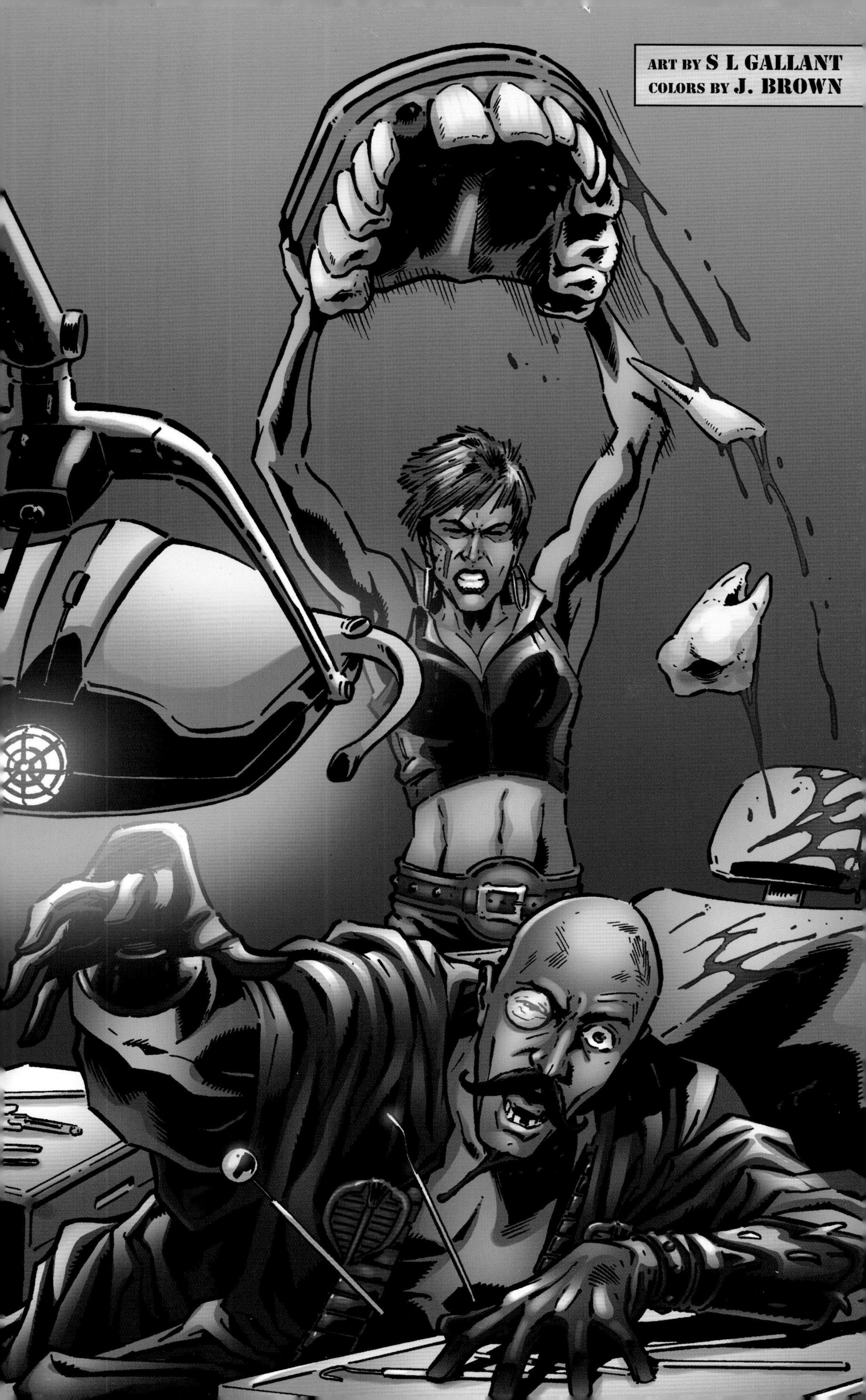
ART BY S L GALLANT
COLORS BY J. BROWN

SKETCH BY **LARRY HAMA**

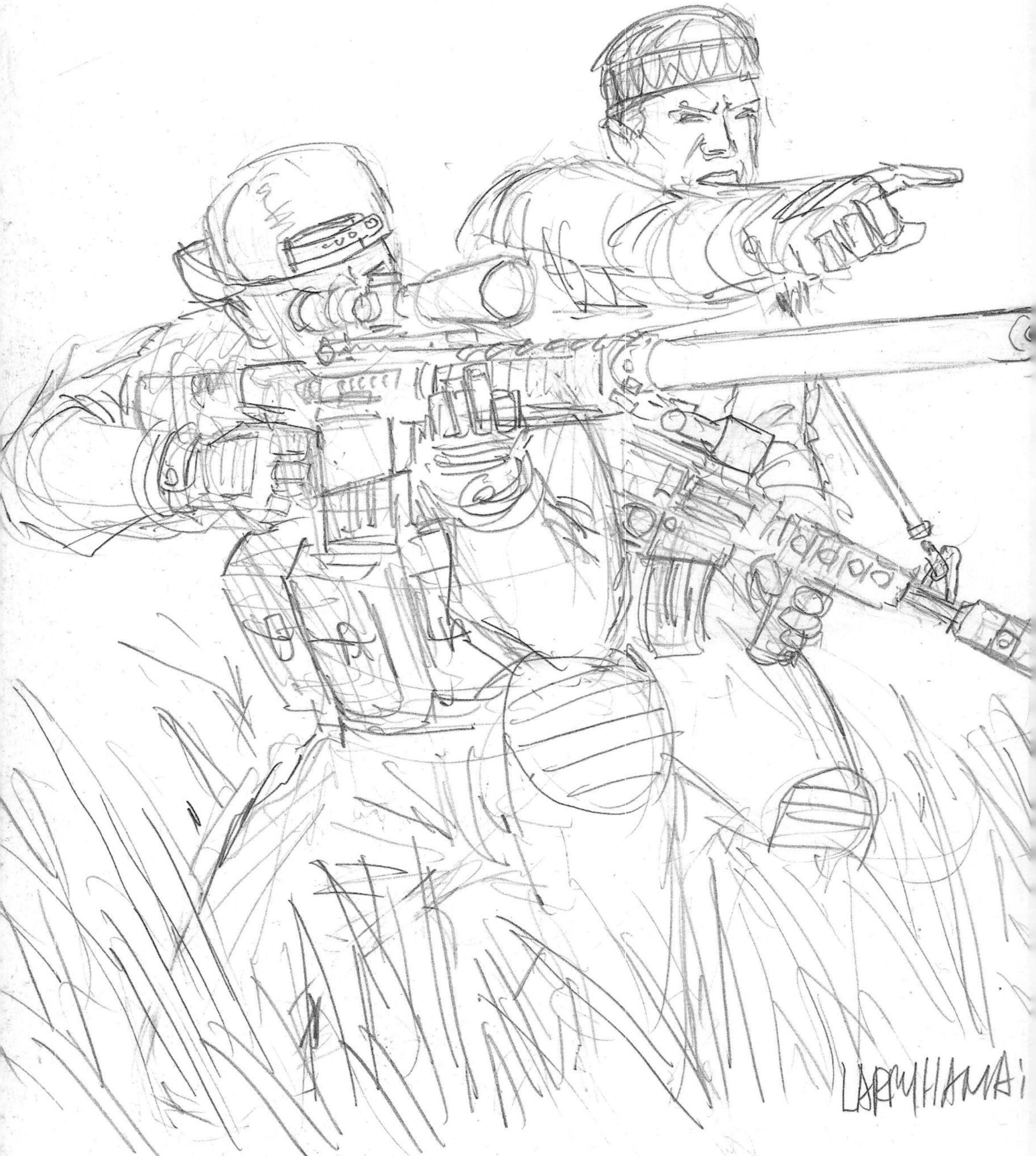
LARRY HAMA

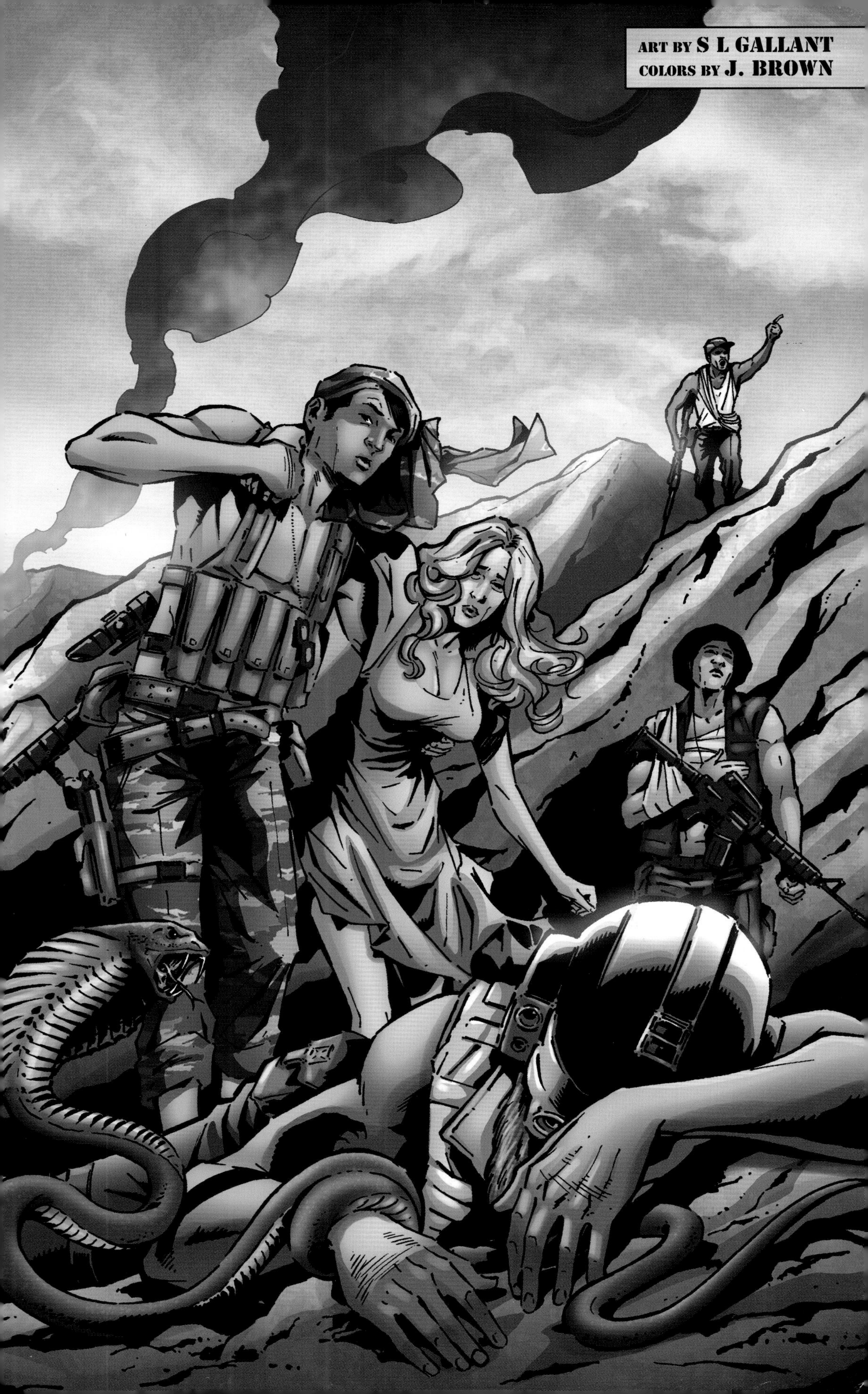
ART BY S L GALLANT
COLORS BY J. BROWN

SKETCH BY LARRY HAMA

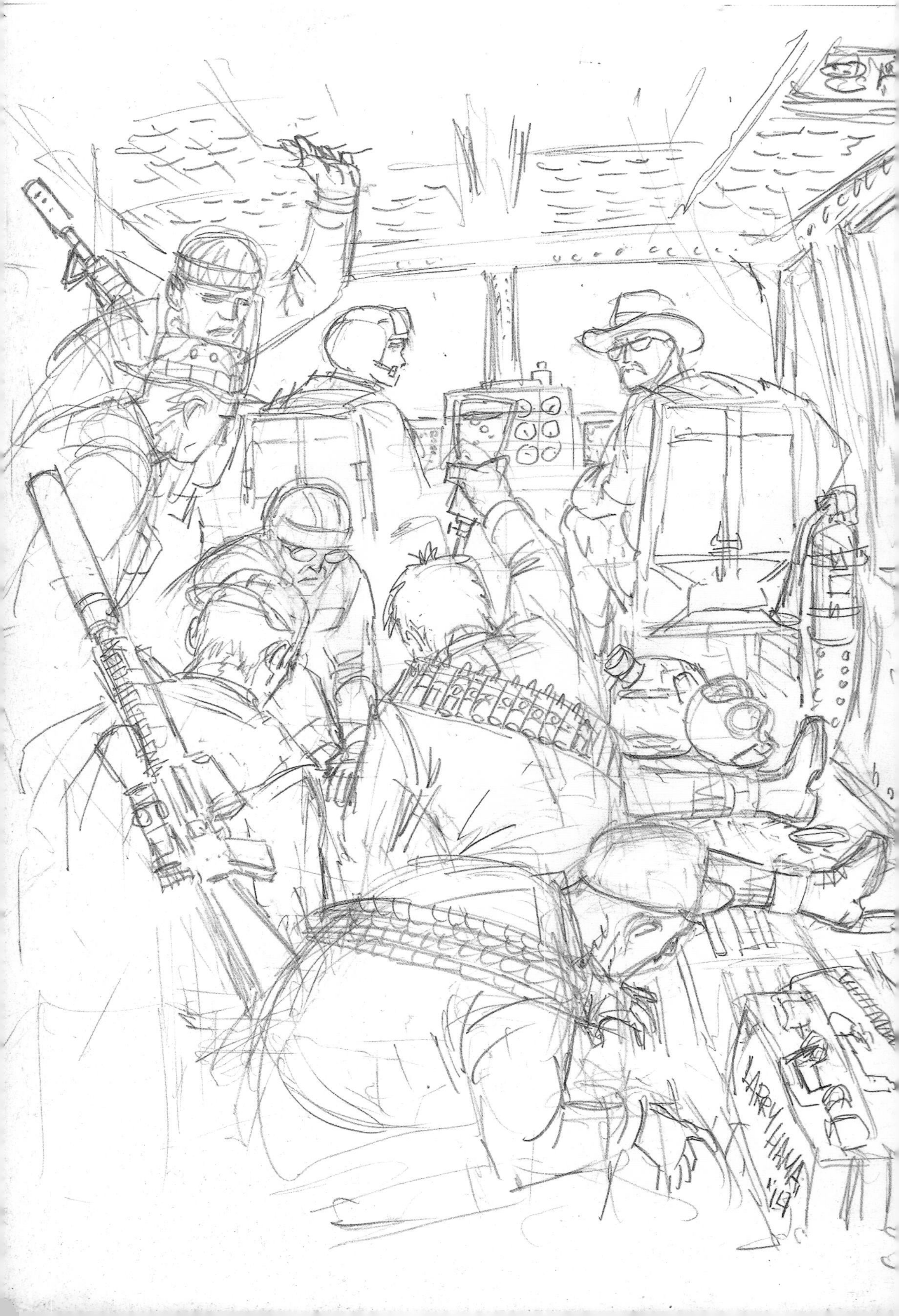
LARRY HAMA '14

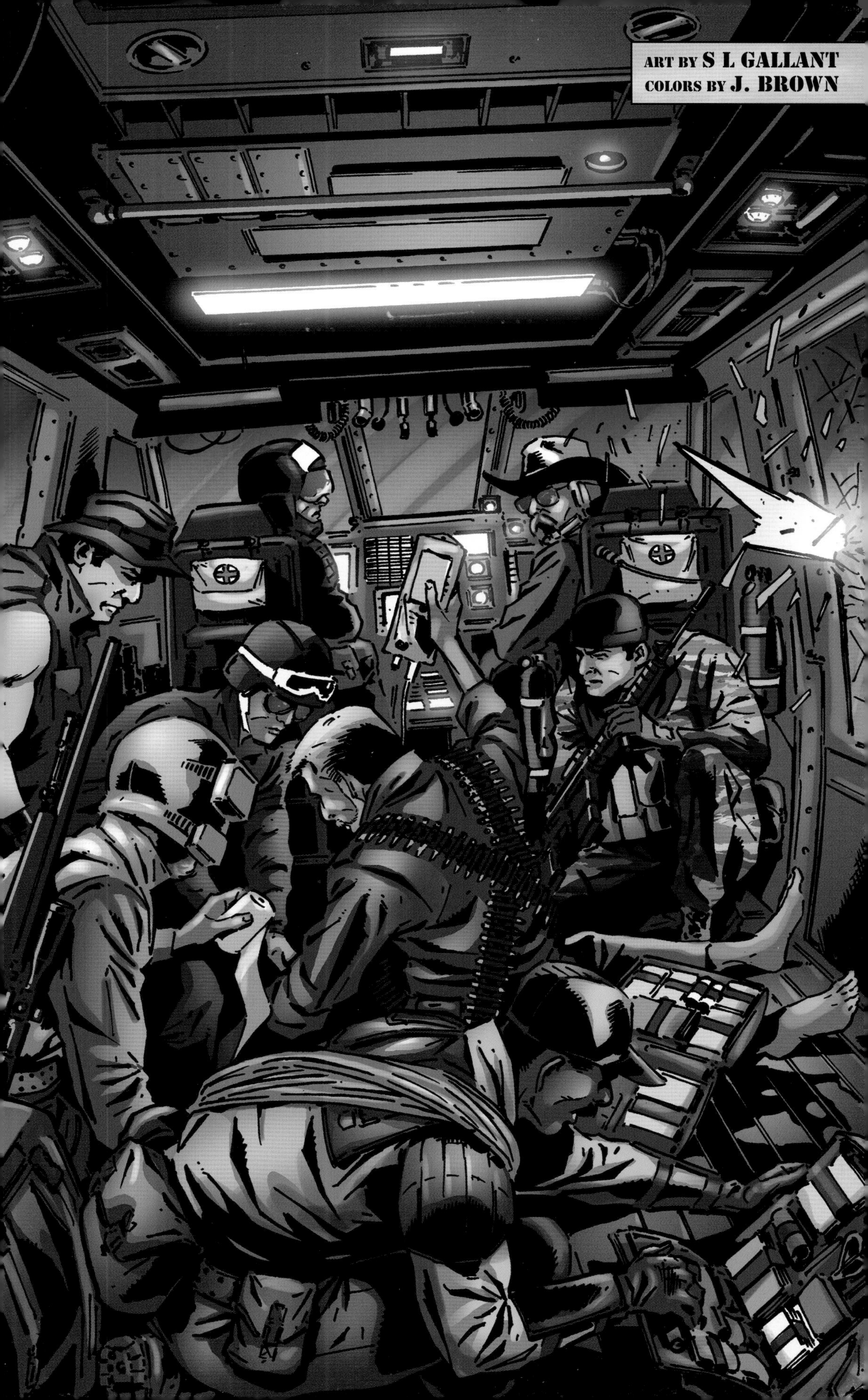
ART BY S L GALLANT
COLORS BY J. BROWN

THE MISSION CONTINUES

G.I. JOE
VOLUME 2:
THREAT MATRIX

G.I. JOE, VOL. 2: THREAT MATRIX
ISBN: 978-1-61377-866-1

G.I. JOE
THE COBRA FILES
VOLUME 2

G.I. JOE: THE COBRA FILES, VOL. 2
ISBN: 978-1-61377-918-7

COBRA
THE LAST LAUGH

COBRA: THE LAST LAUGH
ISBN: 978-1-61377-523-3

G.I. JOE
SPECIAL MISSIONS

G.I. JOE: SPECIAL MISSIONS, VOL. 2
ISBN: 978-1-61377-847-0

G.I. JOE
The Complete Collection
☆004☆

G.I. JOE: THE COMPLETE COLLECTION, VOL. 4
ISBN: 978-1-61377-848-7

G.I. JOE
THE IDW COLLECTION

G.I. JOE: THE IDW COLLECTION, VOL. 4
ISBN: 978-1-61377-931-6